SHADOWPLAY

THE DEVILS IN D.C. SAGA

BOOK 1

ANGEL M. SHAW

Issued in print and electronic formats.

Paperback ISBN: 979-8-9899843-0-5

eBook ISBN: 979-8-9899843-1-2

First edition 2024.

Shadowplay: A Dark Billionaire Romantic Suspense

Editing by Wendee Mullikin, Purple Pen Wordsmithing

Cover images from 123rf.com

CONTENT ACKNOWLEDGEMENT

My books are intended to be read by adults and feature dark, explicit material. I want you to go into this series forewarned that there are some heavy topics addressed—but there's a lot of healing too. And spice. Lots and lots of spice.

Your well-being is important to me, so if you'd like to know the potentially sensitive topics you'll encounter in The Devils in D.C. Saga, please visit my website at http://www.angelmshaw.com/content-warnings.

For more help:

Anyone affected by sexual assault, whether it happened to you or someone you care about, can find support from rainn.org. You can also call the National Sexual Assault Hotline at 800.656.HOPE (4673) to be connected with someone over the phone who can help.

Contact the 988 Suicide and Crisis Lifeline if you are experiencing mental health-related distress or are worried about a loved one who may need crisis support. 988 is confidential, free, and available 24/7/365. To connect, call or text 988, or connect with a trained crisis counselor at 988lifeline.org.

A NOTE ABOUT REPRESENTATION

August, Hunter's son, is an Autistic teenager who uses Augmentative and Alternative Communication (AAC) to speak with others around him. August uses an iPad, but there are dozens of other ways to use AAC.

August's method of speaking is based on a technique called Spelling2Communicate, and the headquarters for the organization that created S2C happens to be in Herndon, Virginia. I'm grateful for what S2C has done for my family, and I'm thrilled to feature this type of communication—and to give space to a character as amazing as August.

Another note: I use the same dialogue tags for August as I do for any other character. So, I write "he says" or "he replies" rather than saying "he types." This is an intentional decision to emphasize that August's mode of communication isn't different from those of us who use our mouths to speak.

Also mentioned in the story is a startling fact: Autistic children are nearly three times more likely to experience abuse. If interested, you can find the 2022 article in the footnote below. [1]

P.S. August is my favorite character. I hope he becomes yours too.

1. Trundle, Grace, Katy A. Jones, Danielle Ropar, and Vincent Egan. 2022. "Prevalence of Victimisation in Autistic Individuals: A Systematic Review and Meta-Analysis." *Trauma, Violence, & Abuse* 24 (4): 2282–96. https://doi.org/10.1177/15248380221093689.

For everyone who sees themself in Winter.

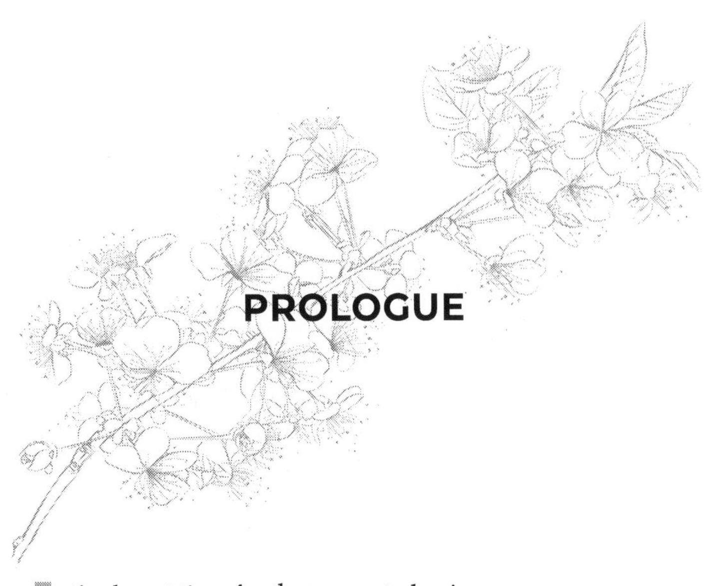

PROLOGUE

It's almost time for the games to begin.

Alone on the shore of Isla Cara, I look up at the mansion tucked in the palm trees. The angry ocean thrashes against the sand behind me as the sun starts to kiss the horizon: purple, blue, orange, and blood red.

When the first bell rings out from the main house, the expansive beach glows as the spotlights on the roof illuminate the contestants' finish line.

It's so bright it almost feels like the middle of the day rather than the edge of dusk.

Dressed in elegant suits and gowns, the exclusive set of guests exit the mansion and make their way onto the veranda. The stone terrace they walk on juts over the sandy beach, providing unobstructed sightlines of the Caribbean.

"This is a billion-dollar view," Father said when he took ownership of Isla Cara. It became his most prized possession.

People have heard of the mysterious Isla Cara, but only a few of the elite have been here. Claimed by Sir Brigham, who came over from England on the Mayflower, Isla Cara is a small, secluded dot on the globe, southeast of the island of Dominica, not far from Martinique.

As was done from generation to generation, my grandfather bequeathed all he owned upon his death to his only son.

Everything, including this godless island.

But I guess that isn't true. There is a god here. His name is Benjamin Brigham.

The revelers on the raised stone deck wear painted faces to allude to their regality. Their blood diamonds are a good conversation piece.

At the center of the crowd is their king—their American royalty.

And I stand on the shore: his son.

"Let's have some fun, shall we?" Father's voice is clear. Even the crash of waves can't drown him out.

Joyful sounds reverberate as the guests jockey for optimal viewing.

Even from my spot below, I hear bits of their excited conversations.

"Six million on the redhead, Tucker," one voice states.

"I think you should bet on the one from Sierra Leone," adds another. "Strong thighs."

"Franklin, you know those kind can't swim."

Raucous laughter blends with the ringing of the next bell.

Far, far off in the sea, a charter boat bobs up and down past the riptide.

Then as the sun waves past the horizon, bodies hit the water one by one as they're thrown from the vessel.

Their screams echo across the water until they enter their salty grave.

One body.

Two bodies.

Three. Four.

More and more and more hit the water.

From their place of privilege on the stone perch, the betters call out their price for a life. Others groan with the sting of a bet lost.

Five. Six.

Twenty-two in all.

I watch for almost an hour as the turquoise water swallows bodies and souls and track the others who make it to shore. This is just phase one of the games.

Next they'll have to evade the hunt. The survivors will make sure they hide well with hopes they make it to morning.

That is, if they want to live another day.

Near the craggy rock cliff, a quarter mile down the shore, a dark body writhes on the pale sand.

I glance at my father, curious if he's noticed the spot on the beach. His back is to the water, and his arms glide through the air as if he were a maestro conducting the group.

My feet move, and soon the bottomless, obsidian eyes of a girl I recognize stare back at me. She has been on Isla Cara since she was six years old.

The first time I came here, I was that age too.

I, the prince of the island. She, a slave.

In the nine years since her arrival, the softness of youthful innocence has become a distant memory, stripped from her being early on with every violation and lash of the whip.

"I made it," she says, panting.

The fact that she did make it is unfortunate. Dying in the ocean would have been a merciful outcome, knowing what the rest of her short life will be like.

I don't say anything.

She rolls to her back and clutches her stomach, her skin shredded by the hidden coral that dots the reef just beyond the shore.

Her wound isn't fatal.

"Why did I fight to get back here?" she asks, looking at the bloody sand between her fingers.

I know she doesn't expect a response from me.

She laughs. It's a bright sound—almost happy, despite the raspy tenor her voice has from the seawater and her screams.

Most of the sun is behind the horizon, and the ambient glow from the spotlights gives just enough illumination to see her face.

The hum of the charter boat draws closer, heading for the dock not too far from us.

One heartbeat.

Two.

Then, voices.

"Help me," she pleads.

I study her face.

"Please," she adds.

I don't move.

"You know what they'll do to me," she says. Her voice is hard. Tense and urgent.

And I do know. I know that the men coming closer, hunting her, will find her naked, bruised body.

Maybe they'll be merciful and end her life there on the shore.

But because she's unable to run, unable to hide, the more likely outcome is that she'll be passed around the massive playroom. I know they will take turns violating her.

I know because this is what happens to prey in the games.

"Help me," she whispers.

My father expects me to join the hunts.

I'm too soft, he says.

So he shreds my flesh to give me tough skin.

"Please," she says. She reaches her shaking hand toward me. "Help me," she repeats.

"I can't help you escape," I tell her.

"I know," she whispers. She tilts her head back. "This is the way."

A dozen emotions flow through me at her words, but the prevailing one? Hopelessness.

How will Father view this betrayal?

I lean down over her, getting closer. So close I could count the dark lashes on her eyelids if we had time. If only we had time.

"What is your name?" I ask her. I have to know.

"Ominira," she replies. Her face smooths out, so all that's left in her expression is the slight upturn of her lips.

"I'm sorry, Ominira," I whisper, reaching for the blade in my back pocket.

Her gaze locks with mine, assessing me. With a sharp nod, she slides her eyes closed.

One more breath. One more heartbeat.

"Thank you," she says, tension leaving her body.

I slit her throat in one sure cut.

ONE
WINTER

O*ne.*

One-two-one.

One-two-three-two-one.

I tap a rapid staccato on the desk as hot air blows from my overworked laptop, warming my numb fingertips. It's midday in the middle of summer, and even though the heat radiating into my studio apartment would usually cause me to sweat my hair out, my whole body is cold.

Eight! Eight-seven-eight! Eight-seven-six-seven-eight…

A wet snout nudges my hand as my dog jumps in my lap. He makes himself comfortable, giving me deep pressure. Even though he weighs all of fifteen pounds, his presence helps bring me down.

Deep breath.

"It's just a fucking phone call, Winter," I say out loud.

Kitty huffs, licking my hand where it grips the desk.

"I hear ya, boy." With one more cleansing breath, I calm my body and feel the pressing levels of high anxiety come down from "I'm about to lose my shit" to "This doesn't feel great, but I've got this."

"Free," I command Kitty, and he hops down from my lap to sit next to my heel.

I rub his silky ear, and he looks up at me, his attention focused on my cues.

The blue "Join Meeting" button glows on my computer screen, and without overthinking it, I click to let myself into the call. I'm face-to-face with my program coordinator a few moments later.

Even though I've never met the woman in person in the four years I've been in the doctoral program, I know her well through the innumerable emails and video conferences we've shared. I try to school my face into a pleasant smile even though my muscles feel tight and like they might spasm at any moment.

"Winter, it was tough to do, but I'm happy to tell you I have great news!" Ms. O'Connor beams at me and claps her hands in front of her face.

Tap-tap-tap.

The air rushes out of my lungs in a whoosh.

"Really?" The relief is palpable.

I clench my sweaty hands in my lap and wish for the millionth time that I weren't such a nervous person. I've always been this way, but it wasn't until I hit my teenage years that my nervousness turned into a panic disorder with obsessive-compulsive features.

Don't think about that.

I've worked hard to manage my symptoms and be able to function in society—to *want* to function in society. So thank God for meds and therapy. And best friends who are there to pick me up off the floor. And a general hope for the future.

Still, being a disabled student has meant I've had to work three times as hard to get just as far as my peers. It's exhausting, even though I've been able to figure out solutions as I've gone along.

With online classes being a regular thing now, I breezed

through undergrad, so it was easy to step into my school's PsyD childhood psychology program.

Everything has been smooth, simple. I finished the master's degree requirements last semester. But now it's time for me to complete my practicum hours: in-person supervised clinical experiences that are non-negotiable to the Virginia Board of Licensing and Liberty Falls University.

The problem is I need to be around people. A lot of people. And while I can go outside and even go to crowded places like the grocery store or the park—with a little preparation and Kitty by my side—the thought of going into a hospital or clinic and dealing with person after person in fifty-minute chunks for ten hours a day feels like my personal version of hell.

I've vacillated between assured confidence and sheer terror over the issue for so long that Veronica and my therapist both demanded that I reach out to the grad board to request disability accommodations.

"The board has decided to honor your request pretty much in full," Ms. O'Connor says, cutting into my thoughts. "They are willing to be very liberal with how you complete your practicum hours. Basically, as long as you have a licensed psychologist sign off on your work and check in with the practicum supervising professor, you're all set!"

She bounces on my screen and does that quick *tap-tap-tap* of her hands again.

"Okay?" I say while trying to temper my excitement. "That's...that's it? I can work with that," I reply again, feeling the tension in my spine release a fraction.

"Yes! Well, there's just one thing—you'll have to do your hours in person, but you get to decide how to do that."

She smiles at me again.

I blink in response.

"But...I can't see clients virtually? Clinicians do that all the time!" I say, feeling my blinking race out of my control.

Blink-blink-blink.

Kitty presses into my leg, alert to my rising distress.

"Yes, well, the program committee was willing to bend on the content of your practicum experience, but it's the opinion of the board that you will get the fullest educational experience and be best prepared for your future as a clinician by completing this part in person."

She lowers her voice. "You know how Dr. Stevenson is," she says in a near whisper.

Well, rip my heart out and set it on fire.

I do, in fact, know how Dr. Stevenson is. He is the professor who tried to kick me out of the program in my second semester of undergrad. I tried to go on campus for my final exam without Kitty. I'd just gotten him and finished service dog training, but I didn't feel comfortable bringing him with me.

It was a stupid decision. A masterclass in how to be self-defeating.

Quizzes and exams could be done online along with the rest of the coursework, but finals had to be administered in person by a proctor. I could have pushed for an exception, but I didn't want to draw attention to myself.

Internalized ableism is a bitch.

Even though I felt comfortable with the material, I had a panic attack so bad I got a nosebleed and ran out of the room. When I returned after taking my emergency Xanax, I told the professor what happened, expecting him to be understanding.

He is a psychologist, after all.

Instead, he looked down his straight nose and cut me to pieces as he said, "If you can't control your mental health, how could you possibly think you can treat clients?"

I passed the exam with a score three points above failing.

Dr. Stevenson was part of the driving force behind my press to finish my program in record time. I wanted to get out of all his classes. But now, he's the chair of the practicum board.

Jesus H. Christ.

I try to take air past my constricted throat muscles.

It's okay, Winter.

"Okay, that's…thank you for going to bat for me, Ms. O'Connor."

She smiles back at me.

"I know this isn't exactly what you wanted, but I do sorta agree with them, Winter. You're going to be a great clinician. You will make an empathetic provider," she says with a sober tone dampening her bubbly delivery. "You've made much progress as a student despite your disability. *And*…I think it's okay if you stretch a little. If you try. If it's really not doable, collect all the data and let's bring it back to the board. Okay?"

Her words are meant to be reassuring, but all they do is piss me off.

Many people *say* they understand anxiety disorders, but they don't. They think I can "think" my way out of panic. I can't. I've done a lot of work to be the healthiest I've ever been, but plenty of days are a challenge still.

I realize I'm biting my nails and lower my hand from my face.

"This is *not* to say you should just 'get over' your disability." She makes finger quotes in the air. "It's more to be curious about what it would look like if you tried. At least you'll know."

"Thank you," I say, my lips feeling numb in a familiar signal that a panic attack might be right around the corner. "Alert," I murmur to Kitty, and he hops back on my lap, ducking his head to stay out of the frame. Part of me feels it's intentional. Every time Ms. O'Connor talks, his ears tense. Her high-pitched, excited tone borders on grating to my human ears. I can only imagine what it does to Kitty.

"You're welcome, Winter." She pauses for a beat. "I've done some thinking—"

Oh, joy.

"—and I have a few ideas on how you could complete your program. If you could find a single subject to work with directly, that would be low stress...low*er* stress, right? I have a friend over at the children's hospital. She's the lead pediatric psychologist there. Since we have reciprocity with the hospital, she's taken a look at her roster of client referrals and picked out a few who might be willing to work with someone with your focus. She'll even act as your clinical supervisor! You can get everything set before the fall semester starts in a few weeks." She finishes speaking and beams, her smile wide.

This is a good case scenario. Not exactly "best case," but you can accept "good case," Winter.

I force the muscles in my face to concoct a smile and say, "Thank you so much for advocating on my behalf. That sounds wonderful."

"I'll loop you and Dr. Wagner together before I leave for the day. But, Winter?" She pauses for a moment. "I'm so incredibly proud of you. You've come so far in such a short time. I can't wait to see what you do this year."

Tears well up in my eyes. Ms. O'Connor, for all her quirks, is the closest thing I've had to a mother figure in this whole process.

We firm up a few more details and end the call after a few minutes. My laptop claps shut as I slam it closed, and I tilt to the side in my armless desk chair as nausea wells in my esophagus. The physical toll of showing up for the meeting, sitting through disappointment, and masking my anxiety means paying for it later.

Or now.

Not today, Satan.

Heading over to the massive wall of windows where the sun shines through at full force, I plop down on the oversized pillow seat in my meditation zone. Reaching for the stone-cased essential oil diffuser, I put three drops each of lavender, vetiver, and clary sage into it.

Kitty settles at my back, pressing into me with a tense position. He's trained to be vigilant to threats that might materialize around me, but mostly, he's alert to threats that may exist within myself.

Focusing on breathing, I close my eyes and turn my face toward the sun, thankful for the powerful rays. I extend my right index finger to my left hand.

I am safe. Trace up my thumb.

I feel calm. Trace down my thumb.

I trust my ability to prevail over hard things. Trace up my index finger.

I let go and trust the process of life. Trace down my index finger.

The scents swirl around me, forcing me to think of nothing but the affirmations.

Breathe in. Breathe out. Repeat.

Finishing my degree means everything to me. For the longest time, no one believed I could go to college and get this close to finishing. Not even myself. But meeting Genevieve changed everything.

I was fresh out of the hospital and fragile in my recovery. She was the first person to encourage me to accept my disorders—to accept my past—so I could move forward and live… even with anxiety as my long-time friend. My weekly sessions with Genevieve have been my anchor for over a decade. She told me I didn't need her blessing to pursue psychology, but she gave it anyway.

But I'm not pursuing psychology for Genevieve. I'm doing it for me. I'm doing it because I know millions of girls and women like me need and deserve support. The support I know I can give because I understand. I more than understand.

Finishing and getting out there to help people…it's non-negotiable.

I can do this. I can fucking do this.

My watch beeps, reminding me to take my meds and eat something. I shuffle over to the kitchen to grab my pill organizer and pour myself a glass of water.

My studio apartment is the first place I've lived on my own. I found the place online and fell in love with the floor-to-ceiling windows facing the busyness of U Street. The Howard University campus stands off in the distance. I still own my parents' house in Arlington, but I haven't been there since…

Nope. Not gonna go there, either.

I settle into a familiar daydream. In it, I take the train to the Tidal Basin and picnic on the lawn in March when the cherry blossoms bloom. D.C. is famous for the cherry blossom festival, but the thought of going to a full-blown festival feels as good as shoving sporks under my fingernails. But in my fantasy, the Basin is empty, and I'm able to lay with Kitty in the spring sun and view the blooms in peace.

And maybe if a handsome man were to walk past…maybe while walking his dog…and the dog got off the leash and ran toward me? Then maybe the man would stop to get his puppy and start a conversation, and one thing would lead to another and…we're in a passionate romance.

Sigh.

"Kitty, we can handle anything," I say out loud to my dog. He circles around and sits at attention in front of me. Tilting his head to the side, he snorts and waits for his next command.

"Relax," I say, petting his head and rubbing his face. When I release him, he saunters off to his dog bed, settling in and cuddling with his plushie.

I open the pill box, take the meds out of the container, toss them in my mouth, and swallow with a big gulp.

There was a time when taking medicine to help my anxiety caused more anxiety. My brain would tell me things like, *What if you have an allergic reaction and go into anaphylaxis?* Fun shit.

But now, after finding the right combination of meds and therapy, I can breathe. The crushing weight of constant anxiety and panic does not weigh me down.

I can go outside. I can get into a car. I can be free. I simply need accommodations.

A rap song about hyping up best friends blares from my phone, vibrating it closer to my laptop. Taking another big gulp of water, I set the glass down and answer my best friend's call.

Veronica Lance and I met on the playground in 3rd grade. I was being teased for the short 'fro my mom gave me after I fell asleep with two sticks of bubble gum in my mouth—gum that migrated into my curly hair.

Veronica came to my rescue when she socked Dominique Jennings right in the mouth and left her sobbing on the playground.

"You look cute. Just fluff your hair because it's a little flat on the left side," she whispered to me as she hooked her arm in mine. With a confident stride, she rushed us away from our crying classmate and to the bathroom.

Even though we both got detention, it was worth it.

She knew what it was like to be one of the five kids with melanated skin in our two-hundred student private school near Capitol Hill. She's been my best friend, my sister really, ever since.

I just wish she didn't need to be my protector so much still.

"*Biiiiiiiitch,*" she says with a long groan.

"What happened now, Rons?" I smile at my loud friend's predictable greeting. I head over to my clothes-rack-turned-closet and pull a pair of yoga pants and a soft T-shirt off their respective hangers before placing them on my bed. I felt compelled to dress in slacks and a button-down for my call with Ms. O'Connor—as if that would impact the outcome. I frown. At least now I can get comfortable.

"James just decided to let me know he's going to Seattle. Guess when he's fucking going, Winter?"

I pull the phone away from my ear and barely get a reply of "When?" out before Veronica interrupts.

"The week I'm supposed to give birth, that's when!" A door slams on the other side of the phone.

I let out a small gasp. "No way! What's he thinking?" I'm concerned, but I'd never tell her that.

"You know he isn't thinking. Why would he think? It's not that he'd ever tell his boss that he needs time off because *God forbid* he tell the Baltimore Thunderhawks they'll have to find a replacement to apply Koban."

"Veronica, he does a *little* more than apply sports tape. He's the team doctor."

"Doctor? You know who needs a doctor? Me! His wife who is pregnant with his first child." She crunches in my ear, and I'm sure it's kettle corn, her pregnancy fixation. She's been blessed to not have morning sickness, even though she just popped positive.

"Well, you know I'll be there, Rons. And James would leave in the middle of the game if you told him you had even a whisper of a contraction." I think. I hope.

The truth is Veronica's husband, James, is not my favorite person. Nor am I his. Veronica met him at the Johns Hopkins satellite hospital where she *was* a trauma ER nurse.

Was, because James doesn't allow Veronica to work anymore. He says it's for her safety, but I say bullshit.

One of James' players suffered a compound fracture, and Veronica stabilized the man. After the patient was sent to surgery, James asked Veronica out. He said he liked the way she commanded the room.

I think he just liked her ass in her scrubs.

To hear Veronica tell it, they connected over their shared love for their work and the fact that they both are part of Black Greek life. They pledged complementary organizations.

"You just have to see him *stroll*, Winter," Rons told me early on in their relationship. I told her I'd take her word for it.

It only took six months of dating for Veronica Lance to become Veronica Palmer. Now, two years later, she's expecting their first child.

Veronica sniffles into the phone.

"Yeah," she says in a small voice. "It's just that…I hate his job. Like, hate it. Loathe the shit entirely. And I *es-pec-ial-ly* hate all the ball sniffers around waiting to hop on his dick at any moment. I just wish he'd quit and work at any other place."

Crunch-crunch-crunch.

"First off," I say while fishing my underwear out of the bottom drawer of my nightstand, "James wouldn't do something like that."

I don't think so, at least.

"And two, girl, you did not just call them ball sniffers!"

She lets out a flat chuckle. "You're right, Winter. I'm just feeling…"

I wait for her to finish, but after a few seconds, I say, "Insecure?"

"Puffy."

"Veronica Marie Lance-Palmer! You are pregnant—with my niece or nephew, might I add. Give yourself a break."

"Win, my jeans don't zip anymore and I'm barely two months pregnant. And I can't even say it's baby weight because the baby is, like, the size of a walnut or something. So…"

I sigh. "Sweet bestie of mine, I won't listen to you put yourself down. Do you need me to come over there?"

"I…really?" Skepticism laces Veronica's voice.

"Yes," I say firmly and clear my throat. "Do you need me to come over? You sound like you need some chocolate and for someone to rub your feet. James is away at training camp, right?"

Veronica sniffles into the phone.

"You'd come over for me?" Her voice sounds watery and tear-filled.

It's a big deal for me to leave my home. It's a process, which is why I only leave a few times a week at most.

Besides getting Kitty ready to work—putting on his harness, finding his paw shoes if it's wet, planning out my route—there are my anxiety rituals I have to complete.

First, there's the ritual of checking all the appliances to make sure they won't set on fire. I have to do this three times, uninterrupted.

Then, when I leave my apartment, I have to check that the door is locked three uninterrupted times. If I don't, I will expect someone to be in my apartment, ready to murder me. It will feel as real to my body as if I were staring down an axe murderer in real life.

Going down the stairs, I must count every single step. With practice, I've learned to count them in my head rather than out loud like I used to. Again, this practice must be uninterrupted. If I miss a step, I have to start over, trudging back up the stairs to count them again.

Once outside, I have to check the vehicle. It's always Uber or Lyft because I don't drive. I know how to, in theory, but I just don't. I've had more than one driver peel off while in the middle of my ritual.

It's a process. But I've come a long way.

There was a time when I couldn't leave the house at all. I'd touch the door handle to leave and blackout from the resulting panic attack. Those times when I'd wake up in the hospital, drugged out of my mind, were the only instances in which I'd see the outside world and anyone other than Henry, Gia, and Veronica Lance.

But I'm better. I'm getting better. I'm managing, damn it.

I will see the cherry blossoms.

"Yes, I would. Actually, I kinda need your help."

In the end, Veronica ends up braving the Monday rush hour traffic to come to my apartment. Not because she doesn't believe I can make the trip over to her home in Adams Morgan, but because she "couldn't stand to stay inside and watch another episode of *Love in the City.*"

So that's how she ends up curled up on my sofa in sweats and a T-shirt at 10 p.m., spilling popcorn crumbs everywhere while watching *Love in the City.*

"I just don't see why they can't let you do all this virtually," she says, swiping the open Diet Coke can off the glass coffee table so fast some of the soda spills over her fingers and lands on the seat.

"I don't understand it either, Rons. Everyone does everything virtually now. Why would this be any different? But I don't want to push it with them and make things harder on me." Sitting on the plush rug in front of the couch, I move to steal popcorn from the bowl in her lap.

She stares at my hand with wide eyes and raised eyebrows.

"Anyway, maybe they have a point," I say, pulling my hand back with caution, a single kernel of popcorn between my fingers.

"The point being that they're ableist fucks?" she says after a beat.

"Veronica!" I laugh and place a hand over my chest.

"I mean, they are! You've done so much for that school, even when you were in undergrad. You've published articles and presented at conferences—virtually, because duh—and now they're sticking to their guns about *this*?" She shoves a handful of popcorn in her mouth and chomps to prove her point.

"I hear you, babe. *And* I think maybe it's okay for me to push myself a little bit more than I have. You know…get out there."

She blinks at me.

"I will set aside the self-defeating rhetoric for now, babe. What does Genevieve the Therapist have to say about it?" I laugh at her name for my long-time therapist.

"I'll talk to her about it in my next session. I feel…not *great* about it, but I feel like this could ultimately be a positive thing. Have faith in me, Rons."

She inhales a little bit and sits up, placing the bowl next to her on the couch.

"I have all the faith in you, Winter. Do you know how spectacular you are? Like, my best friend is a baddie. I know you can do anything! I just— I don't like it when people try to mess over you."

She trails off, and I grab her free hand, squeezing it.

"Thank you for always sticking up for me, Rons. I love you."

"I love you too, Winter. You're one step closer to opening your ranch. Right?"

"Right," I reply, smiling. I let my head land on the sofa, my attention on the screen but thoughts elsewhere. "I'm gonna do it, Rons. One day, I'll have a big plot of land in the country with horses and goat yoga and sound baths and bodywork—"

"And all the other witchy-woo-woo stuff you swear by," Veronica adds.

I roll my eyes and smile.

When I left the hospital years ago, I got the idea to create a place for survivors to mend their fractured souls after trauma —a safe space for healing. The mental hospital's sterile approach was helpful, but it didn't provide what I needed to move forward.

Medication and therapy helped get me stable.

True healing requires so much more—it requires soul work.

Kitty wanders over to me and puts his paws on my shoulder.

"I'm okay, love," I murmur to him. "Off duty."

Veronica grabs the bowl again, frowning and sighing when she sees it's empty.

"Well, let's get to it then." She pops up from her seat, and I stare at her still-flat stomach. It's bananas that she's growing a whole-ass human in there. Veronica has always been fit—her muscular, toned body looked very different from mine until I grew into myself.

My body type didn't get acceptable until the Kardashians made big asses and wide hips popular again. And if I have anything, I have an ass. And a round stomach with a little pooch over my cooch that sticks out when I wear form-fitting clothing.

I'm a comfortable size fourteen, sometimes sixteen.

Veronica ran track-and-field in high school and got a good chunk of money from her college to do the same. I bet if she tried hard enough, her thighs could crack walnuts, even though she's retired from sports. At the same time, she has an ass the Instagram models pay good money for, and her tits are perky perfect C-cups.

I look down at my chest. My G-cups, though full and round, do not defy gravity. I'm grateful for and, at the same time, curse the inventor of the bra.

She snags my laptop from the corner desk and strides back to the sofa. "Ms. O'Connor sent over info on clients, yeah? So, let's see it." She unlocks my laptop, and I rush to close the lid.

"You cannot see private client information. *Sooooorrry,*" I say as I take the laptop from her.

"Yeah, yeah, HIPAA and all that noise. Well, open it up and *you* see what she sent. I'm gonna go get some more pizza."

She stands back up, pivots, and pauses for a second before saying, "Actually, I'm gonna go pee. Then pizza."

I wave her off and re-open my computer. I tap the secure email from Ms. O'Connor, scanning through the message. She looped in Dr. Wagner, and the doctor sent a response an hour ago.

> I have an interesting option for you. I have a fifteen-year-old Autistic male on the floor who is near discharge. The family declines inpatient treatment, and a hybrid program is inappropriate in this case. I've attached the case notes in the portal. Let me know what you think, and I'll begin the referral process.
>
> Dr. W
>
> P.S. I read your last paper on access to alternative communication devices within inner-city Autistic populations. Brilliant work. Thrilled to see what you'll do over the next few months.

I lean against the sofa as Veronica rummages around my kitchen. This seems like a perfect fit for me.

My interest in neurodivergence sparked in Dr. Stevenson's undergraduate seminar of all places. I admit I didn't know much about autism going into the class, and I can now see Dr. Stevenson's delivery of the course material reeked of bias. When we were tasked with a class research project that required us to work with programs serving the autism community, I planned on finishing the assignment and getting through the class.

I didn't plan on finding a deep connection with my clients, even through the barrier of a computer screen. When I learned that Autistic youths are three times more likely to face abuse in their childhoods...it was like part of my mission snapped in place.

Reading over the notes, I learn the client has unreliable speech and uses an alternative communication device to talk. He's just lost his mother, and the circumstances around her death are heartbreaking. The number of transitions he's experiencing right now would be a lot for anyone, much less for someone with his profile.

Even through the sterile case notes, I feel connected to this patient.

I can handle this one-on-one.

This is what you've been working toward, Winter. You can so do this.

I type my response to Dr. Wagner and close my laptop when I hear Veronica sniff in the kitchen.

When she walks into the room, her bright smile contrasts with the tense set of her shoulders. I can't ignore the red tint around her lids.

"What's wrong?" I say, standing up to walk closer to her.

"You know. Hormones."

I raise my eyebrow and say nothing, giving her a long look.

"Listen, I'm pregnant and hormonal. It's fine." Her phone lights up in her tense hand. I flick my eyes down to read the text before she can make the screen black again.

"Everything okay with James?"

Her back stiffens as she says, "Yep," popping the "p" with slight force.

I tilt my head. "Why aren't you talking to me, Veronica?"

"I am, *Doctor Vaughan,* jeez. There's nothing happening. Just James being his usual self, and I have less ability to deal with it without crying." She shrugs. "It is what it is."

I give her another short look before sighing and shaking my head.

"Okay, but if there's something that's bothering you, I'm here to help you. Okay?" She doesn't say anything but leans over to give me a tight hug.

When she releases me a moment later, she says, "I know, sister. Let's just watch some more *Love in the City.* I wanna know what happens with Marc and Jenni."

She shuffles around me and takes up residence back on the couch. Spotting the empty popcorn bowl, she looks at it, then toward the kitchen, and finally at me.

"Um, do you mind…maybe…" She holds the bowl in front of her face and gives me her best puppy dog eyes.

"Yeah, yeah," I say as I snatch the bowl from her to get her more kettle corn.

TWO
HUNTER

The antiseptic stings my nose as I round the corner of the inpatient floor at the children's hospital, but the burning in my face is from sheer anxiety.

Despite the two drinks I had in the hour before landing and fucking the eager flight attendant, restricting her movements and controlling her breath, I still feel like my head is going to pop off my shoulders.

It's clear that no matter who I fuck, how much I drink, or what I take, nothing will erase the mess in front of me.

How the fuck am I supposed to step into parenthood? I can barely take care of myself.

It's been twenty-four hours since I was contacted by state police and told my high school girlfriend and mother of my only child died of a drug overdose. It's been that many hours since I accepted that I need to step into the role of Dad for our fifteen-year-old son.

This new development rocks my shit—tilting everything off-center.

First, to my knowledge, Maiya has been sober for the last decade at least.

Second, I haven't been in my son's life beyond infrequent visits and regular child support deposits.

Maiya was my high school girlfriend—a scholarship kid from the wrong side of the tracks whose presence in my life made my father livid.

I loved the shit out of his reaction.

Plus, if Maiya could do anything, she could suck and fuck a cock.

But then, everything changed when she got pregnant right after graduation.

I did the best thing I could do for everyone involved when she said she wouldn't abort: I gave her money and stayed the hell away.

I would have destroyed him.

The energy in my body pulses and sharpens, looking for an exit out of the prison of my skin. The headache I've nursed since leaving Türkiye sixteen hours ago is in full bloom now. I was in Bursa to finalize the plant details for the European arm of BwP. We're hoping to expand outside of the United States —if we can get the Feds to play nice.

My temples pulse again.

I'm the CEO of BwP, a MedTech company that's grown a multibillion-dollar industrial powerhouse in just over a decade. I run it with my best friend, Leo, as my second in command.

Well, saying I run it isn't really accurate. Leo and I decided it would be best if I operated as CEO and him as COO. The only reason is because with the Brigham name and connections, I was able to get us access to what we needed to grow in a way that Leo was unable to.

He tried. But the gatekeepers kept the doors closed.

I show my face when it's needed to bypass the bullshit. But Leo's the real brains behind the operation. BwP is his baby. So I do what he tells me to, use my connections and influence when necessary, and try to not fuck up the company.

Which is fine by me.

I don't have to worry about many things. I go where I want. I do what I want. It's live and let live over here.

And now I'm going to have to play Daddy Dearest.

I scratch my nose and crack my neck.

Navigating my way to Room P1403, I pass vivid cartoon animal sketches on the walls and try to squash down my discomfort at being here, in this hospital, back in this goddamn cesspool of a town I vowed to avoid.

"H."

Leo's voice echoes off the gleaming floors, and I catch sight of him standing between the metal double doors leading to the locked ward. I shift my direction to catch up with him.

Leo Polanco is often deemed intimidating. It's an unfair and inaccurate assessment. As tall as I am at 6'3", the fact that he's a quiet guy with strong, dark features causes people to assume he's a threat. They're wrong. Sure, he can be a grumpy motherfucker, but the Leo I know has Katy Perry on his Spotify playlist and likes to watch TikToks of otters holding hands in the sea.

It's rare for others to see that side of his personality, though.

Just as I'm the son of a powerful man, so is he. The Lost Boys of the Ultra-Elite.

Over the last few years, Leo has been more serious than relaxed. BwP takes up a lot of his attention, especially with what we have about to hit the market.

Hopefully soon. Hopefully.

"Got a bit of a situation." Leo places his hand on my shoulder, and we walk together. Turning the corner, I look at him and say, "Explain."

"Well—"

"Get the hell out of my goddamn way!"

"Miss!" The pointed voice of a vexed nurse hits my ears, as does a familiar voice I'd also hoped to avoid. At least for a little while.

"Ella is here," Leo says, much like one would say, "You've got gonorrhea."

He rubs the skin above his eyebrows.

Ella Elizabeth Brigham should be demure and respectful, given her breeding. But she's acting now as she always has: loud and demanding. Ella's all hard edges. But my little sister isn't a tomboy anymore, nor is she the girl who was forced to be a debutante, puffy white dress and all, when she'd rather ride dirt bikes and read fantasy novels.

Instead, she stands before me in Chucks, black leggings, and a long-sleeved Henley. She looks very different from when I last saw her in person.

When was that? Seven years ago? Longer?

Her once-unmanageable sable-hued hair, the same color as mine, is in a sleek ponytail that looks like it's vibrating as she rages on the nurse.

She's an adult now. Twenty-two years old.

My little sister isn't my baby sister anymore.

Ella shifts in my direction as Leo and I rush down the corridor. Her acne problem is gone, which makes me happy for her. She was always so self-conscious about it. Her skin is clear, although her face is not—her impertinent scowl deepens as the seconds tick on.

"Ma'am," the nurse spits out, "screaming and cursing will get you nowhere. You are not on the visitor list. Please leave before I have you escorted by security." Two other nurses, both male, flank the nurse, and Ella squares her shoulders.

I butt in before things can escalate.

"Excuse me, I'm August Brigham's father. This is his aunt. She can come in."

The nurse sniffs as I hand over my ID. Leo points to the sticker badge on his shirt, as he'd come in before.

Leo's involvement in August's life is complicated. When Maiya popped up pregnant, he was the first person I told about it. While we both went off to college, he ultimately returned to D.C.

Because he was close by, I asked him to check in on August once. It was his fifth birthday, and I wanted him to have a gift. It was a little helicopter I picked up from a toy shop in London. I don't know what drove me to go into the store or decide to give August a gift, but I did.

While I could have mailed it, I had Leo hand-deliver the present. And years later, he's kept up with August, seeing him often when I can't.

Or, more accurately, won't.

The other nurses roll their eyes as they walk away.

"You'll show her the way then," the nurse replies. "And please know that any aggression toward staff will not be tolerated. You *will* be removed."

With that, the nurse turns away from us and walks over to her computer, sitting on the rolling chair with a huff.

"Right," Ella says. She arches her eyebrow in a way that's so much like our mother. It's uncanny when she does it because she never got the chance to know the woman who birthed us.

I swallow down the memories.

Ignoring Leo and me, Ella enters August's room and stops a few steps from his bed. I brace myself to see my son for the first time in years. When was the last time?

For an hour on his thirteenth birthday. He's fifteen now.

Fuck.

Father of the fucking year.

Sucking in a breath, I turn around. Ella pulls up a chair and holds his hand. The sharp, angry look on her face dissolves as tears stream down her face. Her pale nose is red.

August has always been considered frail. He was born small, slightly premature, but he hasn't jumped any significant percentage on the growth chart from every report I've gotten from his caregivers. In part due to genetics and in part because there are only a few foods he eats.

After nearly a week of dehydration, his cheeks are sunken in, and he looks gaunt. Bandages wind around his hands, and a plastic cover protects the IV site in his right arm.

"Ella," I say after a tense moment, and she looks up at me with watery eyes.

"So you decided to show up, huh?" Her anger takes me off guard, even though I deserve every drop.

"What else was I supposed to do?" I say, genuinely searching for an answer. Maybe she has one.

She sighs and stands back up. Walking toward me, she says, "I don't know, Hunter." She hesitates for a minute before grabbing my hand.

I flinch at the touch.

"It's good to see you, H. I've missed you."

"I've missed you too, Ellie." And it's the truth. Even though staying away was a hundred percent my choice, it doesn't mean I haven't missed the only woman I've ever loved besides Mom.

She would have been killed too.

Ella takes a step back and gives me a warbled smile. Then she hits me across the chest.

"*That* is for staying away so long! And *that*," she slaps me on the arm, "is for not telling me you were in town. I had to hear everything from Dad." I pivot away to avoid her pinched fingers as they make their way toward my nipple.

At the mention of our father, ice shoots down my arms.

He will always know. There's no hiding from him.

"Oh? What do you know?"

"I know that Maiya died days ago. I know August was found after wandering around for God knows how long. I know no one thought to contact me until two hours ago. Me.

His only aunt. The only person in our family who has any regular contact with him."

Her severe frown reappears.

Ella should have been contacted first, not me. I understand why the investigators called—I'm his father and next of kin on his school forms and the area-wide ChildFind database. But I was across the planet, and Ella is right here where she's always been, doing what she's always done: being here for August.

"Help me understand it, Hunter. Why have you stayed away for so damn long? From me? From your son?" The last two words shoot at me like bullets as they explode out her mouth. She crosses her arms over her chest, her stance combative.

I want to fidget under her scrutiny as I think about a way to explain what is unexplainable. At least, not without making me look like a total fuckhead.

But wasn't that the point? Didn't I say that I'd rather everyone think I'm an asshole than know the real reason why I left?

"Maiya and I were toxic," is what I land on. "You remember how she was."

She rolls her eyes, then stares at me even harder.

"Okay, but that still doesn't explain your absence in your son's life, Hunter James Brigham." She pokes me once with her sharp, black fingernail, and her gaze telegraphs what I'm sure are her inner thoughts: *I'm sick of your shit.*

Her mouth tightens. "Is it because he's Autistic?" Her voice is low, but so fire-filled I think she really could incinerate me on the spot.

"Absolutely not!" I reply without hesitation. "I know I didn't understand it when he was first diagnosed, but I've done my best to get educated."

I won't say I'm the poster child for autism allies, but I've taken time to listen to and learn from Autistic people in an effort to know my son.

I didn't get it back then, but I wanted to understand. Even if I couldn't be there for him.

Wouldn't be there for him.

I clear my throat, forcing myself to ratchet down my defensiveness.

"I've taken a lot of time to educate myself. I was the one who got him into that spelling program over in Herndon when those idiot therapists wanted to sit him in a corner forever because he couldn't talk," I say, infusing more calm into my delivery.

For the first eight years of August's life, I watched as report after report came in from the aides and therapists I'd hired to help him, all essentially saying in one way or another that August would never amount to anything. They said I might as well give up on any hopes of him learning because he couldn't learn.

Speech therapists, occupational therapists, music therapists—they'd all given up because his body seemed so out of control to them.

They still came around to collect a paycheck, though.

Holed up in the Waldorf in Manhattan one snowy weekend, I dove down the rabbit hole and found a program so close to August and Maiya that it couldn't have been anything but divine intervention that I stumbled upon it.

Through the new therapy, I learned that August has a lot of thoughts inside him, but apraxia prevents his brain from sending the signals to his body in the way it needs to for speech. There's a disconnect between his mind and his body. The reason why he doesn't speak is more of a motor issue rather than a cognitive one.

There are millions of non-speaking Autistic people who are just like him.

It took a few years, but August graduated from poking out his thoughts letter-by-letter on a laminated board to using a word processor to type and communicate. Over those years, he's become happier and less stressed. He's even said as much.

But now this…

"Sure, H. Money is great and all. But he doesn't need money. He needs—needed—a father." Ella's words pull me back to this sterile hospital room, reminding me that my son is here. And he really does need me this time.

I hold Ella's gaze. "I care. I care about him. I know I've chosen shit ways of showing it, but…" I shrug, not really knowing what else to say.

Her exhalation is short. "It's whatever, I guess," she drawls. She starts to move away, but I grab her arm.

"I'm sorry, Ella. Things have just been insane—busy with BwP. Things with Maiya were getting complicated way before this." That's not exactly true. Maiya and I don't talk. Or, I guess, we didn't talk. As long as the deposits hit her bank account every month, she left me alone. It works. Worked.

"Ever the avoider. Right, H?" Her eyebrow lifts, her sardonic expression socking me in the solar plexus. "Anyway, I know things were complicated. August told me," she says, flopping back down on her chair and pulling her legs beneath her. I sit down too, but pause, looking at her when her statement registers.

"What do you mean?"

"He told me. He talks to me. We see each other all the time. I'd take him out on weekends, for his birthday, yada, yada. He damn near lives with me. Maiya and I weren't 'friends,'" she moves her fingers to make air quotes, "but August *is* my only nephew." She drops her phone on the seat next to her.

"Lives with you? When did this start?"

And why was I not told this?

"For the last year or so. She came to Dad's place asking for more money. She said you were…unresponsive to her needs, and she needed more."

"I was paying her a hundred grand a month for child support," I say with a low breath.

"I know," she says, waving my words off.

Between my business and the fact that my family has more money in their bank accounts than most people will ever see in ten lifetimes, giving someone over a million dollars per year in child support actually puts me in deadbeat territory.

"Wait, so she was taking the child support every month, but not actually taking care of our son?" The back of my eyeballs feel itchy.

Ella doesn't respond; she just does that waving thing again.

"In any event, she showed up at Dad's making a fuss about 'airing the family's dirty laundry,' but you know Dad," she finishes.

I do indeed know Dad.

Ella reaches into her pocket and pulls out a wrapped nugget of bright pink Bubblicious bubble gum. Pulling away the waxy paper, she pops it into her mouth and smacks noisily. I get a flash of her as a teenager.

"So *anyway,*" she draws out the word, "IDK what happened with that situation in the end, but I made sure to let her know that I had no problem hanging with August. She didn't really care either way." She blows a bubble and pops it.

Leo shifts as he leans against the wall. His shoulders are tense, even though the rest of his body seems relaxed.

"Well, I'm glad you've been there for him." I clear my throat.

"Yep," is all she says before blowing an obnoxiously large bubble and popping her gum. "Anyway, I'm not really here for you. I'm here for Augie." She leans forward in her seat to grab August's hand.

"Are you planning on coming to Sunday dinner?" she asks without looking at me.

The anxious energy that's simmered beneath the surface of my skin flares to full force, shooting arcs of electricity through my body. "Sunday dinner. With Dad?"

"Yeah, who else? He requested you be there, H. You should show your face. The prodigal son and all that jazz." She smiles at me as if she's not telling me to deliver myself to the devil himself. But to her, he's just Dad.

To me, he's the ruler and destroyer of all he touches.

"I'll think about it," I say finally.

"I really wish you would. I've really missed you and want to spend time with you before you run off again. This time with August?" she says with a question in her voice. I can't tell whether she thinks that's a good or bad idea.

I don't know how long I'll be here. Or what my plans are beyond today. So all I can say is, "Yeah."

"Well, figure it out. If not for yourself, for August." She shifts in her seat. "So what's the plan?"

"The plan?" I say dumbly. I don't have a fucking plan. My plan consisted of getting back to D.C. without jumping out of the plane while over the Atlantic.

"He's going to need help. A lot of help. When I called *Leonardo*," she says his name with just as much disgust as Leo showed when mentioning her name in the hallway, "he told me that August has not talked at all since he's been here. He's been melting down, hence the sedation drip. So what's the deal?"

Leo clears his throat and says, "I spoke with Dr. Wagner. She suggested he receive in-home therapies rather than going somewhere else."

"Somewhere else—like a home? What the fuck!" Ella yells.

August makes a noise in his throat, and his hand closest to me twitches. At the movement, I shoot Ella a sharp look, and she appears contrite. We're silent for a moment, watching the monitor as his heart rate and respirations stabilize into their previous restful pattern.

"No, more like inpatient mental health treatment," Leo says with a softer voice.

"He's *fifteen*. True, he's gone through a lot this past week, but he will get the best support if he's able to be home with his family," Ella continues.

Home. Something else I'll have to figure out.

"Will you stay at Amelia Manor?" Ella pipes up as if she can read my thoughts.

A wave of sadness threatens to crush me, as it does any time the topic of my mother comes up. I normally wouldn't consider it, but staying at the estate mom left to both me and Ella would work. It's a good option. I shut my brain down when it starts to call up memories of me and my mom at Amelia Manor, picnicking on the thick, impossibly green grass.

"Yes, I think it'll be comfortable for August and me."

"Great. Good thing I've been keeping the property up," she replies. "I'll have a room ready for him by the time he's discharged from this place." She swings her head back around to Leo. "But back to the hospitalization bullshit. What's the alternative?"

"She mentioned getting a therapist to come to the home and basically recreate an intensive outpatient program. With those, you usually spend all day working on your problems, but you go home at the end of the day. With him being Autistic and already needing different therapies, *and* with this new trauma, she basically thinks we can recreate an outpatient program, but at home."

What he says makes sense, even though I struggle with how we'll get this done.

"Did she have ideas on how we can do that? I don't have a fucking therapy team in my pocket, much to everyone's surprise," I say. I feel myself getting antsy.

I pick at the skin on my thumbnail.

"She had some ideas. We'll need to hire someone, but she

has a list. I'll make sure she stops by in the morning," Leo says.

"So it's all settled," Ella declares. Still ignoring Leo, she stands and leans over to give August a kiss on the forehead. He inhales deeply, even in his sleep.

"I'll take care of the hiring part, H. Just be here. Okay?" She wraps her arms around me and squeezes with her head on my chest.

I breathe in her familiar scent of lemon verbena and coconut. "I'll do my best," is all I say.

She's silent for a moment, searching my face. "I know you can do even better," she says before walking out the door.

The room hums with the sound of machines—the IV pumps, the pulse oximeter reading, and August's delicate, slow breathing. I take steps closer to him until I'm beside his bed.

His narrow face and sharp eyebrows look so much like Maiya.

"I see you in him now that he's older," Leo says.

"Maybe," I reply, although I do think he looks more like me now. I take up residence in Ella's abandoned seat. As my body settles into the cheap plastic, soreness seeps into my bones. My palms tingle.

"Tell me about how you found them," I say, not looking at Leo. I'm watching the rise and fall of August's chest.

"She was in a drug house in Baltimore," he says, still leaning against the wall. "It took a while to find her because she left her phone behind at the house in Potomac Mills. August's summer school reported him missing after they couldn't get in contact with anyone for a few days."

I blanch, thinking about the call I might have missed from his teachers. I'm too chicken shit to look at my call logs.

I take my eyes off August and lean on the bed, resting my chin in my hands.

"Why was August there?" I ask.

"I don't know. My best guess is that she didn't expect to OD where she was."

I grunt in reply.

"As for August, the best we could figure out is he left the house where his mom was, probably trying to find help. The police found him five miles away under the interstate. His communication tablet was gone."

I want to vomit.

"Was it Fentanyl?" I ask.

He nods, somber. I sigh and cover my face with my hands.

I tried Fentanyl once, and not of my own choice. It was in some coke I got when I visited Toronto six years ago. It was the first time I got Narcan'd. Thankfully, that experience was sobering enough that I stopped doing drugs altogether. Withdrawals were a bitch, but I got through it. The luxury rehab center in Calabasas helped.

The cravings are a distant memory now. At least, most days.

"She was doing so good, though…" I say. I'm sad that August has lost his mother, that this disease of addiction took her from the world even after being sober for so long.

I rub my chest. When Maiya and I met, she wasn't a hardcore drug user. She was a partier, but she kept her wildness limited to weed and the occasional molly. When we got together, though, I was into drugs. Bad.

Pills brought us even closer together. But when I left her behind, she spiraled while I soared.

The world isn't fair, and I'd have to be dead not to recognize that from the outside, I look like a monster.

Maybe I am.

"We have to talk about the issue of your father," Leo cuts in. He moves to the chair on the other side of August's bed.

My muscles seize up.

"He knows you're in town. He's going to want you to start back up with—"

I give him a searing look. "I will not. I won't go back there." I won't do whatever the fuck it is that he wants me to do.

Won't I?

"Well, how are you going to break the news to Pops?" He leans back, folding his arms across his chest.

Leo hates my father as much as I do. Besides the fact that my father is a racist, elitist fuck, he's also responsible for the shittiest moments in Leo's life.

And mine, too.

"I don't have to say shit," I reply.

"The hell you don't. You don't have an ocean separating the two of you anymore. Plus, you and I both know that if he wanted to, he could have gotten to you at any time, no matter where you were."

I know this. I've always known this. But instead of living in fear of my father and what he can do, I've drowned it out.

Not that my brain doesn't take every opportunity to remind me.

"The fact that he dropped all that info on Ella's lap shows that he knows how to get to you and show who is in charge. You can't outrun this, H. You've got to face up to all of this. Face up to him."

I run my fingers through my hair, gripping the strands at the roots.

Of course, Leo is right. He's always right, though I'll never tell him so. He's a "think first, then act" kind of guy. I'm a "punch first, then think" kind of guy.

We're foils.

"The timing of all this is just fucking great," I say, blowing out my breath.

Leo nods.

Project Panacea is BwP's biggest secret project: a drug using gene therapy to create killer proteins that eradicate cancer for each person. No more blasting people with chemo and hoping it kills the cancer cells. BwP has technology that will encode and then decode cancer cells on the genetic level.

Yes, we're altering people's genes. It's history-changing shit.

"I've got things under control here," I say to him, gesturing toward August and the myriad of tubes flowing from him.

He shakes his head. "With all due respect, you really don't," he says.

Ouch.

"I..." I start to speak and then stop myself. Because he's actually right. I don't have this, even though I want to. "I've got Ella. You really need me at BwP."

"No, I don't need you at BwP," he disagrees. "But you need me here."

"Well, shit, tell me how you really feel," I say.

"You're going to use Amelia Manor, right? We'll set up shop there. It will give me the chance to be with you and August and be close enough to handle things at HQ if needed."

After sixteen hours of travel, I'm too tired to protest or offer any additional solutions, so I nod in acceptance.

We both fall silent. I watch August's breathing.

The plastic chair creaks as Leo shifts, standing.

"Later," he says.

In typical Leo fashion, he's hit his quota of words for the day. After he leaves a few minutes later, I turn off the main lights. The monitors cast a cool glow around the room. August doesn't stir, and the IV machine whirs as it delivers more drugs into his system.

I move over to the couch and unfold the paper-thin blanket and plastic-covered pillow. Setting up for the night, I walk over to August and dare to touch him.

I put my hand on his hair, gently pushing his straight locks out of his eyes.

"I'm sorry, August," I whisper in the darkness. I don't usually apologize to people. Most people don't deserve or require it. But for August…none of this should have happened to him.

Silence greets my statement.

"I've been fuck all to you. But I promise I'll try my best."

Ella's words echo in my head.

I'll try to do even better than that.

THREE
WINTER

School doesn't start for another three weeks, but I'm already finished with the required reading for the next month of classes.

Veronica's told me many times that I spend too many hours with my head in a textbook, but what else would I do? When things are silent and I'm alone, my brain buzzes, energized. Keeping productive and busy helps me to feel fulfilled…and prevents my mind from flipping into an anxiety loop.

It's part of my process.

I'm adding notes to a Post-It in my advanced psychopathology textbook when my phone pings with an email. The bright, happy chime sends a rocket of terror through my body. Kitty jumps up when I do, wagging his tail as he leans on my leg. In my flailing, I accidentally bump into my desk, causing my textbook to plop on the floor. The index cards I've organized over the past hour scatter around my small desk.

"Girl, chill!" I instruct myself out loud, hoping the sound of my voice will cut through the panic and calm my racing heart.

I'm way too on edge.

It's been almost a week and a half since I last heard from Dr. Wagner about the possible case, and my stress has risen in direct proportion to the number of days that have lapsed with no contact.

I *need* this chance.

As time passes, the idea of securing counseling clients and possibly going into a clinic keeps me up at night.

I try to be gentle with myself—to honor where I am in my journey and how far I've come. Because I've come fucking far. And yet, I can't help the frustration I feel when I think about how much of a struggle it is for me to do what I want.

I'm fighting against demons I didn't invite in. I resent the events that have brought me here.

I resent the *fuck* out of them.

But as Genevieve says, I didn't create this story. I'm just a character in this jacked up play.

Woo-freakin-hoo.

Enough is enough. If it's not from them, I'll follow up. It's okay to follow up. It's not annoying. It's expected.

I grab the phone off my nightstand, standing still without looking at it.

In his dark, slightly cross-eyed stare, Kitty says to me, *Wayminute, girlfriend. Take a chill pill. A literal one, if you need it.*

I rub behind his ear.

Canine pep talk received, I open the app.

A renewed surge of adrenaline shoots through me, and Kitty takes a moment to move back, assessing me.

"A-Alert," I say to Kitty as my voice quakes.

Throwing my phone on my bed, I rush to the corner of the apartment. Plopping down with my back to the wall, I stare at the phone from across the room as if the messenger could reach through the screen and drag me down to the depths of hell a la *The Ring*. Kitty automatically settles into my lap, his butt on my thighs and his paws resting on my chest. His little head nestles against my neck.

The Law Offices of Mercer, Statham, and Ryland, PLLC.

Well, fucking shit.

My heartbeat pounds in my ears, and the edges of my vision seem fuzzy and clouded. Overwhelming dread surges through me as it always does when I see the sender's name.

It's just an email. It can't hurt me. It's just an email. It can't hurt me. It's just an email. It cannot fucking hurt me.

Kitty's lick on my cheek tickles enough to cause an unexpected giggle to bubble from my lips. It does a lot to calm me down. Kitty sits beside me, leaning his body against my thigh and putting his head on my lap. I press my palms against my chest and belly and school myself to breathe in and out as deep as I can to a count of three.

One.

One-two-one.

One-two-three-two-one.

I repeat the mantras. As the buzzing between my ears lessens, Kitty moves to put his paws on my bent legs. I crack my eyes open in time to see him tilt his head to the side as if to say, *You good now?*

My energy vacillates, and he tries to climb on me again, ready to provide the deep pressure therapy he's been trained to give when I need it. I scoop him up to cuddle him to my chest. His head goes back to my neck. Patient.

The law firm handling my case only reaches out to me once every three years. It's not that they're reaching out to me that's sending me into a spiral. It's that they're a year and a half early contacting me that's got me off guard. And me being off guard still isn't a healthy spot.

Breathe, Winter. You can handle whatever it is.

"I'm good, Kitty." I rub his velvet-soft ears. "I'm all right."

We sit silently for a few more minutes—as silent as Kitty

can be with his floppy airway—and don't move until Kitty licks my cheek again.

You've got to read the email, Winter.

With cement-filled joints, I unfurl my body to walk back to my bed. Grabbing the phone, I open the message and sit.

> Ms. Vaughan:
>
> The parole hearing for Adam Collins will be on September 23rd at 9:00 AM EST at the Commonwealth of Virginia Correctional Complex, Room 14A. As a petitioner, you can provide a victim impact statement in person or via written submission for the Parole Board's consideration. Please notify this office of your selection and submit any written statements by September 13th at 5:00 PM EST.
>
> You will receive formal notice of this meeting from the Department of Corrections within the upcoming weeks.
>
> Sincerely,
>
> Janice Mercer, Esq.
>
> The Law Office of Mercer, Statham, and Ryland, PLLC

My heart trips over its rhythm. It always does when I have to deal with things related to Adam.

You're mine, my little princess.

A shudder travels through me, but I'm comforted that I managed to stave off a full-blown panic attack.

"Thank you, Kitty," I say. Kitty tilts his head again, and I swear I see him shake his head at me before heading to my nightstand.

He paws open the drawer, grabbing the medicine bottle with my emergency Xanax. He hops on the bed, dropping it by my hip before trotting off to grab a small four-ounce bottle of water from the basket I keep at his height.

He pads over, jumps back on the bed, and drops the water next to the pills.

It's amazing the things the service dog trainers were able to teach Kitty to do, but teaching him to respond to my panic attack cues by bringing me medicine and water is the most mind-boggling task he's able to do for me.

When I don't move to take the pills, Kitty nudges both bottles closer to my hip.

Time for an actual chill pill, babes, his stare says.

I pick up the medicine bottle and decide to take half of my emergency med. Swallowing down the anti-anxiety pill, I squeeze my eyes together so tight that static artifacts dance across my darkened field of vision.

Adam Collins is a name only a few people in my circle know. There was a time when I looked for him around every corner. I'd feel whispers of his hands on my body. I'd smell his sweat. I'd see his eyes in the faces of others around me.

His presence haunted me.

So I buried him—buried him deeply in the dark corners of my psyche, plastering mental bricks and cement in front of the tomb marked "Adam Collins and All the Fucked-Up Shit He Did to Me."

I am in control of when I think about Adam. I control when I have to deal with the aftermath of his actions. I am in control.

But this moment feels so incredibly out of control.

"I will not allow him to win," I say out loud. Kitty huffs as if in agreement—a solid, *You go, girl* said in the exhalation.

I calmly place my phone on my nightstand. Giving myself a few more moments of silence, I feel the effects of the Xanax start to seep into my muscles.

You are in control. You hold all the cards.

I move back to my desk and draft a reply email. Relief

pushes the weight of anxiety off my body when I attach my pre-written statement to the email to my lawyer. With a final hard press of the power button, I slam my computer shut.

Now you're done.

I inhale deeply and hold my breath, feeling the burn of oxygen as it expands my lungs and pushes out my ribs. When I exhale, the mortared wall encasing all things Adam Collins is firmly back in place.

I feel Kitty pad up to me again, nudging my leg in his signal that it's time to go out. A quick glance at the window shows that it's nearing dusk, and I'm an hour late for his evening walk. Luckily, I've trained Kitty to the point where he can do his business at dusk and be good until the morning.

"All right, Thunderbite. Let's roll." I saddle Kitty with his harness and adjust one of the Velcro badges that indicates that he's a working man. Er, dog. I grab my keys, phone, and Kitty's leash and lead us to the doggy park.

It takes us ten minutes to get to the park attached to my building, 110UWest. While I fell in love with my apartment at first glance, the amenities the building provided reassured me that I was making the right decision—even if moving out of the Lance household was terrifying.

The building is new, completed in the last five years. It has a state-of-the-art gym, plenty of outdoor and indoor socializing space, and an elegant entrance with floor-to-ceiling white marble walls. They even have events multiple times per week.

Granted, I use none of these amenities, but I like that they are there. The icing on the cake is the dog park, though.

Being so close to a place important to my mom and dad also feels good. They both went to undergrad at Howard, and while I never went there like we talked about, I feel echoes of their presence just being here.

Kitty stops at my heel when I pause inside the park. He's

still, focused. I take the leash and harness off, and he shakes out his fur.

"Off duty," I order.

He lets out a quick, happy yip, and when a butterfly flutters past him, he darts off after it.

I survey my surroundings, constantly vigilant to who is around me. The park is empty right now; I'm grateful for that. My wrecked nervous system can't handle another scare after all that happened today.

Everything is okay. You are safe.

I listen to my mental instructions and take a seat on the bench.

The gate opens.

A man, well over six feet tall, walks into the park with a Great Dane in tow.

Of course.

I scoot closer to the side of the bench, clutching the railing.

Kitty pauses his play with the butterfly and gets to work when I tell him, "Business."

The look he gives me clearly says, *But, Mom!* and then, with a huff, he starts circling his favorite patch of grass.

"I've seen you here before and meant to ask. Your dog is named Kitty?" The man's voice is deep and slightly accented. I can't tell exactly where his accent is from, but he doesn't have the open, Mid-Atlantic tone so many people in the area have. I observe him and then realize I must look absolutely insane because when I snap my mouth closed, it's only then that I realize I'd been staring at him with it wide open.

"My aunt was blind, and she had a service dog," he provides, even though I didn't reply to his question. I'm grateful he doesn't try to interact with Kitty, even if he's off-duty. I feel terrible when I have to tell people not to touch my dog. He's not just a pet. He's my accessibility aid.

Kitty does his business, and I hop up way too quickly to scoop his poop and throw it away. I freeze in front of the trashcan, staring at the stranger when he whistles for his dog. The action startles me, and my mind and body rocket through the fight, flight, freeze, or fawn cycle.

You can be out of here and back in your apartment in all of three minutes.

"Uh-huh," I reply dumbly.

The man takes pity on me and smiles. A dimple pops in his right cheek, and my brain short-circuits.

Resolved, I scoop Kitty up. I'm steps from the gate—and freedom—when the man speaks.

"Your dog? Did I hear that right?" He nods at Kitty, who I hold in my arms as if he were a grenade. His smile deepens, and of course, another dimple pops out. I'm officially nervous as *fuck.*

"Yeah," I croak. "His name is Kitty. Like after that kid's movie? I like irony, so…" I trail off, and he nods.

"That's cool," is all he says. His dog huffs, and it sounds like a horse.

That's all I need to snap out of my stupor and make a move toward the gate.

"Okay, well, it was nice to meet you!" I say because that's what regular humans say in these types of social interactions. Right? I shuffle toward the exit and awkwardly try to open it while still holding my dog and all his gear.

Suddenly, a hand shoots out from behind me and flips the latch. "I'm Marcus. What's your name?" He continues to smile, and I'm suddenly hit with the thought that something must be very wrong with him because who the fuck smiles this much?

"Wi—Uh, um, Kitty's Mom." I press my lips together, ducking beneath his arm and to the other side of the gate.

"Well, it's nice to meet you, Kitty's Mom!" he calls out as I speed walk down the path toward the entrance of the apartment building.

"Home," I tell Kitty breathlessly to transition him from

work states once we walk into the apartment. He saunters to his bed in the apartment as if everything is normal. Frazzled is the only way to describe how I feel. I head to the bathroom and wash my hands before splashing water on my face.

All things considered, you handled that quite well.

I avoid my reflection in the mirror.

When I walk back into the main room, I hear the tell-tale ping of an incoming message. Knowing that it's after five, it's unlikely to be the lawyer confirming receipt.

And if it is, that's fine.

I decide to face whatever it is and nearly yell when I see an email from the potential client.

Hello, Winter:

This is Ella Brigham, the aunt of the client Dr. Wagner consulted you about. I am scheduling interviews for counseling staff over the next few days. Please use the link below to schedule a time on my calendar.

I look forward to speaking with you.

EB

Biting my fingernail, I look at Kitty, who licks his balls with zero shame. Now that I'm faced with the prospect of an actual interview, I try not to spin as I consider whether I should leave Kitty behind or take him.

No one would ask a wheelchair user not to use their wheelchair. They might as well get the real picture.

Squaring my shoulders, I click through to the scheduling link and secure a time for tomorrow. I'm determined to get the job so I can get this whole nightmare of securing a spot over with.

I can do this. I most certainly can.

FOUR
WINTER

When the car exits the interstate, my palms itch to take my emergency Xanax. The urge to turn around is strong, and I've stopped myself from telling the driver to take me back to the safety of my apartment at least three times over the last half-hour of the trip.

Despite all my accomplishments, I've never had to interview for a job. At least, not a real job interview like this one. The gig I secured at the Trauma Resource Center lab in undergrad was held virtually and super relaxed.

And as evidenced by how I'm trussed up like a holiday turkey, this is anything but a comfortable experience.

You can do this, Winter.

I repeat the affirmation and go through three cycles of my breathing technique before we take a sharp right onto a tree-lined street. Kitty presses into my side. His movement reconfirms that bringing him along was the right choice.

I practiced what I would say to introduce him and why he's there, and I feel somewhat comfortable that it will be well-received. And if it's not…well, fuck 'em.

Tall oak trees line the single-lane road like something out of *Gone with the Wind.* My mom was a huge fan of Turner

Classic Movies, and we would watch Scarlett O'Hara chase after Ashley a dozen times a year.

I'm on my way to Tara.

I chuckle out loud, and the driver—Paul, according to his Uber profile—glances at me for the twelfth time on the mostly silent drive.

I don't blame him. I stood outside his car for a solid three minutes to go through my ritual before I could enter, but he didn't balk at Kitty's presence in the back of his car. Too often I have to relay large portions of the Americans with Disabilities Act at unsuspecting drivers like I'm reciting the Gettysburg Address.

He looked slightly bewildered when I finally did settle into the back seat but didn't ask me anything beyond confirming the address in Alexandria.

I can do this. I can do this well. This won't kill me. This will free me. And if I don't get the job, it's not the end of the world. I can try again.

Resolved and feeling significantly calmer, I take one more cleansing breath and open my eyes to the sight of the sprawling mansion.

Oh shit, it is *Tara.*

To describe the massive home in front of me as merely a house would be a drastic understatement. The estate spans farther than I can see, and I can tell there are multiple buildings on the land.

A cobblestone driveway encases a lavish water fountain with two angels entwined in an embrace at the top of the feature. The double front door has to be fifteen feet tall and is covered in sparkling glass.

A curvy woman who looks like a body double for Bailey Sarian stands on the short stone staircase in a casual bodycon dress. She must be waiting for me.

"Here you go," Paul says, gawking at the mansion as he

gets within a few feet of the stone stairs and the woman. He rolls toward the entrance at three miles per hour.

A flash of anxiety shoots through my body from head to toe, and Kitty puts a paw on my arm.

I can fucking do this, damn it.

Paul looks nervous, like I might break down in his Ford Focus.

I swallow past the dryness in my throat. "Oh, yes, sure." I fumble for my phone to pull up the app to close out the ride.

"Okay, so this is going to sound weird," I begin, trying to both catch Paul's gaze and avoid Paul's gaze. He squints like he is not in the mood for anything weird. Weirder.

"If I paid you"—*Say fifty dollars, Winter*—"two hundred dollars"—*Goddamn it, Winter*—"would you stay here for the hour it will take me to complete this interview?"

I try to smile at him, but I'm sure I look a little maniacal, so I purse my lips to loosen the tension in my cheeks before trying again. Kitty's head joins his paw on my arm.

Paul's eyebrows are in his hairline now.

He clears his throat. "Two hundred…yeah, sure. I'll need it upfront, though. Just to make sure, y'know?"

I take another deep breath and say "sure" more times than is probably acceptable before I get his payment info and send him two hundred dollars.

He comes to a complete stop in front of the stairs.

"Here you go. You'll wait for me here, right?" His phone pings with the payment notification.

"Right. I'll just be on TikTok while I wait for you." He waves his phone in the air before dropping it back in the cup holder.

I smooth my hair back, pinning what I hope is a natural smile on my face.

"Great."

I take one more breath before opening the door and exiting the car.

Slinging my sensible tawny-colored Italian leather briefcase over my shoulder, I do a slight shimmy to pull down my black pencil skirt and make sure my white button-down blouse is tucked and straight. I flat ironed my hair today, parting it down the middle and securing the front pieces behind my ears. I even managed to draw a symmetrical cat eye and apply a thin strip of lashes in one try—a skill only mastered after a thousand hours on YouTube Beauty University.

Clearly, I'm ready to dominate the day.

The woman waiting for me eyes me with a curious look, her gaze sliding to Kitty at my side.

"Ella Brigham," she says, holding her hand out to me. "Thank you for being here and being on time."

I'm not sure what she means by that, and I swallow down any budding offense. Her face gives nothing away. I look down at my wrist and note that it's 1:50 p.m., ten minutes before my interview.

"Oh! Not that I expected you to be late. The last person was an hour late. They said they couldn't find the place." She rolls her eyes and shakes her head slightly.

Ah, I see. I think.

"Sure, I left super early to make sure I made it with time to spare. Thank you for meeting with me, Ella. Er, Ms. Brigham," I say, standing up straighter. I clear my throat. "This is my service dog—"

"Oh, *God*, call me Ella." She finally smiles before her eyes widen. "Sorry, I cut you off. You were saying?"

She bounces on her heels a little bit as she examines Kitty's patches. She must see the one that says, "Eye contact distracts me. I'm workin' here!" because her eyes zip back to my face, and she doesn't look at him again.

"Uh, yes. This is my service dog. Dr. Wagner likely didn't tell you, but I do have a disability, and my dog is one of my accessibility aids. He comes with me, but his presence nor my disability impact my ability to perform the tasks needed."

I breathe in and settle for relaxing my face. I probably look bitchy, but if I try to smile, I'm sure my lips will do that annoying spasm thing again.

"Of course! Oh, gosh, we're all about disabilities here. Wait, that sounded really weird." She loosens a loud laugh, and I notice her tongue is…purple?

"I meant to say, we are very familiar with needing accommodations. Have you met my nephew?"

I start to answer yes and no, because I've read his case file thoroughly, but I, of course, have never met him.

"Lord, of course you haven't met him," she says, bopping her head slightly at her blunder. Suddenly, it occurs to me that I really like her. She's funny. Talking to her is a little like standing in chaos.

Be professional, I order myself.

"Anyway, the point is it isn't a problem or a concern. If you'll just—" A blur with dark brown hair barrels into her.

"Stop running!" Two large men who look physically strong but like they're slow runners attempt to sprint behind a thin teen covered in mud.

The kid laughs hysterically, bent over and clutching his mud-caked hands to his stomach.

The men double down on trying to catch him.

That must be August, the client.

August sprints toward the water fountain, inches from jumping in the small pool when one of the men feints to the side and grabs him by the arm.

"Ow!" August says, and the man swings him over his shoulder, banding his arms across August's thighs.

I bristle at the rough movements.

The other man—a guard, I presume—bends over at the waist to catch his breath.

"Sorry, Miss Ella," the huffing man says. "He was outside

one minute, and the next he was covered in mud and streaking through the goddamn house." Catching his breath, he follows the other man and August around the side of the house.

"Oooookay, then." She shrugs her shoulders and lifts her hands as if to say, *Kids, am I right?*

For an inexplicable reason, I find myself mirroring her pose, and when the realization that I'm doing so hits me square in the face, I drop my hands. Heat crawls up my neck.

"C'mon in."

Kitty, the consummate professional, heels next to me with precision. I, on the other hand, gawk at the massive front entryway as I follow her into this obscenely large mansion. White and gray marble floors gleam in the soft sunlight, and the chandelier rivals anything I'd seen in any of the houses my mom used to bring me to when visiting important political people. Twin staircases frame the sides of the entrance, and beyond them, a wall of windows overlooks rolling hills in the distance.

We don't go far into the foyer before turning to a sitting room a few feet from the entrance.

"Please have a seat. Water? Tea?" She pauses to look at me.

"Nothing for me. Thank you," I say. I take the leash off Kitty's harness, putting it in my bag.

She nods before sitting on the caramel-colored leather loveseat. I follow her lead and sit on one of the complementary emerald armchairs across from her. Then she chucks off her shoes and curls her legs underneath her on the couch. I resist the urge to lift my eyebrows in surprise.

The sitting room is clearly set for just that. Sitting. Artwork that I'm sure costs more than a car adorns the wall, and the high ceilings feature ornate crown molding.

"August's dad will be joining us shortly," she says.

I snap my eyes back to Ella and smile again, rubbing my hands over my hair to ensure I tame my flyaways.

"Okay, so, Winter," she says as she opens a black leather portfolio and pulls out my resume.

"You graduated from Liberty Falls University with your bachelor's and you're in their doctoral program. Childhood psychology, right?"

I nod, not trusting myself to speak quite yet.

"I see you've published articles and are highly recommended by Dr. Wagner. It looks like you've volunteered, but have you actually worked…anywhere?"

She places her hands in her lap over my resume—my woefully underdeveloped resume—and sits with a smile as she waits for my response.

I recall what Genevieve and I practiced during my week of email purgatory.

"Thank you, Ella. Yes, while I haven't held many paid roles as I've been dedicated to my studies, I have worked almost exclusively with children as a volunteer for The Trauma Resource Center in D.C. My focus is on childhood trauma and developmental disabilities, and I've volunteered my time working with clients for the past three years."

I breathe and smile, feeling Genevieve telling me to pace my speech.

"Interesting." That's all Ella says.

Not sure if I should continue, I say, "I created programming for clients ages three to seventeen that involved art and memory recoding. The core of the program I created was a blend of EMDR and somatic bodywork. I facilitated a small group program for teenage girls who faced parental loss."

I don't mention that I've literally never met anyone I've worked with in person.

Suddenly, from deep into the house, a scream rings out, cutting through the thick silence of the rest of the mansion.

My face falls at the suddenness of the sound, and I clutch my hands in my lap. Kitty presses against my leg.

"Okay, that sounds good," she says, but I can tell she's distracted. We both sit in silence for a moment before she continues. She clears her throat before resituating herself on the loveseat.

"Tell me about your experience working with Autistic kids. My nephew is Autistic. He primarily uses AAC to communicate. He hasn't had very many good days lately. That said, he can go into sensory overload. Sometimes, he has meltdowns. Have you ever worked with a kid like that?"

"I've worked with many Autistic kids, some who need lots of additional support or alternative communication methods. One of my kids—"

The yelling starts again, even louder this time. I recognize the pitch of August's voice in the jumble of sounds. A booming male voice that seems to be trying to drown out August's noises with his own aggravated tone is a cacophonous addition.

"Stop!" The man bellows, his voice getting closer to where Ella and I sit.

August's voice gets louder. I can't understand what he's saying, but his urgency tells me he needs something.

"One of my kids, I can't tell you his name due to confidentiality—"

"Stop—párate hijo de la chingada!" I gasp at the agitation punctuating the man's words and feel deep outrage that he's just called a child a son of a bitch. I hear what must be August's feet as they slap against the marble floor. Coming closer.

The man lets out a frustrated roar, and the slap of skin on skin causes me to jump from my chair and rush from the room just as Ella does the same.

I turn the corner from the sitting room into the foyer and

resist a primal yell at the man gripping the small teen by the arms. August dangles a few feet off the floor.

The boy's face contorts, his mouth open in an *O*. Tears fall from his reddened face.

August shrieks and the man squeezes his arms even tighter, impossibly tighter, and shakes him roughly.

"Shut the fuck up!" he yells in August's face, and I snap, completely losing my mind. I am enraged.

"*Stop*!" I demand, rushing forward. Kitty whimpers at my side and I feel him moving back and forth behind me, uncertain what to do. He's a service dog, not a guard dog. "Put him down *now!*" I pull at the mountain of a man hurting this child.

"Down! Now!" I yell, slapping at the man's muscle-corded arms.

He drops the boy. August falls to the ground, grabbing his elbow as it cracks against the unforgiving marble. He makes a sound of clear distress.

"How *dare* you? What makes you think—" I start saying with all the aggravation I feel in every fiber in my body, "—that you can treat a child this way, especially one who literally weighs less than half your body weight?"

I crouch down to August and show him my hands, wordlessly asking if I can touch his arms to see if they're bruised. August lifts his arm, staring at it as I gently put my hands on him. Kitty, finally figuring out some way to help in this situation, skids over, putting his body between me and the hulking man in front of me.

"Who are *you*?" the man says roughly.

I swing my head toward the lump of muscle.

"Who are *you?*" I throw back.

The man scoffs, and I turn back to August. "Are you all right, August?"

"He doesn't talk," the man spits through clenched teeth.

"That doesn't mean you should beat him up, dumbass!

Who the hell put you in charge of taking care of anyone? He's clearly trying to communicate something to you, and you're punishing him for it. You *heathen asshole!*" I'm spitting, quite literally, I fear. Covering my mouth, I gasp.

Ella vibrates with clearly decipherable fury, her eyes pinched tight and her hands balled into fists as she stares at the man.

She looks ready to launch herself at him.

I imagine the only reason she doesn't is because she's not alone. Standing next to her with a hand on her arm is Hunter Brigham.

When I researched the Brigham family last night, a ton of information popped up about Hunter and his father, Benjamin.

Hunter's father is a very attractive man, but Hunter…

He's tall with dark hair and the bluest eyes I've ever seen. Mom and I went to Carmel once, popping down there while on a trip to Sacramento. That's what his eyes look like. They're the color of the ocean off the coast of California—cerulean and stormy, a deep blue. He could be in Hollywood, starring in action movies—hanging off a helicopter or standing between two moving eighteen-wheelers Jean-Claude Van Damme style.

He wears a dark gray suit with a loose tie hanging around his collar. Just from the sheer broadness of his chest and the way his thighs fill out the wool material, it's clear he's stacked under those clothes.

The anger I feel shifts into a confusing tangle of outrage, embarrassment, and lust.

"Um, I—" I'm pretty sure I look like a fish right now.

"Rodrigo, what exactly do you think you were doing?" The god speaks. His voice has a sexy raspiness that reminds me of smoky bonfires on summer evenings. And the menacing tone belying his words causes my stomach to clench.

"Mr. Brigham. I'm sorry, I lost my temper. But you know I'm not a babysitter, and August just doesn't *fucking* listen—" The guard-turned-babysitter cuts himself off, probably finally getting a modicum of self-preservation.

"So your decision was to assault my son?" Mr. Brigham arches an eyebrow.

Ella lurches forward as if to pounce on the man, and Mr. Brigham's hand tightens on her arm.

Mr. Brigham widens his stance.

"I, uh. No. I mean." The man stammers.

"Out-*side*." August whispers this so softly I almost don't hear it. The word bursts from his lips haltingly and with great effort. He rocks gently from side to side.

"I hear you. Let's go," I murmur to him just as softly, my words just for his ears. Turning my head in Ella and Mr. Brigham's direction, I say, "August wants to go outside, and I'm going with him." I don't care that it's presumptuous. But I can't look directly at either of them, so my gaze ping-pongs slowly between their bodies.

"Okay," Ella says slowly as if she can't piece together where we should go from here with the interview. She turns to Mr. Brigham, her back to Rodrigo.

"Handle this," she says to Mr. Brigham in a raspy whisper. I'm unsure if she means me or the mountain off to the side.

I'm sure this interview is over. It's probably not cool to curse out the rest of the staff, but…

I release a puff of air and turn back to August. "Let's go outside. Do you need help up?" I stretch my hand toward him.

He pushes it away.

"No problem. Let's go," I say, keeping my voice light. "I'm Winter, by the way," I say to him, intensely focused on getting the fuck out of the room before violence breaks out. Kitty falls in place at my heel.

After moving down the hall, I notice a door leading

outside to the courtyard and follow August's lead through it. Perfectly manicured bushes surround another beautiful fountain. The courtyard is stunning—but it's clearly meant for adults to enjoy. Everything looks breakable.

There's a hole in the bushes where I can see August dug his way to freedom. Literally. A spade sticks out from another shrub, and a tablet rests on the ground off to the side.

"Kitty, relax," I command over my shoulder, and he is all too happy to saunter over to a patch of grass. He plops down as if exhausted.

I walk over to the tablet on the ground, noting the cracked screen. I press the button to turn it on. It's pulled up to an AAC app, but a few taps reveal the screen is nonresponsive.

"Well, shoot. Is this your tablet for communication?" August stands still next to me. He nods several seconds later.

"I see. Well, that's an emergency, and I imagine it's quite frustrating. We need this fixed ASAP. Let's go tell your family what the issue is. Do you have a backup tablet? Maybe you can log in to your processor with a phone in the meantime if you don't have one?" I turn to face the door to return to the Brighams while talking entirely too much. I stop, lassoed by my anxiety of seeing those people again after I blew up inside.

August pulls on my arm and drags me across the courtyard to the water feature.

"Do you like the water?" I ask him.

He faces toward me and stares in the general vicinity of my left arm. Lifting his arm, he points at the angels entwined at the center of the water feature.

He makes a sharp sound, followed by a long sigh that ends with several vocalizations. I walk around the fountain, hoping something will jump out as a clue to what he's looking for.

An exasperated grunt sounds behind me, and August grabs my hand again. He lifts my arm toward the water feature, and I see it: the cracked remains of a giant replica helicopter. The blades are broken, one completely detached from the helicopter's body and floating in the pool of water.

"Oh, I got it! Your helicopter is stuck. Dang, it's really up there. I see how you got all wet now."

I say all this while kicking off my shoes and rolling up my skirt, still talking too much. If I can save the toy without drowning, I can at least do one thing to help this kid before I never see him again.

"Okay, let me get that for you." I step on the ledge of the water fountain and stretch my right arm above my head, testing the weight of my left arm on the shoulder of the stone statue.

Stretching up on my tiptoes, I snag a corner of the helicopter. It slips from its perch and tumbles toward the pool of water. I release my clutch on the statue and grab the toy midair, flinging it toward the dry grass...which means I go into the reservoir.

Falling hard on my knees, the water splashes and lands all over me. Hair, shirt, and skirt.

Sputtering at the water cleaning out my nasal passages, I contemplate my exit from the fountain when August runs to scoop up the remains of his helicopter.

And Mr. Brigham enters the courtyard.

Great. Just fucking great.

FIVE
HUNTER

In any other situation, I'd be pleased to have a woman on her knees in front of me. I've fucked a lot of women all around the world, even though I've slowed down considerably over the last few months—the episode on the plane on the way to D.C. notwithstanding.

That was more about domination—control—than chasing after a nut. It was about feeling okay in my body. I've taken in enough self-help advice to be somewhat self-aware.

Nonetheless, stunning women staring up at me with wide, pleading eyes is a look I'm used to. So I'm confused and annoyed that I'm unsettled by the beauty sprawled across my foyer.

The woman, who I presume is the interviewee for the therapist position, holds her arms out in front of August's tense body.

Before she noticed me, I noticed her, and I took an irrational and inappropriate interest in the way her chest heaved with every word she spat at the fuckhead to my right.

My attention should be solely on the fucker who just apparently hit or threw or otherwise harmed my son. The fact that I don't know what happened before I walked into the room further aggravates me.

But I'm distracted, and no matter how mature I try to be, I can't help the bolt of lust that arises as I contemplate the angry woman on my floor.

So yeah. Distracted.

Her practical black skirt stretches over her ample ass and hips, and the soft curve of flesh right over her stomach makes her look like a sculpture of a Greek goddess. Her thick, dark brown hair hangs straight down her back from the severe middle part, and her hair looks glossy with the sunlight streaming through the windows surrounding the entryway.

Her medium brown skin looks sun-kissed and supple, reminding me of amber. I'm close enough to her to smell the rose scent wafting from her skin and see deep into her expressive brown eyes. Her eyes display whorls of hazel, just like Tiger's Eye, and they're filled with fury as she protects August fiercely. I can tell that her pillowy lips come from genetics rather than vials of filler.

I'm enamored. I'm disgusted with myself.

Because this is the woman who is supposed to help me with August.

Because I should *only* be thinking about August, but my dick has other plans.

She is a distraction I so don't need.

Part of me is overjoyed at the thought of seeing her every day. Another part realizes it's a fucking terrible idea.

Unfortunately, the overjoyed part, i.e., my dick, has all the blood in my body coursing through it. The rational part, my brain, has left the building, it seems.

Fuck.

A good time to focus, fuckface.

I re-center my brain to be present in the foyer.

Rodrigo stands with his hands balled at his hips, his head downcast. Ella pipes up, "So yeah, you're fucking fired."

"What *the fuck* is going on down here?" Leo's voice echoes against the marble tile as his legs eat up the distance down the hall to where we stand.

"This fucker doesn't know what *child abuse* is," Ella rages, and a red flush crawls up her neck, making her skin blotchy.

"Cállate, pinche puta," Rodrigo spits out, and she whirls around and takes two steps toward the bodyguard, clearly not appreciating him calling her a bitch.

That is the moment in which Rodrigo fucks up.

He steps toward Ella with outrageous aggression, his arm raised as if he'd hit her. I step between the two, ready to make him eat his teeth, when Leo hurls toward Rodrigo and punches him dead in the temple.

The crack of the man's skull hitting the marble floor reverberates, and he drops like a sack.

Ella covers her mouth.

Leo delivers a kick to Rodrigo's kidney and says, "Si te vuelves aqui, cortare tu maldita cabeza." He spits on him.

A growl crawls into my throat.

Leo vows to slit Rodrigo's throat if he shows his face around here ever again.

It's not a threat. It's a promise.

"You two, get him the fuck out of here." Two more of our guards come from the shadows and drag their unconscious comrade out the front door. He leaves a smear of blood on the floor.

That should have been your move, shithead.

"Lydia will have a heart attack seeing all this blood," Ella says, her eyes never leaving Leo.

"I'll take care of it," Leo says. After a few heavy moments of us standing in the foyer, Leo snaps, "No me mires asi."

Ella stares at him with her mouth open, ignoring his instructions not to look at him. Holding her arms to her stomach, she walks away toward the kitchen.

I nod and cut my eyes toward the door leading to the courtyard.

Fuck.

"I need to check on August," I say.

"Tell him I'm sorry. I'm sorry that happened." Leo runs an agitated hand down the side of his face.

I nod again.

Leo may seem hard and cold-hearted, but he has a soft spot for children and women.

I put my hand on the door leading to the courtyard and pause, looking out the glass windows framing the exit.

The woman—damn it, I don't even know her name—rolls up her skirt, bunching it so high I see the muscles in her plump thighs.

The statue in the middle of the fountain holds August's RC helicopter hostage. It sits in the angel's hands like an offering.

This whole fucking house is the biggest, most absurd thing ever, even though Ella has updated the fixtures to bring the antique home into the 21st century.

The estate has four buildings, and our main house now has twelve bedrooms and eight bathrooms.

August and I have only been here for a week, and setting up an outdoor space hasn't been at the top of the priority list. August likes being outside, regardless of the weather. I don't know why he likes it so much. I also didn't know he was so into RC helis, but how would I, really?

I'll have to ask him why. Hopefully he'll tell me.

This whole week he's spent outside, the temperature cooperating and staying bearable. Setting up his outdoor space will be a priority now.

The woman steps onto the lip of the fountain, and my cock twitches in my pants as the muscles of her thighs flex.

Pervert.

I can't hear her clearly, her words muffled as she speaks to August. She holds a whole conversation with him.

That's something history taught me not a lot of people do.

She reaches the helicopter, and in slow motion, I watch as she loses her grip and flings it toward the grass. She goes hands and knees into the water.

In a second, she's soaked.

August rushes off to grab his helicopter. Her dog—a service dog, I guess, from the vest he wears—stands up and moves toward his soaking handler.

I take cautious steps toward the woman.

"Fuuu—Frick," the woman mutters when I'm close enough to hear her.

"Do you need help, Ms..." I shrug off my suit jacket and roll up my sleeves. Her eyes, filled with shock, snap toward me.

"Vaughan. I mean, my first name is Winter. My last name is Vaughan. So Winter Vaughan is my full name. I mean, Winter Leigh Vaughan is my full name, like, my *government* name. Shit, stop talking. Oh shit, I said that out loud." She groans and raises her wet hands to her face before jerking them away, probably remembering her already wrecked makeup.

"Ms. Vaughan," I say.

"Winter. Call me Winter, please," she says in a small voice. Her hands are still up near her chest, almost looking like she's praying.

"Winter." I taste her name on my tongue, then immediately give myself a mental kick in the ass. "I'm Hunter Brigham. Feel free to call me H. It's what everyone calls me." Everyone except my father.

"Would you like help getting out of the fountain?" I reach a hand toward her and grasp her wrist. Her skin is as soft as it looks.

"Oh, shoot, um, yes," she finishes with a grimace. In a second, she jumps up and stands in the fountain. The water almost reaches her knees, and her clothes are soaked.

Her white button-down blouse, which probably seemed reasonable when she dressed this morning, sticks to her chest. I try to avoid staring at the outline of her dark nipples and the lace of her bra beneath the fabric.

Stop perving on the therapist, Hunter.

That would be easier said than done—the warmth of her skin does crazy things to my nervous system.

She steps out of the fountain.

"I will…leave now," she says. Her eyes are wide, and a red flush runs up her neck and pools in her cheeks.

"I imagine you need to get dry," I reply.

"Oh, goodness, what happened to you!" Ella's voice echoes behind me, and I drop Winter's wrist. I didn't realize I still had it in my grip. Ella's eyes ping-pong between us, and that twinkle in her eye that I know means no good reappears —even after all this time apart.

"Jeez, this is a mess. August's tablet is broken. That's part of the reason why he was so dysregulated, I think. Please get his voice fixed ASAP. You wouldn't be cool if someone took your ability to speak away. By the way, do you have backups? If not, you should have several backups." She takes a sharp breath after the racing words trail off.

I resist the urge to smile at her babbling.

Stop. It. Hunter.

"Of course, you're right," Ella says brightly.

"I'll—I hope to hear from you. Heel." She snaps the last part in the direction of her pup. Winter steps around me to scoop up her shoes—black with stubby heels—and rushes back into the house toward the front door.

I should tell Ella to dump her resume. That would be the sensible thing to do.

But after seeing how fiercely she protected August and

how she treated him in the brief moment they were alone, I can't help but feel that she *is* the whole package.

Yeah, and that could also be your dick talking.

"Sooo, that was interesting," Ella says, crossing her arms against her chest. She rolls her eyes and pulls a Now and Later out of her pocket.

"Your dentist bill must be astronomical." I smirk at her.

"Har, har," she says, giving me the middle finger.

I look over to August. He's barefoot and sitting on a sunny patch of grass. A look of pure peace rests on his angular face as he tilts his chin toward the sun. His eyelashes flutter in the breeze that's decided to grace us, and he runs a slow, absent finger around the perimeter of his broken communication device.

He looks completely unfazed by the events of the past few minutes.

"I think she's gonna be great for August," Ella says from behind me.

"What makes you say that?" I turn to her, rubbing the back of my neck. If I can direct my body's sensations to any place that *isn't* my dick, I can likely hold a conversation that requires thought.

"Well, she has some solid experience despite being not quite finished with school. Plus, as evidenced by what happened, she's great with Augie." Her jaw clenches, and her nostrils flare.

My hands ball into fists, so I shove them into my pockets.

"I don't think so, Ella."

She shakes her head at me, her face morphing from agitated to incredulous. "H, we can't keep going on like this. August needs better—he deserves better than this."

"Ella, she's not the right fit. Keep looking. I am his father, and I said no." My words are sharp, and she stares at me, her eyes narrowed to slits.

After a few tense and silent moments, she says as if it pains her, "Whatever you say, Hunter."

She turns on her heels to reenter the house.

And that's precisely why Winter needs to stay away. Because if it's whatever I say, it'll lead to all of our demise.

SIX
HUNTER

Throwing myself into work as CEO is an unusual yet helpful activity. One, because we're fighting like hell to get the FDA to clear us for clinical trials for Project Panacea. So my focus at work is required now, more so than at any other time in the history of BwP.

The other reason is that staying up night and day working across different teams keeps my mind off the one person I should *not* think about.

I will not think about Winter Vaughan.

We're the new kids on the block when it comes to business, especially in the world of medical technology and pharmaceuticals, even though we've been around for more than ten years. And while we've grown BwP to a massive scale over the last decade, the reality is AI has made it so that what takes humans years to figure out, it can compute in seconds.

We have an advantage: Project Panacea. The apparent cure for cancer is in the technology and formulas we own. The secrets to what makes it work are locked up underground in our private parcel of land with proximity to the Pentagon.

We know we have an ace in the hole. But if we don't move

quickly, there's no reason why a competitor can't come up with what we've already figured out.

We'll be edged out of the market, and then everything will go belly-up.

I'll lose the only thing that's truly mine.

And then I'll be back in my dad's mansion filling my day with coke and strippers and whatever else he wants me to do.

I shake my head to clear the impending sense of doom.

"We need this to go off without a hitch," Leo says to Max, our resident hacker and present-day administrative assistant since moving everything to Amelia Manor.

"Easy peasy lemon squeezy," Max says in response, and I nearly burst a lung at the look of pure bafflement on Leo's face. Max is a character. He's lanky and average height. He looks like that one rapper who also acts on that sitcom. He's serious about his work, but he's young and goofy.

An odd bird, as my mom would say. I feel the echoes of my mother's presence throughout this entire estate. There's no avoiding it. No avoiding her memory.

My breaths seize in my chest.

Since reconfiguring everything to stay in Amelia Manor, we reduced the number of people coming in and out of the estate. The more people, the more opportunities for slip-ups. And with that, some people have had to take on multiple roles.

For example, Max. He looks about as thrilled as a call center worker on unpaid overtime to be operating as our assistant in addition to all his other roles. In the hierarchy of our organization, Max is as close to third in command as can be. Not that he wants that title or that responsibility.

He's told me and Leo as much several times over the years. Probably because he enjoys the freedom of his criminality. We found Max in upstate New York eight years ago after being tipped off that the person attacking our porous electronic defenses was a scrawny, barely legal kid living alone with his kid brother. Apparently, Max's parents both ran off at different times, leaving Max and his little brother, Michael, behind.

He ran ransom campaigns to make enough money through Bitcoin to get his brother the treatments he needed for his sickle cell.

Leo and I stared him down in the secluded warehouse we'd had him dragged to, and when he didn't flinch, wasn't apologetic in the slightest, our sentiments toward him changed.

Max has the bravado and courage that I wish I had at his age.

Maybe things would have turned out differently.

We've changed one of the smaller dining rooms into a makeshift headquarters—although saying it's smaller doesn't mean it's small. There's ample open space, at around two thousand square feet, and we had our in-house security team break the room into work zones. In the center is the fishbowl where we have stand-ups.

"The FDA is turning out to be a real pain in the dick, H," Leo says. He usually isn't disturbed by anything. I've seen him face some seriously fucked shit in our younger days, but now he's pinching the bridge of his nose as if he is much aggrieved.

Granted, most of those days we were both high off our asses, doing my father's bidding.

I clear my throat.

"We have people in there, so what's the problem?" I ask him.

"That's the thing, I don't know, but I don't like it. And our contacts inside have gone dark," Leo says.

"Gone dark? What the fuck do you mean?"

"Dark. Oscuro. As in, no one can fucking find them and they've disappeared off the face of the Earth."

My eyebrows shoot up. Max can find anyone. And I'm

confident we will find the lost agents. But the fact that Max doesn't have their locations and, hell, even the last time they took a shit in a briefing on our desks right now means something is going on.

The thing that's always amused me about my industry and Big Pharma is that from the top, everyone is as much of a criminal as any other member of the mafia or the bratva or the cartel.

The top guys at Big Pharma have hit men and politicians in their pockets. They pay off judges and district attorneys and push through legislation that benefits them.

No one is surprised at this, least of all me. But it's curious that there is a line between drug pushers on the street and the ones in suits sitting in boardrooms. It's the same fucking thing.

"I have literally nothing using the usual channels," Max says. Instead of looking scared about upsetting his bosses, he seems excited. It's a challenge that doesn't usually happen for him because most people are woefully transparent with their personal information.

Max can find anything about anyone in a few taps. I believe in him.

"Spend time following the unusual channels then," Leo says. Project Panacea means a lot to Leo, and he's the sole reason why we landed in this industry in the first place.

Leo's mom died from breast cancer when he was a kid. It's a way to honor her, I guess. His mom and my mom were best friends, and that's how we first connected.

I spent many days over at Leo's parents' house. Leo's father is a cruel man, but Gloria Polanco was an angel among mortals. In my loneliest moments, the scent of Leo's mom's empanadas unlocks in my cell memory, and I'm transported to a happier time. One where Leo and I were shithead, bright-eyed kids and none of the realities of Leo's cartel family connections and my father's malevolence touched us.

"In the meantime, see who owes us favors," Leo says to Max.

"You want folks in Congress or other agencies?" he responds.

"Cast the net wide. We need to get this thing out there this year," I respond.

"You got it, boss," he says, returning to his cave. It's actually almost a literal cave with how dark he keeps it. He even blacked out the windows.

That our contacts have gone missing is beyond strange. It's troublesome. Because there's not a thing that happens in our ecosystem that we don't know about.

"Have you heard from him yet?" Leo doesn't have to say his name for me to know that he's talking about my father.

Leo's hatred for my father goes beyond the facts of who my father is or what he represents. His absolute loathing for Benjamin Brigham stems back nearly sixteen years when my father sold Leo's sister, Isabella, to Sheikh Farid Al-Mansoori. Despite endlessly trying to find her, Leo hasn't been able to locate her in all this time.

"Nope," I say, extending out the initial vowel. Leo stares at me, spinning his black phone between his thumb and index finger.

"What, Leo?" I say as I sigh.

"You know I don't believe in coincidences," he says after a moment.

"You think he's behind this?" I wouldn't put it past him. I've been in D.C. for more than a week now when I haven't stepped foot in this part of the country for more than seventy-two hours in years.

I don't put it past my father to interfere with BwP to get my attention.

But then, when has he ever cared about talking with me?

"I don't know what to think." He looks thoughtful for a moment, then he shrugs. "Is August okay?"

I feel the edge of annoyance, guilt, and anger as I recall this afternoon's events.

August being manhandled by someone I employ. August being rescued by a woman I've never seen before in my life—someone who had more compassion and understanding of my son than I've gotten anywhere close to.

The ineptitude I felt when Leo, of all people, came in and rained vengeance on the motherfucker who decided to lay his hands on my child while I stood back and did nothing.

I didn't stand up for August, and I should have. Because I was too busy checking out the counselor's ass.

What the fuck is wrong with me?

"He seemed okay when I saw him before dinner. He took his food and went to his room." Isolating is pretty normal for teenagers, right?

It's probably because he wants nothing to do with you. And why should he?

A knot starts forming in my right shoulder.

"That therapist, though," Leo says, and I jerk my head to look at him. He's wearing a shit-eating grin, making me want to sock him.

In all the years I've known Leo, he's never had to work to get a woman in his bed. I once saw him fuck one woman in a club and then, an hour later, had another three in his penthouse.

It's a level of man-whoring I find admirable but exhausting.

"Didn't really notice her," I reply.

Leo raises an eyebrow in response. "Mmhmm. Well I caught a good look at her when she ran out of here. You wouldn't mind if I hit her up?"

I jolt. Would I mind?

"Do what you want," I say with a shrug that I hope comes off as nonchalant. I stand. "I'm sure Ella has her number," I add, and Leo grimaces. "Anyway, I've got more shit to do. See you tomorrow."

I leave the fishbowl and the office. Leo's guffaws follow me until I'm on the other side of the soundproof door.

BECAUSE I'VE BEEN terrible in this life and probably in my last, it's unsurprising that Ella's curled up in my office chair, scrolling on her e-reader.

"Jeez, you took long enough," she says when I stop short at the doorframe.

"Do you mind?" I emphasize. Striding over to my chair, I tip it forward so she nearly falls out of it.

"Ass!" she yells as she bounces up to her feet. I pull the chair away and sit down.

Spinning toward my computer screens, I say, "Is there a point to your visit, Ella? You know, seeing as you don't live here, yet here you are. In my house. Always in my house."

"It's my damn house, too, Hunter. And if it weren't for me, you wouldn't have any of the cushy shit or clean dishes that I've supplied over the years maintaining this property."

"Your point? You live in Georgetown. Go there."

"My *point* is that your only response should be, 'Thank you, Ella, my smart, resourceful, hilarious sister. I'm so grateful that you're the better sibling.'"

I give her the finger in reply, softening the jab with a smile.

She reaches into her back pocket and flops in the chair across from my desk. She starts unwrapping a pink square. It's a Starburst this time.

"There is a reason for my visit. I was thinking about what happened today, and there are some changes I want to put in place around here."

I sigh, tossing my phone on the desk in front of me. I lean back because it's clear that this will be a lengthy conversation.

"Anyone with contact with August must attend an autism sensitivity training."

I mull it over. "That sounds like a great idea."

"You included," she adds.

I try not to bristle.

"You think I'm insensitive?" I blink slowly.

Not good enough.

"Not that you're insensitive to August. Just maybe a little ignorant to some of his needs."

"I see," I say.

"Hunter," she says between chews, "you haven't been around him like ever. I bet you have spent zero hours around an Autistic child, and even at that, if you've met one Autistic person, you've met one Autistic person." She shrugs. "It's not a personal attack, H. But if you're going to make any headway with August, you must first have a basic understanding. Then you need to get to know August. The whole person…who gets his humor from his aunt, by the way."

My foot taps out a rapid beat beneath my desk.

"I understand."

I am so going to fuck this up.

"*Sooooo,*" she says, drawing out the word. "That brings me to Ms. Somewhat-Soon-to-Be-Dr. Winter Vaughan." She smiles brightly, conspiratorially.

"No, Ella."

"I just don't understand why not, H. She's well-credentialed, has a personal recommendation from Dr. Wagner, and she's great with August. She's willing to jump in front of a massive man who could have knocked her out to protect August. Just give me a reason."

I look at the ceiling to avoid answering her.

"A good reason," she adds.

How inappropriate would it be to tell my sister, *"No, we*

can't hire her because I'm pretty sure I'll get the desire to bend her over the nearest surface every time we're in a room together?"

"Let's keep our options open. I trust you to find viable candidates. But let's move on from Ms. Vaughan."

She rolls onto one hip and pulls a yellow Starburst out of her back pocket. "Ugh, yellow," she says. She tosses the candy toward me, and it lands in my lap.

"Thanks?" I say, picking it up. It's warm from her body heat. Gross.

Picking out another Starburst and evidently pleased with the selection, she unwraps the candy. "That brings me to issue number three."

"How many issues are there, Ella?"

"When are you going to see Dad?"

I suppress a grimace.

I'm a grown man. I own a business worth billions of dollars.

I'm not afraid of my father.

But I never want to see him again. Because seeing him will give him power. And with this power, he will inevitably try to control me. He will exploit any weakness. And now, I have many of them.

A terrifying image of August in the hospital flashes in my mind. Except he's not getting better. He's dead.

"How about the thirtieth of February. Sound good?"

Ella gives me a droll look. "Why are you so mean to him?"

I almost laugh out loud at the simplicity of her statement. There's so much that Benjamin Brigham has done to ruin people. To torture people. And yet, he is the unsaid leader of the Elites. He is the one with his thumb on the millionaires and billionaires and trillionaires in this country—if not around the world.

There's nothing he won't do. There's no line he won't cross.

"We're just not compatible people," I say. For whatever

reason, Ella believes our father to be a loving man. A man who gives anything to ensure her happiness. And he has always treated Ella much differently than he treated me.

He beat me into submission, literally making me bleed until I felt there was nothing left for me to give. I pledged my allegiance to the King through blood-stained teeth.

But with Ella, he earned her submission through overindulgence. And whatever actions he's shown her, she views them as the love a father has for his daughter.

"Well, you should man up and try to build a relationship with him. You need people now that you're parenting, I imagine. Plus, he's getting soft in his old age."

I seriously doubt that.

"He'll likely want someone to take over his business for him, and who better than his son?"

I want to yell, "What business? The business of human trafficking and ritualistic murder?" But Ella looks so eager, so optimistic that I don't have the heart to break her illusions.

Instead, I say, "I'll think about it."

And when she leaves the room, I put my head in my hands and try adamantly to not think about it.

SEVEN
WINTER

"Holy fucking mother of shit!"

I yell as my feet touch the hot water laced with Epsom salt. Kitty runs into the bathroom, where I'm attempting to step into the free-standing tub.

"Off duty," I croak, and he does a double take before stepping outside the bathroom. He sits with his huge eyes trained on me, really taking that whole obedient-disobedience training to heart.

I sink further into the water, and the pain grounds me.

When I exited the Brigham estate, I was dismayed that the Uber driver—whom I paid two hundred whole American dollars to wait for me—was nowhere to be found. Hoping he'd just moved to a shadier spot, Kitty and I began the ten-minute trek down the tree-lined drive only to be further dismayed upon realizing, yep, he's fucking gone.

Dismay turned into near hysteria when I realized my fancy Italian leather briefcase was leaning against my seat in the sitting room of the aforementioned estate. Within said Italian leather briefcase was my iPhone. Kitty sat on top of my sensible heels, forcing me to stop and breathe.

Rationally—okay, irrationally—deciding that facing the

Brighams was more undesirable than facing a hungry pack of wild jackals, I exited the gate and continued walking down the hill toward the convenience store we passed on the way in.

Someone will have a phone. I'll call Veronica, I thought. After all, she's the only person whose phone number I have memorized.

Since I so clearly did *not* dominate the day, I was unsurprised when sheets of rain started to pelt me once I hit the convenience store parking lot.

Kitty's drowned side eye as he tensely scanned for threats made me feel even worse.

Once the rain started, I ran with him clutched to my chest.

Arriving at the convenience store and convincing the clerk to let me use his phone was surprisingly easy. But it wasn't until I got in Veronica's Mercedes, still wet from the rain and fountain swim, that I realized my drenched white shirt clearly showed every bit of my breast, areola, and nipple.

I flashed Hunter Brigham.

Back in the bathroom, I continue cursing as my feet throb and sharp shears of pain streak through my soles and up my calves.

"How ya hanging, sweet stuff?" Veronica's voice comes from the doorway where she stands next to Kitty.

Kitty looks up to her for instruction, and Veronica bends to pet his head.

She was there every step of the way while I trained Kitty almost four years ago. Part of the training is public exposure, so while the trainer was able to start in my home with the Lances, we eventually had to go outside. No matter how tired Rons was from a shift in the hospital, if I needed her to hold my hand while I went to the drug store with a super excitable Kitty by my side, she was there.

And now, she looks at me with so much sympathy my nose burns as the sudden urge to cry snaps into my soul.

For all my talk of this job not being the end all be all, the fact that I screwed it up so royally, paired with the painful walk because my anxiety got the best of me, has me feeling… down.

"Oh, honey," she says, gliding toward me. Overnight she went from flat stomach to a little pooch. It's adorable. But if she tries to hug me, I know I'll lose it.

"Ughhhhh," I say with a long breath before ducking my head under the water. I stay there for a few seconds, listening to the dampened sounds of Veronica sighing and saying what sounds like, "Winter, c'mon."

"Up!" she presses, her voice raised. I sit up and wipe the sudsy water from my eyes.

I sigh.

"Do you want to talk about it?" She sits on the lip of the tub, unfazed by my nudity. We've seen each other naked a million times over the years. When she got an ingrown hair that she was sure was an STI, she enlisted me to look at it before she went to her gyno. And she's definitely seen me naked and vulnerable and at my worst.

I close my eyes against my memories. What a hellacious day.

"I don't really want to talk about it, Rons. In fact, going to sleep and never waking up sounds real nice right now."

Her eyebrows crease in immediate concern. "Winter…"

Sensing my friend's distress, I reassure her. "No, no—not in a…I'm not depressed. I'm not suicidal. Nothing like that," I say.

The crease doesn't move from her eyebrows.

I can't joke with Veronica like that. She'll never find talk like that funny, especially when it comes to me.

I continue, "I'm just being your regular degular melodramatic millennial. For real, Rons. I'll be okay. I'm just really down on myself right now. I let my anxiety control me, and I ended up hurting myself in the process."

In more than one way.

"Can you explain why you thought the interview went so badly? It sounds like you stood up for your client, which is exactly what you're supposed to do."

I swallow, my throat tight.

"Yeah, I guess that part wasn't so bad. It's just that I was yelling and cursing and not at all professional. Then I freaking *flashed* the boss and—"

"Wait, *skrrrt.* Pause. What do you mean you flashed him?" Veronica looks delightfully scandalized.

"It wasn't on purpose. I fell into the fountain and my shirt got wet."

"You…fell. Into a fountain. I thought you were all wet from the rain. Pray tell how that happened?" She's outwardly amused now.

"Ugh, don't worry about it. Just know that it was embarrassing, and I was embarrassing. I am embarrassment."

"Oh, Winter," she says before leaning closer to me to give me a love tap on the shoulder. She slaps her hands on her thighs. "Will you be okay for the night? James will be home in the morning, and I wanted to get the house ready for him." She glances at her smartwatch, frowns, and then looks back at me.

I wave her off. "I'll be fine. I just need to do something about these feet." I raise my leg so my foot is above the water. The blisters formed quickly and many of them have already popped.

She hugs my head and gives me a quick peck on my hairline. "Love ya, sister. Call if you need me."

"I will," I promise.

Veronica stands and pauses in front of the mirror, taking in her profile and gliding her palm over her baby bump. I'm unsure what she's thinking as she stares at her reflection, but something shifts in my stomach as I look at her. Finally, she shakes her head and exits the bathroom. A few moments later,

I hear the mechanical whirr of my apartment door locking, and I sink back into the tub.

If I look at things objectively, the interview didn't go too horribly. I think I answered some of Ella's questions well. But she only got to ask three things before everything went down.

My cheeks warm in embarrassment as I recall how I yelled and behaved in front of everyone. How I behaved in front of Mr. Brigham.

Hunter.

His eyes…

I close my eyes against the memory of Hunter Brigham and how unsettled he made me with just one touch. When he grabbed me, I didn't feel panic, as I usually would when anyone—especially a man—touches me.

When I first got Kitty, I had to switch service animal trainers because being in the room with a man triggered all my sore spots. He was a kind man, so I'm grateful that he took my rejection in stride.

But with Hunter, as I felt his strong hand circling my wrist, for the first time in…forever…I felt secure. Safe.

Insanity, Winter. Pure insanity.

Still, I keep my eyes closed as I think about looking up at Hunter Brigham while sprawled in his ornate fountain. My skirt rode up a bit, and with how tight it was, I know if I moved the wrong way, I would have flashed him.

I heat up in the cooling bath water. He seems strong, like he's athletic but not overly muscular.

I bet he fucks like a god.

My eyes snap open at the thought. My cheeks and chest flush, and my nipples pearl against my will.

"Take a breath, girl," I say to the empty bathroom.

I count silently as my eyes shut again. But despite my efforts to keep Hunter Brigham out of my mind, he slides back in. Except this time when he waltzes into my subconscious, I let him stay. In the fantasy, I kneel in the water fountain, looking up at him as he walks closer. I meet his eyes as I spread my thighs as far as my skirt lets me. It's just me and him in the courtyard, and I feel bold. Powerful.

He stalks toward me, his thick, muscular thighs flexing with each step and says, "Let me see you."

That rough, deep voice of his heats me thoroughly.

I comply, spreading my thighs and pulling my skirt up over my ass to rest on my waist.

"Fuck," he growls.

I open my legs in the bath water just as I do in my imagination.

"Touch yourself," he commands. I run a finger up and down across my slit. He rasps out a low, nearly feral sound as I continue stroking my clit and pushing lower to ease a finger into my sex.

He walks even closer; his confidence and intoxicating presence edges out my vision. I'm close to coming, my essence mixing with the water beneath me.

He puts his hand on his waistband and says, "If you get to come, so do I." He holds my eyes and moves his hand inside his pants to stroke his cock. "Want me to pull it out?"

"Yes," I hiss. The sound echoes around the courtyard and off the tiles of my bathroom floor. His smile is devilish—he's here to pull me down into hell. I know he is.

"Don't come until I say so," he demands, and lowering his pants—

I jerk my hand from my snatch and splash water over the side of the bathtub.

My heart races at the sharp knock at my front door.

Kitty barks wildly, not used to visitors who aren't Veronica.

Another knock rings out, and I determine that whoever is on the other side of the door isn't there by accident and means to talk to me.

"One second," I yell in the direction of the door, sounding

more irritable than I intend. I rip my fluffy robe off the back of the bathroom door.

Walking toward the door and dripping bath water with each step, I deepen my voice and yell, "Who is it!"

That sounds intimidating.

"Ms. Vaughan? It's Ella Brigham. We met today? I brought your belongings. Could you open the door?"

Holy shit, Ella Brigham is at my door.

"You couldn't have called me?" I yell out, my voice at my usual tenor.

"I tried, but you didn't answer," she says back with a slight note of amused exasperation. It's then that I remember that my phone, likely dead, is in the briefcase she probably has in her hands. Duh.

I creep closer to the door and look out the peephole.

Yup. Ella Brigham is at my door. And she's alone.

That thought doesn't make me as relieved as it should.

Maybe because you wanted him *to be with her.*

I shut that train of thought down quickly.

"I wasn't expecting company," I yell through the door. "Just give me a moment to get dressed."

"Okey dokey!" Ella says brightly, and I snort at the unexpected reply.

After sliding into the mustard yellow silk pajamas I'd pulled out before I got into the tub, I take a deep breath and open the door.

"Thank you for bringing my stuff, Ms. Brigham. I'm sorry you had to come all this way." I stretch my arm out to grab the bag from her.

"It's all good, I promise." She still holds the bag close to her chest. My arm hangs in the air, empty handed.

"Um…" I say, reaching out more to grab the bag.

"Could I come in? Can we talk?" she says, and my hand freezes over the briefcase's handle.

Kitty sits next to me, and his huff sounds exasperated. This is cutting into his rest time.

"Is it a requirement for me to get my stuff back?" I raise an eyebrow.

She sighs. "No, but I'd really like to talk with you all the same."

It's my turn to sigh.

She smiles brightly.

"Sure, come on in," I grumble, moving aside for her to walk through.

Once inside, she spins around and holds the bag out as if presenting an award to me. I take it from her, pull my phone out, and put it on the charger.

"Relax," I call over to Kitty, who is more than happy to oblige. The trek through the rain wore him out too, so he curls into himself on his dog bed and closes his eyes.

"Here's the deal, Winter," she says, and I turn around to see her making herself at home on my sofa. Okay, so a long talk. Got it. "I—*We* want to offer you the job. Will you accept?" She smiles at me again with that radiant, perfect Ms. America smile.

I blink, knowing I must be gaping at her.

"You want to offer me the job. Forgive me if this is a dumb question, but why?"

She tilts her head to the side, studying me. "Why wouldn't we offer you the job?"

"Because we didn't even really have an interview?"

"I saw what I needed to see," she says.

"I see," I say, not seeing. At all.

"Here's the thing, Winter," she says, and I'm confused as hell when she reaches into her pocket and pulls out a Halloween-sized Airhead. Cherry flavored, from the looks of it. "I really like you. I like you for August. *August* likes you—he told me so. And I really like how you protected him today."

Another blink from me.

"And Mr. Brigham?" I say, biting my nails.

Her smile tightens. "He's in the loop," she says cryptically.

"I don't know, Ms. Brigham—"

"Ella," she says, cutting me off with a smile. "And we're prepared to compensate you thoroughly." She pulls a folded paper from her pocket and hands it to me. I unfold it, smoothing out the creases, and immediately notice the offer letter and enclosed check. I gasp.

"What's the *50,000 dollars* for?" I don't know if the buzzing in my ears is from my shout or because I'm about to pass out.

Kitty lifts his head, and I put my hand out, signaling for him to stay.

My head starts to spin.

"Consider it a sign-on bonus." She clasps her hands in her lap and sits up straight. She's enjoying this for some reason.

"What's the catch?"

"No catch, Winter. Really. I just want my nephew to get better. To get the help he needs. I know you can help him." Her smile turns sad.

I hum and look over the offer letter. They're offering enough hours for me to complete my required clinical experience and then some over the next two semesters. The salary and benefits make my eyes water. Most practicum placements are paid a hair above minimum wage, if at all.

My parents left behind a sizable inheritance plus the insurance payout when they died. I'm not starved for money. And yet, if this degree doesn't work out and I end up sick again, I'll need to be able to support myself.

The Brigham's offer of a half-million dollars would be an incredible safety net. Or seed money for the Ranch.

You could get started and really do this thing, Winter.

"This feels too good to be true, Ella. And it's been my

experience that when things sound too good to be true, they usually are." I refold the paper.

She nods. "I hear you, Winter. But I hope you'll really consider helping my nephew." I watch her throat work as she swallows. "He needs your help."

I bring my hand back to my mouth but lower it when the tang of blood hits my tongue. Bitten to the quick.

Think of what you could do. Think of how you could change his life.

"When would I start?" I say after a moment.

She bounces with excitement as she jumps up and hugs me. She lets out a slight squeal.

"This calls for candy," she says, pulling a handful from her designer jeans.

EIGHT
HUNTER

To say the month since I'd located August and brought him home has been tense would be an understatement.

There is tension on my part: here I am, thrust into the role of father when I've never fucking done it before.

There's tension on August's part: he is recovering from the physical effects of dehydration and starvation in addition to the dumpster fire that has to be going on in his brain.

August at fifteen is challenging. August as a traumatized and angry teenager, is a whole different ballgame.

"August, breakfast is ready." I stand at his door as music blasts through. His diet is limited to a few steady items he will eat, and I had the cook stockpile them while he recovered in the hospital. So that brings me to standing in my hallway, talking to a door.

I feel like things should be better with August than they are now. But I don't know what I'm doing here.

I'm fucking ill-equipped.

I knock on the door before opening it. August sits on his bed with his iPad on his lap. The king-sized bed nearly swallows him.

I asked Ella what he was into these days besides RC stuff, and I had one of my guards run out to purchase new bedding. We set him up with a computer rig that would make the biggest gamers envious. He hasn't turned the computer on yet, and when he arrived at Amelia Manor, he ripped the blanket off the bed to sleep just with a sheet.

Ella told me it was a sensory issue, but I can only believe it's another example of my ineptitude.

I shake my head against the thought. Yes, I have things to learn. But we're both new to this. It will be okay.

Right?

"August, I have waffles ready for you. I had the chef pull out the Eggos, even though she about had a coronary when she did." I move further into his room. He doesn't look up at me—not that I expect him to—and his fingers move across his tablet.

"I am good. Not hungry." The disembodied voice from his tablet catches me off guard every time. The app he uses to speak for him has a setting that lets users choose the voice types. His voice selection is labeled "American gangster."

"You sure? You haven't eaten much these past few days."

He leans over to his nightstand and snags a bottle of water and a bag of Cheez-Its. "Yes. Goodbye," he says.

I clear my throat before saying, "Yeah, no problem. Talk to you later." I turn around quickly and shut the door behind me.

"He just needs time, H."

I walk toward Leo when I notice him. He stands with one foot on the top step, clearly on his way toward the security office a few doors down on this wing.

"He needs much more than I can give him right now." I feel my shoulders tense up and fight my body to relax them.

He presses his mouth into a straight line.

"Something on your mind, Leo?"

"Yeah, listen." He dips his head down and scratches

behind his ear—his tell that he's uncomfortable since we were kids. "I'm not trying to get into touchy-feely shit with you. But I wanted to touch base with you—"

"Touch base? What are we, on a conference call?" I interject.

"—to make sure you're okay. You know, mentally."

"Leo, if you don't stop, I'm gonna DoorDash you a box of tampons. I'm fine. I'm not sure what the fuck I'm doing here with August. The rest of the shit I couldn't give a flying fuck about."

He shrugs at my words and says, "All right. I'm here if you want to talk."

That's Leo. He knows when to leave me the fuck alone and when to push.

"I think I should call that doctor from the hospital. See if she has anyone else she can recommend to help." I start to move down the stairs.

"I don't think that's a bad idea." Ella appears from nowhere, as she always seems to do these days. She's always here in Amelia Manor. It's like she's fucking haunting the place—or, more accurately, haunting me. "But then again, we had the *perfect* candidate, and you had to blow her off."

I wanted said candidate to blow me in a very different way.

Leo takes the last step and heads back toward the security room. He stops suddenly when the alarm for the front gate activates. It blares for a solid forty-five seconds before cutting off abruptly.

One of our security staff, Jared, comes running down the hallway. "Boss, that's Winter Vaughan at the main entrance. An Uber just dropped her off. The car drove away, leaving her there. She says today is supposed to be her first day working here, but I don't have her name on your visitor list."

Counting to five in my head, I say to Ella without looking at her, "You didn't."

When I finish my deep breathing, I turn to her.

Leo stands at the top of the stairs, amused, and Ella wears a chagrined smile.

"Well, it most certainly looks like I did." She rocks on her heels as a vision of innocence.

"Ella! I *specifically* told you not to hire her."

"Hunter! I *specifically* told you I vehemently disagreed."

"August is *my son*. I get to make decisions for his care."

"Since fucking when!" Ella stops herself, her eyes wide as her statement lands.

Yeah. Since fucking when?

"Um, boss, should I let her in?" Jared asks, to which I snap, "No!" just as Ella says, "Yes, and send the cart down for her."

"Ella, please." I pinch the skin between my eyes and sigh. I'm not going to win this fight. And I know I'm going to lose in more ways than one.

She moves closer to me.

"Brother." She places her hand on my raised forearm. "She's the best for August. They connected—that's something a lot of people don't even *try* to do with him. You want the best for him, don't you?"

Don't I? I've always wanted the best for him. The best doctors, therapists, programs…

Yes, he deserves the best. That's why I've stayed away.

I straighten up. Ella is right. But I sure as hell won't tell her that. She'd never let it go.

"Fine," I say, my eyes landing on Jared. "Do whatever she says." I walk past the group and head toward the office.

Fifteen minutes later, the click of footfalls taps a rhythm outside my door.

"This is H's office. He's in there right now *being antisocial,*" she raises her voice, "but I'll make sure he's out in a minute for your meeting." They continue down the corridor. Another set of feet land outside my office, and three quick knocks precede my door opening.

Leo slips in.

"We need to talk," he says.

"Well, that's never the start of good news," I reply.

Leo doesn't laugh. Instead, he walks over to the sidebar where liquor would be kept. Ella never stocked it, and it's good that she didn't.

When he sees it empty, he plops down into the seat in front of my desk.

"Talk then," I say, rubbing my temples.

"Your fucking father is a piece of work." I look at Leo, and he's seething.

"What did he do now?"

"What *hasn't* he done?" he grumbles and pulls his phone out for me to see.

It's an article from *The Sun-Times.* My father smiles, standing with some important-looking government officials.

"Who is that? They look familiar."

"That would be the FDA Commissioner. Next to him is the Secretary of Health and Human Services," Leo grinds out.

"He's fucking with us," I conclude.

Leo runs a hand through his hair. "He's been sniffing around here for weeks. He hasn't shown his face yet, but I know it's coming."

I rub the skin above my top lip, thinking.

"What would he gain from messing with BwP?" Leo asks.

"Depends on what he's after at the moment. If he just wants my attention, he knows that my whole life centers around BwP. If he has another angle, though…"

I don't have a clue.

"What do you think, then? Do we wait him out to see what he wants, or do we go to him? Be preemptive?" I say.

Leo waits a beat before saying, "Wait it out. Let him come

to us and do what he wants. That will give the guys more time to dig into everything."

I nod. I've left my father alone, and he's left me alone. I know it's a matter of him deciding to not mess with me. I guess my return to D.C. sparked some desire for connection.

Maybe in another world, it would be sweet.

The fact is my father is a bad man who does bad things with other bad people. Not that we're saints, Leo and me. We also work with bad people. But we don't kill people. I haven't killed anyone since leaving my father's clutches.

An edge of remorse pierces through me, manifesting as a pulse in the base of my skull.

All the shit he made me do.

Benjamin Brigham is built differently. He revels in destruction. He gets high off torture. He's a monster.

And instead of slaying him, I've turned a blind eye and let him carry on.

Self-preservation is at the root of the will to live.

But now, my father wants something. I can't stick my head in the sand any longer. Because if I do, all he'll do is fuck me.

When Leo leaves the room, I settle into the reality that my father is about to blow up my world even more than it already has.

NINE
WINTER

I'm not anxious. I'm nervous.

My leg bounces up and down underneath the dining table. Well, to call it a dining table would be utterly absurd. The behemoth slab of Amazon rosewood parading as a table gleams as the wall of windows lets in the sunlight. This thing could easily seat forty people.

We're in what Ella called "the great hall," and I feel entirely dwarfed as I sit to the right of the head of the table.

In that seat is H. Mr. Brigham.

"This parent interview and assessment is pretty thorough, so it will take the entirety of our time together." I try to make my tone light, even though I'm not looking directly at him. I can't. Instead, I make a show of flipping through my yellow legal pad and straighten the various assessments placed on the table before me.

Kitty lies on the floor near my feet.

"I've got everything lined up, though, so we'll be able to get through everything pretty seamlessly." I glance up at him, and I'm startled to see his eyes locked on my face. Which… where else would he look? We're the only two people in this massive room. But still…

When I arrived this morning, I felt a whole heaping of doubt when seven guards stared me down, demanding my identity before my foot even left my Uber.

I only calmed down when a hulking blond with a hard Southern accent put me in the most tricked-out golf cart I've ever seen.

Ella's bubbly personality soothes many ills, so once she greeted me with a warm welcome, I was calm and smiling for the rest of the morning.

But now I'm sharing airspace with Hunter Brigham, and his presence sucks the oxygen out of the room.

Daring to steal more oxygen, I take a deep breath before asking, "Do you have any questions before we begin?"

My eyes lock on his.

"Not at this time," he says. The angles of his stupidly handsome face are sharp, his gaze hard.

"Great, so let's get started." I shuffle more papers. "We'll go through the parent interview portion. Then I'll leave you to fill out the parent questionnaires. I also connected with August's past providers and had a wonderful chat with his occupational therapist."

"Who gave you that information?"

"Oh! I completed my interview with Ella—er, Miss Brigham, virtually a few days ago. She gave me their info." I can see the moment when a wall goes up in his brain.

He replies with a short, "Hm."

"Anyhoo," *Oh, my God, Winter. Anyhoo?* "I've got a lot to go on here, but your input will let us wrap this up nicely."

I pause, waiting for him to say something.

Anything.

I keep going when I realize he's not going to add to that statement.

"Moving on, then. Can you tell me about the pregnancy with August? What was it like? Was it uncomplicated, or were there a lot of concerns?"

He clenches and unclenches his jaw, and I'm mesmerized by the movement. "I don't know much about it, but I believe it was pretty straightforward considering she was an addict." My eyebrows shoot to my hairline and I force my face into a professional mask. I turn to my legal pad to make a note.

"Was she in active addiction during the pregnancy?" I ask. I don't judge people with addictions for their illness. God knows I could have so easily fallen into that path. I try to make sure my voice sounds as positive and nonjudgmental as possible.

"I'm unsure," he grinds out.

"That's okay," I rush to say and face my legal pad again, scribbling notes I'm not sure will be legible. "Let's move on from that. The delivery. Was it a C-section or vaginal?"

"I don't know."

"Okay, how about the first few months of life? Did the mom breastfeed, or was August formula-fed?" I ask this question without looking at H, but I tear my eyes from the paper when his silence goes on for a moment too long.

He's not looking at me, though. He's looking out the window. His face is blank, and his head rests on his fist.

"Whatever you remember, Mr. Brigham." He raises his eyebrow and settles his gaze back on me.

"What do I remember? Well," he emits a somber chuckle. "I don't remember much because I wasn't there. I was anywhere but. I stopped by the hospital to see my son through a window for fifteen minutes and was on a plane to the other side of the country twelve hours later." He sits up in his seat and leans toward me.

"Want to know the truth, Winter? Maiya and I? We fucked. A lot. She gave great head. Grade-A. That's all there was. We weren't a family unit. We didn't have pillow talk or go on dates. It was fucking, plain and simple. Next thing you know, August is here. That's what happened."

I snap my mouth closed and look around to make sure

we're still alone. We are, and I feel heat rising to my cheeks from anger.

"What are you even saying right now? Do you even want August?" My line of questioning is wholly inappropriate, but he opened the door.

"Fuck yes, I want him. I wanted him then too. I saw his face through that damn nursery window and he became the most important person in my entire world. And that's why I —" He cuts himself off, looking back at the window, but this time, he covers his mouth with his fist. I can see the wheels turning in his mind.

"In my world, there's not a lot of space for things like families." The muscles in his face tighten.

He continues on. "These questions…I know you're going to ask me a lot of questions I don't know the answer to," he says, still not looking at me. "And that makes me feel like shit. But that's not your problem." He stands up, and the scratch of the solid wood chair ricochets around the room. "That said, I don't have much to add to the conversation. And I won't be able to fill out these forms." He picks them up and throws them into the crate sitting on the floor near my feet.

He walks away.

I sit at the table, stunned for a full two minutes. My mind spins. He clearly feels *something* for his son. That's apparent whenever you see him interact with August. He's desperate to connect with him. But he talks so poorly about the circumstances of August's birth. About how he showed up as a father up until now. And the sad part is: he's telling the truth. It's not that he's necessarily being hard on himself. These are the facts. This is what happened.

August is paying for the sins of both of his parents.

My anger returns. His father needs to be there for him through this process. Hunter Brigham needs to get his shit together.

"Stay," I tell Kitty. He shakes his head like he doesn't believe me. "I mean it," I say with more intensity.

He lies down with a huff.

I make my way through the estate, following the path of Hunter's departure. After a few turns, I stop in a hallway deep in the mansion.

"Where the fuck am I?" I mutter, and I slow my breathing to try to orient myself.

I hear the smack of what sounds like skin hitting skin, and I'm apprehensive about following the noise. Is he having sex right now?

I don't know why, but my feet follow the rhythmic pounding, and to my relief, Hunter isn't, in fact, in the process of having sex. He's in a gym, and he's trying to annihilate a punching bag.

My relief turns into red-hot shock when I realize the very fortunate/unfortunate news that he's shirtless. If I check myself right now, I know I'll find drool. I was so right in my earlier assessment of him. He has a solid figure that's not overly defined like a bodybuilder's. His stomach is thick with muscle beneath his skin. His arms are covered with tattoos… and scars.

Burn marks?

He must realize I'm standing there because his voice shocks me from my gawking.

"What else do you need, Ms. Vaughan?" He punches the bag again, harder than his previous jabs. And goddamn if his back muscles don't flex with each movement.

I stand up tall, summoning all the authority available in my body.

"Regardless of your presence to date, *Mr. Brigham*," I emphasize his name, "your participation in this process and the following sessions is vital to August's recovery."

In the middle of my speech, he steps down from the platform that houses the punching bag and walks over to the dumbbells. The ones he picks up look impossibly heavy, but he lifts them easily.

"I really have nothing to add to this process." He sits down on the bench and alternates arm curls.

"Well, I disagree. Wholeheartedly, actually. You're August's father. And regardless of what your relationship has looked like so far, you and his aunt are all he has. Don't cut his support system down. Be there." The weights clank loudly as he drops them back on the rack, the sound vibrating off the mirrors along the wall nearest to us.

"What do you need from me, Winter?" My chest warms at him using my name.

"I need," *a lot of things from you.* "I need you to come to the caregiver sessions with Ella so we can discuss your progress and come up with ideas to engage with him." I take a breath. "And figure out how you two can build a relationship."

His left knee pops up and down rapidly, and he grunts when I stop speaking.

"And I think you could really benefit from one-on-one sessions with a counselor. Someone who can help you process your trauma and emotions. I can help you."

His head snaps my way when I mention one-on-one sessions. It wasn't something I'd thought about until the words came out of my mouth. I don't think I can actually offer him counseling sessions. Not legally or officially, anyway.

"Or," I say, rushing to fill the silence. "I can connect you with a few great referrals who can work with you individually. It's, um, it's up to you." I bring my hand to my mouth and start nibbling on a hangnail.

Hunter stands up and walks toward me. When he's a foot away, he stops, places his hands on his hips, and looks down.

"And if it goes nowhere? If it turns out that August will always hate me and my presence hurts more than it helps? Goddamn it," he says, rubbing his hand over his mouth.

He walks back to the dumbbells and sighs, his back to me. He may not like it, but I hear the vulnerability in his tone. He isn't looking at me, but I can feel it. This strong, powerful man is scared. Maybe he wants this to work.

Compassion floods me. Uncontrollably, my feet move closer to him.

"We just need to give it time." I place my hand on his forearm.

His gaze snags mine at the touch of my hand, and I find myself wholly ensnared. The foot between us seems to evaporate, and I feel the intimacy of his nearly naked body so close to mine.

So close.

His smell—cedarwood, smoke, and sweat—wraps around me, and the room starts to spin.

Down, damn pheromones!

I pull my hand from his arm.

"Oh, sorry. I shouldn't have—okay, wow, I should really get going." I step back several feet and find myself at the doorway. I clutch the doorframe so hard my fingertips ache. "I'll be by in the morning. I'll evaluate everything from Ella's interview and assessment submissions tonight and present an action plan to the three of you tomorrow. Okay, bye!"

I whip around and shockingly find my way back to the great hall without getting lost. Stuffing everything back into my tote as quickly as possible and bringing Kitty to heel, I swing my bag over my shoulder. I damn near run to exit Amelia Manor.

I'm forty feet down the driveway when I realize I never scheduled an Uber.

Fuck.

TEN
HUNTER

I shouldn't be surprised when I walk into my office a little later to find my phone and instead find my father sitting at my desk.

You don't put off Benjamin Brigham. Once I knew he knew where I was, it was only a matter of time.

Now's the time, I guess.

The only thing making this reunion at all positive is that Ella's in the room too, and she claps with a bright smile when I enter.

"Hunter, since you won't go to Dad, I decided to bring Dad to you!" She looks so eager, so innocent in her efforts to bring us together that I can't be mad at her. I walk over to her, giving her a brief hug.

"All good, Ellie. Give us a minute?" I say gently.

Her eyes twinkle and she practically skips to the door.

"Absolutely-tutely! I'm gonna raid your kitchen, H. Toodles!" And then she's gone.

"Hello, Father," I say with all the formality I can muster. "Thank you for coming to visit. Shall I prepare a room for you in the *master* wing?"

He smirks, his eyes narrowing.

"Son," he says. "It's about time you've chosen to return."

After stopping to flick on the fireplace, I sit in the wing-back chair across from him. It's not cold outside, but the chill in the air is from the man sitting across from me.

"What do you need?"

There's a decanter on my desk that wasn't there before.

"I think it's time we catch up and talk about what's happened in your absence. Things have been busy." He taps his finger on the whiskey tumbler in his right hand.

It's incredible how a person who shows so much cruelty can be so relaxed. So unbothered.

I sit back in my chair, mirroring his lazy pose. He lets out a dull laugh.

"Cut the shit, Hunter," he says suddenly, not moving an inch. "It's time you started taking responsibility for your duties to this family."

Fire licks up my calves and thighs, and the muscles in my back and stomach clench at the mention of responsibility. The burns marring my body pulse in memory.

"What responsibilities? I have done my part, and I want nothing to do with you," I say, trying my damnedest to control the amount of venom in my voice.

He acts as if I said nothing, lifting the glass to his mouth and taking a slow sip.

"You are Hunter Brigham. No matter how much you may detest your name, and no matter how much you fuck around Europe or Asia or Central America, the reality is you are a Brigham. You've been given wealth, status, protection," he drawls as he taps the glass again. "I've given you time to sow your wild oats. But that time ends now. Welcome back, son. It's a pity it's under such terrible circumstances." His eyes lock on mine.

"Maiya. That was you," I say.

He gives me a closed-lipped smile. "I didn't do anything

to your whore, Hunter." He shrugs, unaffected. "She made her own choices."

Another slow sip.

"Let me guess, you just gave her the options to choose from. Right?" The tension in my jaw starts to thump, matching the agitated thud of each of my heartbeats.

For not the first time, I contemplate ending my father's worthless life. I could slit his throat and dance in his blood as his life spills all over the hand-knotted Persian rug.

Why don't I?

Right. Because I'm weak. Because ultimately, when it was time to stand up against him, I did nothing. And then I ran away.

"My son was there for days with her dead body. Why? What did you get out of getting rid of Maiya?" I don't expect him to give me a straight answer.

"You are so damn dramatic, Hunter," he says, looking bored at this line of questioning. "But I'll bite. You needed a little bit of a wake-up call. And I know you have a soft spot for that child of yours."

"Ever heard of an email?"

More silence as he takes a leisurely sip.

"What do you want from me?"

"It's not what I want, Hunter. It's what you will do." He places the glass on the marble coaster next to him. "Your days of gallivanting around the world are over. You will stay here, in Amelia Manor. I'll do you the favor of not requiring you to stay at Brigham Estate. You're welcome." He tilts his head toward me as if to say, *Aren't I the greatest?*

He continues. "You will stop this idiocy of ignoring my phone calls." He sits silently, and I nod, as expected.

"And congratulations. You're getting married to Blair Winthrope."

I choke on my spit. "What?" I cough and try to reconcile my father's words.

"I was quite clear, Hunter," he snaps.

"For what reason do you need me to marry *anyone*, particularly Blair Winthrope?"

This is so far from what I expected him to demand from me. I'd met Blair a few times over the years. Fundraisers, the country club, and other places where young people are seen but not heard. It's been well over a decade since I last saw her. She and her father attended a banquet in Manhattan that I happened to go to. My memory recalls her as tall and thin, with red hair and a perfect face that could only be from the end of a surgeon's knife.

He gives me another closed-lipped smile. "Blair and her family present an interesting opportunity for me. So you will marry her. And I need you to give me heirs. Not defective accidents that should have been aborted."

"You would do well to never speak about my son again," I spit at him.

He rolls his eyes, and I swallow against the band of rage that's choking off my air supply.

"If you don't want to marry, you have free choice. Do what you want."

A trap.

"Say whatever you're going to say, Father."

"You're so busy with your company. It would be a shame if that were to go under."

I arch a brow at him. "The FDA?" I ask in a flat tone.

"No one wants a cure for cancer," he says.

"Tell that to the people who are dying from it."

He waves off my words.

"Nonetheless, I can do some interesting things with this new opportunity with the Winthropes," he says.

"Care to share with the class?"

He appears to think about it for a moment before saying, "Nah."

"Motherfucker," I grumble under my breath, clasping my hands together behind my neck.

"Think of it this way, you'll get to start over again. Build a family the right way from the start," Father says brightly.

"What the fuck do you mean by that," I say in a low, dangerous tone.

Father's smile is slow, derisive. "I'm sure you know what I mean, Hunter."

Dread drops in my stomach like an anvil.

August. He's talking about August. Hurting him, getting rid of him.

Never. Never again will August get caught up in my father's bullshit.

I could kick him out right now, tell him to fuck off and run away with August, hell, with Ella too. But the reality is, there's nowhere I can go that Benjamin Brigham won't be able to find me. And when he does…

I have to play this smart. I know as soon as I bring in Leo, he'll have Max following the threads of this conversation so we can get a step ahead of my father.

Somehow.

…How?

Until I have a plan, I have to keep August safe.

"Fine," I say. I don't have to voice the words, but I do anyway. "I'll do it."

"Excellent," he says with no heat.

Father gets up from the chair and glides over to me. "I'll be in touch, son. In the meantime, keep this," he rears back, giving me an open-handed slap across the face with my phone in the same palm, pressing it into my skull, "nearby."

The ring on his pinky glints against the flames—a heavy gold band centered with an onyx eye surrounded with intricate geometric shapes. It's a flashy, outdated choice for a man who considers himself a fashion icon. But I've never seen my father without it.

My cheek pulses. Not from his slap but from the memory of that same ring cutting into my flesh with the force of his strikes. There weren't many times that he would choose his fists over any other torture device, but his delight came from making me bleed, however he managed to do so.

And with that final order, he leaves the room.

I sit silently for several minutes, staring at the flames.

Helplessness threatens to drag me under as a simple thought rings true: my father knows no boundaries. There's nothing his power cannot achieve.

When am I going to stop letting him control me?

I run a hand down my face.

The fire overheats me, burning my eyes the longer I stare at it. So when a knock sounds at the office door a few minutes after my father's departure, it's for the best. Any longer and I likely would have damaged my corneas.

"Was that who I thought that was?" Leo's incredulous voice comes from behind me, and I sigh heavily before turning to meet his gaze.

"Yep. Benjamin Brigham in the flesh."

"So he finally decided to show himself." Leo moves to take over the seat my father vacated, loosening his tie at the same time.

"Ella brought him over. She thinks I'm mean to him." My lips start to go numb, and I turn to face the fire once more.

Leo makes an indelicate sound. "When are you going to stop hiding the truth from her?" Leo presses, his voice laced with anger.

"What's with all the questions, Leonardo?" I shoot back. I catch it when he raises an eyebrow in reply.

There's so much to what I just learned that I don't know where to begin sharing. I groan for a solid three seconds before adding, "Guess who's getting married."

Leo lets out a choked sound, sputtering for a moment before rasping out, "Certainly not you?"

I nod grimly.

"Fuck! That's fucked. But wait, why are you…"

I give Leo a hard look, telegraphing that the answer is obvious.

"He's basically holding BwP hostage," I reply.

"Ah. So the FDA was him."

"Yep," I say, rubbing my temple.

Leo grunts, a short, frustrated sound. "We can get around him. You don't have to do this, H."

"But I do," I croak. "He's also threatened August. He was behind Maiya's death."

Leo explodes out of his chair.

"I shouldn't be surprised, and yet…*shit*," he presses.

He paces across the room, putting his hands on his waist as he moves from one side of the room to the other. A flurry of tense Spanish streams from his mouth.

"So you see why I have to see this through." I rest my head against the back of my chair, lolling to the side to observe his agitated steps. I'm tired. So tired.

"There might be something…" Leo says once he stops moving.

I hum, indicating for him to continue.

"Something interesting happened to me last night." He's curiously calm now.

"Did you pick up a girl and she let you put your monster dick in her ass on the first try?" I guess.

He rolls his eyes. "No," he says dryly. "I met a new potential friend."

I raise an eyebrow.

"Misha Hroshko was in VIP at Krush last night. He sat down in my section for a talk."

Both eyebrows are raised now. "No shit?"

"Yep," he says. "He didn't say much, just that we had a mutual friend of a friend and that he'd be in touch to discuss opportunities soon."

I blow out a breath. "That's not cryptic as fuck," I mutter.

Misha Hroshko is like the Ukrainian boogeyman. The average person wouldn't know Misha by name, especially here in America, but he's the type of silent ruler that everyone should fear. Misha is the leader of the Mafiya, the Ukrainian organized crime unit that currently has a stronghold on imports and exports through the Black Sea.

Many years ago, I saw him at Isla Cara. He was nearly always silent, never partaking in the drugs or the girls from what I could tell.

The fact that he was so different from the other men who were there, so reserved and separated, confused my teenage brain. It scared me if I'm honest.

"I think it's about your father," Leo says in an even lower voice. "I think he's got his eyes on him too."

I pause, processing his words. "I mean, it only makes sense," I add.

The fact that he randomly showed up in Leo's section isn't benign. It's worrisome.

"Regardless, he wants something from us. Or you," I finish.

Leo nods.

"I think it's better to figure out what he wants sooner rather than later," Leo says. "And maybe he can help."

I zone back in, realizing I'm nodding.

"Set up the meeting," I tell Leo.

He nods in confirmation. "Done deal."

Leo stays with me in my office for a few more minutes before heading out for the night. He is staying in one of the guest cottages not too far from the main house.

He invited me over for a drink or three, but I declined.

Now, I'm back in silence. Just me and the dying fire.

I am so, so fucked.

My recipe for success against my father has been through classic avoidance. I haven't had to deal with his high-handed plans for the last several years because I've always been somewhere else, leaving an ocean and at least half a continent between us.

But now, he's got me here.

If it were just BwP he wanted to screw over, I'd let him. In a heartbeat. But he has his eyes on August. And I will protect my son no matter the cost.

I close my eyes and focus on blocking my mental tirade. Breathing deeply, the lingering smell of whiskey transforms into the scent of roses. Umber hair with soft curls passes into my field of vision. Winter left it curly for her first day working. I see her lips. I see her eyes. I revel in her presence.

I've never been around a woman like her—one who honors her vulnerability and yet is so strong and resolute in how she moves through this world. She intrigues me. I'm curious about her.

I'm more than curious. I'm...infatuated.

The pressing weight of the silent room fills the empty space in my ears, amplifying into a persistent buzz. Everything feels so out of control. I feel out of control.

I lean forward with my head in my hands.

"I hate this," I hiss out loud. But obviously, no one is here to care.

I pull out my phone, staring at the blank screen for several heavy moments before unlocking it. I'd uploaded Winter's contact information after she left. Doing so took me a full ten minutes of contemplation.

Now, I'm grateful I did it.

I don't allow myself to stop. I pull up her info and fire off a message.

I may not be able to control my father, or BwP, or whether August will hate me forever.

But I can control seeing Winter.

Somewhere along the line, the lust that I so clearly feel

when I think about her got an added layer: I like her. I want to know more.

I've been with a lot of women and I started fucking way before I ever should have.

You know what that was.

I screw my eyes shut at the thought, focusing on seeing Winter's face in my mind's eye. In the fantasy, she's dancing in the rose garden where I used to spend so much time with my mother.

Her soft smile calls me in; her eyes are open and guileless.

I allow myself to dive into the fantasy for one, two, three breaths.

And then, I shut her out.

My father left his whiskey glass on the side table, and I finally unlock my joints to walk over to the abandoned tumbler. Only a single square ice cube remains, mostly melted in the time I've sat in the room.

I raise the vessel to the light, staring at the fractals that cast as I do so. Each perspective shows a different picture. It's a simple kind of beautiful.

Channeling the frantic energy born from my impotence in this situation, I use all my force to rocket the Baccarat crystal toward the fire, shattering it into a thousand pieces.

ELEVEN
WINTER

Genevieve gave me homework after the weekly Friday session we had today, which she hasn't done in a while.

Her challenge for me is to come up with ten things that would make me feel like I'm living full-out.

"Don't limit yourself," she said, "put down the things you think are small and the scary-as-hell things that make you feel like you're gonna throw up just from writing them down. Go wild."

I tap my pen against the leather Moleskine journal on my lap. I've just come in from Kitty's afternoon walk, and he snoozes happily in the corner.

At the top of the page, I write "Winter's Life List" and underline it. A car honks outside my window, laying on the horn. Another vehicle picks up the battle, and soon yelling joins the noise. Kitty lifts his head but settles back into sleep when everything is silent.

1. Explore U Street

Even though I've lived here for almost two years, I haven't explored much past my building. These days, I go out an acceptable number of times every week.

Hell, I even go to work now.

I smile at the thought.

But the fact is, my default mode is to limit myself to short jaunts to specific stores, and only when I can't coordinate delivery.

I tap my pen against the notebook again and groan in frustration when I can't think of a second thing.

And you're supposed to come up with nine more.

I flop against my bed, throwing the notebook next to me.

A citrus essential oil blend swirls around me. I draw in the scent, feeling the burn of the trapped air, then force all of my breath out of my lungs.

Orange gives clarity, but I feel as clear as mud.

Breathe.

Repeat.

Repeat.

What do you want, Winter?

Slowly, images form, becoming vibrant the more I focus on them behind my closed eyelids.

Cherry blossoms.

Taking a picture of my passport as I board a plane.

Getting a manicure and pedicure with Veronica.

Laughing.

Loving.

Blue eyes flash in my mind, and I snap up on the bed.

"No good will come from fantasizing about your boss, Winter," I say out loud. Kitty huffs in response in his sleep.

I grab the notebook again and revisit my list.

1. *Explore U Street*
2. *Take a cooking class*

3. See the latest art collection at the museum
4. Visit the Cherry Blossom Festival next spring

I chew on my pen, thinking about the crush of travelers who will flood the Tidal Basin for the festival.

Genevieve said to be wild.

5. Kiss someone on New Year
6. Run in a marathon
7. Go sailing
8. Visit Paris again

My breath catches in my throat.

My eyes snap toward the wall and lock on the image of me and my mom. We're standing in front of the Louvre in Paris, and I have my arms wrapped tightly around her waist. She stretches her arm out high with the digital camera in her hand as she tries to capture both of us in the picture. She's wearing jeans and a white button-down shirt—casual for the Representative. She put her curly hair, which naturally straddles the border between blonde and brown, in a high ponytail. A relaxed, happy aura fills her light brown eyes. Her smile, usually absent under the constant stress of her work, lights up her chestnut-colored skin. I love this city. I love this moment.

And then he…

I put the journal down again and lean over my thighs, resting my head on them. Breathing is hard at this angle, but taking a break from the biological need of inhalation feels soothing. When the strain is too much, I sit back up.

I am here. I am safe.

Kitty hops on the bed, snuggling into my side. I pick the notebook back up again.

9. Go on 15 unique dates
10. Have sex

I look at the last one again. There are a lot of ways I can write the last entry. Ultimately, I revise it.

10. ~~Have sex~~ Make love while in love

A few hours later, I take Kitty out for his evening walk and lose my mind.

Or, more accurately, decide to face the crush of U Street on a Friday night. Kitty trots down the sidewalk, his head held high and on a whole 'nother level as his paws tap against the pavement. He's focused because his harness is on, therefore he's working, but I can tell he's excited to experience something new.

I've been depriving him of so much with my reclusiveness.

I don't have a target in mind. I just want to see the few blocks around my apartment building. After crossing the main street—*since when do our crosswalks talk at you and light up when you walk across?*—I spy a cute indoor–outdoor café that doubles as a bookstore…and wine bar?

I stop in front of it and look at the marquee illuminating the store name: Dichotomy.

"What do you think, Kitty? Should we go in?" I'm murmuring, talking under my breath to my dog. He's a quiet pup, so when he lets out a quick, loud bark, I laugh.

"I'll take that as a yes."

I walk into the store, and immediately I'm smitten with this place. It's dimly lit to set the mood, and dark wood bookcases line the shotgun-shaped store. Like a booklover's dream, a ladder runs across the entire right side, and higher shelves house more books and other bookish items.

On the left is the wine/coffee bar, and the barista—*or bartender? Bartendista?*—presents a flight of red wines to a group of women.

The coffee side is closed, but the wine bar is fully open. That makes sense, seeing as it's 7:30 at night.

"Are you sitting out on the patio?" a voice calls from my right. I choke, clutching my chest when I practically jump.

"Are you following me?" I take three quick steps back as Kitty immediately moves in front of me. I stop when I realize: one, the man is wearing a striped apron, and two, he has a name badge that says, "Marcus."

"No, I'm not?" he says with a healthy dose of confusion. Luckily, Marcus doesn't seem to take offense at my idiocy. Instead, he smiles. Those goddamn dimples pop again.

"I—I'm sorry. I wasn't expecting to see you here after seeing you in the dog park all those weeks ago."

"It's all good. I work here. Actually, I own this place. But we're a little short-staffed tonight, so I'm manning the bar and the store's cash wrap." I nod for entirely too long.

"This place is really, really cool!" I say a little too enthusiastically.

Jesus Christ on toast, get a grip!

"Thanks a lot." Pop goes the other dimple. "I haven't seen you here. Is this your first time visiting?"

I keep on nodding.

"Well, look around. If you'd like a glass of wine, it's on me."

"Oh, I don't drink," I say, starting my sentence entirely too loudly but finishing in a small voice I'm sure he can barely hear.

"That's okay. We have mocktails and a few other nonalcoholic drinks." He waves his hand toward the chalk menu posted above the bar.

I smile again, feeling more relaxed. A little bit. Marcus is nice. And he smells like my dad's beard balm, which calms me.

This is what making friends feels like. Flex the muscle.

"Nostalgia requires me to order a Shirley Temple," I say, turning back toward him. He smiles down at me, and again, I wonder if he's a little unhinged or maybe he finds me amusing?

...Attractive?

"Coming right up. I'll bring it out to you." He nods before going around the counter to talk to his other bartender.

I make my way back outside, finding a spot away from the foot traffic. I sit at a wrought-iron table, taking in the scene as Kitty sits on the ground behind me. The patio has three other pockets of customers seated—two couples and an older man reading a Bible. The couples are engaged in deep conversations by the looks of it, and one pair holds hands over their wine glasses. The man leans in to kiss the woman for a few long seconds.

I look away.

"Here you are, one Shirley Temple. I added a few more cherries to it. I thought you'd maybe like them." Marcus places the drink on the table with a napkin and a wicker coaster embossed with the Dichotomy logo.

I look up at him, and he winks at me.

He just fucking winked at me.

"Thank you," I say. I'm not sure if I'm smiling or frowning or what the hell my face is doing, so I grab my drink and move to take a massive gulp before I say or do something embarrassing.

More embarrassing.

"Let me know if you need anything else," he says, walking away.

I sit stunned for a few minutes.

Was he...was he flirting with me?

My phone jumps in my back pocket and rattles against the iron chair. When I unlock the screen, I fight to resist a gasp.

I have an email from Hunter Brigham.

I contemplate whether or not I should open it for two minutes before snapping out of it.

I'll take you up on the session. Tuesday at 11 a.m. is free for an hour. Talk to you then.

H

I curse the word vomit that's resulted in Hunter Brigham signing up for a session with me. The ethical and legal thing would be to refer him or see if another colleague could take him on.

I feel entirely too attracted to him to make this a good idea. But at the same time, the thought of not spending more time with him feels devastating.

Is this the start of a new obsession, or is this just lust? He probably isn't even interested in me like that. I mean, why would he? He probably has wealthy socialites and celebrities on his arm and warming his bed every night.

I groan softly and rest my head on the table. This is so inappropriate. And the fact that I feel so goddamn conflicted, torn between what I want and what's right…

What Would Veronica Do?

I respond to his message.

I've got you down.

Winter

Then, as if summoned, Veronica calls me.

"How has your first week gone? I haven't talked to you in forever, it feels like," Veronica asks.

It *has* been forever—or at least it seems that way. Between Veronica's doctor visits and my traveling back and forth to the Brighams, we've struggled to stay in contact outside of a few texts here and there.

"It's been great," I say. I'm not exactly lying, but I'm not telling the truth, either. Going through the family and therapist reports gives me a solid picture of who August Brigham is. But so far, August hasn't engaged with me much. Or at all.

And the fact that his father is never around when I am, but I can always smell his cologne throughout the house is…

"Why do I feel you need to say more, bestie?"

By the sound of rustling and cursing on the other end of the line, I can tell that Veronica dropped her phone.

"Veronica?" I reply once I hear her breathing in my ear.

"Yeah, I'm here. What's with the new job? What aren't you telling me?"

I take a sip of my drink. "Well, it's fine. The client is great. It's just the family is a little challenging," I say.

"Say more," she replies.

"Well," I pick a safe place to start. "His aunt is a little eccentric."

"Hmm, okay. But then, you're eccentric, right? Is that such a bad thing?"

"Maybe so, maybe no," I reply.

"Okay, sooo…" I visualize her on the other end of the call, circling her hand in the air to urge me to get to the fucking point. "What's the real issue, then?"

I take in a deep breath and take another drink to stall.

"Well, the client's dad is…" Hot. Brooding. Makes me cream my panties.

What the fuck, Winter.

"The client's dad is a little difficult sometimes."

"Is he bullying you?" she asks, the words bursting over the phone.

"No!" I reply a little too loudly, and the old man looks up

from his Bible over the rim of his glasses. I mouth "sorry" to him before continuing.

"No, Veronica. He's not bullying me. He just makes me feel a little…" I search for the word.

"A little *what?*" Veronica adds.

"A little unsettled." I finish.

Veronica is silent on the other line for several seconds before saying, "Please be specific about what that means." Her tone is serious, dropping a few levels and I press the phone tighter to my ear.

"I'm unsettled because he's a very handsome man." I will not tell Veronica about starting one-on-one sessions with him. I absolutely will not.

Because you know it's wrong.

She takes another few seconds before responding. "How does that make you feel? To be 'unsettled,' I mean."

I think about it. Genevieve and I started to talk about my attraction to H, but I quickly changed the subject. One, because there's an ethical gray area. While he isn't my client, he is my client's father.

And two, because I have never talked to Genevieve about sex like that. And it feels *awkward* to start having those conversations now, so far into our relationship.

"I feel okay with being unsettled," I say. "I think I'm ready to be unsettled."

Veronica goes mute again until I hear her sniff.

"Rons, are you crying?"

"I've told you once, I've told you a million times. I'm hormonal, bitch!" We both laugh over the line.

Finishing my drink and fishing out the last cherry, I ask, "How was your visit with James?" I tie the cherry stem into a knot with my tongue—a trick my mother taught me when I was a kid on a trip to the Kentucky Derby. They'd served Shirley Temples, and I had so many I got a stomachache from all the sugar.

"It was fine," she says.

"Just fine?"

"Yeah, it was a quick trip," she finishes.

I twirl the knotted stem between my fingers and mull over her words. The last time I tried to press her about her husband, she shut me out. I don't want to push her emotionally right now, especially since she's pregnant.

"When will I see you next?" I change the subject.

"Next weekend sometime?"

I smile. "Sure, I'll take you to this great little café, slash bookstore, slash wine bar. It's right down the street from my house. In fact," I pause for dramatic effect, "I'm there right now."

"You are not!"

"Yep, I sure am." A taxi presses its horn as a pedestrian jaywalks. "Did you hear that?"

She sniffs again. "I'm happy for you."

I'm happy for me too.

TWELVE
WINTER

I'm unnerved at how long it took me to get ready this morning. My routine was all the same: wake up, take Kitty out, make coffee, prepare Kitty's things and my supplies for the day, get cleaned up, and leave the apartment.

But when I faced my reflection in my bathroom mirror after spending forty-five minutes diffusing my curls and applying lashes, I felt foolish.

Silly.

I'm going to spend an hour with Hunter Brigham. Alone. Talking.

Holy bananas.

But now that I'm standing on the steps of Amelia Manor waiting for one of the staff to open the door, I'm self-conscious. Half of my wardrobe is currently on my bed, strewn about after my frantic search for the right outfit combination.

I rarely go to the mall or anything like that, but I love online shopping. I have a lot of clothes for living in a studio apartment.

I smooth my hands over my floral linen dress and pull the

sides of my soft cardigan together, praying I look casual and approachable rather than dressed up for no reason.

I don't want Hunter to think I tried too hard for this simple meeting.

Didn't you, though?

Kitty shuffles closer to me in his seated position, leaning against my freshly shaved legs. His presence helps knock a bit of the edge off. Which is a good thing because as soon as the door opens, I find it hard to breathe.

Hunter stands in the entrance. His charcoal gray suit can only be custom made, and because he doesn't wear the suit jacket, the unbuttoned top of his crisp white shirt stands out. Between the open panels of fabric, the edge of his chest tattoo peeks out.

With air trapped in my lungs, I try to form words past the constriction when he saves me from further embarrassment.

"Winter," he says. And when he smiles, I feel like I can relax again. The pensive, troubled look he wore for most of our parent meeting is gone. He looks…happy.

I'm glad for it.

"Where do you want me?" I ask after he ushers Kitty and me inside.

He gives me an unreadable look, and I want to smack myself because damn if that wasn't a provocative statement.

"Let's try the sitting room. It has a pocket door that we can close for privacy," he says. I freeze, suddenly having to face the idea of us being secluded together.

"Or not. It's all good," he adds quickly.

I face him, biting my lip. "It's okay, we wouldn't want someone overhearing or interrupting us."

No, we certainly would not.

Once in the room, I tackle the main issue.

"So first, I want to clarify. I'm not a licensed therapist yet, so it was a poor choice of words when I said I could take you on for a session. I can only provide services under the supervision of my advisor. I could ask for her to add you to my practicum…or I can be here as a friend to talk to. Would you like me to explain the differences between the two?"

I go for a gentle smile, but I'm distracted by the tremor in my hands.

"Lay it out for me, Winter," he replies, leaning back on the loveseat Ella sat in when interviewing me.

I clear my throat, patting the side of my leg to wordlessly get Kitty to jump in my lap.

"Well, if I'm to be here in an official capacity, that means that we will have to create super clear boundaries about what I can and cannot share with you in this space about August. Feedback sessions on August's progress will be separate from our sessions together. Does that make sense?" I raise my hands to my mouth, prepared to bite my nails, but I lower it to run through Kitty's fur. My dog lets out a pleased huff.

"That makes sense," he says. "What else?"

"Um…" I look around the room and feel heat rising to the apples of my cheeks.

"I mean, that's the main difference. We couldn't have a personal relationship outside these doors."

He raises an eyebrow.

"A personal relationship?" he asks, and there is a thread of amusement in his question.

Oh, God, he's laughing at me.

"Not that you'd want to connect outside of this professional arrangement. I don't mean—I mean—"

I'm flustered, stammering, so I'm grateful when he breaks my diatribe by saying, "I understand what you mean."

I pull Kitty closer to my chest.

We're both silent for a moment and I'm grateful for it. He glances away, and I want to think it's because he knows I need a break from the intensity of his eyes on me.

With a deep breath, I ask, "Which one do you want?"

His eyes slide back to me when I begin speaking, and he bites the side of his lip for a moment.

"Let's be friends," he says. He smiles, and I can't help smiling back.

"Okay, Hunter. Here's to being friends."

The silence is comfortable as we look at each other in the wake of that admission. When I was here last with Ella on the day of my fateful interview, I only had a moment to take in a few of the room's details.

Now, I can't say if anything has changed. All I can see is Hunter.

Hunter, who is now my friend.

"Well, *friend*," I say, testing out the word. "How are you?"

His laugh falls flat.

"That's a great question," he says without sarcasm.

"Isn't it?" I reply, giving him space to think. When he doesn't respond for a full minute, I say, "I'm not here to psychoanalyze you or diagnose you. I'm your friend, right? Friends talk about how they're doing."

His lips twist before settling into a smile. "You won't psychoanalyze me?"

"Well, not officially. Just in my head, though."

His smile is gentle. "You're funny, Winter Vaughan."

I smirk back at him. "This? Catch me when I'm warmed up. I'm hilarious."

Then I wink.

I wink!

Who even are you?

"I don't doubt that for a second," he replies.

"So don't avoid the question. How are you?"

He *tap-tap-tap*s a finger on his thigh several times before saying, "I'm sustaining." He inhales deeply, holding it for a second before expelling it.

"My whole life has changed in a matter of a day. I've gone from traveling the world, doing what I want when I want, to being tied down. I don't leave the house—I've brought the business here. Things are stressful at work, but when are they ever not stressful? Plus, all I want is for August and me to be able to move forward, and it feels like I'm doing everything wrong." He runs his fingers through his silky black hair, and I squeeze my thighs together involuntarily.

Skirting around his statement about August for now, I ask, "Do you like your work?"

He barks out a quick laugh.

"That good, huh?" I respond.

"It's not that I don't like my work. I do. We're doing some great things. Some world-changing shit. But am I passionate about it?" He thinks about it for a moment. "No, I'm not."

"So why do you do it?"

"I—" he cuts himself off, rubbing his thumbnail over his top lip. "I'm not really sure. At first, we started the business out of revenge. To right a lot of wrongs in this world. But now it just gives me a goddamn headache."

Revenge?

I nod. "I get that."

"What about you? Why did you get into psychology?"

I startle at his question, not expecting him to ask anything about me. But then again, this is supposed to be a friendly conversation, right? Not a counseling session.

I'm not his counselor. I'm here as his friend.

Yeah, keep telling yourself that, sister.

I consider his question. Even with our budding friendship, I won't tell him everything.

I would *never* tell him everything.

"My parents died when I was a kid. Their death really impacted me," I say.

He frowns. "I'm sorry that happened."

I shrug. "It happens," I say. I desperately want to change the subject. I twirl a loose thread from my cardigan around my finger.

"After finishing high school, I decided I wanted to help people, so I got into psychology." I pause for a moment. "How did you end up here with August?" I ask.

"What do you mean?"

I blow out a breath, reversing the direction of my twirling finger. "What happened with August's mother that resulted in you being absent all these years?"

He blinks. "Wow, going for the hard-hitting stuff right out the gate, huh?" The corner of his mouth quirks up in an imitation of a smile. It doesn't reach his eyes.

When I don't fill in the silence, he continues on. "Well, I was an idiot to start." He chuckles, rubbing the back of his neck. "And Maiya and I, we weren't healthy people in any sense of the word."

"You mentioned she was in active addiction when she had August," I add, wanting him to fill in the gaps in the story.

"She was."

"And you?"

"I was too. But I wasn't as bad as she was." He pauses for a moment. "No, that's actually a lie. I was just as bad as she was. Probably worse if I'm really honest. I just was able to…"

"…function?" I fill in for him.

"Yeah," he confirms. "But I had a lot more resources than she had."

"Ninety-nine-point-nine percent of America has fewer resources than you, H."

He nods before saying, "Fair enough."

We lapse back into comfortable silence, and I usher Kitty off my lap. He settles at my feet, relaxed yet alert.

"Are drugs part of your life now?" I ask.

"Not really. I haven't gotten high in over a year, and that was just weed. I haven't touched the hard stuff in six years. The only substance I use now is alcohol."

I hum. "What attracted you to her? Besides…how did you put it?"

He flushes and seeing him embarrassed does something to my already overheated lady bits.

"Yeah, I'm sorry for how I handled all that the other day."

"Apology accepted," I reply. "Now answer my question."

"Has anyone ever told you that you're persistent?"

"It's a great quality to have, H. The question." I arch an eyebrow at him, and he laughs.

"She never asked a lot of questions. She didn't talk much."

"I see," I say. Probably because she always had a mouthful of his cock.

And now I'm flushed and thinking about Hunter Brigham's cock.

"She didn't expect my attention or anything like that. She was just there, and she let me simply exist."

The look in his eyes grows distant, and I know there's more there.

"Could I ask a tough question?" I ask.

"Your questions haven't been tough enough?" He doesn't look off-put. He sighs and leans deeper into his seat. "Sure."

"Why did you walk away from August?"

He's silent for several heavy moments—the only sounds in the room are our breaths.

"I was never too far away from him. I don't know if that makes it better or worse. I kept up with everything he was doing. Anything he needed, I got it for him. But mostly, I was afraid I couldn't take care of him and keep him safe," he says finally.

"Safe? Take care of him? You have more than enough resources to take care of one child. Were you threatened to be disowned if you didn't drop him?"

"No, nothing like that," he says.

"Help me understand then. Because I see a man who feels deeply, and it's obvious you care about August. I'd say that you even love him because if you didn't, you wouldn't be trying this hard to build a relationship with him. So what's this about?" I feel flustered, and I try hard to regain my composure.

"The best way to hurt someone is to find their weaknesses. August is a weak spot for me," he says resolutely.

"You make it sound like you're in the mob," I say, mostly joking.

His silence makes it so that I'm not.

"I'm not in the mob, Winter," he clarifies.

"Thank God for that."

He smiles and then shrugs. "So, what's your story, Winter? Have you lived in northern Virginia all your life? Big family? Friends? Boyfriends?"

Am I hallucinating, or did he sound a little growly when he said, "boyfriend?"

"I've lived in Virginia forever, but I have an apartment in D.C. now. I don't have a big family, but I have a best friend who is more like a sister."

"I see," he says, echoing my phrase. "And the last part of my question?"

He leans forward, putting his elbows on his knees. He pushes his sleeves up, exposing his forearms. I damn near faint. The tattoos on his forearms stand out in colorful whorls in his skin.

I want to analyze them up close. Then I want to lick them.

Get. A. Grip!

"What was it again?" I blurt out.

"Is there someone you're going home to after this?" All of a sudden, his face looks grave. And instead of feeling fear, I feel like I'm vibrating.

And as is my M.O., I opt for humor.

"As a matter of fact, there is," I say smugly.

His face falls slightly, and I don't think too deeply about why that is. "Ah, I see. Is it serious?" he says.

"Very. He's with me twenty-four-seven. We do so much together—share meals, back rubs…I love him."

"Got ya," he says, leaning back and looking away.

"His name is Kitty," I say.

His gaze jerks back to me.

"Your boyfriend's name is *Kitty*? What the hell kind of name is that?"

I can't help it. I burst out laughing. It's one of my loud, full-volume laughs that echoes off the walls around us. I cover my mouth and snort when I try to suppress my laughter.

He raises his eyebrow at me.

"Yup, Kitty. And I wouldn't say he's my boyfriend. He's way too furry for that."

Humor floods his face. His eyes flick down to my dog at my feet before settling back on my face. "I see. So this is Kitty, I take it?" He nods his head in Kitty's direction.

"Yep," I reply cheekily.

It hits me right then that I'm comfortable with him. Kitty's relaxed, and a quick look down shows that he's panting with his tongue out, looking at Hunter. When Kitty looks back at me, I swear he grins.

"He's a Cavalier King Charles Spaniel. At first, the service animal trainers wanted to pair me with a Golden Retriever. It was a nice dog, but I saw Kitty's cross-eyed, happy face and fell in love."

"How long have you had him?" he asks.

"A little under four years."

"Hm," he replies with a gentle smile. His face is so expressive. I think back to the time we sat together in the great hall —his face showed everything. I wonder if he knows his expressions give him away.

I know he wants to ask me the same thing everyone else does.

"I have an anxiety disorder," I say simply, calmly. Usually, trying to explain this stresses me out because people judge mental health issues so harshly. But with him, I feel safe.

I know it's crazy, but I do.

"I'm mostly in remission from the worst of my symptoms. But that's only because I have tools. Kitty is one of them." I lean down to rub his silky ear. "Some people think it's impossible for a psychologist to also have a mental health disorder. I think it helps me to relate to clients. I know what it's like to struggle, not just because I've read about it in a textbook, but because I've lived it. I know what it's like to manage this condition."

I'm not looking at Hunter, feeling like I've shared entirely too much. I don't want to see his expression in case I'm wrong. In case I've read the entire scenario wrong.

"That makes sense," he says softly. I snap my head up, and instead of pity or skepticism, his eyes shine with what I can only imagine is compassion.

We're both silent for several moments. His head rests on his fist as he leans into the arm of his seat.

I keep rubbing Kitty's ear.

He lets out a small, humorless chuckle.

"What?" I ask. I don't know why I'm whispering, but I am.

"Nothing, you're just…" His voice is just as soft, raspy.

"I'm just what?"

"Unexpected," he finishes.

These feelings I have for Hunter Brigham? They're unexpected too. And I'm way over my head here.

"H," a voice says, and I only stay in my seat because Kitty jumps in my lap, probably reacting to the sharp spike in my heart rate.

Standing at the entry of the sitting room, a large, unreasonably attractive man takes up most of the door opening. He's wearing a suit, like Hunter, but he wears a jacket and a cocky smile. I'm unnerved by his sudden appearance.

I look over to Hunter, who stares at me intently. His eyes

roam over my face, and something he sees causes him to frown. Hunter spins to face the intruder.

"What's up, Leo?" His words are friendly enough, but his tone is anything but.

"Just stopping to let you know I'll be out for the rest of the afternoon," the man, Leo, says casually. He leans against the doorframe, and I see Hunter raise an eyebrow from my position facing his profile.

"I'm sure you could have texted that information," Hunter says through clenched teeth. The sudden flip into aggression doesn't feel great, but even with Hunter showing this edge of agitation, I don't feel scared of him.

This new guy, though…

He looks like he hurts people for fun. But when he speaks, his tone is teasing and lighthearted.

His aura is confusing.

"Probably," Leo says, still loose in his delivery and obviously not going anywhere. "I couldn't pass up an opportunity to officially meet the person helping August." He unfolds himself and saunters over to me.

"Leonardo Polanco," he says, holding his hand out to me. Kitty sits up in my lap, creating a physical barrier between me and the man.

I swallow. I don't need to be afraid right now. Hunter wouldn't allow me to be hurt.

I feel foolish to have this level of trust in a man I've just met, but here we are.

"Down," I whisper into Kitty's ear, and he moves to sit at my feet. I scramble to stand and shake Leo's hand.

"Winter Vaughan," I say back, and I must be losing my mind because a low growl comes from Hunter's direction. My eyes shoot to my hand where Leo grasps it. He rubs the inside of my wrist, and while it doesn't feel terrible, it's clearly not something I want.

I only want H's hands on me.

Wait, what?

I look to Hunter for help, but when my eyes land on him, his gaze is intense and locked on where my and Leo's hands meet.

"I'm sorry we didn't get a chance to speak. But I'm grateful you are here. Dr. Wagner had wonderful things to say about you. You're close to finishing your degree program, yes?" Leo's accented voice takes on an intimate, smoky tenor.

I try to pull my hand back, but I'm unsuccessful against his firm grip. He flips his hold so the back of my hand faces up, almost as if he intends to press a kiss to my palm like in the movies.

Please God, no.

"Not particularly," I say. "Two more years and then I'll have my post-doctoral internship to finish."

"Hm," Leo says. "Were you injured when you fell?"

I shake my head and say dumbly, "Fell?" I pull on my hand that he's still grasping, but he doesn't let go.

"Yes, when you fell in the fountain. You did fall in the fountain, right? Did I hear that correctly?"

Even though I don't think he means to embarrass me, a wave of mortification washes through me. I jerk my hand back, cradling it to my chest.

"Leo." Hunter's hard voice snaps in Leo's direction, and I look at him gratefully. H sits on the edge of his seat, and at his gaze, Leo takes a step back.

Amusement is clear on Leo's face. "My apologies, Winter. I'm an ass," Leo says, and I see that heartbreaking side grin slide across his face.

Leonardo Polanco is trouble. Flirty and troublesome.

"It's okay," I squeak. This has officially tipped over into "too much for me" territory.

Hunter moves suddenly, standing and taking the two steps to get in Leo's face. Hunter doesn't say anything to him, he just grabs him by the thick bicep and hauls him out of the room.

Walking backward, Leo faces me as he points to Hunter's back, his expression saying something along the lines of *Can you believe this guy?*

Once Leo's frame passes the threshold, Hunter turns to me briefly. "I'll be right back," he says over his shoulder.

Then he's gone.

I sit down again for a few minutes, absently rubbing Kitty's soft fur after he jumps back on my lap. His soft chuff brings me out of my daze.

I frown. Despite Leo being breath-stoppingly handsome, his advances feel discomforting and unwelcome.

I don't like how he came at me. But he seems like he has a sense of humor.

Maybe.

I look at my watch, surprised that H and I have been talking for more than an hour. My phone beeps, reminding me that I have a virtual meeting with my practicum coordinator and Dr. Wagner in two hours.

I'll barely make it back if I run into traffic.

I pull out my phone, tapping the prompts to schedule a ride, when Hunter bursts back into the room and slides the door closed quickly.

He turns to me with his back pressed to the door.

"I'm sorry about that," he says. He keeps his distance. "I could tell you were uncomfortable. I told him to leave you alone."

I bite my lip. "You didn't have to do that," I reply.

His face takes a strange look that I have a hard time reading.

"Do you want him to…not leave you alone?" His words are level, but my hypervigilance allows me to see his fists tighten slightly.

His knuckles are a little red.

"No. I mean, yes. I mean, I don't want him to treat me like a pariah, but I also don't want him rubbing on me." I cast my eyes down in the direction of his feet and suck my bottom lip into my mouth, worrying it.

Hunter makes a noise when I release it, and my eyes snap to his.

The look in his eyes is so intense, so focused, that I find myself having a hard time breathing. And it's not from anxiety.

I blink once, twice, three times, and then I stand to grab my bag and Kitty's leash. The spell is broken.

"I understand," he says when I'm facing him. His voice is even more hoarse. "Friends?"

The question takes me off guard. I know we said we'd be friends, but defining what that means is…

"Friends," I say resolutely. I hold my hand out to him, expecting him to shake it. But when he presses his hand to mine, it's a move more intimate than I could have ever expected. It's overwhelming.

"Beautiful," Hunter says. And I relax into the friendly embrace.

THIRTEEN
WINTER

Working with August starts slowly.

My first challenge was convincing Hunter and Ella that having security shadowing August's every step was contributing to his dysregulation. Ella agreed right away, but Hunter was not fully convinced. We compromised that if August were on Amelia Manor grounds, he would be free from his detail.

We sit silently for the first six biweekly sessions: August plays video games on the massive 85-inch TV screen for much of the ninety minutes we've agreed on. I take notes and try to engage him by asking questions about the game. I set up a space for Kitty to rest and instruct him to remain there for the entirety of my time with August.

"I really do not feel like explaining this. It is distracting me," he says during the second session.

"Fair enough," I say and sit back in the leather chair in the corner of his game room.

For our third meeting, he meets me at the door of the game room at the start of the session.

"Did you get Hunter to stop having people follow me

around?" He has the words waiting on his tablet, so he taps his iPad once to say the entire sentence.

"I asked him to, yes," I reply brightly, thrilled that he's talking to me at all.

"Okay," he replies, and before I can open my mouth to respond, he runs out of the room and down the hall. I wait for him for twenty minutes, expecting him to return.

He doesn't.

I try to engage him again on session six, picking up the controller. As soon as I sit down next to him, he stops pressing the buttons in his hands and shoots a look my way so quickly I can't tell whether I've actually seen it.

"Do you mind if I join in? I've been studying your plays and think I can hold my own." I try to look relaxed, but I'm honestly running out of ideas to get him to connect with me on any level.

He huffs and taps a few keys before logging off. After hopping out of his gaming chair, he goes into his bedroom. The door shuts just shy of a slam.

Later in the afternoon, I call Veronica for her opinion.

"Let's say you were trying to connect with a fifteen-year-old boy. His interests are gaming, RC helicopters, music, and ignoring the hell out of his therapist. What would you do to try to engage him?" I fight the urge to bite my nails—I've already got them down to the quick again.

"That's tough," Veronica says. I hear the chatter of the nail salon workers in the background. I look at my neglected toes. I give myself a pedicure once a month, pulling out the pumice stone and my favorite gel polishes. I want to be pampered, not just by myself but by someone else. I want to laugh with Veronica as we get our toes done. Maybe I'll add a manicure so I won't be so tempted to bite my nails off.

"At the end of the day, you need to seem really cool to him. Is there something you could bring and show off to him?" she finishes.

I hum as I think of what could possibly draw him in so much. Later, while scrolling on Reddit for the latest tech news, I find the name of the game most Redditors are going crazy over and get excited when I recall *not* seeing it on his shelf.

"Rons, I need a huge favor," I say as soon as Veronica picks up her phone.

I tell her my plan, and she connects me with a friend of her husband's who has exactly what I need.

When August walks into the game room, I sit in his chair, headset on and controller in my hand.

"What are you doing?" he asks.

"Hm?" I question, turning my head slightly toward him but not taking my eyes off the game. I shoot down a particularly nasty-looking zombie who pops up on the right of my screen.

August takes a step closer.

"Is that *Doom of the Zombie Galaxy IV*?" he asks, and I fight the urge to giggle. His voice is still set to American gangster, and the way it says "zombie" in a New Englander accent gets me.

"Mmhmm," I say, glee rising in my chest.

"How did you get a copy of that? It is not due to be released for another three months." I glance at him, and his face transforms. I see him smile for the first time ever.

"I have connections," I say cryptically, shooting another zombie and throwing a grenade into an abandoned building.

August is silent for a moment.

"Can I play?" he asks.

"Of course," I reply, sliding a controller in front of the seat next to me without looking.

He sits and grabs it with one hand while placing his tablet on his lap with his other.

We play in silence for the next few levels. Finally, I ask, "How long have you been into video games?"

He makes a few moves before tapping out his response with his other hand.

"I have been gaming since I was ten. Aunt Ella got me my first PlayStation."

"That's super cool," I say.

We're silent for a little longer before he asks, "Are you a gamer?"

"Not usually," I reply. "I prefer to read books or draw or color."

"Coloring?" He twitches, then gives his version of an eye roll.

"Yeah, like in adult coloring books. It's something I got into when my parents died."

His head turns sharply in my direction. He looks at me soundlessly before saying, "Your parents died too?"

He puts his controller down. I do the same.

"Yeah, they died when I was twelve. Car accident."

He nods somberly. "I am sorry."

"Thank you," I say.

"So you know what it is like then."

"To lose a parent? Yes, I unfortunately do. We're…" I laugh a little and shrug, "part of a crappy club, you and I."

The corner of his mouth tips up, and for a second, he looks exactly how I imagine Hunter did at August's age.

"It is a real shitty club, Winter."

At least he's calling me something. Progress.

"I agree. It is shitty. And for a while, it felt more than shitty. It felt impossible to get through."

He looks away from me and fidgets with the silicone rings attached to his pants. He picks up his tablet.

"I do not," he begins, then he lifts his hand from the keyboard. "I do not know what to do with myself. I have always felt like I did not fit in with everyone." He lifts his hand, shaking it back and forth a few times and cracking his neck as he allows his body to stim. "The world is not set up for people like me. It has not been. And now I am just floating around these days."

He rocks back and forth in his chair. I turn to face him fully and lean forward to put my elbows on my knees.

Listening.

"Being here with my…" He lifts his hands from the tablet again, slapping his leg in a quick three-tap staccato. "…sperm donor is shit," he finishes.

He tosses his tablet onto the table in front of us and gets out of the chair. Walking in circles, he alternates between walking and hopping, switching directions often over the next minute.

He jumps over to where he left his tablet and types furiously. He emits tiny grunts as his fingers fly over the screen. When he's done, he taps the "Speak" button forcefully before throwing the tablet back on the table, returning to his track on the other side of the room.

"He has never given a shit about me. I have hardly talked to him in all these years. I was alone with her, and do you want to know the messed-up part? It is that I wanted to be with both of them. I wanted to know what a family is like. But I was left here alone like trash. I am trash to them. And to everybody in the world."

His chest rises and falls quickly, verging on hyperventilation. I put my hands up, trying to soothe him. "August, I'm here with you. I can say this with certainty: you matter. You are not trash. Your life has value."

He turns in the other direction, walking back and forth across the length of the room. He's vocalizing and a blur of movement. I stand still and silent. Then suddenly, he stops in front of me. Tears stream down his face.

"August," I repeat. "I am here. I won't say I know how you feel because only you know how you feel. But you are not alone in your feelings."

His whole body shudders. He walks back to the tablet and

grips it in one hand, swinging it back and forth. I have a momentary fear that he might chuck it across the room like a Frisbee. When he pauses again, his fingers tap quickly on the tablet. "I keep having dreams about her. But not her when she was alive. Her dead. What that looked like. What that smelled like."

He drops the tablet on the plush carpet and wraps his arms around himself. The pained sounds he makes come from his soul. There is no mistaking this level of anguish.

I approach him. When I'm a foot away, I pick up the tablet and say in a low voice, "August."

He stops and looks in the direction of my torso. He sways from side to side.

"Do you want to tell me about the dreams? I'm here to support you as you talk about it in any way you need."

After a moment and without looking at my face, he grabs the tablet from me, holding it to his chest. After another moment, he flips the device over and hovers a hand over the screen.

"I need to run," he says. He vocalizes again, and something splinters inside my chest at the devastation in the sound.

"Let's go together," I say.

"Alone," he says as he exits the room.

I stare at the open door and allow my shoulders to slump. This is the furthest I've gotten with him, so I try not to be too disappointed that the session ended how it did.

I scribble a note on a sticky pad I grab from my bag.

Try to not wreck my high score.
See ya tomorrow, August.
-Winter

"Come," I say to Kitty, and he slowly walks over to me.

His head droops a little, and I feel like he's just as bummed about August's sadness as I am. Looking down at my phone to schedule a ride, I'm only a few steps outside the game room when I smack into a wall.

A solid wall.

A solid wall that smells like cedarwood and campfire smoke.

A solid wall that smells like cedarwood and campfire smoke and with ocean eyes that reflect a look I know entirely too well.

Grief.

I haven't seen Hunter in a week, and it's been three weeks since our private discussion in the sitting room. But I haven't stopped thinking about him. Haven't stopped thinking about the intimacy of our conversation or how easily it all flowed.

Hunter Brigham has taken up a lot of space in my mind.

"H," I say. "Did you run into August?"

I don't realize I'm still quite literally plastered to him until his hands circle my upper arms. "Yeah," he says. His chest rises and falls, pressing against me.

"Did you hear all that then?" I whisper.

"Yeah," he says. It takes a moment, but his face clears to an unaffected look, like he doesn't care that his teenage son just verbally eviscerated him. But I can tell from the sag of his shoulders he's taking August's words hard.

I step back and immediately my body protests the action. "Do you want to talk about it?"

He's silent for a few moments with his eyes closed. When he opens them, storm clouds brew in his gaze.

"Nah. It doesn't matter," he says. He even sniffs and shrugs his shoulder.

I roll my eyes. I take his hand, pulling him along.

He doesn't ask where we're going. Just like I don't focus on how his big hand feels pressed against mine.

We reach our destination in a few minutes, and I breathe in the smell of the ornate garden around us.

"I did some exploring the other day to find some places for August and me to change the scenery. But he hasn't wanted to do anything except play video games." I smirk as I walk deeper into the garden, my eyes on the wrought-iron bench shaped like a butterfly.

"This was my mother's favorite place," Hunter says.

I sit down and place my bag at my feet. "Play," I tell Kitty and he's all too happy to bolt off down the path. We're about an hour from dusk, and I'm grateful that the late September sun is slightly obscured by cloud cover.

"I can see why," I reply.

"Ella's updated Amelia Manor over the past few years, but this garden still looks the same."

"Do you not spend a lot of time out here?" I look around and marvel at the dozens of roses around us. Lavender-blue, apricot, and dark red rose bushes surround the garden in staggered arcs, centering on where we now sit. Birdbaths scatter around the garden, and on the far wall, ivy and honeysuckle climb up the trellis.

"I don't. I haven't been out here since I was a kid."

I tilt my head, studying him. There's more to the story there, but I don't push.

"August shared a lot with me today. What did you happen to hear?" I try to keep my face and posture open and non-judging.

"I heard—" He runs his finger over one of the flowers. It's a deep, velvety red rose that makes me think of dark sheets and sensual lovemaking.

What the actual, Winter?

I hear my inner Genevieve *tsk-tsk-tsk*ing at me.

He continues speaking. "I heard that he hates me. That he's fucked-up about his mother's death. That he feels alone. Abandoned. And he's right. I did fucking abandon him."

He plucks the rose from the bush, brings it to his nose, and then crushes it in his fist.

I don't say anything about his actions. Instead, I say, "Yes, you did."

His head jerks toward me before looking back at the rose. His jaw visibly clenches.

"You did abandon him. You did avoid interacting with him for the majority of his life. You say you have your reasons, but intent doesn't erase the impact of your actions. He did go through an incomprehensible trauma with his mother's death." I blink at him. "These are facts about the past. Facts we cannot change."

I stand up and walk toward him. I take the crushed rose from his hand.

"But the beautiful thing is we have a chance to make the future better. To heal. To grow." I remove the bulb from the stem, cradling the bloom.

"I bet you think I'm the biggest piece of shit, don't you," Hunter says.

I look up at him, and his eyes are full of emotion. His hands twitch slightly, and I notice pinpricks of blood on the palm that crushed the rose. He shoves his hands in his pockets.

"No," I say simply.

His eyes narrow as he looks at me.

"I don't think you're the biggest piece of shit. I think you truly believed the choices you made were for the best and that any alternative was unacceptable. And while I or someone else in your position might have made different decisions, they were *your* choices to make."

Finally, he looks away from me, his angular jaw tilted up as he looks at the flock of birds hopping from tree to tree near where we stand.

"I don't need to know your reasons because honestly? You're the one who has to live with them. And it looks like you've been living with those decisions for a long while. And feeling the consequences."

He looks back at me now, and the full force of his gaze unsettles me as it always does.

"What matters to me, to the world, and most importantly to August is what you choose to do from here on out. Will you continue to be the sperm donor? Or are you here to be his father? A father to a deeply traumatized, lonely, growing teenager? A father who does better every day?"

I fold my arms, proud that I told him the truth without sugarcoating it. Without trying to make it palatable or easy to swallow. Because I sense people don't tell him the truth and it's about time someone did.

The uncomfortable, raw truth.

"I don't know what that even looks like, Winter." His voice is soft and serious. "I don't know how to make this right." He's looking right in my eyes now, and I feel his gaze shoot down into my soul.

"It starts with you being with August. Like, really being with him. It starts with atonement."

"Atonement," he repeats.

"Yes, you need to acknowledge the harm you've caused and act to make it right from here on out. You make it right by doing better every day."

"Will you—" He cuts himself off, tilting his neck from side to side as if to release the tension.

"What, H?"

"Will you help me? With this?" He says the words so softly that I find myself leaning toward him to hear.

Or maybe it's the magnetism of everything that is Hunter Brigham.

"It's hard for you to ask for help, isn't it?" I ask.

He looks at me for a heavy moment. "I don't like having weaknesses," he says.

"Everyone has weaknesses. That's what it means to be human."

We're close, breathing each other in.

"I'm glad we're friends," he whispers.

"Me too." Another moment. Another breath in and out. For an unexplainable reason, I'm trembling.

"So you'll help me?" he asks. His voice is so soft, like a caress across my cheek.

"Of course, I will," I whisper back.

My only explanation for what happens next is that we both devolved into pure insanity.

Because when his lips touch mine, I know I'm completely, utterly, and thoroughly lost.

FOURTEEN
HUNTER

I know I'm making a grave, horrible, terrible mistake as soon as our lips touch.

Not because she should be off limits.

Not because she is too good to wrap herself up with someone like me.

But because as soon as her lips touch mine, the most precise voice I've ever heard screams into my consciousness:

This one is yours.

I press into her, and the taste of her citrusy lip balm and that unique taste I determine is all Winter Leigh Vaughan explodes on my tongue. I need more.

I crave her.

My hands go to her cheeks, and she presses her hands against my chest before grasping a fistful of my shirt.

And then my undoing happens when she shyly presses her tongue against the seam of my lips.

"Winter," I say, reluctant to break away from her.

"H, I—" She presses her lips against mine again, and I walk her toward the tree next to us. Her back hits the bark of the Virginia pine, and I groan when she moans against my mouth.

This one is yours.

Our mouths are a tangle of lips and tongues and teeth, and her hands roam over my chest and shoulders. I rub my hand down her side, pushing my palm over the fabric on her stomach to cup right beneath her breast.

She further damns me to hell when her leg bends at the knee, the action causing her pelvis to tilt and press right against my erection.

I grab her thigh and press against her more, and her groan turns into a whimper. I can't help but rock against her. My dick is eager for the promise of the heaven I'll find when I sink into her.

She's riding my thigh, and with her rose scent and the natural version around us, her movements are liable to drive me insane.

This one is yours.

I allow myself to fantasize about the things I've only allowed space for in my unspoken thoughts. For years the desire has been a general yearning, but now, everything transforms into a concrete vision: Winter in my bed. Winter in my home with August. August and I being father and son. August accepting and forgiving me. The three of us laughing with Ella on warm summer nights with my new, growing family around me. All of us living a peaceful life filled with Christmases and birthdays and happy kids that look like the perfect blend of both Winter and me.

All of the shit I've been running from for decades will cease to exist. I'm free to love and live.

With one hand, I feel the rise and fall of her ribs beneath the supple skin of her midsection, and my other roams to grab a handful of her plush ass.

She presses against me harder, and a long groan comes from her throat. I rock against her, and she acts as a counterpoint. The press of my black jeans against my cock is rough, bordering on painful, but I won't stop for anything in the world.

I'm lost to her.

Winter.

Our movements become even more frantic, and I ghost my hand over her ample breast. She gasps into my mouth when I palm it, squeezing to feel the weight of it. The gumdrop nipple I've been fantasizing about ever since I saw her dripping wet in my fountain presses against my palm. I bring it between two of my fingers, squeezing her breast and rolling the flesh with precision.

"Hunter…" Her voice is breathless, and I grin against her lips.

Perfect.

I go back to kissing her, inhaling her, and the hand on her ass moves up her side and to the back of her neck. With one hand on her breast, I use the other to cradle her head. She rocks faster and faster against my thigh, and I move against her until her muscles tighten, and she's screaming in release.

She breaks our kiss, panting.

As am I.

Her eyes snap closed, but I take in every feature of her face. The gentle smattering of freckles across the bridge of her nose. Her long lashes. The upturned shape of her eyes. The soft, plump lips that are now even more pronounced from our kissing.

For the first time in my life, I want to be gentle with a woman—to release the need to control everything about our interaction. This desire is foreign, completely different from what I'm used to.

And yet, I need to be safe for her.

I lean in to kiss her again, raining fragile pecks across her eyes, cheeks, and lips.

"Wait," she says, turning her head away from me.

I cradle my head into her neck, freezing in the position.

We're pressed together so completely that our breaths sync. When she breathes out, I breathe in.

This one is yours.

"Hunter. Mr. Brigham." She pulls away from me and lowers her leg. She places her soft hand against my chest to push me back a few steps. "This isn't…this isn't right." She doesn't look at me.

"I'm so unprofessional. This is unprofessional. I should—"

I cut her off, my voice soft despite the inferno raging beneath my skin.

"Stop. Stop, Winter." I place my hands on her shoulders, sliding them up to cradle her cheeks. "It's all right. I promise it will be fine."

"It is *so* not fine. This crosses all kinds of boundaries. I—I have to go." She walks around me, rushing to scoop up her bag, yelling commands at Kitty to follow. She bolts to the garden door, determined to go back through the house.

After she passes through the doorframe, I unlock my muscles to run after her. I catch up with her in the foyer.

"Winter, wait. *Goddamnit,*" I swear at myself, and she freezes when I utter the word.

Breaths saw in and out of her chest as if she's run a marathon.

"Wait, I'm not angry at you, I…" I don't know what to say. It's probably as confusing for her as it is for me. All I do know, with crystal certainty, is that Winter Vaughan and I are fated to collide.

I just hope we both survive the crash.

I take one step closer to her and then another and then another until I press against her back.

She trembles.

"Are you scared, Winter?" I ask, placing my hands on her shoulders. I so want to pull her back to me. To hold her close.

"Of you?" She makes a grim sound in her throat. "No, I'm not afraid of you."

I bring my face close to her ear, and the floral scent is strongest near her neck. "Then what are you afraid of, Sunbeam?"

She inhales sharply but then is silent.

"Nothing." She goes silent again. "Everything."

And with that, she walks out the front door.

I stand in the foyer for what could be minutes or hours.

It's not until Leo's hand claps on my shoulder that I stop staring at my front door.

"H. You good, brother?"

No, I'm not good. I've never been good. And I'm certainly not all right.

"Could you make sure Winter and Kitty get home safe?" I say and head toward my office.

My mind is not clear; it's a jumble of thoughts. The only one I can pull out of all of them is:

This one is yours.

And that fucks me more than anything in the world.

I SIT in my office for far too long after Winter leaves. My body wants me to drink or hit something until either option forces me to lose consciousness. I don't do either. Instead, I pore over the financial records for BwP's last fiscal year. There's no real need for my inquiry except this:

1. Gives me something to do, and numbers are my singular strong suit.
2. Will give me a head start on understanding the outsourcing scheme the VP was going on about in last week's meeting.
3. …I don't know what I can say for the third point.

As I said, there's no real need for the activity.

I run my hands through my hair, staring at the double monitors in front of me as I analyze the success of our last funding round. The same funding round our investors are getting antsy about with the delays to Project Panacea.

My phone rings, which startles me for two reasons. One, it's the landline I never use and honestly didn't know was actually hooked up to anything. Two, there is no one on this earth who I expect to have the number.

My hand hovers over the phone for a moment before I pick it up.

"Brigham," I say shortly.

"Hunter Brigham, a pleasure to connect," says an unmistakably Slavic voice. I pause.

"Hroshko," I say.

"Tak," he confirms.

"I was expecting to speak with you, but I was not anticipating you calling my home office," I say. I'm on guard because I'm *off* guard. His communication to this point has been with Leo. And now he's calling me?

"Well, I wanted to discuss an important issue with you regarding your father," he says.

I balk. "Clearly, you're not worried about this line being secure," I say.

"Of course I'm not worried," he says simply.

Well, okay then.

"Your father has made some people very, very mad," Misha says.

"Oh?"

"Yes. Some people believe that it would be better if someone else were to…take the reins, as you may put it."

"I see," I reply. I feel no emotion toward this conversation, which is only a curious observation. It dawns on me, and not for the first time, that any affection or loyalty I might have had toward my father burned away when I was a teenager.

"It has come to my attention that this may be something you also would be interested in, seeing as his behaviors have impacted you in multiple ways." Shit, this man knows everything about everything. He probably knows how long my dick is too.

"Anything is possible," I say back.

"Hmmm," he says. "That is interesting. There are some things you may have access to that will make this process easier," he says. Now he's talking in riddles.

But I wouldn't dare express confusion to a person like Misha Hroshko.

"I see," I say again. "Perhaps this is a discussion better suited for in person," I say smoothly. My only reason is to buy some time.

Always with buying fucking time.

He hums again. "I suppose so. Well, this transition is anticipated to happen very quickly, as more parcels will be impacted if there is a delay."

Parcels. He means humans. Women, children. I've known my father has dealt in human trafficking. And at the end of my time with him, I knew he was getting into even darker shit.

At least Misha sounds disapproving.

"Got it," I say hoarsely.

"But I agree, a meeting is in order," he says. "I'll be in touch." He hangs up.

The phone doesn't even emit a dial tone—it's silent in my hand. I return it to its cradle, dumbfounded.

I've been contacted. Talk soon.

After sending the message to Leo, I lean back and close my eyes.

Why couldn't my father be a regular white-collar criminal and embezzle a few millions?

My office door is open, and even in the expansiveness of the mansion, I hear the *clomp-clomp* of shoes hitting the stairway. Knowing it can only be one of a few people, I deduce it's likely August.

You should check on him.

I swallow against the thought. His words run through my brain at the same time.

"I was left here alone like trash. I am trash to them. And to everybody in the world," he said. And even the comedy of the accent echoing from his tablet couldn't soften the blow of the raw truth in his words.

I am a piece of shit.

I know this about myself. I haven't cared much about many people in my life, but when I'm able to be honest with myself—truly honest—the people I care about, I care about deeply.

Ella.

Leo.

Mom.

...and August.

The day he was born truly changed me, no matter how cliché that sounds. Maiya and I weren't communicating at the time. I didn't show up for her labor and delivery, not that she wanted me there. From what she told me the last time we'd spoken, all I needed to do was send the checks on time for our son. I was a terrible person to Maiya.

I can admit that now.

Sit in that shit, Hunter.

Before boarding my plane to California the day after August was born, I walked into the L&D ward and met my son through the glass window of the nursery. I don't think Maiya or anyone else knew I was there.

I stood there for several minutes, feeling every breath enter and exit my lungs. The day before, I'd spent my time getting high and fucking different girls. Their faces are unmemorable.

But when I looked at August, I felt several things simultaneously. I felt the responsibility of having created a life. An entire human being that carries twenty-three of my chromosomes. I felt regret that I'd been so reckless in how he came to be. I felt guilt that I wasn't a better person to his mother. I felt fear at the knowledge that I'd ultimately taint this perfect person on the other side of the glass—that his proximity to me, my affection for him, would ultimately be his death sentence.

Just like my mom.

There wasn't a doubt in any part of my soul that the best thing for August would be to provide him with as much as I could—as much as would befit a Brigham—and stay the fuck away.

If it didn't seem like I valued him, my father would ignore his presence.

It felt like the safest option, even though the logic was flawed. I deeply regret that choice.

Because the years I spent wasting away my life doing drugs and chasing meaningless relationships came at the cost of knowing my son.

I've hurt him significantly. It's idiotic that I couldn't see this outcome when I decided to walk away—that I couldn't see that August might…need me.

"Others might have made different decisions, but yours are yours to live with, Hunter." Winter's voice rings through my brain, and I fight against a new wave of regret.

I put my head in my hands.

I can't do anything about Winter, at least, not tonight. But I can do something about August.

Atonement.

I move to the kitchen where I hear dishes clinking together. When I round the corner, he puts two Eggo waffles in the toaster. He stands in the dark, swaying slightly while he waits for them to warm.

"You missed dinner," I say softly, not wanting to startle him. He jumps anyway. Spinning around, he jerks his hands up toward his ears, clasping them over the sides of his head once he spots me. I stand still for a moment, giving him time to acclimate to my presence.

When the Eggos pop out of the toaster a few minutes later, he removes his hands and finally grabs his tablet.

"Yes, I went for a walk." He grabs a plate, preparing his Eggos. Instead of walking back to his room with them as I expect him to, he turns to place his plate on the island. His tablet is next to it.

"You heard my session with Winter." This is more a statement than a question.

"I heard a little bit of it," I say. "I wasn't trying to eavesdrop."

"I have the right to privacy in my therapy sessions," he says matter-of-factly.

"Yes, you do," I say, nodding in agreement. "I won't listen in again," I promise him.

He doesn't react to my statement. Instead, he proceeds to cut his Eggos into perfect squares along the natural score lines of each waffle.

"What's it about Eggo waffles that you like so much?" I ask him, trying to settle on a safe topic.

"They are the same every time," he says. "Homestyle Eggos are the same wherever. The size is always the same. The texture is always the same. I like predictability."

"What would happen if you were to try a homemade waffle? Or one from a restaurant?" I ask.

He gives me a brief, droll look, his gaze landing in the vicinity of my left shoulder, before rolling his eyes and putting a square into his mouth.

"No syrup or butter either?" I ask him.

"I do not have to explain my preferences. Asking is rude." He glides his fingers over the tablet, and I hold my hands up in apology.

I'm batting a thousand, and I'm just talking about some goddamn waffles. "I'm sorry," I say.

He continues to eat.

Atone.

"August," I say. My voice is low, and I feel like my throat is closing—an itchy, tingling sensation that causes me to wonder if the next breath I take will be my last.

"I am so sorry," I say. I stare at him, willing him to give me some sign that he's accepting where I'm trying to take the conversation.

Where I'm trying to take our relationship.

He just continues to eat, popping square after square into his mouth.

"Okay," he finally says. I feel my shoulders drop. He doesn't say any more.

"I am going to bed," he says after he puts his empty plate into the sink.

"Goodnight, son," I say to his retreating back. He stops, and his shoulders rise.

"Do not call me that. Ever." He doesn't turn to look at me.

Then he walks away.

And I'm left standing in the dark.

FIFTEEN
WINTER

I walked to the front gates of Amelia Manor in a daze. I've been standing at the entrance for a solid five minutes, phone in hand. I'm unable to make my fingers tap the options to order a ride, so when Leo pulls up beside me in a blacked-out Mercedes G-wagon, I'm conflicted.

"I'll take you home," he says.

"Uh," I say, shivering as the temperatures fall quickly now that the sun has fully set.

"I promise you're safe with me to drive you into the district. Plus, do you really want to sit out here in the dark while you wait for an Uber?"

No. No, I really do not.

I get into the passenger seat without a word.

The drive over is mostly silent until we cross over the Potomac River. Kitty nestles in my lap.

"Sooo," Leo drawls. "Wanna talk about what happened?"

I roll both lips into my mouth, pressing the flesh into my teeth.

"What's there to talk about?" I say after a solid minute of silence.

Leo laughs. "You two are so alike," he says, his voice filled with amusement.

I don't say anything, I just turn toward the window.

"For what it's worth, he's really different when you're around. He even punched me for making you feel uncomfortable."

I swing back around to face him. "Come again?" My face must reflect the horror I feel.

"Yeah," he waves his hand in the air, a quick flick of his wrist. "I knew I was poking the bear. He's really twisted up about you."

"He *punched* you?" I repeat, still not understanding but also pushing back the entirely fucked-up part of me that perks up a bit that he'd punch his best friend over me.

"Again, like I said, I deserved it."

He takes the roundabout near Foggy Bottom, and I'm grateful to only have a few more minutes on this ride from hell.

"Anyway, you seem like a relationship girl," he says, and I open my mouth to correct him when he puts his hand up to silence me. I snap my mouth shut. "And I think my boy actually likes you, but he's not really up for much beyond a physical thing. You know, with everything going on."

I nod several times, then lean into my fist, propping it on the windowsill. I say nothing more.

He pulls up to my apartment building but parks instead of dropping me off at the front.

"You don't have to walk me in," I say. My throat feels dry.

"Yes, I do. I'll see you to your door."

"This is my door. The front door to the building where I reside, in fact," I say, pointing to the brightly lit glass façade of 110UWest.

He sighs and says nothing as he opens the door.

I follow behind him because what else can I do? And I try

to keep my eyes on his broad back as we move through the lobby.

Suddenly, the energy around the space feels strange. Heavy. I turn back to look out the glass windows. There's nothing out of the ordinary.

Chill out.

"Everything okay?" Leo's voice is unexpected, and I jump. "Woah, gallita."

He moves his eyes around the lobby and out toward the street. His eyes narrow and his face changes before my eyes. The friendly, joking man from the ride over looks terrifying as he assesses our surroundings.

I barely register the feeling of Kitty's paws on my leg or the fact that Leo just referred to me as a little chicken.

All my consciousness centers around the slamming of my heart against my breastbone.

I take a step away, picking up Kitty and whirling around to walk backward.

Leo looks at my face, and something in it has him putting his palms out in front of him.

"Hey," he says, his voice gentling. "I'm not going to hurt you, Winter," he says. Then he smiles, and his face shifts again.

I'm losing it. This day has all been entirely too much.

Dr. Stevenson was right. I'm not cut out for this. And that has me stifling a sob—trapping it inside my ribs.

"Let me see you to your apartment. He'll want me to make sure you get in safely."

I nod, my lips numb. Kitty licks my chin.

Leo ushers me toward the elevator, and of course Marcus exits when the doors slide open.

"Kitty's mom! How are you this evening?" he asks, his dimples immediately on display. I clench my teeth so hard no sound comes out.

"That good, huh?" His eyes flick to Leo, and I'm grateful when Leo gestures for me to enter and the doors slide closed.

"Well, this is me," I say when we reach the seventh floor, as if he didn't already know which apartment is mine since he's been leading the way.

He waits quietly as I unlock the door. Once I enter the apartment, I turn and say, "Thanks for the ride."

"You're welcome, gallita." And then he's gone.

I lock us in, resting my head against the solid wood doorframe for several minutes.

"Kitty," I say, not lifting my head from the door. "What the hell have I done?"

Vexingly, I feel the burn of tears in my eyes, and I'm angry when I feel them fall.

I'm angry that when I was in Hunter's arms, I allowed myself to let go so dramatically.

I'm angry that it would be so ethically wrong for me to be with him.

I'm angry that I feel so much for this man that I cannot have and should not want.

I'm angry that I don't regret any of it in the slightest.

Kitty crawls into my lap once I sink to the floor. I cry and cry until I can't breathe through my nose and a headache forms behind my eyeballs.

And then, I do the only thing I know to do. I call Veronica.

Two hours later, I'm curled up on the sofa with my head in Veronica's lap and slathered in a serum-soaked face mask. She brought over chocolate, Dr. Pepper, and Hot Cheetos—my period cravings for when I'm feeling particularly crappy.

I guess they'll work in this situation too.

Veronica runs her fingers through my hair, gently detangling my curls with a wide-toothed comb and braiding them into medium-sized plaits.

An early 2000s chick flick streams on the TV, but I'm not paying attention.

"As much as you know that I'm always down for an indoor girls' night, the fact that you looked like you got stung in the face by bees when you opened the door leads me to believe that something happened today. And while I can be patient—"

My side eye cuts her off.

"Okay, so I'm able to be patient *with you*. But I'm dying here. So let me ask this first question. Are you okay now? Clearly, you weren't okay earlier. But we'll get to that."

I sit up so I can look at her fully. Only a small section of my hair is unbraided, and I move to finish working on it myself.

"I'm okay now," I say.

She expects me to add more and leans forward to stare into my eyes when I don't.

I peel the sheet off my face and rub in the serum.

"Okay, thank you for that answer. I guess," she says. She rolls her eyes. "Okay, so question number two. What happened?"

I finish the last braid and grab the silk elastic to pull my hair together at the top of my head. Without looking at her, I say, "Well, I made an ill-advised decision that ultimately resulted in my emotional turmoil."

She looks at me, her face blank, until she says, "What the *hell* are you saying, Winter?"

I put my hair bonnet on, securing it at the front with a bow.

"I did something stupid. Very stupid," I say.

"You? Stupid? I doubt that, Win."

"No, Veronica, I did something really, really, really stupid."

Her eyebrows shoot up, and she says, "Well, shit, tell me what happened." Her voice has a thin, strangled cast.

I breathe in and out and in again before finally saying in

one breath, "I kissed my client's dad and let him feel me up while I dry-humped his leg and came on a tree."

I look at her.

And she looks at me.

And then she says, "I'm trying to compute the words you said and the order in which you said them, but I'm having a really hard time."

I get up from the couch and walk to the bathroom, desperately trying to avoid this conversation.

"Winter Leigh Vaughan, don't you run away from me," she says, and she grunts as she tries to get up from the couch to follow me. She's only about four months along, but her newly acquired pelvic dysfunction diagnosis makes moving quickly painful.

"Veronica, you heard what I said. Please don't make me repeat myself."

I turn on the tap and squirt too much toothpaste on my toothbrush. I shove it in my mouth anyway, focusing on cleaning all thirty-two of my teeth.

"Okay, so let me recap. You kissed your client's father."

I nod.

"The hot one," she continues.

I nod again.

"And you did some…heavy petting."

I pause for a moment and then nod.

"Okay, following. And then you came on a tree?"

I spit out the toothpaste and add, "Against a tree. I was pressed against a tree."

"Ah, I see. I was worried about you getting splinters in your cooch."

I choke as I laugh at the unexpected image, sputtering into the sink.

"This is not a time for jokes, Veronica!"

I rinse my mouth out only to look up and see her smiling at me as if she's just won the lottery. Or been told that there was an endless supply of boiled Chesapeake Bay crab in the lobby.

That girl does love her seafood.

"Why are you smiling?" I ask, dismayed.

She presses both hands on her chest and then steps back into the living room, splaying her hands wide and spinning around like Julie Andrews at the beginning of *Sound of Music.*

"I'm smiling because *you kissed Hot Daddy*! And you did *sexy things*! And you *came*! I'm so fucking happy for you!" She spins again and then clutches her belly, a grimace passing across her face.

"What's happening!" I rush over to her and she waves me off.

"It's okay," she says, breathing slowly. "Just a little cramp."

She stands up more fully, rocking her hips from side to side. "See? It's already gone. Nothing to stress about."

I hover next to her, watching her every move.

When her face and body finally fully relax, I unclench enough to breathe.

"Sorry, I was…" I turn to tidy up our mess, needing my hands to be busy. "I was a little worried is all."

I feel her walk up behind me.

"Winter."

I turn to her.

"I'm okay." She gives me a look of understanding that I close my eyes against.

"I'm so grateful for you, Veronica," I whisper.

"I love you too, Winter. You're the sister of my heart, and I'll always be there for you," she replies.

We're both crying now.

"Shit, now we're both a mess," I say.

"Well, *I'm* hormonal. What's your excuse?"

I laugh and throw a pillow at her.

VERONICA SLEEPS OVER, and I give her my bed for a few reasons. One, while we could fit in my king-sized bed, we both like our space. Two, Veronica runs at approximately 150 degrees, and if I get an inch too close, she's liable to kick me off the bed. And three, Veronica has always been a wild sleeper.

So when we both wake up in the morning, we feel better.

"I want to take you to that café I promised to bring you to," I say to Veronica once we're both dressed.

"Oh, my God, I'd legitimately merk someone for a blueberry scone. Like, homicide in the first degree. Do they have blueberry scones?" She looks at me as if my answer will make or break the survival of humanity.

"Well, let's go see," I say.

When we finally settle on the outdoor patio, Veronica beams from ear to ear as a fresh blueberry scone appears before her.

"You weren't lying, babe. This place is cool," she says, breaking the scone in half.

Dichotomy looks different in the morning daylight but no less cool. Lush vines of ivy and wisteria weave through the electrical lines where the Edison bulbs are strung. They've pulled a few carts with discounted books toward the front entrance. I picked a copy of *Their Eyes Were Watching God* from the shelves. Planters at the patio's entrance have milkweed, lavender, and verbena. Butterflies hop from flower to flower.

Dichotomy is peaceful.

"I'm so glad I found this place," I say. I opt for a salmon bagel with lox, and I'm stunned by the flavor of the wood-smoked fish resting on top of the homemade cream cheese. Kitty stands on his hind legs, sniffing the air and whining for a piece of my salmon. I tell him to get down, but his sad eyes compel me to give him a small piece of the fish.

I'm smashing it between my fingers to double check for bones when we're interrupted.

"Hey, neighbor. Feeling better today?" I hear from my left shoulder.

Looking up, I see Marcus standing near the table.

Marcus and his goddamn dimples.

"This is awkward, but," he leans closer. "You *do* know you've never told me your name, right?"

I feel a blush crawl down from my hairline. Or maybe it's sweat.

"You're neighbors?" Veronica calls out. She's eyeing Marcus down, but not in the way that I'd expect. Her face is unreadable.

"Yes, we met in the dog park a few weeks ago, and he's the owner of this fine establishment," I say, raising my hands toward Marcus as if I were showcasing a prize on a game show. "Marcus, meet my best friend, Veronica."

He smiles, and dimple one and dimple two pop out.

"Are you enjoying your meal?" Marcus asks, but he's not looking at me. He's looking at Veronica.

She nods, then she averts her gaze.

"I'm glad," Marcus says. He straightens up. "Well, I'm off for the day. Just came in to check the inventory that came in last night. But I'll see you around. Right, neighbor?"

"Sure thing," I reply. I can't help but notice that Marcus is trying to regain Veronica's gaze.

He gives up and taps his knuckles on the wrought-iron table. Then he leaves.

"Those dimples should be illegal," I say to Veronica, picking up my iced tea. It's not just regular southern iced tea. It's basil and raspberry-infused tea with lemonade.

"Eh," Veronica says. "He's all right."

I rear back. "You don't think that drop of six-foot-three

goodness deserves more than an 'all right?'" I lean over to put the back of my hand on her forehead. She bats it away.

"Was he handsome? Sure, I suppose. But lots of men are. Anyway, let's talk about you and Hot Daddy." The flush travels from my face down to my chest.

"Could we not, Rons?" I cover my eyes.

"Oh-ho-ho, we most certainly will."

"Ugh," I say, extending the sound as I slouch deeply into my chair. "Veronica, I don't know what I'm going to do. I obviously can't show my face to him again."

She leans toward me abruptly. "And why not?" She's trying to keep her voice low but failing.

"Because, Veronica, he's my client's *father*."

"So? He's not *your* client."

"Surely, the licensing board will frown upon this."

"Who the fuck says they have to know?" She waves her arms around to make her point. "But first, I need a name."

"Why?" I jerk, adrenaline rushing through me.

"Because I'm going to Google him, duh!" Her phone is in her hand, and she's looking at me with blatant expectation.

I put my hand over hers and lower her phone. "No need because I need to stay away from him." I bite my fingernails again, choosing to attack my thumb this time.

"No, you need to nut," she says entirely too loudly, so loudly, in fact, that Kitty skitters to a hyper-alert position in search of threats. I look around quickly. Thankfully, the patio is empty.

"Take your hand out of your mouth, Winter. What I'm about to say is vitally important."

I drop my hand and turn to face her more fully.

"Winter, I love you like a sister. No, not like a sister. You *are* my sister. And I say this with so much love. *So* much love. But you need to get your back blown out in the most serious way." Her face is so severe I can't help but laugh.

It's loud, full-bodied.

"Okay, but…maybe it doesn't have to be him?"

She leans into her seat, contemplating the question. "Well, I do agree you should play the field. Who are your other prospects?"

I gaze off, looking at the butterflies flitting around the outdoor space. Even though I try to imagine any other man instead of H, he's all I can think of. The look of lust in his eyes. The feeling of him pressed against me, his cock…

I shake my head. It needs to be someone else.

I think back to my list.

Maybe this first time shouldn't be with someone I love.

"Maybe Marcus would…" I trail off as she inhales sharply. "What, Rons? You don't think he'd be interested?"

She chews on her lip for a moment. "No, he'd definitely be interested. He *is* interested. It's just that…I get the sense that he's a fuckboy. You don't want to get caught up in that."

"Don't fuckboys stay unattached? Isn't that exactly what I want?"

Veronica looks worried as she thinks about what I say but is saved from having to respond when a waiter comes up to us.

"Here's your chocolate chip cookie," he says. He's dressed in total hipster fashion. Wire-rimmed glasses frame his face, and his skin looks like he's never seen the sun. He has on a black button-down shirt and black pants, which I'm sure is part of his uniform, but on top, he wears houndstooth suspenders and a green tweed bow tie.

"We didn't order any cookies," Veronica says.

"It's from a gentleman. The barista told me he placed the order but said he had to leave. He requested that we give the cookies to you."

I look around for anyone who might have ordered the cookie for us.

"Did you see what he looked like?" I ask. I analyze the anxiety bubbling up in my stomach right now.

Is it necessary for this to make you nervous, Winter? Why are you scared right now?

In the distance, two birds fight in a tree.

"Nah, I didn't. I'll ask the barista for you, though?" He looks back at the line of customers who suddenly appear at the cash wrap.

"It's okay," I say. "Thank you for the cookie." I look at the bakery item as if it were radioactive.

"You have a secret admirer," Veronica says, taking a big bite.

"Yeah," I reply. But I can't shake the feeling that's not a good thing.

SIXTEEN
HUNTER

"Someone better be dead," I grumble. My eyes pinch closed against the early morning sunlight.

Ella traipses through my bedroom, singing at full volume and, for an unknown reason, speaking with a British accent.

"Oh, brother, wherefore art thou," she says dramatically as she twirls through the room, opening window curtains.

I groan and throw a pillow in her direction before turning over and throwing the blankets over my head.

"H, wake up. We need to talk."

I slide my hand from under the covers and shoot her a one-fingered salute.

She gives a shocked gasp.

Moments later, what feels like an earthquake hits my room —except it's Ella jumping on my bed.

"What the fuck, Ella!" I roll over and sit up, gripping her ankle and pulling her down on the bed.

"*Hunterrrrr,*" she drawls. "For real, I need to talk to you."

I rub my eyes.

"What. Do. You. Want?" I say through gritted teeth.

"Damn, you're still grouchy in the morning, aren't you?"

"Ella, get to the goddamn point."

"Right." She flips her hair behind her shoulder. She's dressed casually today with jeans that look fashionably baggy, a soft sweater, and a chunky scarf. Her long hair is pulled up in a high ponytail that still reaches her shoulders, and she uses a folded bandana instead of a headband. October breezed by and it went from hot as hell to fall in what feels like a blink.

I forget how beautiful autumn is in Virginia.

"It's about August." I look at her fully now.

"What about him? Is everything okay?" Despite seeking him out, I haven't been able to connect with August much over the past few weeks. He's either in his game room with his headset on, or he's with Winter. Which means she's just as much of a ghost as August.

Not that I have a plan to engage him once we are in the same room. How can I even begin to repair the damage of life lost? How can I make it right—the fact that I've left him alone to navigate this world?

How can I make him understand what I can't even talk about?

Winter's words echo in my mind: *atonement*. I have to stop feeling sorry for myself.

And I have to stop my incessant thoughts of Winter Vaughan. It's time to focus solely on August…even if I dream about the feeling of her body pressed against mine and the bright sound of her laughter.

"Well, Augie is a competitive RC helicopter racer," Ella says.

I didn't know that about him, and resentment at that lack of knowledge settles in my stomach.

She continues, "And there's a meetup he'd been planning to attend for months. Before all…this happened." She bites her lip. Lips that I notice are faintly blue.

"Ella, you have *got* to slow down on your candy consumption. It's barely"—I look at the clock on my nightstand—"eight a.m., and you've already got stained lips. You're gonna get diabetes."

She grimaces and rushes toward my ensuite bathroom. She turns on the taps, and I see her grab a spare toothbrush out of the top drawer from my vantage point in bed.

"Anyway!" she shouts from the bathroom after brushing. "I planned on going with him, but I thought it would be great if you'd go with him too." She walks over and peers down at me, standing at the side of the bed.

I think about it for a second. I've been searching for a way to connect with August for weeks and coming up blank.

"What time is it for?" I hop out of bed, pushing Ella back as she yells, "Ewwww!" at my nakedness. She covers her eyes and twirls to leave the room.

"Be downstairs in ten minutes, freak!"

This could be a good time for both of you.

The drive to the small airstrip in Reston is quiet, and we're in the Range Rover I delivered to the estate. I'm grateful to drive because it gives me something to do with my hands.

"How many people do you expect to be there, Augie?" Ella turns in the passenger seat to look back at August.

"I have told you, Aunt Ella. My name is August." He switched to a British accent, and the voice sounds like a butler in *Downton Abbey*.

"Sorry, I forgot that you're a *teenager* now," she says while bringing her hand to her chest with dramatic flair.

I clear my throat before looking in the rearview mirror at my son. His head is down, engrossed in a video on his iPad.

"August, how long have you been racing?" I ask. He looks up from his tablet, his face turned toward the back of my head. He returns his gaze to his video.

After several minutes, I try again. "Have you been with this group for long?"

He sighs and flips the screen on his tablet.

"Yes," he responds.

I squeeze the steering wheel and look over to Ella. She gives me a soft, encouraging smile.

Things are silent after that until we reach the field. August jumps out and rounds the vehicle to get the metal hardtop helicopter case out of the back. Then he walks off toward the group of people a few feet from the small airstrip—the hood of his puffy jacket flops against his back as he skips away.

"Just be cool, H," Ella says after putting on her gloves and zipping up her Patagonia coat. She pulls one of the folding chairs out of the back of the car.

"I'm just getting used to all this," I grumble.

She looks at me with an arched brow. "You know how to talk to people, I'm sure of it. Just talk to him like a regular human," she says. She hands me her chair while I grab the thick blankets she packed to protect us from the cold.

I shut the trunk.

"I'm going to get some drinks for us," Ella says, nodding toward the concession stand on the other end of the airstrip.

The field is often used for small-scale competitive air shows and RC aircraft meetups. There are pockets of dozens of people spread across the area, and a table sits under an awning. Ella mentioned there'd be a competition later today.

"Sure," I say as she walks off.

I head toward one of the groups of people near where August stands. The group he's with all have tablets out, and I realize they're all using alternative communication to talk.

My kid has more friends than I do.

I open a chair for Ella and myself, drop the blankets in her seat, and settle in to watch August. The realization that he's grown into an independent person with interests and friends and hobbies isn't lost on me. He's managed to grow into a nearly adult human.

I may not have been there for him over the last fifteen years, but I can be there for the rest.

Yes, I can.

I feel movement near my shoulder and say, "I hope you got alcohol, Ella." But as I turn, I don't see Ella.

Instead, my father is there.

He doesn't say anything as he throws the blankets on the cold ground and sits in Ella's seat. I look across the field and Ella is still in line, about seven people deep, tapping her phone screen.

"It's a great day out, even though it's cold. Don't you think so, Hunter?" My father looks laughably casual. A knee-length black wool coat complements his leather gloves, charcoal gray pants, and black loafers. Unironically, he has Ray-Bans over his eyes despite the low sun visibility.

I can still feel the malice in his gaze.

"What are you doing here, Father?" I say in a low voice. I don't want to draw attention to us. Specifically, I don't want August to notice the man beside me.

Protect August.

"You've been avoiding me again, Hunter." He crosses an ankle over his knee, the picture of nonchalance.

I don't respond. I *have* been avoiding him. He's called a few times and even sent a message for me to contact him through Ella. But every day that my team can't find anything about why the Winthropes are entangled with my father, the more my anxiety grows.

He flicks a piece of invisible lint off his pants.

"I'm granting you a lot of leeway because, well, I did give you life. And I don't like to waste my time, so I won't enjoy ending you after thirty-four miserable years on this planet. And yet," he turns to me, methodically taking the glasses off his face, "I will still end you if I see fit to," he finishes.

I stare at the cold eyes that are so much like mine.

He's smiling.

I want to carve it off his face.

He looks directly at August. "He is such a delicate boy. Isn't he?"

My esophagus spasms.

"Well!" Father claps his hands on his thighs and stands gracefully. "That's enough drama for the day." He hands me a card from his inside coat pocket.

"Be here at 8 p.m. sharp. Don't embarrass me."

And then as if he were never here, he's gone.

I clutch the card in my hand, not looking at it.

Minutes later, Ella bounces up toward me.

August's group assembles their helicopters, and a few hover them above the airstrip to perform flips in the air.

"They had hot chocolate, but they didn't have the kind with marshmallows. Who does that? Anyway, I got us a few." She hands me the steaming insulated cup, and I take it from her with numb fingers. She plops down next to me, taking a sip of her drink as she settles the blankets over her legs. She also pulls out a box of Nerds.

"What do you want to do after this?" she asks.

"I have no idea. But I have plans."

"He just showed up at August's meet?" Leo paces back and forth in front of the unlit fireplace in my office. My palms itch to take a drink, and I eye the new bottle of Macallan in the corner.

"Yes, out of nowhere. Then he threatened August again and left."

Leo runs a hand through his hair, sighing deeply.

"Has he told you what he wants? It has to be much deeper than marrying you off and making heirs."

I look up at Leo from where I'm slouched in my desk chair and say, "Max and his team are looking into Blair and what her family is up to. The bigger question is why get married at all, and why her?"

"It can't be just to punish you. Something is happening between him and the Winthropes. I'd bet money on Daddy Winthrope," Leo says.

A memory flashes back to Isla Cara. Morris Winthrope, with a girl young enough to be his granddaughter, laughs—loud and vile—as he bets on two naked girls fighting to the death.

Disgust bubbles beneath my skin.

"Hmm," Leo says. He's deep in thought. He sighs, and it's an unhappy sound. "In the meantime, you know what you have to do, right?"

I close my eyes, hoping that the words won't annoy me as much if I don't have to look at him.

"What, Leo?" I ask, sighing.

"You have to go along with all of this. Be amenable and active in the process. Nice. At least until we can figure out a way around this."

"What the fuck," I mutter. My head throbs under the stress of the situation.

"H, we're stuck here and don't have many options. You have to play his game until this is over. Otherwise, he will continue to get aggressive to get you in line."

The problem with playing his game is that I lose all around. I lose if I marry Blair because what else will he want me to do if I do this?

I shudder.

Plus, if he decides to really retaliate…

August's life is at risk. We're all at risk.

The anger I feel morphs into cold fury.

"The only way to get rid of this headache is to get rid of him," I say. I look directly into Leo's eyes. "Nothing we do will stop him. Nothing we do will keep August safe or keep BwP safe. The only way to nullify his power is to knock him off the throne."

By force.

Leo is silent for a long while. "If you get rid of him, you'll need to have someone else lined up to take the helm. Otherwise…" he doesn't finish his sentence, but I do mentally.

The devil we know may be better than an uncertain successor.

"Misha Hroshko," he says.

I rock my head back and forth on the headrest of the leather chair. My father's influence has been present for as long as I've been alive. And yet, it wasn't until I reached puberty that it reached God-level.

"You think he'd take over?" I keep my eyes on the ceiling. The thought of ending my father isn't a new one. But now that we're actually talking about doing it…a strange feeling settles in my stomach—a sharp edge of apprehension, relief, and another emotion I also don't want to look at too closely.

"It's probably what he wants. He's already said pretty plainly that my father has pissed off some people and it's time for him to be a non-factor. But getting him into power will take more than just influence. He needs some kind of leverage over your father's minions."

I allow myself to think about Isla Cara again. "I don't know if it's tapes or videos or what it is exactly, but on Isla Cara, there's what he calls 'insurance.' It's records of the misdeeds of some very important people. If we got ahold of it…"

"Then we'll have enough dirt on the people your father runs with to keep them in line." Our gazes collide as the plan formulates between the two of us.

I rub my hands on my thighs.

"Leo, I'm gonna need a drink for this. And I need you to not say shit about it."

He presses his lips together but ultimately nods solemnly.

At 8:45 p.m., I sit across from Blair Winthrope in the main dining room of the Appleton Country Club.

My father has been a member his whole life, as was his father, and his father before him—probably back to the Niña, the Pinta, and the Santa Maria.

I'm familiar with the setting.

The gilded chandelier, Persian rugs, and Italian leather furniture scream subtle opulence. Both in-your-face and understated with how much wealth drips from each corner of the room, but always unsaid.

The chateaubriand with béarnaise sauce sits untouched in front of me while Blair takes small tastes of her lemon and herb-crusted sea bass. Both our glasses are filled with chardonnay, and I'll leave my regret for testing the bounds of my sobriety and drinking not one but four glasses of wine for tomorrow.

"I think spring weddings are lovely," Blair says.

Everything about her is delicate. Her skin is like porcelain, unblemished and fragile. Her red hair is muted—a pale copper in the room's dimness. Her green eyes, straight nose, and straight teeth all present the perfect image of what a Winthrope woman should be.

Admired from afar but untouchable.

In response to her statement, I raise my glass to my lips for a healthy drink.

She sighs, her mouth tightening slightly.

"Listen, Hunter," she says.

I don't tell her to call me H.

"I know this isn't the most romantic situation. For either of us," she says softly. "But I am willing to make the best of it. And I hope you can too."

I look over the rim of my wine glass. When I lean back in the chair, my vision swims a little.

"Let me ask you, Blair. Do you want to marry me?" I blink at her, waiting for her response.

She appears to contemplate her answer. "I want to ensure that my family is well-regarded and has a stable place in society."

What a fucking non-answer.

"It's a simple question, Blair." I place the glass back on the table, but I nearly miss and it lands slightly on the edge.

A slight flush comes to her face. Even that is delicate—just two twin spots high on her cheeks.

"Hunter—oh, what the hell," she says, huffing and crossing her arms over her chest. "No, I don't want to marry a transient, sometimes drug addict who has fucked half of Europe."

My eyebrows are in my hairline, I'm sure.

"What, you don't think I've heard? People talk, Hunter." A flinty look appears in her eyes.

"I've heard a lot about you, Hunter Brigham. The majority of it is unsatisfactory. But you know what you haven't heard about me?" She leans forward in her chair and lowers her voice even further.

"A lot. I have secrets too." She lifts one corner of her mouth in a closed smile.

"Care to share?" I ask.

She looks at me for a moment before leaning back in her chair. "Not yet. But maybe one day."

She takes her first sip of chardonnay.

"But to answer your simple question, Hunter. No, I don't want to marry you. But I have my reasons why I am. Reasons, just like you have for going along with this whole thing."

A sad look crosses her face, and I stare at her momentarily. Maybe she's mixed up in this whole thing too.

I feel myself starting to have sympathy for her.

"And, importantly, you are a Brigham. So even though

people think you're a degenerate, you're a prime catch," she adds.

There go those sympathetic feelings.

"If we can make this work and tolerate each other, I think we can get through this marriage thing just fine. We can come to an understanding." She reaches across the table and grabs my hand.

Immediately, images of Winter's palm touching mine after I stood so lost outside August's room come to mind. Flashes of her in front of me, against the tree, wrapped around me, our mouths seeking, seeking, seeking…

I pull my hand away from Blair's. "An understanding," I say. "I'm sure we can come to agree on something."

She looks at me and smiles.

I feel movement at my shoulder, and expecting the server, I turn to face the intrusion. My eyes meet none other than Morris Winthrope.

"Daddy," Blair says gently, moving her seat back soundlessly to hug her father.

"Princess," he says, ghosting the approximation of a kiss over her cheeks and releasing her embrace.

"Hunter Brigham," he says, sticking his hand out to me, and a mixture of training and ego forces me to stand and match the man's height.

"It's been a long time," I tell him. I force my mind to clear all thought, because if I don't, I'll have a replay of his depraved crimes running in my mind.

Morris smiles enigmatically, and the sight causes sickness to well in my stomach.

Morris Winthrope hasn't aged much since I last saw him, and it's difficult to know if it's from science or genetics. My bet is on science.

His reddish-blonde hair sweeps away from his strong face in an elegant haircut, and his green eyes are even more piercing than Blair's. He's a tall, wide man, and he reminds me of an ox.

I've seen him dish out unimaginable pain.

I force my eyes to stay open as I lose the battle to forget and the vision of him driving a harpoon through a child's abdomen crystalizes in my consciousness. The smell of the angry sea and metallic blood still assaults me. His triumphant laughter rings in my ears.

My hand flexes in his grip, squeezing.

Winthrope's smile twitches almost imperceptibly, and he is the first to drop his hand.

"We'll be seeing a lot of each other now, though. Won't we?" He isn't actually asking a question.

Winthrope raises his index finger in the air, still looking at me, and three servers immediately materialize to change the place settings, adding a seat for him. Winthrope sits, and I do the same.

God, just strike me down now. I know I've done some bad shit in my life, but just kill me now.

A server brings my soon-to-be father-in-law a glass of brandy without him having to ask. He picks it up and takes a sip. The ring on his pinky gleams in the soft candlelight, drawing my attention to it.

Gold and onyx, just like my father's.

Blair and Winthrope talk in muted tones, my brain involuntarily tuning out their conversation. I can only focus on the gleaming stone that draws me in—the center of the eye. The longer I stare at it, the more unease settles in.

Nothing sets it apart from the ring my father wears.

"We'll have much to celebrate soon. Uniting our families and creating a strong lineage," Winthrope says, drawing me back in. He raises his glass as does Blair. I pause for a beat, Blair's gaze hardening the longer she stares in my direction.

Get with the program.

I plaster a smile on my face. "Of course. To much happiness," I say.

"And prosperity," Winthrope adds. Looking at his face, it looks too perfect, to editorialized.

Clearly, there's so much more to this whole situation. More to this whole fucked-up world.

And I'm in over my head.

When we all lift our glasses, I drink until mine is drained.

SEVENTEEN
WINTER

August is quiet and still on the drive over to Potomac Mills. We're both bundled up in scarves and coats, but the blast of the heater causes a bead of sweat to roll down my back. Thanksgiving sped past, and the streets have Christmas lights strung around the light poles.

We should be in a mood of Christmas cheer. Instead, the energy is somber. I don't want to move because August seems fragile, like he's a moment away from melting down. Kitty shakes his head from side to side, sniffing in the hot air before putting his face on the seat where he rests.

August requested this trip—he wanted to go back to the home he lived in with his mother for most of his life. I wasn't sure then and I'm not sure now if this is a good idea, but it's important to August.

I don't say no.

August's maternal grandparents never had a funeral for his mother, instead choosing to quietly cremate her and bring the remains with them to Florida where they've retired. August hasn't said how he feels about it—the lack of closure—despite my trying to bring the topic up several times in our sessions.

Two bodyguards follow our SUV as we amble down I-95. August's driver, Jared, talks with August's new guard, Rex. I haven't seen his original guard—the one who shook him—since that day in the foyer. Rex has a kind face, speaks softly, and moves intentionally—despite being at least 250 pounds of solid muscle.

We pull up to the home, and sadness washes over me. I'm not completely sure why. It's a three-story colonial with tall white pillars on the front. There are four black rocking chairs on the porch, and thick canvas covers the plants, protecting them from the frost. Someone, probably Hunter, is keeping the property maintained. Still, the home looks dead. Desolate.

I shiver, and it has nothing to do with the December chill.

"Do you want to go in?" I ask August slowly and in a low voice. I don't want to startle him. He stares out the window with an emotionless glare. I know his expressions are deceiving. His face often gives nothing away, but his words express the depth of his feelings.

"No," August says.

I nod.

He opens the door and I scramble out after him when I see the two guards in the other car exit. Tossing a command at Kitty to stay, which he gleefully does, I wave the guards off, forcing them to go back into their vehicle. They look at each other, then back at me, standing still outside their SUV. When I give them a fierce glare and put my gloved hands on my hips, they roll their eyes and return to their seats.

I stand next to August. "Do you want me to wait in the car too, or am I good to stand here with you?"

He's silent for several seconds, probably a minute or two, before he says, "Whatever you want."

His eyes return to the colonial home. "I'll stay right here next to you," I say, taking a step closer. "If you want to talk or need something, I'm right here."

Then we are both silent. The clouds of our exhalations rise from our bodies, charting a course toward the sky.

August rocks side to side, distributing his weight from one foot to the other. Without saying a word, he leans his body against mine. I press back against him firmly, giving him a foundation. Absorbing his sadness.

A few minutes later, August spins around and reenters the car. He looks tired, but after driving in the opposite direction of Amelia Manor for a few minutes, he decides to ask, "Where are we going?"

I smile slowly. "We're going to have some fun."

The look he gives me is disbelieving until we pull up to the activity center in Tyson's Corner.

FuryFusion is completely empty by my request, which put what I'm sure is a sizable dent in the business credit card Ella gave me for the outing.

I assess August as he takes in the space, his eyes darting from the axe-throwing stations to the doors labeled "Rage Room" and the sign pointing to the indoor paintball park.

"Ready, Aug?" I ask, putting a hand on his forearm, which I know is a safe zone to touch him.

His eyes sparkle as they dart around. Then he jumps away, skipping through the space as he checks out all the features.

Circling back to me, he laughs and stims, I think happily, as he raises his tablet from where it hangs around his shoulder. "This place is cool. Thank you."

"No problem, bud," I reply. "Wanna do something with me?"

August shrugs, then nods his head. "Yes."

I guide us over to the tall table near the Rage Room. "Relax," I tell Kitty, taking off his harness. I hand him over to Rex, whose face lights up at being on dog duty.

August waits for me near the table, looking at the stack of cheap white plates I purchased for this activity.

"I have this idea that I got from another therapist. I want us to go into the Rage Room and smash these plates." I explain, opening the pack of Sharpies. August looks at me skeptically, giving me an expression that's so like Hunter I clear my throat to focus.

"But instead of just smashing plates, I want us to write on them. I'll write them for you if you tell me the words, but I want you to think about all the things that make you feel sad or pissed off or hopeless or any other feeling that you just can't shake. We'll pretend these plates represent that thing. Then we'll smash the hell out of 'em."

A sudden fear rings through me that maybe this isn't the best idea. That maybe his super-literal brain won't connect with this activity. But I release my trapped breath when he says, "Okay, let us break some shit."

Grabbing our gear and the box of plates, I scoot everything into the particle board-covered room. After sweeping a spot to make doubly sure it's clear of sharp bits, August and I sit on the floor.

"Okay, do you have some things in mind?" I ask August.

He taps his cheek three times, pauses, then taps it for another three.

"Hunter," he says. I nod, writing on the plate in big block letters, trying my damndest to keep my face neutral.

"Cool. Another one?" I ask, and he taps again.

"Moving. Not being able to go to school in person this semester. I hate virtual school," he says, spilling the words forward.

"Okay, 'moving' and 'virtual school.' What else, August?" His face starts to turn red, and he rocks from his crisscrossed position on the floor.

"Drugs. Money. Bad people. Stolen futures. Broken promises..." He continues on until we have a stack of thirty plates and he's rocking back and forth, holding his abdomen as if his guts would spill out alongside his words.

"Where are you now, August? What are you feeling?" My voice is gentle, my gaze settled on his chest, not his face, to save him from the intensity of eye contact.

"It is so much, Winter," he confesses. His stims increase, and I see the energy, the storm brewing inside him.

"You wanna break all of it into pieces? Do you wanna let it go?" I ask him, holding out the insulated helmet, safety goggles, and thick protective suit.

"Hell yes." He jumps up, dressing immediately.

Once we both have our suits and helmets on, I turn to August, wordlessly handing him the plate.

"You wanna destroy this one?" I look down at the word on the plate.

"Yes," he confesses.

"All right," I say. Then I take a step back and bellow, "August lets go of broken promises!"

August laughs, the sound muffled but still loud. He throws the plate at the wall, and it smashes into a thousand pieces.

He shrieks, running around the room and clapping. "Next," he says quickly. I hand him another plate. He reads the word, then looks at me, nodding.

"August lets go of disrupted routines!"

He smashes it and summons a roar from deep in his chest.

"Feel it, August!"

It continues on like that for ten more minutes before he stalks over to the plates. He takes the remaining armful, then pauses. His breathing is labored and fast, like the plates weigh a ton.

He reads the one on top, then chucks it. Then he does it again. And again. And again.

When he gets to the last plate, he doesn't immediately chuck it after he reads. Instead, he hands it to me. He nods at me after I read it silently.

"August lets go of hate!"

I give the plate back to him, and he pitches it to the wall. When it shatters, he moves over to the mallet leaning against the wall. And with more strength than I thought he could possess, he swings the mallet up and pulverizes the broken pieces.

He slams it over and over and over until he falls in the ceramic dust.

Then he throws off his helmet and goggles and unzips the protective suit.

Once he's free, I see his muscles spasm.

Then a count: One. Two. Three.

August wails.

The sound is so loud, so sorrowful that I can't help the tears that spring to my eyes. I rush over to him, stripping off the gear until the suit hangs on my hips.

"Get it out, August. I'm here for you," I say in his ear once I'm on the floor next to him.

He starts up another guttural moan, his voice broken by the sobbing tears. He collapses completely now, his body giving up and falling into mine. And I hold him.

We sit there for a long while, long enough for my butt cheek to fall asleep, but I don't move a muscle. I keep my hands on August, giving him solid pressure to orient himself to the present.

His tears and sobs slow, and with trembling hands, he reaches for his tablet.

"I really miss my mom."

I inhale and exhale loudly, bringing air into my nose and out of my mouth.

"I know, August. I know, and that's okay. You are safe to feel whatever you feel. I'm here to help guide you through this."

He drops his tablet on the floor and goes so still that after a few minutes, I think he's sleeping, passed out from the emotional onslaught of the day.

Without any indication, he sits up, his nose red and eyes bloodshot.

"Can we get McDonalds?" he asks.

"Of course, dude. It's whatever you want," I say.

He gives me a small smile. "Then I want ice cream too."

My smile widens. "Done deal."

It's only eight thirty when we get back to Amelia Manor after the activity center, but since it's a Friday, finding an Uber back to my apartment proves to be a lost cause.

August stops in the foyer and gives me a brief hug. A first for him.

He taps on his tablet. "Thank you." He bounces off to his room.

I consider wandering around the mansion in search of Ella but decide that I'd rather shove razor blades under my fingers than accidentally run into H.

Hunter.

Mr. Brigham.

It's been months since The Incident, and I haven't seen him except for a few sessions with August. If not for those sessions, I'd believe I'd made up his entire existence as some kind of fucked psychosis.

Because the prevailing thought I've had over the last several weeks is how much I want to do it again. How much I want to do more with none other than Hunter Brigham.

Delulu, for real.

I haven't stopped thinking about him and the press of his body against mine. At my lackluster birthday party, which only included me, Veronica, and Kitty at a Halloween-themed Rocky Horror Picture Show, I blew out my candles and wished I could be the type of woman to take Hunter up on the promise of wild, hot, amazing sex.

I'm officially out of my twenties. Hello, thirties. And I'm in virtually the same social state as I was fifteen years ago.

The thought is sad. So, so sad.

I want to make more friends. I want to go out more, be more social. Hell, I want to date. I want to have strings-free sex. I'm letting my life pass me by. I refuse to do so.

So I do want to see Hunter Brigham. Eventually. But I don't want to make now, when I'm covered in sweat and splatter from the indoor paintball session, the first time I see him after coming on his leg.

Embarrassment shoots hot through me, and Kitty jumps up on his hind legs to snag my attention.

"I'm okay, love," I murmur to Kitty.

I text Ella.

Are you at Amelia Manor right now?

I tap my fingers on my thigh in a triplet rhythm. *TAP-tap-tap. TAP-tap-tap.* Her reply comes through five minutes later, after I've thoroughly analyzed the art on one of the far walls in the foyer.

It's a Basquiat, which is cool AF. There's a lot to look at in the image.

No, girl, I'm on campus. You okay?

Shit, that's just great. I pull up the app again, cycling through all the rideshare apps on my device. No such luck. Fuck.

Can't get an Uber out. Do you mind if Kitty and I crash here for the night?

Her reply comes seconds later.

I don't mind, but why not ask H? 😉

I grimace, contemplating my response. I don't want to say

*I creamed on your brother's pants, and now I'm avoiding him...*but I also don't want to lie.

I can't find him. But I wanted to check with someone before I start hitchhiking back to D.C. LOL.

Don't do that. Use the guest room. There are a few spare sets of clothes for you to use.

I relax.

Make yourself at home.

Permission granted, I head to the guest room a few doors from August's game room.

I'm covered in paint. My hair is crunchy, and I decide to shower when I look at the blindingly white comforter and sheets.

Not that it's a hard ask.

My muscles melt as the water cascades down from the five showerheads in the massive stall. It's stocked with the most luscious soap, and I opt for using the conditioner to protect my hair after rinsing out the paint.

Clean and refreshed, I wrap myself in a towel and grab the shirt and sweatpants Ella left behind in the dresser. It's a tight fit over my ass, but they'll work.

Kitty's curled up on the bed of pillows I made for him, snoring. He's certainly made himself at home.

I'm drained. The Rage Room was exhausting, but after eating DoorDashed McDonalds and immediately heading to axe throwing and paintball, I almost needed an inhaler.

I plop on the bed and reach for my phone.

"Did you know that you can reach a stage of pregnancy in which you just leak tiny dribbles of pee every time you walk?" Veronica says when she answers my call instead of "hello."

"No, I didn't know that," I say. And I'm not quite sure I wanted to know that, either. I clench my inner muscles in an involuntary Kegel.

"Welp, that's the stage where I'm at," she replies. She sighs for a solid three seconds.

"I was just checking on you, baby mama. James comes in tonight, right?"

There's rustling on the other end and then a giggle.

"Actually, he came into town earlier today. He surprised me," she says. The happiness in her voice vibrates over the line.

"That's so sweet! Why are you answering the phone for me, though? Go be with your man!"

"I'll always answer the phone for you," she replies. My smile turns sad.

"Rons, you *do* know you don't have to answer the phone for me all the time. If you're busy, that's okay." It's important to me that she knows that. That she knows that she can live her life and enjoy it without constantly worrying about me.

"I know, I know," she says.

But I'm not sure she does.

"Are you settling in for the night?" she asks, changing the subject.

I look around the room. "Well, actually..." She's going to flip her shit when I tell her that I'm sleeping doors away from Hot Daddy.

"Well, what?" she presses.

"Well, I'm," I lower my voice, "I'm still at my client's house."

"Isn't it kinda late?" she asks. I can tell her attention is elsewhere.

"Well, I'm actually spending the night," I say.

She's silent for a beat and then practically yells, "What!"

I shhh her. "Jeez, Rons, my eardrums."

She lowers her voice to a whisper, "Are you going to fuck Hot Daddy?" She sounds delightfully scandalized.

"No!" I say forcefully. "I'm staying in the guest room. I couldn't get an Uber out."

"Well, I could come get you. Actually, no. And not because James is here but because I really, really, really, and I mean really, need you to get dicked down in the most serious way."

"Veronica!" My phone beeps with the low battery signal. Five percent left.

If this don't beat all.

Make that four percent.

"Listen," she says while I scour through my bag, hoping against hope that I have a charger. "Just make sure to use a condom and demand that he gets you off. It's the twenty-first century. Faking it is unacceptable these days."

I throw the bag on the bed in frustration when I don't find one.

I run a defeated hand down my face.

There's a charger in the game room.

Turning toward the door, I say, "Rons, my phone is going to die, but I'll catch you in the morning." I put my handle on the doorknob.

"Be safe!" she says.

Opening the door, I say, "I'm not going to fuck my boss!"

"Thanks for sharing. It's good to set boundaries."

But the voice doesn't belong to Veronica. Hunter Brigham stares me down.

My phone goes dead in my hand, and I stand frozen in the doorway, clutching it close to my face. He reaches out, removing it from my grasp.

He walks toward me, and I step backward, only stopping when my legs hit the edge of the bed.

When we both stop, breathing in sync, he breaks the silence.

"Ella told me you're crashing here tonight. I just wanted to see if you needed anything," he says.

I don't know whether to curse Ella or send her a gift basket. He places my phone on the nightstand.

"Can we talk, Winter?"

No. No, I don't want to talk, Hunter. I don't want to look at you with your beautiful eyes and smile and see everything I cannot have.

Everything I should not want.

"Yes," I say instead.

He takes my hand, and I gasp slightly, but he gently moves me to sit on the side of the bed. Then he goes to sit on the armchair across from me.

"I wanted to start by apologizing to you."

Of all the things I was expecting him to say—hoping he would say—this is not it.

"Okay," I reply, unsure what else to add.

"You are right that we should maintain a professional distance. And I shouldn't have kissed you that night. I shouldn't have taken it that far, no matter how much I wanted to."

I'm dying. I'm dying inside because while he's saying exactly what he should be saying, everything within me is devastated that he's being honorable.

"It's okay. I wasn't innocent in all that, either. It takes two..."

"Yeah," he says. He rubs the back of his neck. "I just...I never want you to feel like you have to do something you don't want to do."

He pauses, still looking me in the eyes.

And then, something snaps within me: the knowledge that it's not me keeping myself from doing what I want to do. It's the past. It's...*him.*

"Who says I didn't want to do what we did?" I whisper,

my lips trembling. I clutch my hands together in my lap to keep them from shaking.

The mood in the room shifts instantly. His gaze tracks over my face before roaming lazily down my body.

When his eyes snap back to mine, the focus in them singes me.

"You tell me, Winter," he says just as softly.

I inhale deeply, drawing in his scent and getting high off his presence.

"The ball is in your court," he continues, and everything about his tone, his presence, honors the delicacy of this moment. "You'll have to tell me what we do from here. Because here's what I want," he says.

He gets up with purposeful movements. "I want to kiss you. I want to taste you. I want to feel you around my tongue, my fingers, my cock."

I gasp, and he stops a foot from me. He's still, but his intensity fills the room.

"Can I say that to you, Sunbeam? Can I say how I want to make you come over and over, harder than you did with me back in my rose garden? Can I say how I want to hear you sigh and moan and be wild with me because I know that's what you want? I can see it so clearly on your face. You want to be wild, but you're holding yourself back."

And then, because it's exactly what I needed but didn't know, he kneels before me. And his hands land on my thighs.

"You disappeared," I whisper, averting my gaze but still feeling his presence surround me.

"I tried to give you space. I didn't want to scare you any more than I already have." He reaches his hand out to me, and I close my eyes when his palm caresses my cheek.

"I'm not scared of you, Hunter. Of all the people I'm scared of, you're not on the list." My words are so truthful, and the muted delivery doesn't soften them.

"Sunbeam," he says on a breath. "You're going to have to tell me. You're going to have to say the words. Do you want what I want too? Or do you want me to step back? To leave you alone? I will do either because while I want you more than I want my next breath, I want you to have everything you need too."

He's inches from my face now, kneeling between my legs. I don't even know when I parted them or when he moved into the space.

The tension of the moment is thick between our bodies.

"I don't know why I feel like this with you. But I do. So tell me," he says on an exhale. "Yes or no?"

I search his face for a reason to say no. For a reason why I should continue to deny the inevitability of us.

"H," I say. "Yes."

As soon as the word is out of my mouth, his lips are on mine, swallowing my doubts and worries and anxieties. He leans me back across the bed, his hands cradling my face gently—a perfect foil to the harshness of his kiss.

I taste his lips with my tongue, and when he groans, the sound surges straight to my center.

"I've been dreaming about you, Winter," he whispers in my ear, ghosting kisses down my neck and across my collarbone. "Do you know how many mornings I've woken up rock-hard from dreams of your body pressed against mine?" He lifts my shirt to right beneath my breasts and looks at me for confirmation to take it off.

I bite my lip, nodding. He removes it.

"God," he whispers, and I fight the urge to cover myself as my breasts start to splay to the side. I cross my arms over my chest.

"Arms up," he snaps, and the raw dominance in his tone has me drenched in a second. He pins my arms to the bed and my back arches at the motion.

"These breasts, I will dream about these breasts," he says and lowers his head to suck my nipple into his warm mouth.

I feel like I'm on fire.

I'm wet. So wet, and he's barely kissed me.

"H, I—"

"Do you know how many times I've washed my cum down my shower drain thinking of your moans? Thinking about how you came so hard with me and how I'd do anything to see that again?"

I moan, the need to touch him and feel him so potent I can taste it.

He moves to suck my other nipple, and when he removes his grip from my wrists, I run my hands through his thick hair.

"H, please, I need—" I choke on the rest of my sentence, rational thought cut off when I feel the hard length of him pressed against the most intimate part of me through the protective layers of our clothes.

I don't feel fear. I feel nothing but lust.

"Do you want to come again, Sunbeam?" His voice is a hard rasp.

I nod my head, not daring to speak.

"Let me feel you this time." It's equal parts a command and a request. He pauses at the waistband of my sweats, waiting for my answer.

I bite my lip and nod again. I'm unable to say the words—it's a swirl of lust and an emotion I refuse to acknowledge that chokes off my vocal cords.

"Thank God," he grates, pushing a slow hand past the waistband of my sweats.

When his fingers ghost over the hard nub of my clit and down my sopping pussy lips, I can't help the loud near shriek that explodes from my mouth.

I'm thrashing and moaning. This is what will make me lose my mind.

Not my parents' death.

Not all the fucked-up shit that's happened since.

This. Hunter Brigham with his fingers against the most private parts of me.

"H, it's so good," I say breathlessly, amazed I can utter a complete sentence.

"God, it is. You're so wet. You're so perfect. You feel—" He stops talking, sucking hard on my neck as he thrusts a thick finger inside me. I clench on the intrusion.

"Fuck, you are so insanely tight, Winter." He looks at me, and his eyes are glassy. He's as drunk on this moment as I am.

I don't respond, but I reach a hand down the front of him and, with the last iota of my sanity flying out of my brain, I grasp his dick against the rough fabric of his jeans.

"Shit!" he says, his breath stuttering, and he adds another finger inside me. The stretch is so exquisite, so overwhelming, that when he presses the heel of his hand against my clit and curves his fingers up, I come immediately. Squeezing the life out of him, I can't help but scream his name.

"Hunter, *God,*" I say. My teeth chatter, and my hold on his dick flexes. I'm coming so hard that the edges of my vision darken and become hazy as pinpricks of stars flash.

"Shit-shit-*shit,*" he says as he rocks against my hand. Seconds later, he tenses on top of me, sucking my neck deeply and gentling the motion of his fingers inside my pussy.

In the quiet aftermath of what just happened, we're both silent. Unmoving. My hand is still on his softening dick; his fingers are still firmly inside me.

And I cannot bring my brain to a state of coherence.

He's the first to move, pressing his lips against my cheek.

"I'm fighting embarrassment that I just came in my pants," he says with a soft chuckle.

I focus my eyes on his face when he pulls back.

His boyish smile looks so vulnerable my heart thumps over in my chest.

He slowly pulls his fingers from me, and I turn ten shades

of red when he slowly brings them to his mouth, sucking them like the taste is the best thing he's ever experienced.

I'm mesmerized by him.

I bring my hand to his face, and he closes his eyes, leaning into my palm. After a moment, he leans down to kiss me. It's slow this time, seeking, and an unknowable amount of minutes pass before we both come up for air.

He leans his forehead against mine. "I'm going to take a shower." That playful smile comes back to his face. "Stay with me tonight." He's not asking a question. It's a plea.

Our eyes are so close our eyelashes could kiss. I whisper, "Okay."

He kisses my nose.

Moving toward the bathroom, he strips off all his clothes before reaching the ensuite door.

Again, I'm overheated by the pure strength of this man's body. He turns slightly, one hand on the doorframe, and says, "I just need a few minutes, Sunbeam. Join me if you want." With that, he smirks and heads to the shower.

I sit silently for a few minutes, absorbing the massiveness of what's just happened. I feel my sanity knocking on the door of my consciousness.

So I do the only thing I can do in this situation.

I get out of the bed.

I RAN. Almost quite literally.

I grabbed my stuff, scooped up Kitty, and hightailed it out of Amelia Manor while H was in the shower. The frigid air burned my lungs as I ran down the drive and all the way to the convenience store where the same clerk I flashed all those months ago gave me a phone charger to use to schedule an Uber.

Three hours later, I walk into my apartment.

After I put my phone on the charger, I strip off my clothes and walk to the bathroom. Turning the taps on as hot as they'll go, I step under the shower spray, letting the water soak my hair.

I sit on the tiled floor. And then, I allow myself to cry.

The reasons why I cry are a jumbled mess in my brain. I'm crying because I'm happy and terrified and angry and grieving. I'm crying because I could have said yes and kept saying yes to all that happened tonight. But I chose to stop.

The truth is, I needed some space. I want Hunter. I can freely admit that I want him *badly*. But I need to go slow. And if I'd stayed, we would have had sex.

I'm not ready for sex. I thought I was, but as the heat from Hunter's body faded, disgust and self-loathing washed over me so thoroughly that I swallowed bile.

So yeah. I thought I would be ready, but I'm so not.

The water starts to cool, so I peel myself off the shower floor. Once I'm back in bed, I reach for my phone.

I have five calls and three texts from an unknown number. I've been sending Hunter's calls to voicemail, but I finally feel the courage to look at the texts.

Where did you go, beautiful?

This came right when I'd scheduled my ride.

This is H, by the way.

This one came right after I'd gotten into the Uber.

Winter, where are you? All my calls are going to voicemail. Did I do something wrong?

This one came right when I'd walked in the door.

My finger hovers over my keyboard, contemplating what to write to him. He didn't do anything wrong. Neither of us did anything wrong. But I'd played myself if I thought I was ready to take that next step. How can I explain to this sex god that I'm scared of having sex with him? My phone vibrates in my hand as another text comes through.

At least let me know you're safe.

I start to type and then stop, erasing what I wrote.

Ah, good. I see you're typing. So you are alive? I don't have to send out the National Guard?

Despite my messed-up mind, I laugh a little.

I'm safe.

I press send before I can rethink the message. And because I'm a psychopath, I find myself eagerly waiting for his response. He starts and stops typing several times before the dots on the bottom of our chat disappear altogether.

Good.

My breath seizes in my chest. I don't know what to say, but I want to say something.

I'm sorry.

I contemplate what even to reply when more texts come in.

Don't be sorry. I feel like I went about things the wrong way with you, and I rushed you.

I don't want only sex with you.

I want to spend time with you. Get to know you. I'm sorry if it felt like I just wanted you for a hook up.

I'm about three minutes away from an asthma attack at this point. Each text message heightens my confusion and anxiety.

Are you saying you want to date me, Hunter Brigham?

I bite my nails while I wait for his response. He replies almost immediately.

Yes.

I can't help the smile that spreads across my face. I'm giddy.

This is what you missed out on in high school.

I might not be ready for sex with Hunter today, but I might with time. No. I know I will be ready with time. I pull my finger from my mouth and type my reply.

I'll consider it.

I chew on my thumb cuticle. He says he wants to get to know me, but....Sighing, I finally bite the bullet, deciding to be truthful.

And the truth shall set you free.

I've never dated before.

You've never dated? Or you've never been on a date?

I think about my reply before I send the message.

Both.

He starts and stops typing a few more times. Then, finally, his reply comes through.

Is it strange if I say that I love that?

I can't help the smile that passes across my face. Two minutes later, another text comes through.

Okay, so. Hi. I'm Hunter. My middle name is James, so Hunter James Brigham. I'm 34. I've been a shithead for most of my life, but in the past few years, as I've grown up, I've learned to be…a little less of a shithead. I'm a work in progress. I like numbers and math; I hate reading, but that's because it took several years for anyone to notice that I needed glasses. I wore contacts forever until I got LASIK. I don't like onions. My favorite place is Santorini, Greece. I want to introduce you to a woman I met there. She makes the best Greek food ever. Do you like Greek food? My favorite color is green. My favorite dessert is chocolate cake. I love photography, and if I wasn't doing what I'm doing now, I'd probably be a photographer. The most scared I've been was when August was born. The second most scared I've ever been was when I base-jumped off the side of a cliff in Norway. I love dogs, but I've never owned one.

That's the short summary about me. Tell me about yourself.

I breathe deeply as I re-read his text. There's so much to unpack in all of it, but I set that aside to sit with the fact that he's sharing. He wants me to know about him. And he wants to know about me too. I start to type.

Hi, Hunter. I'm Winter Leigh Vaughan. But you already knew that since I rambled about my name when we first met. I just turned 30 in October. I don't have many friends except my best friend, Veronica. I love to read, specifically the classics. Sense and Sensibility is my favorite Jane Austen novel. I love roses, which is why I love your mother's garden. I love to color, and I have a ton of adult coloring books around my apartment. I'm sorry to say that I have perfect vision, but I suck at math. I've never been to Greece, but I traveled a lot with my mom. Santorini sounds like a dream. I love Greek food. I love crystals and many alternative practices like yoga, meditation, and tarot. I promise I won't read your natal chart unless you ask. I don't have strong opinions about onions, but I do love French onion soup. If I weren't a therapist, I'd probably still be helping people in some way. The most scared I've ever been was…

I stop typing, not wanting to say the honest answer—that the most scared I've ever been was today. This evening, when I was in his arms. Even realizing *that* moment was when I was the most scared has me shook.

I back out the last sentence I started to write.

My favorite season is spring and one day, I want to catch the cherry blossoms in bloom down at the Tidal Basin.

I read over my response before hitting send. I stare at the screen for a few more minutes before deciding that the action isn't healthy and that I need to sleep. My phone beeps right after I snuggle under the blankets, and I pick it up to open the message.

When was your birthday?

Usually, low-key birthdays with Veronica and an ice cream cake fill my soul just fine. But this year, on what's supposed to be such a milestone, I just found myself feeling grumpy.

October 24th

He's quiet, not even the text bubbles show, and I feel my heart rate rise. It's not like I did anything wrong having a birthday.

That's your fawn response, Winter.

I pull the sachet of lavender from my pillowcase, bringing it to my nose. My phone pings, and I look at it immediately.

Happy belated birthday, beautiful Winter.

I feel his words as if he were whispering them in my ear.

I look forward to getting to know you. Sleep tight, Sunbeam.

I turn my phone off and do just that.

EIGHTEEN
HUNTER

I don't buy her flowers. Instead, I go to the greenhouse and pick the most vibrant set of roses on the bushes. Most of the flowers in the garden are covered, winterized against the cold, but the hardier flowers inside still maintain their blooms.

Choosing the pink and white Rugosas was easy, taking me only fifteen minutes at each bush. But I spent half an hour going through our Mordens before landing on a few perfect orange Knock Out roses. While I bundle them up on the kitchen counter, Ella waltzes in, because of course.

"Ooh, pretty!" she says, smacking on a stick of gum. Doublemint, from the smell of it.

"At least you're avoiding the red dye number 40," I say to her under my breath. She still hears me and mimics my words.

"I'm assuming those aren't for me or August. Probably not for Leo. So who is the lucky lady?" She hops up on the counter, swinging her legs.

I don't respond right away. Instead, I focus on trimming the stems and placing them in the crepe paper I snagged from our housekeeper this morning.

"Could they be for one pretty curly-haired therapist?" She scoots her butt across the counter until she's sitting almost on top of the flowers. I look up at her, arching an eyebrow.

"Holy shit! They are, aren't they!" she says, clapping her hands like a seal. "Are y'all a thing? I swear I felt chemistry between the two of you. Oh, my God, tell me the details," she says when she grabs my arm and starts shaking me.

"Jeez, Ella. What are you, twelve?" Heat creeps up my neck, and for once in the longest time I can remember, I blush. I fucking blush.

"Hunter," she drawls.

"Yes, they're for Winter," I say.

"And you and Winter are…?" She leans into me when she asks.

"Winter and I are…" I search for the right word. Winter and I are giving each other powerful orgasms. Winter and I are dancing around our insane attraction for each other. Winter and I are…

Falling for each other.

What the actual fuck?

"…dating. Winter and I are dating." When I look at Ella's face, her eyes are misty, and she's looking up at me as if I've said the most romantic thing ever.

"Calm down, Ellie," I tell her quietly, tying a bow around the paper-wrapped bouquet.

"I am calm! I'm just happy for you, is all. And her. And August. And me!" She hops off the counter. "I feel it important to warn you, though: don't do anything that will mess up August's recovery. If things go south…just don't let them go south in an explosive way that touches Augie, okay?"

I chew on her words for a minute. *If* things go south… aren't they destined to go south?

Not always. This one is yours.

I push back the faces of Blair and Morris Winthrope from my consciousness and focus on the display of blooms. "I won't," I promise Ella. "Now, if you'll excuse me, I have to deliver these flowers."

Ella smiles brightly as I leave.

"Use condoms!" she yells out from the kitchen, and one of our guards looks up from his seat near the front door. His eyebrows shoot up, and a knowing smirk crosses his face. I ignore it.

When I find myself at her apartment building an hour later, I'm seriously reconsidering my entire plan for today.

Suddenly, I'm nervous. I'm never nervous.

Are you saying you want to date me, Hunter Brigham? She texted. And even though I should have left her alone, I should have said no, I couldn't. It was like my mind and body rejected the idea of not being with Winter. So I said yes. Even though this fucked-up engagement to Blair Winthrope hangs over my head like a tornado about to drop and wreck all my shit up.

The valet waves at me from the passenger side window. Taking that as my cue to stop idling in front of her building, I get out, hand him the keys, and square my shoulders as I enter her lobby.

I'm four steps past the entrance of Winter's building when I run into someone. Not someone—Winter.

"Hunter! What are you doing here?" she asks once she rights herself. The flowers are crushed a little as I inspect them, but I get distracted by the feeling of tiny paws settling on my pant legs.

"Oh! Down, Kitty!" Winter says.

I hear a masculine voice chuckle near us.

Turning, I see a tall and entirely too smiley man who legitimately looks like a superhero in a blockbuster movie standing near Winter.

"I will never get over that dog's name," he says.

And much to my annoyance, Winter gives him a gentle grin.

I stand even taller.

"Hunter Brigham," I say, sticking my hand toward the man. He takes it, and I grip his hand firmly. Not too tightly to seem paranoid, but firmly enough to stake my claim.

"Marcus Law," he replies. He's still smiling, and that unsettles me.

"Marcus is my neighbor. He owns an amazing café bookstore down the street from here." With Winter's soft hand on my arm, I start to relax. I look at her and am pleased she's looking back at me.

Only me.

Insecure much?

"It's nice to meet you, Marcus," I say, calming down. I release his hand.

Why the hell am I so amped up? Why am I feeling so goddamn awkward?

I am Hunter Motherfucking Brigham. I do not do awkwardness.

"Are those for me?" Winter cuts into my internal beratement, and I remember the flowers.

"Yes," I say, not wanting to explain that I spent an hour in my mother's garden picking the exact right flowers for her. At least, not wanting to explain that with Muscle Marcus in earshot.

Luckily, Marcus saves us all by moving on. "Don't let me get in the way of you two lovebirds. Hunter, Kitty…" He pauses for a minute. "You know, I can't keep calling you Kitty's Mom. Will you give me your name now?" He shows his too-straight teeth, and I find myself irrationally wanting to punch them all down his throat.

Clearly our unstated truce is over. Fuck this guy.

Winter rolls her eyes and says, "It's Winter."

"Winter," he says, drawing out her name. I step closer to my girl.

Yes. My girl.

I feel immense satisfaction when her body presses gently against mine.

"Well, it's been a pleasure. See you around the café, Winter." And with that, he gives us a tiny salute and heads out the front door of the building.

"So..." Winter says, drawing out the word.

I face her fully, taking her in. She has her North Face unzipped, and she's dressed in a white cashmere turtleneck, light denim jeans, and snow boots. Her hair is pulled into a high ponytail, the riot of curls pulled back sleekly only to pouf out of the hairband. Her face is bare of makeup, and for the first time in the bright morning sun, I see the freckles on her nose and the small mole above her right eyebrow.

She looks stunning.

"So..." I say back to her. I can't contain my smile.

"You never said what you're doing here, H. Not that I'm not happy to see you. I am. I was just wondering what brings you into the city, specifically U Street. This doesn't seem quite like your vibe." She stops talking when I pull her into a hug.

I let her go way too quickly.

"Why are you nervous?" I ask. I cup her cheek, and she closes her eyes, leaning into my touch.

Yes. Just...yes.

This one is yours.

"I'm not nervous."

I give her a look.

"Okay, you make me nervous! I told you I haven't done this before and feel awkward. Like, are we going steady now? Am I supposed to wear your letter jacket?"

I laugh at her rambling.

"Winter," I say quickly. "Will you go out on a date with me?"

Her eyes widen.

"Yes, of course. Wait. Like right now?" She looks around

the lobby as if a passerby could help her navigate this situation.

"Yes, right now. Unless you have plans already?" I let the question hang in the air, aware that I didn't consider that she'd have plans for her Saturday.

"No!" she says in a rush. "I mean, I planned on working on case notes to send to Dr. Wagner, but no, I don't have any plans." She blushes. "What do you have in mind?"

"Well, I was thinking we'd go to artTech first." Her eyes light up.

"First? artTech?"

"Yes, it's an immersive art installation. Right now, they have a Renaissance display on roses."

Her cheeks pinken, and I'm addicted to the sight.

"That sounds amazing," she says wistfully.

"Then I thought we'd head to the indoor market to see if we can get you some crystals to add to your collection."

She's beaming now. "Okay, the art installation and the market. Sounds fun," she says.

"By then, I figured we'd be hungry, so I thought we'd get lunch at La Maison. Maybe you could get French onion soup."

"But you hate onions," she whispers, drawing closer to me as I step toward her.

"I'll have something different," I reply with a shrug.

She bites her lip, and I want to draw it between mine.

"Maybe not onions. This is a date, after all," she says. Her eyes sparkle.

I realize that I'm enamored with everything she does. She could clip her toenails, and I'd probably find that sexy too.

Jesus fucking Christ.

"Then I thought we could go to a movie. Because a dating rite of passage is to have a movie theater date, so we definitely need to check that off the list."

"What would we see?" she asks.

"Hmmm. Probably a scary movie. That way if you get scared, you can curl into my arms. It's all very strategic, you see."

She purses her lips, and twisting them into a grin, she says, "I don't like scary movies though. The principle is stupid."

"Scary movies are stupid? Some of the classic horror films are literal cinematic canon."

She sighs, rolling her eyes. "Sure, I guess if one looks at it objectively as an art form. But it makes zero sense to me to pay to be frightened."

I laugh at her reasoning. "I guess rollercoasters and haunted houses are out for us, huh?"

"Exactly," she says brightly.

I don't know if she knows it, but she rubs her hand on my chest, and the feeling drives me wild. It seems like an absent motion, though, but the fact that she's giving me small touches, small moments of care and intimacy, makes me feel....

"Anything else?" she adds, quirking her eyebrow.

I rally myself to think clearly again.

"I was thinking we'd come back to your place so we could change for dinner. I have a suit in my car."

"A suit?" she says. Her voice is a little squeaky.

"Yes, then I'm taking you to dinner at Tavalia."

"I've never even heard of that place, but it sounds fancy."

I chuckle. "It is, and it's new. But I've heard good things about it. But it might be one of those places where the chef is making artistic statements with the menu."

She bounces on the balls of her feet a few times.

"Okay, so this is a whole day date?" Kitty shakes his fur, the buckles on his harness clinking together.

"Yes, all day. Can I have you?"

She looks into my eyes for a moment, searching. "Yes, you can have me, Hunter."

I smile.

SPENDING a full day on a date with Winter doesn't feel as awkward as it would with any other woman. I'm sure of it. I wanted to test a theory: would spending more time with her make my interest wane or would my feelings grow stronger?

The feelings I have for her are entirely new. I've felt affection and affinity for people before. My friends. August. Ella. But with Winter, this is something very different.

I'm drawn to her, connected to her. I want to breathe her in and never let her go.

This one is yours.

"Before I let you in," she says as she brings her phone up to the mechanical lock on her apartment door, "just know my place isn't huge. I wasn't expecting guests, so it may be a little cluttered."

The lock whirrs, and Winter opens the door slightly, turning back to me.

"I'm excited to see your home, Winter," I say simply.

She smiles.

The apartment is quiet when we enter. We'd stopped by the service animal trainers who placed Kitty with Winter. They offer boarding for service dogs, and Winter decided to drop Kitty with them for the evening.

I told her that I didn't mind Kitty coming with us to dinner, but she guaranteed me that she'd feel more comfortable going to a fancy place without eyes on her because she's toting a dog.

"Legally, no one can bar your entrance. Furthermore," I say.

"Furthermore, H?"

"If anyone were to try to block you from going anywhere, I'd annihilate them."

She sighed and said, "There you go sounding like you're in the mob again."

In the end, she decided boarding him for the night was what she wanted. I didn't push her on it.

Winter spins around the small living space of her efficiency and flops her arms at her sides. "Well, this is my apartment," she says. She's right, it is small. But the space is comfortable, and just how I imagined Winter's apartment would look.

Her bed is on the far side of the room, separated by a folding screen. A dog bed sits near the floor-to-ceiling windows, and there's a great view of U Street and the university. She has what looks like a meditation space in the center of the wall of windows. Crystals and candles form a circle around a plush, oversized pillow. In front of it, there's a large ceramic bowl.

After seeing her excitement at the crystals and incense I bought for her at the market, this feels a hundred percent Winter.

"It's great," I say. My smile is genuine.

I lift the flight bag higher on my shoulder, which snaps us out of our trances.

"Why don't I take the bathroom to get dressed, and you take the room. I'm sure you'll be much quicker than I am. Not that I'll take a super long time. I just need fifteen minutes, tops."

She's fidgeting again, and I see her picking at her thumbnail. I step closer to her, and her breath hitches.

"Take the time you need." I grab her hand and squeeze it lightly to stop her from picking.

She heads to the clothes rack and grabs a black dress before reaching for a sparkly silver jumpsuit. She bites her lip.

"What should I wear, H?"

I drape my flight bag over her bed and walk over to her. "What do you want to wear, Sunbeam?"

She blushes again.

"Why do you call me that?" she asks.

I smile at her. "I'll tell you later." Then I place a kiss on her forehead. I want to kiss her more but stop myself. "What do you want to wear?"

"I have not the foggiest idea. What are you wearing?"

"I have a navy suit."

"Okay, so not black then." She flicks through a few more dresses before pulling out a gold satin wrap dress. It looks formless on the hanger, but when she clutches it close to her chest and beams at me, I say, "That one is perfect."

She moves to her shoe rack, snags strappy heels, and heads to the drawers next to her bed. She pulls out black lace, and my mouth goes dry.

"I'll be just a minute!" she says before shutting the bathroom door firmly.

As I pull off my shirt and toss it on Winter's bed, I don't resist the urge to pull one of her pillows to my nose...and accept that I'm thoroughly over my head.

NINETEEN
WINTER

When I close the door to the bathroom, I turn on the shower. Not to use it but to drown out the sounds of my unhinged babbling.

I pull my phone out of my pocket.

"Veronica," I stage-whisper as soon as she answers.

"Winter? Why are you whispering?"

"I'm in my bathroom," I rasp out urgently.

"Are you afraid the soap will hear our conversation?"

"No. Hot Daddy is here."

"What!" she yells down the line, and I slap my hand over the phone while frantically clicking the side button to lower the volume.

"He's in the next room. He's taking me on a date. Well, this is, like, part two of our date today. Part three? We've spent the whole day together, and I'm *freaking out.*"

She's silent for so long that I say, "Hello?" and pull the phone from my ear.

She blows her nose with a loud, prolonged honk.

"Jeez, Rons," I say, laughing.

"Winter, I am so proud of you," she says between hiccuping sobs.

I give her a moment. "Veronica, please pull it together. I really need your help."

She sniffs and sighs. "Okay, sister mine. What do you need?"

I switch to FaceTime and hold up the dress. It's a gold wrap dress with long off-the-shoulder sleeves in silky satin. The panels of the skirt bunch at the hip, clipped together with a crystal-encrusted clasp. The collar is low, a V-neck that stops in the middle of my breasts, and the slit up the side will border on obscene with the size of my hips.

I got this dress from an online boutique when an ad popped up on my social feed. I have never worn it.

"I gave him a choice, and he picked this dress."

"That's hot," Veronica says.

"Veronica! Do you not see the problem? My tits and ass will fly out of this dress," I yell-whisper.

I don't think much about my body. After my parents died, I was so disconnected from myself that I felt completely separate from my human form. My therapists told me it was dissociation, and it took a while for me to tap into my senses.

But before my parents died, my mother tried hard to instill a good sense of body image and self-esteem. She told me once shortly before she died that her mother always counted calories and passed that along to my mom.

On top of that, my grandma had mom in pageants from a young age. Mom swore she wouldn't have me in anything like that. Grandma died when I was very young, but she always talked about my mom's naturally dark blonde hair, fair brown skin, and hazel eyes with a strange amount of pride.

Mom was Black, as was her mom and dad. But they always said that the "creole genes" were responsible for Mom's random variation in coloring. More than once, I've heard people say that my mom could "pass," but I didn't understand what that actually meant until I was much older and she was gone.

I think that's why Mom chose to go to an HBCU. To hear Mom tell it, Grandma didn't want Mom to be around Black people, although she would never say anything so crass out loud. Grandma chose to surround herself with people who didn't look like her. Mom said she didn't want me to have that complex, so she made sure I knew and celebrated my culture. I'm a few shades darker than Mom was, and she made it a point to tell me I was beautiful every day.

"I don't see a problem with anything! Except you probably shouldn't wear panties," Veronica says.

"Good thinking, no visible panty lines." I turn to hang the dress on the hook on the back of the door.

"No, so that way if he decides to finger-bang you under the table, he has easy access," she says with complete seriousness. I snap my head around to look over my shoulder at her face on the tiny screen.

"Veronica!" I hiss, super conscious that Hunter is on the other side of the door.

"Don't act all innocent, Little Miss I'm-Gonna-Come-On-A-Tree."

"*Against* a tree, Rons." I cross my eyes and stick my tongue out at her, feeling a sense of giddiness rotate in my belly.

"To-may-toe, to-mah-toe," she says. "Listen, stop making the man wait. Get fresh, get dressed, put on a lil makeup, and stun this man so hard that he forgets his name."

"Veronica, has anyone ever told you you're too much?" I ask.

"Nope! But then my response would be to go find less." She shrugs, and I blow her a kiss before ending the call.

Since the shower is running, I pull my hair into a shower cap and step under the spray. And then for a reason I don't analyze too closely, I shave my legs and tidy up my bikini line, trimming everything super short. Veronica has been harassing me about getting laser hair removal down there, but the thought of some stranger staring at my hoo-ha for several sessions is way too much for me.

I take the quickest shower known to man and rush through an abbreviated skin-care routine. After putting subtle makeup on and twisting my hair into a high bun that I hope looks sexy rather than messy, I stare at the dress.

I'm actually, literally, really about to do this.

I pull on my lingerie, grateful that I have the type of bra that will keep my girls lifted without showing any straps, and I take the dress off the hanger.

Here goes nothing.

I stun myself when I look in the mirror. This is a version of myself that I've rarely, if ever, seen. The sexy, smoky makeup and lashes. My plumped lips. The dress cascading over my breasts and hips. I look hot.

This will definitely draw attention.

I don't know if I want that or not.

I turn to look at my ass and realize I was right about the VPL. I take the panties off and then put lotion on my arms and legs, spending a good amount of time on my heels and between my toes.

With the strappy gold heels on my feet, I breathe deeply and open the goddamn door.

Hunter is looking at his phone, a frown creasing his eyebrows. The look on his face doesn't detract from the fact that there's an absolute god in front of me.

Hunter in a T-shirt and jeans is drool-worthy. But this man, with his broad shoulders, muscular thighs, and *goddamn his arms,* clad in a bespoke suit has me literally mute.

After a few seconds, he looks up from his phone and does a double take.

"I—" he starts to say and then stops. As his silence continues, I start to worry.

"Do you think this dress will work for the restaurant? Maybe it's too showy."

"If you think about taking that dress off and putting anything else on your beautiful body, I will make your ass so red you won't be able to sit down tomorrow."

His words, his voice—so low and growly—do something to me. I should be scared. This man just threatened to hit me. So why do I feel wet between my panty-less thighs?

"Oh…" I say dumbly. "I just don't want to stick out if it's too much."

He walks forward, crowding me where I stand outside the bathroom.

"There's no way you wouldn't stick out anywhere you go."

A niggle of doubt weaves its way through me. He's from a completely different world, one where he can move without thinking about whether he'll be judged for the color of his skin or his level of education or if he speaks perfect English.

Even though my family has worked hard to establish an undeniable place in society, people who look like me have never been welcomed at the table. We've taken a seat, but no one lets us forget that someone else should be sitting there but isn't.

And Hunter, with his wealth and family ties and privilege, is in a place so incredibly distanced from mine that I feel untethered.

I know how to move in white spaces. I know how to move in affluent spaces.

But what am I walking into with him?

The feeling of Hunter's hand on mine brings me out of my thoughts. I look into his eyes and see the depth of his admiration beaming out.

"You are so beautiful," he says. He caresses my cheek.

"So are you," I say, and I want to smack my head.

He smiles, and I notice wrinkles around his eyes for the first time. "You think I'm beautiful, Sunbeam?"

"Yeah," I say. All of my common sense has clearly left the building.

His hand rubs the fabric at my waist, and my brain fizzles and pops. He pulls me close to him, our chests touching.

I press my hands into the fabric of his suit.

He leans down, running his nose up the side of my neck. When he reaches my ear, he whispers, "You smell delicious, Winter."

My legs literally shake, and I become self-conscious about making my dress dirty with my arousal. I should have worn panties, because if I leave a stain on the satin I will die on the spot.

Winter Leigh Vaughan. Cause of death: Mortification by Bodily Fluids.

"Oh, God."

I realize too late that I just said those two simple words out loud.

"No, Sunbeam. It's just me." Then he kisses me.

My whole body feels sensitive—like he could blow on me, and I'd come. I've never, ever felt this with anyone else.

I'm in so much trouble.

I don't care about my lip gloss or that it's getting smudged. His hands roam over my body, and when he grips my ass with both hands, he groans in my mouth. It's the most deliciously masculine sound, and I moan in return.

I gain a little sense when Hunter moves us toward the couch. "No, we'll get all wrinkled," I say. I might be slurring.

"Good thinking, Sunbeam." The side of his mouth kicks up, and I see that the blue part of his eyes is almost gone—edged out by his blown pupils.

He turns us in the other direction, toward the kitchen. "Yes, let's g—" I squeak when he lifts me onto the island in one smooth movement. My hands go to his muscular biceps and holy crap, feeling his muscles bunch under the fabric of his suit jacket is everything.

I'm dizzy.

"Winter." I feel the way he growls my name down to my toes. "Will you let me taste you?" He runs his hand up my spine and to the base of my neck, cradling my skull. His face is so close to mine that it feels like I can hear his heartbeat.

Or maybe that's mine that's racing.

And still, he's waiting for my reply. Patient despite the fire burning in his gaze.

My head lolls back, and I tilt my chin toward him. "Yes, H. Kiss me," I say. I beg.

When I feel him move back, I snap my eyes open. He's removing his jacket, taking a moment to unbutton his wrists.

"Good idea," I say breathily. "Wrinkles. Bad." Clearly forming words are hard.

But then all sense flies out of my brain when he kneels on the floor, his face level with my legs. And my crotch.

Holy hell, I see where this is going. Embarrassment at just how incredibly wet I am and the fact that no one has gotten so closely acquainted with my lady bits in this way has me sitting up straight.

"Oh, God, you don't have to—"

"I told you, baby. You call me H." Then with firm yet gentle hands, he spreads my legs apart. Wetness coats my thighs and trimmed pussy hair.

"No panties," he murmurs. He lands a kiss on my inner thigh, near my knee. "Do you always get this wet?"

I flush, shame coursing through me. I start to close my legs.

A hand to each of my thighs gives me pause. "Do you really want to shut me out?"

He rubs my thighs up and down, and I'm so sensitive, I

whimper. Each pass of his palm tugs on a string directly connected to my cooch.

"You're not going to let me look at the most beautiful cunt I've ever seen in my life?" He runs his finger from my opening up to my clit, and I damn near collapse. "Answer the question, Sunbeam."

"We're going to be late for dinner," I say breathlessly. If he applies an iota more pressure, I'm gonna—

A slap to my thigh has me choking down a strangled shriek. The sound echoes off the walls.

"Answer the question, baby," he says softly. His voice is a caress, followed by sucking kisses up my thighs, closer and closer to my weeping slit.

"No. Yes. I don't know. I don't do this," I say.

He flattens his tongue, licking the crease between my thigh and pussy.

"Don't do what, Sunbeam?"

"I don't have anyone look at me like that. No one except my gynecologist."

He growls again. His eyes are hard, locked on mine.

I'm hyperventilating. I'm going to die right here—legs spread on my kitchen island.

"No one but you, H." I swallow, lust coating every part of my body. "But I think I want that from you."

I feel flushed as the words leave my lips, a burning cast across every inch of my skin.

"You think or you know?" He's leaning back now, his eyes locked on mine but his thumbs pressing into the sensitive skin where my groin meets my upper thighs, rubbing up and down.

"Yes, I want it. I want you to do that to me."

He hums, long and low. "You really shouldn't have told me that, baby."

"W-why?"

"Because I'm gonna make you addicted to me eating you

out morning, noon, and night." And with that, he leans forward and licks me from opening to my clit.

And I'm mortified that with five strokes, I'm screaming his name, my hands involuntarily flying to his hair. When I grasp at the strands, he groans deep, and the vibration makes me shiver.

"Oh, my G-g—" I cut off with a shriek when he slaps my inner thigh again.

I look down at him with my hazy vision, and the teasing arch of his eyebrow makes me want to laugh and cry and moan and come all over him.

He pulls back from me for a moment.

"Not God, Winter," he says with his face against my wet flesh.

I shake my head. "Hun-*ter*," I say on a broken sob.

"Good girl," he growls, and I nearly collapse against the table at the words.

"Oh," I groan on a long breath when he attacks my pussy by sucking my clit into his mouth. But when he presses his finger against my opening, barely breaching me, somehow knowing that I needed more, but not to push me all the way, I come.

I collapse on the island, my head hanging off the opposite end. I'm perplexed at how loud I'm moaning, how my legs are quaking around his head, the soft flesh jiggling.

"Again, Winter," he says, his mouth following me up the island before pulling me back into position with my ass at the edge of the counter. He attacks my clit and pushes his finger in and out, still barely breaching me.

"H, you don't have—" I scream. I fucking scream. Because when he slaps my pussy, my whole sheath contracts around his finger, and he takes the opportunity to curl his finger up.

"I said again, Winter. At least one more." He's whispering against me, his whole face between my legs.

When he suctions my clit in his mouth, sucking and

licking and adding delicious pressure inside me, I do what he wants. I come again.

I come hard, tears springing to my eyes at the fact that I don't feel shame or disgust in this moment like I often do when I orgasm. Even if the feeling has lessened over the years.

I feel powerful. Feminine.

I did that. I brought this powerful man to his knees for me and loved it.

"Hunter." I pant as tears track down my face and leak into my ears. "Please," I say. I don't know what I want him to do. But I plead with him nonetheless.

He peppers kisses on my lower lips, then on my pubic bone, my hips. He leans over me, and through hazy tears, I lock my eyes on his. I'm lying flat on the island and my back protests at the unforgiving granite.

My shaky hands reach toward his face.

He kisses my palm, his eyes fluttering closed. His lips are shiny with my essence.

I reach my other hand toward his belt. "I could—"

He grabs my hand. "No, Winter."

"Why? I need to return the favor."

"First, you don't need to do anything. And two, if you touch my dick right now, I'm going to fuck you. I don't think you're ready for that. And I also don't want to fuck you on a kitchen counter."

I pull my hand back, putting it over my heart.

"What we just did was perfect. That's what I want, Winter." He kisses my other hand.

After a pause, he says, "Still worried?"

The moment is intimate, tender.

"Worried about what?" I echo his tone.

"When you came out of the bathroom, you were worried. I could see it on your face. Has anyone ever told you that you don't have a very good poker face?"

I blush.

"Like right now." He leans down and gives me a chaste kiss on my cheek. "What were you thinking about?" His eyes are clear and trained on me. "Friend. Tell me," he says with a slight smile.

We're friends…and we're lovers.

Lovers.

"I was thinking about how we're planets apart when it comes to our social circles. Our cultures. I was thinking about how we can make this work. If we can make this work."

The honesty shatters the moment. He pulls me back into a sitting position, but before I sit up fully, he tells me to wait and steps into the bathroom. A moment later, he returns with two washcloths and my panties.

He steps between my legs. "Lean back a little, baby," he murmurs.

I comply.

He uses the warm washcloth to clean my arousal off my legs and pussy lips. He pats the area dry with the other towel.

"Do we have to go to dinner?" I whisper, not looking at him. It's not that I don't actually want to go. It's that I'm feeling self-conscious and wrinkled and sensitive. I just want it to be the two of us a little bit longer. Not to sit in a room with a bunch of bougie people.

He helps me put my panties back on and helps me hop down from the island. He leads me to my bed.

"Let's cuddle," he says, surprising the hell out of me.

"No dinner?" I ask.

He toes off his shoes. "While you look so gorgeous, and I want everyone to see you right now, the conversation we're about to have is important, and I want to have it while holding you. Plus, there are forty different apps we can use to order food right to your door." He lays down on the bed and motions for me to join him.

I think about it for a few seconds.

"We'll save Tavalia for another date." He grins.

Do I want to go out and feel awkward, or do I want to stay inside with comfortable clothes pressed against this man?

I'll take door number two. "Okay. Could we get dim sum?"

He smiles broadly. "Absolutely. I love dim sum."

I gasp. "Really?"

He nods.

"It's my favorite food," I say.

He leans over to kiss the back of my hand. "We're fated," he says.

My heart quivers.

I get dressed in an oversized Howard T-shirt and boy shorts. Snagging a wipe, I do a perfunctory job of removing my makeup. I'll do my double-cleanse routine later. After I light an oversized candle, I turn off the lights.

"We're worlds apart, huh?" Hunter says when I'm pressed against his side in the bed. The darkness feels comforting.

"I mean, yeah," I say with a tiny laugh. "You are the definition of the .01 percent, Hunter."

"You wound me, Sunbeam. I support social programs, and I think I should be taxed way more than I am. I'm actually quite liberal."

I gently hit his chest.

"I wouldn't be with you if I thought you were bigoted, H." I'd looked him up as part of my interview prep. He has supported several political initiatives to lower maternal mortality in childbirth, fund Head Start, and promote Universal Healthcare.

"Thank God for that," he says.

"It's just that you were brought up in a completely different reality than I was raised in."

His body tenses at the mention of our childhoods.

"It's not even just about money, even though that's a

mindfuck in itself. Google said you have a hundred-billion-dollar net worth?"

He gives me a significant look. "Don't believe everything you read online." He kisses the top of my head.

"Okay, sure," I drawl. "But it's an issue of culture too. I'm Black—"

"Noooooo!" he says with a grave frown that quickly turns into a grin.

"Hunter, I'm being serious!"

"I'm sorry, you're right." He turns to look at me more fully.

I lay my head on his arm.

"Do you know what it means to be with a Black woman? It's not the same as being with a white woman with a tan," I say. I chew my lip.

"Winter," he says, then he looks to the ceiling, appearing to think. After a moment, he looks at me again. "I think your Blackness is beautiful. Not in a weird, fetish, I-wanna-wear-your-skin kind of way."

I snort.

"I think everything about you, Winter Leigh Vaughan, is beautiful. I've had relationships with women of all colors and nationalities."

I can't help but notice him trip over the word "relationships."

"I know that I, a white man, operate under a certain set of privileges that I have not earned. And it's unfair."

He pulls my lip from between my teeth with his thumb. "Stop distracting me, baby."

I purse my lips before rolling them both between my teeth.

He laughs. "I'll never know what it feels like to be you. I haven't been in your skin or in your family or community. But I promise that I'll learn. I'll try my best. I'll listen to you.

And if you tell me that I'm fucking up in any way, I'll listen so I can fix myself." He kisses me on my forehead, his lips lingering.

"And if anyone in my world treats you with anything less than the utmost respect, I will end them." His eyes glitter in the dim moonlight coming through the big windows.

"Again with the mob talk."

He doesn't say anything. He just kicks the side of his mouth up in a smile.

"I'm not in the mob," he says. The way he ends the sentence makes it seem like there's more to the story.

"Is there a but in there?" I whisper.

"But since we are dating, I feel like you need to know what comes with being with a man like me."

I sit up, turning on the bed to look at him as he reclines. He looks relaxed, unbothered, with one arm behind his head. The way his muscles bunch makes me salivate.

Focus, bitch!

"What *is* it like being with a man like you?" I bring my thumb to my mouth but quickly lower it.

"I'm not in the mob, baby. But my business may or may not have relationships with some nefarious people," he says, unaffected.

I gape at him for a moment. "Nefarious people....So *you* aren't in the mob. But you're—" I search for the right word. "Mob-adjacent?"

He smiles again, letting out a small laugh.

"That's one way to put it." He places his hand on my knee, drawing dizzying circles on my skin with his thumb.

"Are you going to tell me what 'mob-adjacent' means?" I ask, fighting the urge to scoot closer to him so that his hand could go higher on my thigh.

"As I'm sure you can imagine, industries like mine aren't known for their integrity. To get things through and to get anywhere, honestly, it's about who you know. And it's not just other wealthy people. It's powerful people. Sometimes it's dangerous people."

I think about it for a moment. Maybe it makes me a silly bitch, but Hunter telling me that he runs with some rough people causes me to clench my thighs together.

Whoopi Goldberg in *Ghost* pops in my head.

"Am I safe with you?" I ask.

"Very," he replies, and his voice is low, gravely. Serious.

He stands up from the bed suddenly, and I miss his warmth.

"Where are you going?"

Is he leaving?

He starts to unbutton his shirt. When his thick abs are revealed, and he reaches for his belt buckle, he says, "Just getting comfortable for bed."

I can't help it. I ogle him so disrespectfully.

"Has anyone ever told you you're built like the lead singer of Imagine Dragons?"

"Who?" he asks with a laugh.

"The lead singer from—hold on." I grab my phone, tapping over to Google. "This guy."

I show him a picture of a shirtless Dan Reynolds.

He flicks through the Google image results. "Why does he never have a shirt on? Regardless, we look nothing alike. And I don't usually keep a beard," he says.

"I wasn't talking about shoulders up," I say with a laugh. I repress a shiver at the thought of Hunter Brigham with a beard. His face scratching up against—

"Keep looking at me like that, Sunbeam. See what happens," he says. His voice is low, and his eyes are trained on my chest. My nipples poke through the shirt now that they're unbound from their prison.

I pull the blanket up to my chest. "I won't! Scout's honor."

I hold up my hand and he laughs. "That's the Vulcan symbol, baby."

I suck my teeth and flop back on the bed. Still chuckling, he gets under the cover, joining me.

I feel entirely too comfortable pressed against Hunter Brigham's body.

"Let's get dim sum tomorrow," I say with a yawn. Because nothing will make me remove my body from his.

TWENTY
HUNTER

My phone chirps and it wakes me from my sleep. It's the tone I set for Leo. It must be important if he's messaging me at this time of night. I roll to face the nightstand and lower the light on my phone.

> Update. Talk ASAP.

I suppress a hard exhale, not wanting to wake Winter. Pressing the side button to darken the screen, I put my phone back on Winter's nightstand as quietly as I can and roll over to spoon her again.

"Wha'shappening?" she slurs in her sleep.

"Nothing, baby, go back to sleep," I whisper in her ear. I run my hand up and down her arm.

"I love you call me baby," she mutters, and for a second, my breath catches in my chest at "I love you." She means, "I love it when you call me 'baby,'" but for a moment…

What the fuck am I doing here?

I scrub a hand down the side of my face, feeling the prickle of my five o'clock shadow against my palm.

I know why I'm here in Winter's apartment and why we had the most incredible day yesterday.

Winter and I simply go together. She's my person. I think I'm her person too.

That leaves the most fucked-up question of all: what am I doing with Winter when I'm the most unavailable I've ever been?

Blair's face pops up in my mind, standing beside my father.

I hold Winter closer and close my eyes with her scent in my nose.

When I open my eyes again, sunlight ricochets around Winter's apartment. I roll on my back to look at the windows, and the fact that there are no curtains is appalling.

I groan and cover my eyes with my forearm. The sound or the movement causes Winter to stir.

She rolls onto her stomach, slinging her arm around my chest and snuggling into my body.

This presents problem number two. My cock is so hard it hurts.

I don't want to draw attention to my plight, but if she were to look down, she'd get an eyeful. So I pull one of the pillows from beneath my head and put it over my lap.

"Good morning, H," she says, tucking her face into my armpit.

"Good morning to you too. What are you doing?" I ask her, chuckling.

"I, um, morning breath," she says finally, still talking into my armpit.

"Well, I'm sure my armpit doesn't smell any better than your breath. And—" I pull her face up to look at me. "I don't care." I crunch down to kiss her forehead.

She lays her head on my chest, looking up at me. The way the sun frames her face makes her look like an angel.

She kisses my chest, bounces from her bed, and runs to the bathroom.

I sink back into the pillows, arm swung over my eyes again. I'm sending someone out to get her some goddamn blackout curtains today. And to make sure these windows are one-way.

The image of her pressed against the glass while I fuck her from behind pops into my brain. A bead of precum pearls at the tip of my dick.

"Do you mind if I hop in your shower?" I yell out to Winter. It's not that weird, right? We did have an active day.

She doesn't have to know that I'm a stiff breeze away from jizzing on my chest.

She pokes her head out of the bathroom, toothpaste foaming on her lips as she brushes her teeth. "Sure thing," she says, her voice garbled.

I take some deep breaths, willing my dick to go down. I plan on blasting the shower on cold until the damn thing shrivels.

It's not that I don't want to have sex with Winter. It's that I know she's a runner. If she gets scared, she will run away from me, and I don't know that our relationship is at the point where I could reel her back in.

Not that I should reel her back in. If she runs, I should let her go.

"Here are some towels. I put a new toothbrush on the counter. Do you want me to throw your clothes on a quick cycle so you have something clean to put on? I don't mind." Her smile is effervescent, and as she stands before me in her soft shirt and shorts, loose strands of hair curling out of her braids, a boulder shifts in my chest.

She trusts me. She's comfortable with me. And I'm completely lost to her.

"Thanks, Sunbeam. That would be wonderful." When she turns her back to grab my clothes off the floor, I take the towels off the bed and stand up, using them to cover the tent in my briefs.

She turns around just as I'm bundling the towels in front of my crotch and says, "Do you want me to throw those in too?" Her eyes flick down toward the area of my dick, and I see her flush as her eyes pop back up to mine. "I really don't mind," she says, her voice lower.

"You know, that'd be awesome. Let me take them off in the bathroom and toss them out if that's okay?"

Goddamn it, I haven't been this damn awkward around a woman since I was a pimply preteen.

"Yep! Sure!" Her voice is bright, and she turns around again.

Once inside the bathroom, I don't waste time. I brush my teeth, scrubbing them so hard I might draw blood. Then I turn the shower on. Cold. I toss the boxers outside the door with a rushed, "Thanks, Sunbeam," and step directly under the cold stream.

My breath seizes in my chest, and I resist the urge to yelp. After thirty seconds of my self-imposed Arctic plunge, I slowly turn the water temperature to something more tolerable.

At least my erection is gone.

I grab some of Winter's soaps. She has four different kinds, all smelling like flowers. She also has skincare products and gadgets propped in a basket suctioned to the shower wall. Everything is lined up, pristine, the labels all facing at the exact same angle.

I pick up the soap that smells the least like a garden and lather my body when the door opens. I don't dare look over my shoulder.

But when the shower door opens and closes, I drop my head to the tiles.

"Sunbeam, I don't know if you want to be here with me right now."

I feel her body move closer to mine, and she puts her hand on my back.

"I've always wanted to shower with someone," she says. "And I saw that you, erm, you were *awake* this morning, and I thought I could help you out." Her voice shakes a little bit, and I turn to face her, one hand over my growing dick.

I try to ignore the fact that she's completely naked. I put my other hand on her face, forcing her to look at me. "I told you. Let's take it slow. We don't have to do anything." She blinks at me, water beading on her eyelashes, making them clump together.

She leans into me slightly but doesn't touch me.

Then she steals my entire soul when she drops to the floor, settling on her knees.

"I want to taste you, H. Can I taste you like you tasted me?"

I still, my muscles tense. My dick doesn't get the message that we're not coming out to play today, and it lengthens under my hand.

"Sunbeam—*Jesus*!" My head drops back as she bats my hands away, grabs my dick, and leans forward to run her flat tongue up my length from the base to the tip.

"I want to. Please." She looks up at me with so much emotion in her eyes. I can't help but notice the quake in her chin.

"I know you haven't dated, but have you ever done it before?"

A look flashes in her eyes before she says, "I don't know what I'm doing. You'll have to show me." She takes the thick mushroom head of my cock into her wet, warm mouth.

"You're doing an amazing job so far, baby." I widen my stance and tilt the showerhead away from her body. My muscles twitch, but it's not a hundred percent from being wet and cold.

"Tell me what to do, H," she whispers, kissing tentatively along my shaft.

Okay, so we're doing this.

My dick rejoices by twitching in her soft palm.

"Stroke it with one hand. Like this," I take my hand and palm the base of my dick, rotating my wrist up so that it's a tugging, twisting motion.

"Like this?" She mimics my motion, replacing my hand with her own. I bite my lip to not moan like a bitch.

"Y-yeah, that's perfect. If you want to keep doing that alone, that's great, baby. You don't have to put me in your mouth." My eyes feel like they're crossing, so I tilt my head back and close my eyes.

"No." She stops stroking. I look down at her, and she's frowning. "I want to suck it."

My dick jumps at her words. Goddamn, if her saying "I want to suck it" doesn't solidify my place in hell, I don't know what will. There's no way being with her isn't a sin.

"Keep stroking, and then put the tip of me into your mouth and suck and lick. Get me all wet. You can put as much of me in your mouth as you want," I instruct.

She starts stroking my dick again, and the look of concentration on her face concerns me a little, but then the thought flies out of my head when she brings half of my dick into her mouth. And sucks.

My dick is a respectable eight inches, so it's not like I have a third arm down there. But it's thick, and her lips stretch around the girth. The sight is one I will recall on my deathbed.

I put my hands on my hips, not wanting to grab her head. Not wanting to thrust. I want her to take her time and do this at her own pace.

"God, baby, that's such a good job. You're doing such a good job," I say. Thoughts are hard, and the tingling at the base of my spine lets me know that I'm about two seconds away from coming.

The praise does something for her because she gets into sucking me off even more, working her mouth over me and keeping a steady pace as she strokes my cock.

"Pull back, baby," I tell her. I put a hand on her shoulder when she doesn't let up. I try to not grip her too hard. "Baby, I'm gonna come in your mouth in a second if you don't pull back."

Her eyes flick toward mine, and goddamn if she doesn't suck harder. She moans and I nearly die on the spot when I see her spread her legs wide on her knees, one hand massaging her spectacular pussy. That's all it takes for me to blow in her mouth. I groan this time, and it's loud against the tiled shower stall.

"Fuck, Winter," I grind out. My muscles tense at the force of my orgasm. My hand is still on her shoulder.

When I come to myself, I see that she's swallowed the mouthful of cum. And she's waiting on her knees, an unsure look in her eyes. She bites her lip.

"Was that okay?" she whispers.

Our gazes are stuck together, magnetized to the other. And just like last night, a wealth of emotions cross her face.

Something in my chest breaks. Because it's at that moment that I know that it's not just that she's scared of this intimacy brewing between us. She's scared of sex, period.

"Baby," I say when I pull her to stand. I wrap her in my arms, and she puts her head on my chest. "You did perfectly."

I feel her smile.

Once we lather up and rinse off, sharing goofy smiles in the mirror when we exit the stall, she pulls a robe on while I wrap a clean towel around my waist.

"There's coffee there if you want it," she says, pointing to the pot next to the stove. She's wrapped her hair in what looks like a T-shirt, and she pads over to the washing machine hidden in an alcove behind a set of folding doors.

As the droplets of water dry on my skin, I allow myself to analyze this serene moment. Watching the curve of her back, her delicate neck, I feel a wave of panic wash over me at the thought of something happening to her.

Of her being harmed by this shit with Blair and Morris and my father.

She looks at me over her shoulder, jerking when our gazes meet.

"What?" she asks with a laugh.

This one is yours.

I'm never letting her go.

I watch her ass jiggle as she takes the tiny load and moves it over to the dryer.

She jumps when I'm right behind her. "H! You scared me," she says, trying to turn.

"Did you ever sit on the dryer when you were younger to make your pussy feel good?" My body is pressed against hers, my front to her back. I ghost my nose up the side of her neck.

She blushes. "No, of course not!" She glances away from me.

"Well, today is a day of firsts, then." And then I sit her on the dryer and eat my breakfast.

"AH, brother. Doing the walk of shame, I see." Ella leans against the doorjamb at the front of Amelia Manor. She smiles as I approach, and I toss my keys to one of the guys who will park my car in the garage at the back of the property.

"Not a drop of shame here, Ellie."

She rolls her eyes as I push past her to enter the home. I

drop my flight bag over the back of one of the living room chairs and keep walking.

My first order of business is to find Leo. I called him on the drive over, and he started talking in code.

I find him already in my office.

"What's the latest," I say to him.

"There's finally proof," he whispers.

"Be specific. Proof of what?" He arches his eyebrow at my tone and pulls his phone from his pocket.

"Sit down. You'll want to once you watch this."

I take his phone to my side of the desk, a video pulled up already.

I sit and press play.

My father looks as regal as he should, given his status. He's dressed in a three-piece dark gray suit, and I notice the backdrop of palm trees. He's on Isla Cara.

The camera captures him right in the center, but it looks like the novice videographer hides behind some type of gauzy material. Things are hazy, but I can still see so much. At my father's feet are a dozen naked bodies—chained together but silent.

He snaps his finger, and the form closest to him shifts. A woman. A girl.

A young—too young—girl.

Blonde hair like sun rays.

The girl bows at his feet. Her head is so low her torso almost touches the floor. I can feel the coldness of the tiles just as sharply as if I were there.

He pulls the girl up to her knees by her hair. He unzips his pants, fishing his dick out.

"Suck," he says. I fight down bile as I see the next part. I look away.

A few minutes later, he finishes, and I glance back to the phone. She's buttoning him up, and he pats her head.

Like she's a dog.

And then the camera goes black.

Leo and I sit in silence for several minutes. Finally, I clear my throat and look at him.

"What do we do with this, Leo?" My throat is dry, and the high I rode when I left Winter's house this morning is gone.

My father is a pedophile. A rapist. A human trafficker. And he gets away with all of it because he has money.

Blood money.

For not the first time, I want to give everything away—anything that isn't earned from BwP.

And even that…

"FBI?" Leo asks and I flinch.

"You know how that will work out," I reply. He closes his eyes against my words in a long blink.

"Why do people connect themselves with him? It's because they know he's powerful and can protect them if something were to go south. So this video isn't gonna do shit to sway people to turn against him. We have to control them by instilling fear," I say. Even if we manage to off my father, people will run scared, searching for someone to cover their sins.

"We can't make a move right now. I wonder if he knew this was being filmed," Leo says.

"There's a strict no electronic device rule on Isla Cara. When people arrive from the boat, all of them are confiscated and kept in a safe off-property." I sink further into my chair, spinning the now-locked phone between my fingers.

"So the question begs, how did they get a camera in there, for what reason, and—"

"Why did they send it to you?" I add.

"That's the biggest question. I have no idea who sent it or from where. Max is working on tracing everything, but even he was confused."

I raise my eyebrows. I don't know who could if Max can't track it down.

"This all smells. It feels like a trap, Leo."

"You're probably right," he says. "But still, what do we do with this information?"

I drop my head against the headrest. I'm now in possession of child abuse material. It's supposed to be used as evidence against my father—something to leverage.

"Trace it and lock it down. It's time to get in touch with Misha Hroshko again."

Leo leans back in his chair.

"This is bigger than us at this point. And honestly, if we're going to bring him down, it needs to be now."

Leo sighs as if the weight of the world is on his shoulders.

"Fuck! Why couldn't your dad just be a guy who fucks his secretaries?" He runs a hand down his face, and I chuckle.

"Oh, to be so lucky," I say.

TWENTY-ONE
WINTER

By the time Tuesday rolls around, I'm a mess.

I'm a mess not only because we got a random bout of continuous icy rain yesterday, forcing Kitty and I to stay indoors. Or because staying inside wouldn't have bothered me two months ago, but now it feels suffocating.

I'm a mess because the few days consisted of me falling in love with Hunter Brigham.

I'm aware that sounds crazy. And I know that I've never been in love at my big age of thirty years old, so how would I know?

But I know I'm two steps away from the edge of falling head over feet in love with H.

We text and talk on the phone all the time now. We talk about our pasts, likes, dislikes, and love for August. It feels good to have the space to think about what I say to him and his messages to me. In the relative safety of my apartment, I can smile and laugh and occasionally hop around the kitchen at something adorable that he says.

What can I say? I'm making up for lost time.

Or maybe you're being very naive and are about to get your heart pulverized.

My phone pings on the bathroom counter as I style my hair and do my makeup. I've chosen a white square neck blouse that highlights my cleavage and wide-leg wool pants in a burnt orange color. It'll pair nicely with my tan knee-length wool coat. My gold watch and dangly gold earrings to match finish off the outfit. Casual and comfortable enough to handle the frigid temps, professional enough for therapy, and sexy enough that if he decides to pin me against a wall and ravish me, he won't have much to fuss with.

Who even are you, Winter?

I pick up my phone.

I can't wait to see you. Just an hour until you're here.

I smile wide.

Me neither.

Cancel your Uber.

Why?

I have a ride waiting for you downstairs.

I raise an eyebrow. Ready to go anyway, I put on my coat and make quick work of harnessing Kitty. I got him a long-sleeved Christmas-themed sweater to wear and matching booties to protect his feet from the cold ground. Grabbing my bags, we head out the door. When I reach the lobby, I immediately notice the shiny G-wagon idling outside the automatic doors of my apartment building.

A man I've seen at Amelia Manor waits for me.

"I assume you're here for me?" I ask as if the sign he's holding wouldn't be enough notice. I shake my head and text Hunter.

You are too much, H.

The man opens the door, and I slide into the back of the car.

I want to make sure you arrive safely. No more Ubers for you.

I roll my eyes.

Okay, Dad.

It's never really been my thing, but if you wanna call me Daddy, I wouldn't object.

I laugh, and the man in the driver's seat glances back at me.

I'll see you in a bit, baby.

"What's your name?" I ask the driver.

"Mario, but everyone calls me Rio, ma'am," he replies.

"Oof, ma'am. Please call me Winter."

Rio looks to be in his late thirties, maybe a little older, but not by much. He's tall and has a lean build, but he looks like he could more than hold his own in a fight. He's dressed in all black, just like I've seen the other security staff wear around Amelia Manor.

"Yes, ma'am," he says, and I chuckle.

We drive a bit before I realize I entered the vehicle without completing my ritual. And I didn't count the steps on the way down. Nor did I complete my ritual of locking my front door over and over.

The realization doesn't cause me overwhelming anxiety. And that in itself is mind-boggling. I pet Kitty's fur to ground myself against the revelation. I don't feel the compulsion to have Rio turn around so I can lock my door again. Nor do I want him to stop so I can check the tires.

I just want to get to Amelia Manor.

Wait until I tell Genevieve about this.

We pass the ride in a comfortable silence, and before I know it, we're pulling up to the estate.

Murder hornets, rather than butterflies, take up residence in my belly.

Standing at the front entrance wrapped in a wool coat and a dark gray scarf is the person I long to see. H.

When I exit the car, he nods to Rio and waits for him to drive off before grabbing my hand and bringing me closer to him. I look around to make sure we're alone, and he gently grabs my chin, forcing my eyes on him.

His gaze is soft. "Hey," he says.

I smile. I breathe. "Hey," I say in reply.

Still holding my chin, he brings his head down to mine and kisses me.

If anyone else were looking at the scene, they'd likely say it was a tame kiss. But for me, it was anything but.

Even though his lips are gentle on mine, the riot of emotions the simple action evokes causes me to skip toward that precipice gleefully. And when he ends the kiss and puts his forehead on mine, holding me close as if I'm important to him, I swan-dive over the edge.

My heart is gone—packaged up and hand-delivered to none other than Hunter Brigham.

I step back, reluctant to part but needing to add some space.

"You know I'm here to work, Hunter," I say with mock annoyance.

He smiles even brighter.

"I know," he says. "I'd like to join you for the session with August if that's okay."

Now it's my turn to beam.

"Of course, but only if it's okay with August," I reply. Hunter has attended a few of our sessions in the past, but it's been tough to get August to be as open when his father is there as he is when we're alone.

"I'll see you inside." I move around him to enter the house but stop short when I spy Ella's face pressed against the glass.

"Oh, shit," I say and jump when I feel Hunter's hands on my shoulders behind me. He sees her, and Ella waves through the glass front door.

"Well, we *are* out here for everyone to see. Might as well let them see, right?" Hunter says, and I whirl around on him.

"Hunter, this could be bad if people found out. We talked about this. We can't be out officially until after August's therapy is done or I reach the end of my practicum."

"I won't tell anyone!" a voice pipes up. Ella's head sticks out a crack in the front door. She's smiling from ear to ear, and I look up at Hunter in time to see him roll his eyes.

"Ella. Discretion, please," he says. She pops her bubble gum in reply.

Shaking myself, I step around them to find August. I locate him in the game room. He's playing the game I brought and, from the looks of it, dominating it.

"Wow, you've gotten up there, Augs."

August doesn't take his eyes off the screen but takes his right hand to tap the quick-fire button for "thanks" without looking.

I sit in the gaming chair beside him and wait until he finishes the current level. Kitty goes to his usual spot. He knows when we're in this room, he's off duty. He takes his chew toy, and I grin when it starts squeaking rhythmically.

August puts the controller down without my asking and picks up his tablet.

"How was your weekend?" he asks, and my eyebrows shoot up, caught a little off guard. August rarely asks about my day or anything like that. Those types of details aren't usually very important to him.

"It was good. Restful, with all the rain we got."

"Yes, that is how I was able to get up to level fifty-eight," he says. "I was hoping we could do something."

I sit up straighter in the chair, curious about his sudden shift in topic. "Oh? What do you have in mind?"

He taps his cheek for a few seconds, his face a mask of concentration, before tapping on his tablet.

"I was hoping we could make pizza. But not pre-made pizza. We could go get the dough and sauce and toppings."

"Sure, August. That sounds cool. Why do you want to make pizza, though?"

He looks away from the tablet, tapping his cheek again.

"My mom and I used to make homemade pizza together."

I don't say anything to that, waiting for him to add more. When he doesn't, I ask, "How often did you make pizza with her?"

"A few times a month, usually on Fridays." He pauses. "When Mom found foods I liked to eat, we tended to eat them a lot. Pizza was always fun to make, and she said it felt fancy to spin the dough in the air like in the movies."

I smile at him. He puts his tablet down.

"Can I come?" Hunter's subdued voice comes from the doorway of the game room. He stands there in obvious discomfort, moving from crossing his arms to putting them in his pockets and then back to crossing his arms.

August looks in his general direction before tapping his cheek several times. He turns to me.

"Would that be okay, August? If Hunter joins?" I keep my face friendly and open.

"I would really love to make pizza with you, August." I glance past August to where Hunter stands in the doorway. Hunter's face is open, emotions plainly warring on his face. But as the seconds tick on without a reply from August, Hunter's face smooths, his mask up again.

Oh, Hunter. You have to stay open, love.

August doesn't say anything right away. He turns his head in Hunter's direction and then back to mine. Finally, his gaze returns to the screen in front of him, and he blinks. After a full minute, he picks up his tablet and says, "Bring your wallet."

Hunter grins.

WE PULL into the parking lot of the Wegmans just as the clouds roll in. The weather forecast doesn't call for rain until later today, but it's already getting dark with heavy cloud cover. It's unseasonably warm at ten degrees above freezing, which saves us from the risk of sleet and freezing rain.

August instructed us to go to Wegmans, and only Wegmans, because that's where he'd go with his mom. He further demanded we go to *his* Wegmans back in Woodbridge. I think the long drive did us some good.

The trip was quiet, but not tense. Kitty sat in the back with August. He indicated interest in Kitty a few months ago. He told me he'd always wanted a dog, but his mother didn't like them. When I explained that Kitty is a service dog, he found the training process fascinating.

At the next session, he educated me on the topic of psychiatric service animals for a solid hour.

"Do you have the list, Augs?" I look in the back seat

toward August. He's tapping away on his tablet and finally says, "Yes. We need flour, yeast, oil, tomato sauce, mozzarella, and pepperoni."

August's hand returns to Kitty's fur, petting him around the harness he makes quick work of putting on.

Kitty smiles happily.

"Easy enough," Hunter says. His eyes fix on August's reflection in the mirror. I don't think August notices.

August opens the door to exit, and we all follow him.

Outside the store, a man dressed in a baggy Santa suit rings a bell next to a donation bucket. When people walk past, he wishes them a Merry Christmas.

I search my bag for some spare change, but hear the man exclaim, "Thank you, sir! Merry Christmas!" When I glance up, Hunter slips a folded bill into the can.

"Don't mention it," Hunter says in a gruff voice. He turns to find me, and something in my expression causes a strange look to pass over his face. His cheeks turn pink, and I'm not totally sure it's from the cold.

I drop the quarters I found at the bottom of my bag in the can, and we walk inside.

"Do you want fresh pepperoni from the deli, August?" Hunter asks him while grabbing a small cart. August hands me Kitty's leash.

"No. We need the Hormel stuff."

Hunter and I look at each other. "Okay, sounds good," Hunter says.

The store is in full Christmas mode, and I feel a slight pang of concern that Christmas is almost three weeks away. I usually spend the holiday with Veronica—whether it's with her parents or alone in her townhome with James. But Veronica's parents are sailing around the globe right now as part of their retirement plan, and James is taking Veronica on a babymoon to a cabin for the holiday. I don't know what my Christmas plans are this year.

I stare at the back of Hunter's head. Hunter shouldn't factor at all into my plans, right?

Right.

Bing Crosby plays over the speakers, an old-timey Christmas carol. When we walk past the seasonal aisle, everything smells like cinnamon and cloves.

August waves a hand in front of his face, clearly displeased with the scent. Eventually, he skips down the aisle to get away from the olfactory assault.

As we follow August through the aisles, he picks up ingredient after ingredient with impressive efficiency. We're done shopping in ten minutes.

Hopping into a checkout line, we have everything loaded up on the belt when August says, "We forgot the active yeast!"

He slaps his head, vocalizing his upset, and Hunter gently grabs his arm, attempting to hold his hand.

The move must shock August, because he immediately stills. His face and body show signs of obvious distress, but I'll have to ask him later how he feels about the handholding.

"It's okay, I'll get it, August," Hunter says brightly.

August tugs his arm, and Hunter releases his hand.

Hunter's brows lower a fraction, but he's quick to correct his look. "Be right back," Hunter says in a calm tone.

"No, Hunter, you stay." I give him a significant look. "You stay here with August." He nods.

Picking up Kitty in a football hold and twirling around, I make a beeline for the aisle with the yeast. Spotting it, I reach for a packet on the top shelf. I snag it with my free hand and spin back around, bumping into a man.

I move around him and take a few steps down the aisle, saying, "Sorry!" but when I turn to face him, the words die in my throat.

The man's back is toward me, his head turned to watch my retreat over his shoulder. I only see half of his face—most obscured by his hood. But his eyes. The shape of them, the malevolent intent in his gaze…I know.

Adam.

It's only a glimpse, but it's Adam.

The man turns away and walks down the aisle as if nothing happened, and I stay there, rooted. Frozen.

You've got to move, Winter!

Kitty whimpers, wriggling in my arms to lick my cheek. I ignore his movements.

I jump and run to the checkout line.

August and Hunter have the items on the belt and are waiting for me. Hunter gives me a concerned look when I reach them.

I'm shaking.

"H-here," I say, throwing the packet on the conveyor belt and clutching Kitty to my chest so hard he yelps.

I don't know what to do with my body, and I don't realize that my teeth are chattering until Hunter's face materializes in front of me.

"Winter, what's going on?" His eyebrows are drawn down over his eyes. He puts a hand on my arm, and I jump back, knocking into the magazine display.

Glossy pages and chip bags fall to the floor.

"I'm sorry!"

Adam is in prison. Adam is in prison. Adam is in prison in prison in prison in prison—ADAMISHERE.

Inhalation is impossible with the constriction in my lungs, even though I'm starved for air. My vision tilts, and everything looks stretched and warbled. I can't focus. I can't orient myself in space. My tongue swells, blocking off my throat. Every scar on my body sears with remembrance.

"I'm so sorry. I'm so sorry," I yell. Or maybe I whisper. All I know is one second, I'm staring at Hunter as August paces with the grocery bags in his hand, and the next, I'm in front of Hunter's car with Kitty licking at my cheek.

Fat raindrops smack against my chilled skin.

"Breathe, Winter." Hunter's voice goes in and out. The car doors are open, and the engine idles while we all stand outside the vehicle.

I try to suck in a breath, but it feels like a band is tightening across my chest.

ADAMISHERE.

ADAMISHERE.

ADAMISHERE.

I bend over at the knees, dropping Kitty, unsure if I'm going to vomit or scream. I clutch my head, trying to calm my racing thoughts.

ADAM IS HERE. *Suck in air.*

Adam is in prison. *Exhale air.*

ADAM IS HERE. *Suck in air.*

You don't know that you saw him. Adam is in prison. *Exhale air.*

Adam is here. *Inhale air.*

Adam is in prison. *Exhale air.*

Adam is in prison. *Breathe.*

Adam is in prison. *Release.*

My hands shake as the adrenaline merges into mortification. I don't want to look at either of them. I'd rather die than look at either of them.

I plop myself on the cement bumper in front of Hunter's Mercedes, covering my face with my arms as I prop them on my bent knees. Kitty tries to wedge himself into my lap but fails, so he settles in front of me between my slightly spread legs.

I feel Hunter move and hear the sound of doors shutting. A moment later, a blanket covers my shoulders, and mercifully, the drizzle stops pelting me. I see Hunter standing over me with an umbrella from the cracks between my arms.

"You don't have to tell me what just happened right now,

Winter," he says. He looks around the parking lot. His eyes are narrowed, assessing.

I'm so embarrassed.

"But something here set you off. And I want to get you to a place where you feel safe. So will you get in the car? Or do you need a few more minutes? I'm good here either way."

I clear my throat. "I'm sorry," I say. My voice sounds strange in my ears.

"I…I have panic attacks sometimes. I haven't had a full-blown one in a long time, and I guess today was the day to end my streak." I try to go for a self-deprecating tone, but it just ends up sounding sad.

A sob breaks out of my throat. I lower my arms and look at him. At my movement, he looks down at me, and instead of a look of disgust, he's looking at me softly.

I cry harder.

"Sunbeam," he says softly. "Let's go home." He reaches a hand to me, and I take it.

Kitty stands too, staying close to my heel.

Instead of pulling me toward the passenger seat, Hunter holds my hand and asks, "Is it okay if I hug you?"

I nod.

Without a word, he pulls me into his arms, one hand still holding the umbrella. Protecting us from the elements.

I bury my face into his chest.

He doesn't say anything. He just holds me as the rain falls.

TWENTY-TWO
HUNTER

I'd think she were asleep if it weren't for her iron grip on my hand while I drive.

My brain centers on the reality I've been avoiding for several days. The reality that I'm supposed to marry Blair Winthrope in a few months, but I'm in love with Winter.

I can admit it to myself now.

I'd laugh if it weren't so incredibly fucked-up.

I glance at the side of her face and note the restless tick of her jaw. Kitty lay in her lap, eyes closed. When we got in the car, she told me she needed to take an anti-anxiety pill she'd been prescribed, so I gave her a water bottle.

Now she's in a strange in-between state.

There's only one thing to do in this situation—I have to get out of this mess with my father and Blair, and I need to do it immediately. Like, now. I just don't know how the hell I'm going to accomplish that. At least, how I'm going to achieve that and keep BwP, August, and the rest of us safe.

I need Misha Hroshko to get in contact with us. For all his energy around connecting with Leo and me all those months ago, he's annoyingly silent. I can't take down my father on my own. That's asking for all of us to get slaughtered. We're playing chess here, but circumstances force me to play checkers. Not even checkers. It's like I'm playing a game of jacks.

A headache starts to form, throbbing in my temples.

August pipes up from the back seat, "Are you and Winter in a romantic relationship?"

I glance at him in the rearview mirror, unsure how to answer that question. I want to be honest with him because lying to him will only cause more strife in our relationship. But I also don't want him to think I'm hanging around him only because Winter is there.

I finally decide to be honest with him. "Yes, we are dating."

I listen for the sound of his fingers on the tablet screen in response.

"Does that bother you?"

I risk a glance in the rearview mirror again, and he taps his cheek as he looks out the window. We eat up miles of interstate before he says, "I like Winter. She is kind." He picks his hand up from the tablet, flicks his fingers a few times, then resumes typing.

"Just do not mess her up like you did my mom."

I close my eyes in a long blink. Opening them, I catch his eyes again and say, "I won't." I look at the side of Winter's face. "I promise."

August doesn't say anything else. He pulls his headphones out of the seat pocket in front of him and tunes me out for the rest of the ride.

When we arrive, Winter is still dozing. August hops out of the car—literally—as soon as we get the garage door closed. Winter blinks at me sleepily when I rub her shoulder to wake her. Her expression is flat. The happy, joking Winter I know and love isn't there.

Love.

I focus back on Winter's face.

"Why don't you nap in my bed," I say.

She nods and exits the car robotically, Kitty following her steps.

I need to know what's wrong. I need her to tell me what happened in the store. I don't believe that she just slipped into a panic attack randomly, even though that does happen from what I've learned about anxiety disorders over the past several weeks.

My gut tells me that something specific set her off, triggered her. I need to know what it is.

Winter stands in the entryway of the garage, waiting for me. I take her cold hand and lead her up the back staircase to my bedroom.

Neither of us takes time to inspect the suite, even though it's her first time here. I simply lead her to the bed.

She takes off her shoes and rolls under the covers without saying a word to me. Kitty settles into her side.

Her body is still; her eyes shut. Nothing disrupts her static position except the gentle up and down of her breathing.

Kitty presses deeper into her side and cocks his head to give me a look.

"I don't like it either, Kitty," I whisper.

He whimpers in reply, putting his head down on his paws. I resist petting him solely because he is on duty right now supporting Winter.

I lean over and place a gentle kiss on her temple. She doesn't move.

"Rest, Sunbeam," I say.

Looking back at Kitty, I say, "Look after our girl."

When he huffs, I finally feel like I can exit the room.

I'm three steps down the hallway when I hear a pointed hiss. "What the hell did you do to Winter? I swear to God, if you mess with her head, I will put Nair in your conditioner."

I stop and sigh, not turning to look at Ella.

"I didn't do anything to her, Ella," I say over my shoulder, then I continue my stride down to my office. I need to do something I should have done long ago: read the file on Winter Leigh Vaughan.

"Really," she deadpans. "That's why she was laughing and kissing you four hours ago, and now she's catatonic?"

I grab the file from my desk drawer and sit down to open it.

In it is a picture of Winter. It looks like a candid shot of her on a walk. Kitty is in the frame—his leash in one of her hands and a water bottle is in the other.

I move to the first page of text and read her family history. I remember when her mother, U.S. Representative Katherine Vaughan, died with her husband in a car crash almost two decades ago.

She couldn't have been more than a kid. Not even a teenager when that happened.

I stop reading when Ella's tiny hand slaps over the pages. Her long black nails score the paper.

"May I have your attention, *please,*" she growls.

"Ella, sometimes I really wish you'd mind your business," I say, pinching the bridge of my nose.

"Mind my business? Well, how about this business, seeing as it pertains to our family. You're getting married?" Her words are so full of rage, I struggle to keep my eyes open to face it head on.

"Ella, there are things you don't understand."

"Don't patronize me. Answer the damn question. Are you getting married?"

"On paper, yes." Maybe. Hopefully not. My throat feels tight.

"On pa— What *the fuck* does that even mean? What. Are. You. Doing. Hunter? What did you do to Winter?" I've never seen hostility like this in my sister's eyes. Her whole face flushes, blotches of red fusing together on her skin, moving up to her ears.

In a perfect world, I could tell Ella what's going on. I'd be able to confide in her that our father is a monster and all the fucked-up shit he's doing. All the fucked-up shit he has done. What he'll do if I don't comply, and how I'm going to make this all right.

But the words die in my throat.

I lean back in my chair. "Ella, I don't know what to tell you. I wish I could explain more, but just know it's a..." I search for the right wording. "It's a business situation."

"What the fuck," she whispers, enunciating every word and looking away from me.

"As for Winter, I didn't do anything to her. I promise you. At the grocery store, she stepped out of line to get an item we forgot. When she came back, she was in full panic mode. I wasn't going to harass her with questions right as she's coming down from hyperventilating," I say pointedly.

Ella stands up straight. "Fair enough. It's just—" She looks away from me and down to the floor. After a moment, she looks at me again. "It's important to me that August gets what he needs. I believe that Winter is the person to offer that help. And I don't want you screwing things up so she leaves. Plus, she's a nice person. A good person. She doesn't deserve to be hurt. As for you getting married, can I just say how fucked it is that you're obviously stringing Winter along?"

"I'm not trying to string her along or mess up with her, Ella. I have no intention of doing that ever," I say.

"Ever?" Her eyebrows are in her hairline.

"Ever." We stare at each other, a face-off. "Just trust me," I say.

She looks at me for a long moment, then says, "I'm in the goddamn *Twilight Zone*."

Throwing her hands up, she steps back toward the door. Opening it, she says, "Make this make sense, Hunter. Because none of this shit does." Then she leaves, slamming the door with her departure.

I dive deep into Winter's information, moving along to

learn about Mr. and Mrs. Lance, Veronica, and Veronica's husband, James.

I frown when I read all the shady shit James Palmer's involved with but set it aside for now. Not my circus.

Twenty minutes pass when a scream echoes through the house. I'm up in an instant and running toward it.

"Please! I'm sorry!" I'm at my doorway and see Winter thrashing in the bed. Kitty barks in short yips, trying to jump back up onto the bed. It looks like Winter might have kicked him to the floor with her uncontrolled movements.

I take a step closer to the bed. Her eyes are wide open, unfocused. She's dreaming.

Or rather, she's trapped in a nightmare.

"Please, Adam, stop! Don't!" She's sobbing, slamming her fists down on the bed over and over. She flings her arm over her head, hitting her hand on the wooden nightstand. She screams, and I do the only thing I know to do.

I pull her into my arms.

"No!" she screeches in my ear. She swings wildly, her hands scratching at my face.

Kitty yips, finally making it back on the bed and jumping on Winter's chest, but she pushes him off and rolls away from me, curling into a trembling ball. Kitty moves to put his face in the crook of her shoulder, but Winter pushes him away again, and he half-tumbles, half-hops from the bed.

Spinning in a circle, Kitty whines and shoots under the bed.

Stepping back, I say her name as loud as possible. "Winter! Winter, wake up, you're dreaming." I repeat her name a few more times until her body stills. She sinks back into her pillow, screwing her eyes shut. After a few deep breaths, she opens her eyes again.

She doesn't look at me when she says, "I hurt you just then. Didn't I?" Tears track down her face as she stares at the ceiling.

I cross the room slowly to flick on the fireplace. It's cold in here. I should have made it warmer for her. More comfortable. Maybe she wouldn't have had a nightmare just then.

Stop. Focus on Winter.

I turn away from the flame but continue moving slowly so I don't spook her in her fragile state.

"You got a few hits in," I say. I smile to let her know it's okay, even though she's not looking at me.

She closes her eyes again, and more tears roll down her cheeks. I sit back on the edge of the bed. She doesn't move away. That's progress, I suppose.

"You didn't hurt me too bad, though." My hand lands on the comforter right next to hers.

"I'm so, so sorry," she says. Hiccups break the words up, and she turns her head away from me.

Slowly, I take my pinky and run it against the side of her hand. Her breathing stops, but she doesn't move away.

I add another finger and then one more until my hand rests on top of hers.

"Winter, look at me, please."

I wait patiently for her to turn her head.

She does, but her eyes don't open until several seconds later. They're swollen and red-rimmed, and her nose matches the color.

"I can take it. I've had much worse." I give her a slight smile.

Her lips part.

"You can stay here as long as you want because you have a place here," I say. *With me,* is what I don't say.

"Today has been…" she sniffs and purses her lips in thought. "A rough day," she finishes.

I rub circles on the back of her hand.

"I know," I say. "That's why you're going to tell me what happened."

TWENTY-THREE
WINTER

"Tell me what happened," he repeats, settling more on the bed.

His eyes blaze like the fire in the hearth, and I feel more heat coming from his body next to mine than from the fireplace.

Everything in my body tells me to lean into him—to trust what I've learned about him.

How he cares about his son.

How he caught me in the grocery store. The tender touches and quiet care he's shown me every day…even when it feels like he's as unsure what to do with the feelings developing between us as I am.

Yet still, I curl in on myself, pulling my hand from beneath his. "It doesn't matter what happened. I got triggered by some old shit. It was so long ago, and I—"

"Winter," he says gently, cutting me off. He reaches out and wraps his hand around mine. I realize I'm biting my nails. The taste of blood registers on my tongue. I don't need to look down to know that I've bitten them to the quick again.

With cautious movements, he lets go of my hand.

I give him a bewildered look when he kneels on the floor.

When I hear him make kissing sounds and pat the soft rug beneath the bed, I realize he's coaxing Kitty out of the hiding place he's found.

When Kitty appears, Hunter stands with him, giving him reassuring rubs on his ears and belly. After a moment, he places my dog back on my lap. Kitty wastes no time hopping up to place his body against my chest, resting his head on my shoulder.

"I'm sorry, Kitty," I whisper into his fur. I don't want to look at Hunter.

I'm embarrassed and angry and…wounded.

"I haven't had a night terror like that in years."

I pause to search my memory. The last one was the day Veronica moved for college. The nightmare kicked off a three-day period of sleeplessness. Staying awake for seventy-two hours contributed to all the stuff that happened later.

"It's been a really long time. I don't think Kitty's ever seen me have one," I say with a chuckle. It's devoid of all humor.

I gather the courage to look at Hunter, to assess his face, even if looking him in the eye is impossible.

When my eyes land on his chin, I see his lips are quirked slightly to the side. It's a soft look.

"Winter, I'm going to sit over there," Hunter points to the wingback chair in the corner of the room near the fireplace, "and I want you to tell me everything. I want to know everything about you. And based on your reaction at the store, I know there's more to your story. Something threatens you, and I won't tolerate you being threatened."

He's standing over me, but I don't feel intimidated by him. Still, I avert my gaze.

I'm quiet and take a moment to glance around Hunter's room. The Xanax I took a few hours ago is still heavy in my system, but I still take note of the massive space. The ceilings soar at least twenty feet, and the walls are painted a forest green except for the exposed red brick wall shared by the fireplace. The king-sized bed beneath me is bigger than the average mattress, and I'm surprised his sheets and comforter are white. There's a camel-colored duvet thrown at the foot of the bed.

Hunter grabs a glass from the side table near the fireplace and presses on a panel near the set up. Camouflaged in the wall is a fancy drink fridge, and Hunter pulls out a glass bottle of water. He pours some in a glass and hands it to me before sitting on the fabric-covered chair. The gas fireplace runs. I still don't feel warm.

"I know it will take a lot to earn your full trust, Sunbeam. But I want you to know I'm here to carry your secrets and hurt. I want all of it."

He stretches a leg out in front of him, leans back into his seat, and looks at me. Waiting.

At the certainty in his words, I feel the pain in my throat unravel.

"Why do you call me Sunbeam?" I question.

He smiles and doesn't answer for a long moment.

"Because you glow like the sun. That was my first thought when I saw you in my foyer." His mouth quirks up in a rueful smile.

I find myself smiling back, but I feel lost when the smile falls from my face.

"It's *a lot,* H."

"That's okay, Winter. *I* am a lot." He traces the pattern on the arm of the chair in slow movements. "Tell me."

I breathe in and out and close my eyes. When I open them, my gaze immediately collides with his.

You can trust him. Telling the truth will not hurt you.

"My parents' car accident was on the New Jersey Turnpike. They were driving home from a weekend in New York —The Hamptons. A semi lost control in the rain and ran right into them. They died on impact and were both flung from the car."

Hunter simply says, "I remember the news when your mother died."

"It was all on CNN and MSNBC. Up until then, she was getting ready to run for the Senate, but then, she died. All these paparazzi were trying to take pictures of me coming out of school, and it was…it was a terrible time in my life."

"That does sound like a terrible time. More than enough to traumatize someone, especially a young child."

I swallow, feeling the searing tingle in my sinuses that tells me tears are imminent.

"What else happened, Winter?"

I take a large gulp of water.

"I was sent to live with my father's sister and her husband. My mom was an only child, and her parents died when I was really little. My other grandparents were too old to care for a kid. They were in their eighties when my mom and dad died," I say.

"I was sent to live with my aunt Margurite and uncle Louis. They lived in Bethesda but decided to move into my parents' house to keep things consistent for me. So they sold their house in Bethesda and moved into my parents' house in Arlington…along with their son, Adam."

I look down at the glass again and am dismayed to learn it's empty. When I glance at the oversized glass water bottle, Hunter follows my eyes. Slowly, he stands from the chair and moves to pour more water into my cup. Just as smoothly, he returns to his seat.

"Drink," he says.

I immediately take another large sip.

"Keep going, Winter."

Swallowing, I say, "I eventually got into a new sort of normal. Veronica has been my best friend since forever, so I always had the Lance family as a support. But my aunt and uncle were just…there, ya know? They weren't ever overly affectionate, but they'd been that way even before my parents died. We didn't see them often, just on holidays and big events like my mom's swearing-in."

We both sit silently for a few seconds, nearly a full minute, before Hunter says, "Keep going, baby," in a low, quiet voice.

My eyes snap to his, and in that moment, I come to terms with telling this man about the most horrible point in my life.

"Adam, their son, was twenty. He'd tried to go to college but flunked out his freshman year. He went back to live with my aunt and uncle a few months before my parents' accident, and rather than moving out when they sold their house, he decided to move with them to Arlington."

I lick my dry lips, feeling for the cracks.

"Adam and I never really talked much. He is seven years older than me, and even though we didn't have the biggest family ever, he didn't want to hang out with a little kid, you know?

"When he moved in, he was always in a strange mood. Like he was angry to be in my parents' house, but also, he was living rich because of all the money and extra cars my parents left behind. So it was confusing. He was confusing."

I take a chance and look at Hunter. His face is impassive, but his eyes are a little glassy and very focused on me.

"I— I was a little dazed by him at the beginning. He was a popular guy when he was in high school. A fairly talented basketball player. He always had a girlfriend, and I admit I—I had a c-crush on him." Admitting this part took me years to get through with Genevieve. The guilt I harbored that I invited everything I went through still lingers.

"It started with little things. I thought they were accidents. I'd trip over his foot, or he'd break a glass in the kitchen, and I'd step on it. But then his hurting me got more intentional. He'd grab me and squeeze until I had bruises, and he'd say—"

I love how fragile you are, princess. I could snap your bones with such little force.

I stop as a cold shot of adrenaline rushes ice to my face. "He'd say all kinds of things."

My eyes are closed now, but I open them again to ward off the flashes of images steeped in terror and pain.

I feel Hunter stand before I see him do so. When I look at him, his back is to me as he focuses on the fire. After a big breath, he turns around and runs his free hand through his hair.

"What else, Sunbeam?" he says. His features are tight.

"You know, H, it's okay. It was all bad stuff. More bad stuff. We don't have to revisit it. And he's gone—long gone from here." I move to place my glass on the nightstand and sit up on the edge of the bed. Instantly, he's right in front of me, crouching down.

My body sways toward his, an ever-present effect of the intoxicating energy that is Hunter Brigham.

"I need you to tell me everything, Winter…" he whispers, his voice raspy. Then with slow, intentional movements, he places his hands on my arms.

I shiver.

He must mistake my movements for anxiety rather than a confusing mix of desire and shame. He moves back to stand in front of the fire. "I need to know what I'm dealing with," he says, schooling his features back to an open, undemanding mask.

"Why, Hunter? I promise I'll leave before any of this touches August or you. I'll go back and never leave again."

I'm spiraling. The hurt, elemental part of my brain screams at me to flee. But the conscious part, the part tied to my heart, wants to stay here and be protected by this man. I want to lay all the pain and ugliness at his feet. I want him to willingly pick it all up, so I won't have to carry this baggage alone anymore.

"Why?" he rasps. "Because you matter to me. Because

you're important. Because I want to help you—to keep you safe. And I can only do that if I know the whole story."

I gently sway from side to side as the effects of the medicine and the rush of adrenaline seep out of my muscles.

"Okay," I say. *Okay. Here we go.*

"It didn't take long for Adam to start coming into my room and abusing me. First, he'd touch me—my breasts, then my…" I search for the right word to say, "vagina."

Clinical, but good. Clear.

"Then he'd have me perform acts on him. Sexual acts. But he was angry because I couldn't do it right. He would hurt me so bad. He'd be so rough that I thought I'd choke and die. Then he started raping me."

The gentle clinking of glass pulls me out of the dissociative state I feel myself drifting toward.

Water appears in my cup.

Hunter sits down next to me on the floor, clears his throat and nods at me as if to say, *keep going.* He reaches forward, putting the glass bottle on the nightstand.

I take a steadying breath.

"He raped me for months whenever he felt like it. The middle of the night was the most common time. But then he'd started doing it during the day whenever we were home alone. Sometimes when we weren't. He became obsessive. Possessive."

I clear my throat. It's tight and dry, and I sip the water, holding it in my parched mouth for a second before swallowing.

"I'd resigned myself to get through it until he either went away or I left the house for college. Yes, that was a far time away at that point because I was, what, thirteen, going on fourteen when it all ended? But whenever he did what he did, he threatened me. He told me that if I told anyone, he'd kill me. And I believed him. He had a knife and he'd make sure I saw it every day. And to make his point, he'd cut me."

My hand goes to the side of my calf where a particularly long, thin scar still hides in plain sight. I battle my brain to stay in *this* moment. To replace the sensation of my blood spilling hot over the steel blade with the warmth of the fire and the feeling of the mattress cradling my body. I wiggle my bare toes, grounding myself against the plush material beneath my feet.

I am here. I am safe.

"Like I said, I'd accepted it all. Until one day, I got sick. It was the beginning of the school year. I was so stressed because I'd just started high school. I was at school and not feeling well all day and the day before. In third period, I'd rushed to the bathroom in so much pain. I sat on the toilet, and so much blood came out. My mom told me about periods before she passed away, but I hadn't had one until then, even though Veronica and my other friends started getting theirs around age ten. I passed out in the bathroom stall. Veronica found me when I hadn't returned to class after fifteen minutes. If she hadn't, I would have bled to death."

I've been staring at the fire for God knows how long, and I risk looking at Hunter. His breathing is shallow, but his eyes are fixed on me.

"You were pregnant," he says.

"Yes. Five months along, the doctors said. After they got me to the hospital and I woke up, they told me I'd had a baby girl, but she'd died inside me long before I'd gotten to the hospital."

I pause. I swallow.

"The doctor said it just like that. He didn't try to be sympathetic or sensitive when he delivered the news. Just, 'your baby died. Sorry about it.' They gave me an emergency C-section because the placenta had detached, and I was hemorrhaging to death." I let out a dry laugh. "Death would have been one way out, right?"

He doesn't laugh back.

"The nurses weren't kind to me. I mean, I guess I looked like a fucked-up stereotype. I was a black girl from D.C. who was not even fourteen years old and pregnant. They weren't overtly rude or hostile, but…"

"You needed someone to lean on."

"Right. I needed…softness? Compassion? They sent in the social worker, which is routine in these situations. My aunt and uncle were in the room when I woke up, and they were *not* happy. They kept asking me who I'd been with, how long had I been 'whoring around,' as my aunt put it. I was answering the social worker's questions, and my aunt and uncle kept interjecting. I was clamming up. Finally—her name is Shawna, the social worker—she had them leave the room."

I release my tensed muscles and run my hands up and down my legs over the linen-covered scars that remain—one of the physical reminders of what I went through.

"She looked at me when we were alone, and without saying a word, she hugged me." I force my eyes to look at him again.

"It had been so long since I had a real hug. My aunt and uncle never hugged me. Veronica did, but this one was different. It was as if my mom were there. So I told her everything. After that, the police got involved, and they did DNA testing on the remains and confirmed that Adam was the father."

"The state took me out of my aunt and uncle's home. But they still lived in the house—my parents' house—until they died a few years back. I was sent to live with Veronica's family. That was the best thing that could have ever happened to me."

I take a big breath, not really ready to share what happened in the aftermath of everything. But I do it anyway. Hunter's scent wraps around me, and I'm grateful for his presence, right next to the bed rather than across the room. I'm feeling warmer. His proximity grounds me.

"After everything that happened, I really struggled." I look down at a spot on the floor, not wanting to meet Hunter's eyes. "It was so…anti-climactic, you know? Like all this drama, and when he was sentenced it was like, what happens now? I started to get really sick. My anxiety was bad. Really bad."

He puts his hand on my cheek, turning my face to meet his. "There you are, Sunbeam. You can look at me."

I settle my eyes on his mouth.

He takes my hand and kisses my fingers.

"I went from having panic attacks all the time to much worse. I was having panic attacks several times a day. Then I couldn't leave the house. I couldn't leave the house at all." I flick my eyes up to his. "I finished high school virtually to the best of my ability. But I...I couldn't leave the house for years."

He rubs my hand with his thumb. "What changed?"

I crack a small smile. "Veronica left for college. She stayed nearby, but when she left her parents' house to move into the dorm...I spiraled." I close my eyes against the memory of trying to leave the Lance house. In my sick brain, I planned on showing up at Veronica's dorm to show her that I could make it without her. I felt abandoned, even though Veronica never left me. Not in the way I felt. As soon as I stepped over the threshold of the front door, I blacked out. I woke up in a bathtub, soaked in blood. I'd dissociated and harmed myself badly.

"I went to the hospital for a little while. It took a few weeks for me to get stable. I was…not well when I went in. But then I met my therapist. And I started to come out of it all. I started to heal."

"And then you decided to help others." He grins at me.

"Yeah," I say quietly. "But it took me several years to get to that point."

He doesn't say anything else. He kisses my palm.

I take a deep breath, feeling the stretch as I inhale as much air as I can to compress my diaphragm.

I exhale with a therapeutic sigh and Kitty moves to snuggle in next to me. My hand plunges into his fur.

"Adam…. He's serving time right now. I've been a little stressed because he's up for parole again." I fight against the swell of anxiety that settles in my stomach. "But he got twenty years. He still has time on his sentence. I thought I saw him. In the grocery store, I mean. I bumped into a man who looked just like him, but it couldn't have been him because—"

Adam is in prison.

"It wasn't him. My nervous system just needs to calm down." I look at his hands. They're clasping mine again. "This helps," I say, and I rub my thumb against the rough skin of his wrist.

"Winter," he says, pulling me up to stand. I sway a little bit. My muscles twitch. "I am so sorry you went through that."

I shrug. An accustomed response. "It's okay. It happens. It happens every day, actually."

"No, Winter. It's very much not fucking okay. And I'm sorry." He reaches a hand up to my cheek, and with a gentleness that feels opposite to the hardness of his body, he caresses my skin. "I'm sorry you were unprotected. I'm sorry you were hurt. I'm sorry you were cast away. I'm sorry you had to defend yourself and grow up far faster than you ever should have. I'm sorry that your brain was forced to create an isolating and stressful defense mechanism to keep you safe from harm again. I am so sorry, Sunbeam. You are so brave. You've saved yourself. You're living. But you have something now that you didn't have then. You have me."

I look into his eyes, and with every word, I feel the tears well up and crest over my eyelashes. For all the pain, humiliation, and torment I've experienced for decades…I know I'm abundantly lucky to have this man in my life. He's here. He's with me.

Mine.

"I know I just told you some fucked-up shit, Hunter. But could you kiss me again?" My lips tremble.

He smiles at me.

"I'll kiss you again and always, Sunbeam."

And then his lips crash into mine

TWENTY-FOUR
HUNTER

A shaft of light peeks through the tall blackout curtains and lands across her fingers. I've never paid much attention to a woman's hands before, but if there's one word I can think of for hers, it's "elegant."

I spoon behind her, holding her body to my chest, and the arm that's not holding her has long gone asleep, tingling underneath her pillow. They could chop it off for all I care. Her face is smooth, and the troubled furrow to her brow is absent. She looks peaceful.

After the heaviness of last night, I just wanted her to relax and get undisturbed sleep. So I made her a bath. I pulled out all the frilly shit Ella stocked under my sink and dumped anything labeled for relaxation into the water.

When she stood in front of me, fully naked and not hiding anything, she allowed me to catalog her scars.

There were so many of them. On her stomach, her thighs, on her back, her upper arms.

She shook as I looked at her. Keeping eye contact, I knelt before her and kissed every one of them. When I saw her C-section scar, just a tiny, puckered line at the top of her mound, I kissed it with reverence.

She cried. I kissed her tears.

I close my eyes and press my face into the riot of curls draped across my pillow. Her hair still faintly smells like roses, and the coils tickle my nose. It took everything within me to maintain composure last night as she haltingly spilled her past to me. I wanted to rage and maim and kill as I processed every word. Her abuser. Her aunt and uncle who are long dead. I wanted them all to bleed and suffer. I wanted to hold together her broken pieces, the parts that she's stitched together day by day, year by year, so she can move forward and live. I wanted to weep in the face of her raw, haunting honesty.

Slowly, I drift my hand from beneath her breast to her lower belly, right where her womb would be. My pinky grazes her scar. I allow myself to envision our future. The perfect child she would give me. The love we'd have for them as we blend our family. It feels impossible, but I can't imagine a world where Winter and I aren't together and a family, whatever that looks like. So I allow myself to dream.

She stirs, and I press against her more firmly and say, "Good morning."

"Hmmm, good morning," she replies, reaching out in front of her in a long stretch. "What time is it?" she asks sleepily.

I pull my arm up, letting the movement activate the digital face of my watch. Holding it in front of both of us, I tell her, "Just past ten a.m."

She hums and smiles before her face crashes into a frown and she jolts upright.

"Oh, my God!" Her hands rush to her hair. In the dim light, I notice it's a little flat on one side. "Oh, God, this is—shit!" She rakes her fingers through her hair.

I grab my phone off the nightstand, tapping the screen to quickly access the home system to open the curtains.

She spares the window only the briefest of looks before scrambling to pull back the covers.

"What is it?" I'm slow to process because I'm having a great time staring as her bra-less tits dance beneath the T-shirt I got her to sleep in the night prior.

"My hair is—I didn't do my hair right last night."

"Do your hair?" I ask with a yawn.

"Yes, I—" she lets out a frustrated groan. "It's a—it's a Black thing, all right?" She reaches underneath the pillow with one hand, the other holding her hair tightly on the top of her head.

"Well, help me understand. I want to understand." She finds the hair tie, says, "A-ha!" and quickly secures her hair. Settling back into the pillows, she sighs and says, "Really?"

I place my hand on her bare thigh. Her skin is so fucking smooth. "Yes, really. I want to know all the things."

She starts biting her fingernail. "I got my hair wet but didn't do it before we went to sleep."

"Okay, give me a little more info here."

She blows out a breath and says, "I needed to do my hair to keep it from tangling and frizzing. I should have re-added the moisture to it with oils or creams since I'd stripped my hair of them when I soaked in the tub last night. I usually braid my hair into a few big braids for sleep. My pillow at home is satin, but when I sleep on regular pillows, I need to wear a bonnet and tie my hair up. But obviously, I didn't have any of those things and I've never done," she waves her hands in the space between our bodies, "*this* before."

My head spins a little at the multi-step hair routine, but I make a mental note to get a list of all the supplies she needs so I can have them here by the end of the day.

I smirk at the last part of her spiel. "Oh? And what is *this*," I say, amused. My hand travels higher up her thigh. She opens her legs slightly.

"Um, sleeping with a man at his place. I mean, in the most literal sense, right? And also, even in the figurative sense. And—what are you doing, H?"

"Hmm?" My hand disappears beneath the hem of her shirt, rubbing her inner thighs so close to her crotch my mouth starts to water.

"You're awfully close to my..." she trails off, and I lazily draw my eyes up her body, snagged by the hard tips of her nipples pressing through the shirt.

"Pussy. Your pussy, Winter. Say it." I look at her directly in the eye as I run thumb over her seam with a whisper-soft touch. She went to bed in an oversized shirt and nothing else. I feel her heat against my fingers.

"My *pussy*." She whispers the last word.

"Yes, and to answer your question, I'm playing with your pussy. Is that all right?" I rub in circles now.

"Y-Yes, that's f-fine." She leans back, catching herself on her hands, and I sit up further.

"Winter, I want to take things slow with you. Savor you. We need to build trust in this space especially. And at the same time, I want to make you feel good. Is that okay?"

She nods, biting her lip.

"Good girl." I remove her shirt. Her nipples are large and surrounded by dark areolas. I want to suck on them *badly*. "Sunbeam?"

"Huh?" She asks, her eyes half closed.

"I want to suck on your breasts. Is that okay?"

"Yesss," she says, drawing out the last syllable as I pull her over my body to lick the tip of her breast with my tongue.

"Oh, *God*," she says breathlessly.

I don't say anything except moan. I fucking moan.

The taste of her skin—slightly salty from sweat but so sweet—makes me want to stay with her in this fucking bed forever.

I need to get her pussy in my mouth.

"Come here," I say. My voice is gruff, deepened by the strength of my desire for this woman.

She jolts and places her hand on mine. "Um, do you want to have sex?"

Seeing her tension, I bring my hand to her neck and caress her cheek with my thumb.

"Not yet, Sunbeam. But I do want to make you feel good. You can tell me to stop anytime, and I'll stop." I kiss the tip of her nose. "What I really want to do," I say, placing soft kisses on her cheek and down her neck, "is to kiss," I press my lips to her racing pulse, "and lick," I place my lips to the shell of her ear. "And suck your pussy until you come on my tongue."

Before she answers, I kiss her on the mouth, and she pushes against me, our lips fighting for dominance.

Breaking away, I say, "What do you say to that, baby?"

She nods up and down, panting. "That sounds…yes."

"Okay then," I say. I sit up to adjust my position on the bed, and she looks around as if lost.

She straightens her legs and, if possible, presses even more deeply into the bed.

"Nope, not like that."

She sits up military straight and clasps her arms around her knees. "Where do you want me then," she asks, confusion lacing her words.

I see her closing herself off, and that simply won't do.

I lay back flat with my head on the pillows. "Here."

She looks me up and down. "Where?"

"Here," I say, pointing to my mouth.

"You want me to…"

"Sit on my face? Yes," I say simply, taking her hand and pulling her toward me.

"What! That's not a thing people actually do."

"I can assure you it is most certainly something people do."

"But how will you be able to breathe? I'll suffocate you! I'll—"

"I'll be able to breathe just fine. If death by suffocation were to happen because you smothered me with your pussy, I'd die the happiest man on earth. Now sit on my face, Winter." I pull on her waist and leg before deciding to go to her. Even though it means laying sideways on the bed, I move to situate my head near her crotch.

"Are you...are you sure, H?" She's got her hand back to her mouth, biting on her nail again.

Looking at her from my upside-down vantage point, I take her hand and place it on my bare chest, right over my heart.

"I have never been more sure of anything in my life, Sunbeam."

She blinks hard one, two, three times before darting her gaze around the room. She releases a short breath when her eyes land on Kitty curled up in the dog bed I'd snatched from August's game room.

"Stay. Off-duty," she commands. Kitty raises his head, tilting it to the side and assessing her. I reach over, putting my hand on her thigh and rubbing her silky skin with my thumb.

"I mean it! Relax. Stay. Do not move from your dog bed." There's a slight, quivering tone to her voice, and Kitty focuses on her for a few heartbeats before chuffing and readjusting his position to curl into a ball facing the wall.

I'm going to give that dog so many treats for this.

"Okay," she says, but I'm not sure if she's talking to me or psyching herself up. "Okay," she repeats.

She lifts up slowly on her knees. Taking that as an invitation, I move into position and sigh as her glistening cunt hovers over my face. I fight back the urge to drool. Looping my arms around the juncture where her thighs and pelvis meet, I say, "Sit down and enjoy."

She relaxes a bit more, and blindly shoving a pillow under

my head, I tilt my chin to give her a long lick up her seam, starting at her hard button.

"Oh, holy shit!" she says. A full-body roll goes down her back, and she goes from sitting up straight to leaning over my body. Her face is inches above my aching cock.

Reaching down, I quickly swoop my dick to pin it beneath the waistband of my boxers. I'll deal with that later. In the shower. With the smell of her still on my face.

My dick twitches, and precum starts to bead against my neglected tip.

I return my attention back to her pussy and lazily settle in to lick around her clit.

"H, that's—oh, my God, that's amazing." She starts to rock her hips above me slowly, and I'm glad she can't see the beaming smile I'm wearing right now.

"Hmmmm," I say, drawing her into my mouth in a wet suck. The taste of her explodes on my tongue, and I decide right then and there that she's my new addiction.

Reaching up, I place my index finger against her pussy, teasing the entrance. She rocks harder against my mouth and finger.

"Oh, H, I need…I need…"

I understand what she's not able to verbalize, and I slowly press my finger into her, gauging her response. When she lets out a low groan followed by a rush of her wetness against my face, I move my finger in and out of her impossibly tight cunt.

"Oh, *fuck,* H. This is—" A louder moan cuts off her sentence as I put another finger into her.

Popping off her clit, I use my thumb to rub it as I say, "I want you to come all over me, Winter. Do you think you can do that?"

"Uh-huh," she says, nodding and pressing back against my fingers.

"What do you need from me to get there?"

"What—I mean…what?"

"Tell me what to do to get you off, Winter," I demand, slowing my pumping fingers until they're resting right against her entrance. She groans in frustration.

"What do you want from me, H?"

"I want you to tell me. To use your voice. Demand that I do exactly what you need me to do to give you an orgasm so good you see stars. So, what do you need from me to get there?" I punctuate the end of my sentence with a gentle kiss to her clit and a nip at her inner thigh.

Pushing my fingers back into her torturously slow, she stutters out, "I want—oh, God."

I press my thumb against her clit, rubbing in firm circles.

"I want you to push t-two fingers in and out of my... *pussy.*"

"Good girl." I reward her good work with a firm push of my fingers and a quick caress of her G-spot. "And?"

"And...And *I want you to suck hard on my clit,*" she says on one breath.

Immediately, I pull her clit back in my mouth and pick up a steady rhythm with my fingers, twisting them and pushing against the most sensitive parts of her with every pass.

My cock leaks against my stomach, but I don't care if I bust in my underwear like a kid. It will be worth it to see Winter come undone on my tongue.

"Fuck, Hunter, I'm gonna...I need to—"

She presses her body flat against my torso, and I about die when I feel her puckered lips against the head of my dick, licking it with tentative strokes.

That's it. Game over. I push my dick against her mouth, and she sucks the tip like I'm sucking her, and I feel her hands grab my balls and shaft inside my underwear.

She hums a long moan, her voice escalating higher and higher. She arches her back and pops off my dick, screaming, *"Hunter!"*

Her sheath flutters on my fingers and tongue, and she gets

impossibly wetter. Her walls clamp down on my fingers, squeezing as I suck and press on that spot she loves so much to prolong her orgasm.

Panting and rocking against my mouth, she collapses back down against me and reaches for my dick again. Taking half of it in her mouth, she pumps only twice before I rush out, *"Lean-back-if-you-don't-want-me-to-come-in-your-mouth."*

She hums and sucks harder. Not even a minute later, my cock twitches in her wet warmth as I flood it with my cum. She hums even louder, and I feel my dick press against the back of her throat as she swallows me down.

I rub her back in firm circles as she catches her breath and I come down from the soul-stealing blow job she just gave. Eventually, she rolls off my body and lays flat on her back, staring at the ceiling.

"That was…" she says with a small smile, panting.

"Everything?" I put a possessive hand on her thigh.

"Something like that."

"Come up here," I say, pulling on her arm, and she moves to lay her head on my chest. Putting my arms around her, I breathe deeply.

"Thank you, H."

"For what, Sunbeam?"

"For being you," she says and yawns. She settles against me, and a few moments later, she's asleep.

All I can think is, "Ditto."

AN HOUR LATER, I close the blinds and let Winter sleep. After all she's been through in the past twenty-four hours, she needs it. Kitty stretches lazily before padding over to me where I stand near the door.

"You know I've never had a dog?" I say to Kitty and he

gives me the doggy version of an eyebrow lift. "I've always wanted one. You're a really cool pup to have around," I finish. He huffs and jumps back, sticking his butt in the air and his front legs and chest close to the ground. His tail wags, playful.

The wagging picks up to double time when I reach down to scratch behind his ears. Figuring he needs to do his business and eat, I lead us in the direction of the garden.

"Mr. Kitty!" a deep male voice echoes when Kitty and I hit the foyer. I follow Kitty's progress as he trots away from me and toward August's guard, Rex.

"Miss Winter isn't around?" Rex asks as he bends down to pick Winter's dog up. Kitty isn't wearing his harness, so it's safe for Rex to assume that he isn't working.

"Resting," I reply shortly. I've been on guard with anyone who is around August after what happened with his old detail. But Ella thoroughly vetted Rex, calling him a gentle giant. I haven't received any reports of anything bad happening.

August seems to like him.

"Where's August?" I ask. He clears his throat and erases the playful look he's giving Kitty from his face.

"He's in the kitchen, sir," he replies. I nod.

"Mind taking this one out for me?" I point to Kitty. "Let him into the kitchen when he's done with his business so he can eat."

A look of happy surprise settles on Rex's face. "Oh, yes, of course, sir. It's no problem," Rex rushes out. Kitty lolls his head back over his shoulder, panting with his tongue hanging out in a goofy look.

Dude, get outta here, is what I imagine the look translates into.

I pivot on my heel and head toward the kitchen.

My phone beeps, alerting me to an email, and by the time

I'm steps from the kitchen, it beeps three more times with more messages. I've wasted most of the day away.

Well, not a waste.

Memories of Winter in my arms slide through my brain.

I am in love with Winter Leigh Vaughan.

How long until this all explodes?

I stop at the entrance of the kitchen because August stands at the island. He's dusted flour on the countertop and kneads a ball of dough. He's wearing blue medical gloves as he works.

"August," I say, clearing my throat. He pauses, not looking at me. I contemplate giving him his space. Letting him do the thing that gives him peace and happiness. This is a moment he spent with his mother. I don't want to ruin any more memories.

Atonement. Winter's voice echoes in my brain. This is step one.

"Can I help you make the pizza?" His hands still, and I hold my breath. He makes several different sounds in his throat, and I'm not sure if they are voluntary or not. But then he nods.

I go to the sink to wash my hands, and when I dry them, he turns to do the same after pulling off his gloves. Once his hands are dry, he grabs his tablet.

"I need to make the sauce," he says. Just then the oven lets out a short *beep-beep-beep*, indicating that it's preheated.

"Isn't the sauce already pre-made?" I ask.

He shoots me a short look and then goes to the cabinet where the spices are kept.

"We have to add spices," he adds quickly. He pulls oregano, basil, onion powder, garlic powder, and Italian seasoning from the pantry. Then he pulls a bowl from the cabinet and places everything on the counter.

I continue to knead.

"Do you like any other types of pizza?" I ask. He ignores

me, emptying the jar of pizza sauce into the bowl. He then adds two shakes each of the spices.

"My favorite type is Hawaiian," I say to fill the silence. He pauses his work and then moves to his tablet.

"You would like something like that," he says.

I chuckle. "What? Do you find the pineapple appalling or is it the ham?"

He taps his cheek. "I do not like either. Putting both on a pizza is just stupid."

My chuckle turns into a laugh.

"The dough is ready. Roll it out into a circle," he says.

I do as he says.

We fall into another silence. It's not as tense as it usually is.

Be brave.

"August, I'm not happy about the circumstances that brought you here to live with me. But I'm glad that I get to spend time with you."

He freezes and stops grating the cheese for the pizza for a full thirty seconds.

"I want to spend time with you, August."

He hesitates before he says, "I cannot say the same."

I nod, my mouth forming a straight line.

Atonement.

"I am sorry." I stop rolling the dough and look at him.

Placing my palms flat on the counter, I lean forward and repeat. "I am sorry, August. I am sorry that I treated you so shittily. I am sorry that I've been a shit father, and I know it sounds like I'm seeking sympathy, but I'm not. I'm just stating the facts. I've been horrible to you. I was horrible to your mother. And," I swallow against the jumble of words, all the words I want to say. "I can't make up for the past. I can't change the past. But I would like the opportunity to make the future better for us. For you and me."

I wait for him to do anything. But he just resumes grating the cheese.

"Right, that's…that's all I wanted to say right now." I go back to rolling the dough. Head down, I feel him shift. Then his tablet activates.

"If this pizza is good, we can make one next Friday."

And that's the best thing I could possibly hope for.

TWENTY-FIVE
WINTER

I take two days off this week to get my mind straight. As soon as I got in the car back to my apartment, I scheduled an emergency session with Genevieve.

"Adam is still in prison, though. Right, Winter?" She looks at me with concern. She's usually calm and impassive for our sessions, but her brows are creased this time. She's worried about me.

"Yes, I'm sure that he's in prison. He's up for parole, but there's no way they will grant it. My lawyers said so." I've bitten all my nails down to the quick at this point, so I move over to the cuticle. Gross.

"Do you think you actually saw him, Winter?"

I don't know.

"It's logically impossible for him to have been there. So, no. I don't think I saw him. I think I'm going through a lot of stress and change right now, and it's triggering my nervous system."

"What's got you so stressed then, Winter?"

I blow out a breath and motion for Kitty to jump in my lap from where he lays on top of my bare feet.

"I met someone," I say softly. I bury the lower half of my face into Kitty's neck, looking up at the screen.

Her eyebrows surge up. "Oh? How long have you been seeing this person?"

I bite the inside of my cheek. How long has it been?

"I've known him for a few months, but things didn't get serious until about two weeks ago."

"I see," Genevieve says sagely.

She does that irritatingly effective thing of waiting for me to add more to the conversation, so I do.

"It's…we've…gotten more physical than I thought I'd be comfortable with," I add.

I turn to face my apartment window. It's snowing today. We got a foot of snow overnight, but now it's just flurries.

I always have found flurries to be so peaceful. Their trek to the earth is more of a lazy release of precipitation into the atmosphere. It feels like a happy accident from the heavens.

She waits in my silence for a few more seconds before saying, "Say more on that, Winter. What did you think you'd be the most uncomfortable with?"

"We haven't had sex," *yet,* "but we have done a lot of other stuff. Almost everything but sex."

She nods. "And how does that level of intimacy make you feel?"

Scared. Exhilarated. Like I'm flying. Like I'm in love.

"Confused," is what I ultimately say.

"That's understandable. And maybe a little fearful?" she inquires.

I nod in response.

"It makes sense that your nervous system is messing with you," she says. "Plus, Veronica's getting pretty advanced in her pregnancy, right? I imagine that's also got you feeling…"

She offers me the opportunity to finish the sentence. "Emotional. I feel very emotional about her baby." I'm whispering now.

"And that makes sense," Genevieve says just as softly.

"When will this stop being so hard? Stop being so impossible?" I'm annoyed when I feel tears fall toward my lap, landing on Kitty's back. I don't want to cry. And yet, here I am.

Genevieve adjusts in her seat. "You are in transition. You've gone through several life-changing events, and it's taken you time—necessary time—to pick up the pieces. To find a sort of equilibrium in your new normal. But now you're in another life shift. You're doing the tough thing of looking life in the face and saying, 'I want more.' You're facing your monsters, and with each step, you're turning them into mice. Do you know how incredible that is? You're not weak. You're brave."

I'm crying openly now and reply, "But I feel so scared, Genevieve."

"Bravery isn't doing things without fear. It's feeling the fear and moving forward anyway."

I let that settle into my spirit. Into my soul.

"I receive that," I reply. And I do.

I PUSH down my awkwardness as I walk through the front door of Amelia Manor. I feel like all eyes are on me—that everyone knows I'm boning the owner of the house. I feel like even Rio gave me a sly smile when he picked me and Kitty up in front of my apartment building this morning.

"Hey there, stranger." Ella calls over to me, and I square my shoulders when I see her bounding down the stairs.

"Ella, I'm so sorry you had to see me behaving so unprofess—" I startle when she lunges at me. But instead of socking me in the face, she wraps me in a tight hug.

"Oh, my God, stop that right now!" She pulls back from

me and smiles. Her lips have a slight red tinge to them. She pops a half-eaten candy cane into her mouth. "Plus, you and my brother? I ship it," she says, winking.

I blush. "Thank you?" I'm completely mortified.

She loops her arm through mine and walks me up the stairs toward August's game room. As we ascend the stairs, I take in the giant Christmas tree in the middle of the foyer. There are boxes underneath it. I wonder if the boxes are for decoration or if there are actual presents inside.

"Augie is in here," she says when we're standing outside the game room door. "He's been asking about you for the last few days."

"Oh?" I reply. "What exactly has he been asking?" I'm so worried that I've added another layer of drama to his already stressful life.

"He's just been asking when you're coming back. If you're coming back. He seems okay," she replies.

I nod and make a mental note to let him know if I ever take time off or deviate from the schedule. I don't want him ever to think I've abandoned him.

Ella leaves me at the door to the game room, heading down the hallway. I see the back of August's head when I open the door. He sits in front of the television, controller in his hand. Kitty makes his way to his dog bed, sighing happily.

"Hey, August," I say, sitting in the chair beside him.

He doesn't acknowledge my presence. A few minutes later, after he's killed a few zombies, he turns to me, putting his tablet close to his face.

"Where were you?"

He puts the tablet down and turns to look at the television screen. The game is paused, his character bouncing from side to side.

"I'm sorry I didn't tell you I would be gone for a few days.

I needed some time to…rest after everything that happened at the grocery store."

He doesn't say anything, but his jaw clenches and unclenches, just like his father's.

He picks his tablet up and puts it down a few times. It's like he wants to say something but is unsure how or what to say. Finally, he picks the tablet up again and says, "That was weird what happened at the grocery store."

I smile. "Yes, I'm sorry if it upset you."

"Why did you freak out like that?" he asks.

I consider what to share with him. How much is appropriate.

Don't you think you're a little past propriety, little miss "I'm-Gonna-Sit-On-My-Client's-Dad's-Face"?

"I have Generalized Anxiety Disorder," I say. "For the longest time, I couldn't go anywhere. I couldn't leave my house. That was years ago when I was that impacted, and I'm so happy that I can get out and go places now."

He doesn't pick up his tablet to respond, so I continue speaking. "Sometimes, I have panic attacks. A lot of the time, they come out of nowhere. Sometimes, they're caused by stress. I saw something in the store that caught me off guard and sent me into overload."

He nods sharply once.

"I'm sorry you had to see that, August."

He taps his cheek several times with his index finger.

"It is okay. I kind of understand. My body goes into overload sometimes too. I want to stop it from doing whatever it's doing, but it does what it does. I feel out of control."

I nod back at him. "Exactly."

He taps his cheek again. "So Hunter did not do anything to upset you? To hurt you?"

I tilt my head, looking at him. "What makes you think your dad would hurt me?"

Tap-tap-tap.

"He hurts people," August says simply. I don't say anything.

"He hurt my mom," he adds.

I process that statement. "What do you mean by that?"

"I mean," he begins, "he broke her heart. She would tell me so all the time."

I nod. "I understand how that can happen. How did you feel hearing that?"

He's silent. "It made me hate him. My mom was so sad. When she started getting back into drugs, she would talk about him all the time. I realized that he ruins people," he finishes.

"I get that too," I say softly.

He starts tapping his face vigorously, then he finally says, "Hunter said you two are dating. Is that true?"

He jumps up and starts pacing near the corner of the room. I watch him stim and wait patiently to see if he will return to his seat. Plus, it gives me time to think. He had to have seen us hugging outside the car. Once he does sit back down, I reply, "We are seeing each other. Does that make you uncomfortable? Would you rather we didn't?"

August sits, rocking back and forth in his gamer chair. After a moment, he says, "He seems different with you than I thought he would be."

I try not to look too deeply into that statement.

"Will you still work with me if you date him?" August asks.

I smile at him. "I'll be here for as long as you want me to be, August. I promise you'll still have the same confidentiality we've always had. Anything you share with me will stay here unless you want me to tell anyone else."

His body stills, and then he relaxes back into his chair.

"Play with me." August says. He puts his tablet on his lap

and picks up both controllers. He hands one to me, and I say, "I hope you're ready to lose."

He looks at me out of the corner of his eye and says, "Not a chance."

TWENTY-SIX
HUNTER

It's ignorant to forget about Blair and my father, but for the first time in what feels like forever, I've been committed to living.

I've dedicated the past few weeks to connecting with August, inch by inch. He's even let me play a video game with him, even though he didn't talk to me the entire time and he soundly beat me in every match. Which I could tell delighted him.

Winter and Kitty spend many of their days and nights at Amelia Manor, which is a totally novel experience—having a woman in my space as a permanent fixture. I don't hate it.

I'm as new to the dating thing as she is, in all honesty. But I'm finding it exhilarating to plan different excursions for the two of us around the area, simply for the excitement of seeing her joyful reaction. The day before yesterday, she and I finally went to Tavalia, and the chef indeed was making statements with his food.

After we left, we stopped at a dim sum restaurant that had excellent ratings on Yelp and filled up on dumplings. Afterward, we went to a small live music venue to hear an indie singer-songwriter perform an unplugged set.

Our mouths made love in the dark corner of the music hall, and when I got her home with me at Amelia Manor, we held each other, talking in hushed murmurs about life, until the sun came up.

I allowed myself to forget the terrible realities brewing outside of my permeable bubble, but I can forget a lot when I have Winter in my arms.

I can forget that my father is using me as a pawn in one of his fucked-up games.

I can forget that I've killed people at my father's order and that I've wrecked lives.

I can forget that I've deeply hurt my son with my abandonment, and now I have the impossible task of making it right.

I can forget.

Until I can't.

"I like the gold-embossed invitations with the ivory card stock over the cream ones. What do you think, Hunter?" Blair looks at me with bright eyes. We're sitting in the upscale meeting room of D.C.'s most sought-after wedding planner. It's the day before Christmas Eve, but that does little to dissuade Blair Winthrope from calling me into the heart of the city for a wedding meeting.

Despite the slushy, frigid weather, Blair looks immaculate, as always.

I'm sporting a five o'clock shadow and a stress migraine.

The migraine cropped up as soon as I saw her wearing the pear-shaped diamond engagement ring on her left hand. My mother's ring. My father must have given it to her.

"They're nice," I reply.

Her eyes flicker as if suppressing an eye roll.

"We can get 500 printed in the next month. The save the dates have also been prepared for your final approval." The wedding planner leaves the room to grab the save the dates, and Blair and I find ourselves in an uncomfortable silence.

"You know," she says after a full minute. "You could at least pretend to like me a little. The whole disinterested fiancé thing isn't that unusual. But playing it like you hate my guts is just weird."

I look at the side of her face. Her back is straight—as if someone shoved a stick up her ass. And maybe they did. She's pointedly not looking at me, but her eyes are sharp.

The wedding planner's return saves me from having to reply.

Blair and the woman—I think she said it was Marianne or Maria or something like that—ooh and ah over the prints while I sit and contemplate what I must have done wrong in a past life to end up in this spot.

But if things were different, you wouldn't have Winter.

I close my eyes at the thought. Do I have Winter? Will I have Winter when all this is said and done? And how the *fuck* am I going to explain all this to her?

"Hey, babe, I know you're super vulnerable right now, and I'm so stupidly in love with you, but there's one little issue…"

I swallow against the ball of anxiety. Of all the things my father has taken from me, losing August or Winter would be the things I wouldn't get over.

Then you better suck it up, buttercup.

I draw in a long breath and sit up to pay attention to the conversation.

"On your itinerary for today, you have a meeting with the event coordinator to choose the color scheme for the wedding, your engagement photo shoot in the next hour, and you need to approve the menu for the engagement party at the end of next week."

My head jerks. "Next week?"

Blair looks at me, and her eyes narrow slightly. "Yes, honey," she says with a tight smile. "Remember we chose next week? I know you have those meetings the following week, so that's why we chose New Year's Eve." Her voice raises slightly on the last few words.

I smile back at her, my mouth just as strained. "That's right. My apologies."

She turns back to the wedding planner, who taps on her iPhone.

"Blair, hair and makeup are ready for you. Hunter, you can also meet your stylist," Marianne/Maria says.

Blair pulls her phone out when we leave the wedding planner's office, and we ride down the elevator to the first floor in silence.

She doesn't try to engage with me. Once the doors open, she pastes on a friendly smile and waves at the stylists and crew that litter the large ballroom.

The people who planned this whole thing—Blair, the wedding planner, who knows—decided that our nuptials requires all the pageantry that any other wedding for people with last names like ours would require.

They've converted the ballroom into a full-scale studio. Separate hair and makeup stations line the room's far end and a craft table with food and drinks is on the other. In the center are three different stages with ornate backgrounds and expensive-looking furniture.

"Mr. Brigham, right this way, please." A young guy who has to be in his early twenties damn near runs up to me and tries to whisk me away. I follow behind him, and I can tell he's slowing down so he doesn't outpace me.

Three minutes later, I'm in a chair, tilting my head back and getting powder slapped on my face. An assistant shows the photographer and another person three different tie options when the air shifts.

"I need a minute with my soon to be son-in-law," a deep voice says with a sure cadence. Morris Winthrope.

I lower my head to watch the man's entrance.

Everyone scatters, and even though there were five people

milling around the small dressing station, we're completely alone in seconds.

Morris walks further into the room, rounding my chair and standing with his back to the lit mirror.

"Hunter, I was hoping you could spare a moment to speak with me," he begins with a friendly tone.

"Well, Morris, seeing as you've cleared out the room, why not." I attempt an unoffensive tone.

He releases a closed-mouth chortle, but he still looks amused. He leans against the makeup table, crossing his arms.

"My Blair has told me that there are some issues with your engagement. I told her that couldn't be and surely there was a simple misunderstanding. But when Blair is upset, I will always intervene. And my Blair is upset."

He leans closer, his arms still crossed. His face morphs, the friendly look edged out with quiet aggression. "What's the problem, Hunter?"

I swallow. "Problem? There's no issue, Morris," I say through numb, lying lips. There are all the problems in the world. But I can't solve any of them without help.

Where the fuck is Misha Hroshko?

"Oh, good." He stands up to his full height, straightening his suit jacket and cuffs. "Because if there were a problem, we'd definitely have to solve it, wouldn't we? The show must go on," he says.

"Nope," I say with lighthearted emphasis I don't feel. "Nothing happening at all that I'm aware of."

I'm quiet as he assesses me. His head tilts to the side as his eyes roam across my face. Then with a quick breath, he straightens again. "Hunter, you've been away from this place for too long. We haven't spent much time together, but I know you never cared for politics. What I think you fail to realize is that every facet of your life is political."

"How so?" I ask, clearing my throat.

He smiles. It's cold. "You're a Brigham. I am a Winthrope. Surely you can see the benefit of the two most powerful modern American families uniting in marriage and blood?"

I want none of this.

"It'd be a political win," I reply.

"Yes, very much so." He leans forward, lowering his voice. "Can I tell you a secret, Hunter?" he asks conspiratorially.

"Sure," I say. *Fuck off,* I think.

"Next month I'm announcing my run for President." His eyes sparkle, and I notice the flush that comes to his cheeks at the words. The air around him changes, and it feels almost sexual.

"Ah. Let me be the first to congratulate you. I wish you much success."

He does that head tilt thing again.

"When we win, it will be world-changing," he says in a low, energized voice.

His confidence is unsurprising. He is a powerful man in his own right. Born from a long line of wealthy businessmen, he's known as a mogul in the world of business.

He owns hotels, restaurants—hell, I think he even started a college at one point.

But from the way he talks, it doesn't feel like he's manifesting his win. It's already been assured.

"We all have a part to play in this election process, Hunter." He walks over to the basket of small water bottles in the corner of my station. He tosses one to me and I catch it. He uncaps his bottle, drinking it down in five big gulps.

"I know the way this marriage came about isn't the most romantic," he says. His tone comes off almost as if he cares.

He's an actor.

"But you'll find that your commitment to this process will be well-rewarded." He tosses the empty bottle into the waste bin, sinking the shot.

"Anyway," he says, taking a step toward me—to where I sit, still unmoving. "Just remember, when you're in the spotlight like we are, we're always being observed. Watched." My brain immediately goes to Winter. We've been public with our dates because I haven't wanted to hide her, to keep her locked away. I want to shout our love to the world like Tom Cruise on Oprah.

Now, I find deep regret at my idiocy. Does he know about Winter? Who knows about Winter? I'd already set Winter up with security, but is it enough?

Dread congeals in my gut, twisting my intestine into a searing knot.

He places his hand on my shoulder, and the black onyx stone at the center of his ring sparkles in the set lighting.

"Be careful, Hunter," he says. His expression is open. But his gaze? Lethal.

I fix my lips to tell the biggest lie of my life. "I am committed to your daughter, Sir."

He squeezes my shoulder tight before releasing me and stepping away. "Wonderful. Well, enjoy the shoot. Blair looks stunning, if I may say so. I tell you what, if she weren't my daughter, she'd be exactly the type I'd go for. Consider yourself lucky."

He winks at me, and I swallow down disgust at his lecherous statement.

"Right on," I say. My whole face is numb.

With that, he exits, and the team returns to the station, hurrying through their checklist to get us back on schedule.

When I slip on the navy suit, looking at the ceiling as a photographer's assistant straightens my tie, I accept that I'm not in a David and Goliath fight. It's more like I'm the fly, and they are the spider.

And I'm trapped in the web.

"FOLLOW THE PLAN, H. Follow along with the marriage shit until we can get your father out of the way," Leo says, his voice low.

We're sitting in a diner in Vienna, Virginia. The insane routes we took, then hopping on the metro until the orange line ended, meant we could feel safe enough to meet where we knew no one would follow us.

Still, we're sitting in the back of the diner, baseball caps pulled low, untouched cups of coffee on the counter in front of us.

I'd laugh at the cliché if things weren't so deadly serious.

"Leo, I'm over it at this point. Why can't we just walk up to him at his next dinner and put a bullet in his head?"

Leo looks at me sharply.

"Well, first, I'm not sure you'd want to spend the rest of your life in prison. Luckily, Maryland and Virginia abolished the death penalty."

"At this point, I'm already in prison. I'm signing my life away, my fucking sperm away, and—" I look around the diner. The rest of the customers aren't paying any attention to us.

"This isn't permanent. It's a means to an end, H. I'm getting Misha on board and tracking down who sent us that clip and why. We have one shot to get this right. Be patient." Leo grabs a sugar packet and pours it into his coffee.

I rub my temples. Getting through to Misha Hroshko is taking forever. There's been no movement since our last conversation.

He has what we need if we're going to overthrow my father, but he's all but ghosted us.

"It's not just you who stands to lose against your father.

You have the Brigham name and wealth behind you, but I have nothing. Nothing except BwP."

The reality is that we have nowhere near the power, resources, or influence to knock my father off his throne and not get killed in the process.

It's a fucking lose-lose situation.

Resentment at my powerlessness in this story chokes me.

"This is all so fucking convoluted at this point. There's BwP. Now there's the fact that Morris Winthrope and my father are planning some kind of presidential alliance born out of my offspring with Blair. Misha might not even help us. We're always two fucking steps behind." I swing to slam my fist on the table, pulling the punch at the last second to avoid attracting attention.

"Be patient," Leo says. "Misha Hroshko will—"

"We don't even know where Misha Hroshko is or what he really wants. Plus, you want me to be patient—you're not the one who has to do all this shit," I say.

The mix of aggression and testosterone swirls between us, the volley of our words against each other landing harder with each swing.

"And who's fault is that?" Leo crushes the empty sugar packet with his fist.

"What the hell do you mean by that, Leo?"

He doesn't say anything.

"What the fuck do you mean by that, Leo?" I repeat.

He explodes, his voice a barely constrained hiss. "I mean that if you hadn't ratted your mother out all those years ago, maybe we wouldn't be sitting here *right now.*"

I stare at him, anger and rage and shame at the long locked-away sin rising to coat my skin.

Leo knows almost all of my secrets. Except this one. He doesn't know what really went down the night my mother died, but he has enough information to make assumptions.

He's not far off.

"How dare you say that to me, Leonardo? Do you think that I could have stopped him? That she could have stopped him? That the judicial system—the same system that he has in his pocket—could have stopped him? What could I have possibly done?"

"Well, step one: don't fucking tell your father your mother's plans. Maybe she'd be alive, and maybe he wouldn't be."

The world tilts on its axis at my friend's words. He looks like he regrets them as soon as the words leave him.

"Hunter—"

"I had no other choice. You know what he was like," I mumble, my lips numb. The burn marks marring my body pulse with the memory of how I got them.

The torture I endured at my father's command.

Amelia Brigham was too gentle to be Benjamin Brigham's wife. That's the truth. My mother was raised much like Blair was: to be beautiful and unapproachable. To be seen but never heard.

But when she learned what was happening at Isla Cara—the corruption, the crimes against humanity—on top of what was happening in her home, she discovered her bravery. She, along with the FBI, created a scheme to catch my father in one of his many crimes.

Her bravery was not rewarded.

Father learned of her defection, and she was taken out before anything could come of her strength.

The official record says that Amelia Brigham died in a boating accident. I know that is untrue.

And the reason for her death? It's because I couldn't be strong against the immutable power of Benjamin Brigham.

He pressed, and I bent.

Leo is quiet and says, "I know you didn't have any other choice, Hunter." He sighs wearily like he's exhausted. "I'm sorry I said that."

I laugh dryly, not letting it go. "You, *especially* you, know what he did to people. You know what he did to *me.* I was just a kid—a kid he tortured until he got the information he wanted."

My coffee is now cold, not that I would drink it anyway.

"Let's talk about the plan from here," Leo says.

"What's there to talk about? Play along with this sham. Figure out how to take him down—*if* we can take him down. Pray Misha Hroshko will deign to work with us. Then we move on," I say. "BwP is safe in the meantime. August is safe in the meantime. I just have to suck it up."

I force my brain to *not* think about all the things I lose with this plan.

All the pain I'll cause other people by following through.

Specifically, I try to not think about Winter.

Leo's phone buzzes, and he abruptly leaves the table when he reads the caller ID. When he doesn't return fifteen minutes later, I determine he's gone for good.

The waitress comes by and removes the coffee cups.

"I don't mind you staying here, honey, but my shift ends in ten minutes," she says pointedly. I nod and drop a hundred-dollar bill on the table.

"Thank you, sugar!" she shouts as I exit the diner.

The sharp point of the freezing rain threatens to pierce my skin as I make my way back toward the train. Every step resonates, acting as an anchor point to my emotions.

I don't ever allow myself to think about my mother. I don't allow myself the privilege of doing so. Of being a keeper of her memory.

Because despite wanting to protect her, wanting to see her succeed in her quest to rid the world of my father, I still told him everything he wanted to know.

Limp, broken, literally flayed open on the marble floor at Isla Cara, my bruised lips spilled my mother's secrets.

By the next morning, she was gone. Dead.

I can't quiet my thoughts, so I don't try to.

He's right. I did kill her. I had my chance to take down Benjamin Brigham. I failed.

I walk back toward the metro, deciding as I stand on the platform whether to follow the path back toward Amelia Manor, or to change course, ending up on the green line to take me further into D.C. In the jumble of my choices, one thought rings plain: I'm so completely alone.

I always have been.

And I always should be.

TWENTY-SEVEN
WINTER

When the banging on my door starts at 8 p.m., I know it can only be Veronica. Primarily because she's tried to reach me five times over the last two days, and I've been completely unavailable.

Delightfully unavailable.

Detouring through the kitchen, I open my apartment door. I catch her mid-knock and glaring down at the man dressed in all black and sitting outside my entryway. His earpiece points to him being security, which is probably the only reason why Veronica doesn't have her Reebok shoved up his ass.

In contrast to the security guard's all-black outfit, Veronica wears a Christmas sweater and leggings. The sweater is amazing—it's covered in pompoms and is a green, red, and white monstrosity. A reindeer head covers her protruding abdomen, and the apex of her belly serves as Rudolph's nose, complete with a red pom.

"Merry Christmas Eve-Eve to you too. Come on in, Rons," I say. I hand her a bowl of pre-popped kettle corn, and her eyes light up. Peace offering.

"You are so lucky I love you, Winter, because so help me,

if you disappear for forty-eight hours again without a word, I will find you and shave your head bald!"

She waddles to my sofa, and I nod to the man outside my door before closing it.

Last week, Hunter told me he would be making changes with everything that's going on. One of those additions is twenty-four-hour security and a chauffeured ride wherever I go. I even saw Rio's handgun peeking from his shoulder holster when he opened the door for me to exit the car this morning.

"It's great to see you too, Rons," I say suppressing an eye roll.

She plops down on the sofa, pushing aside my holiday-themed pillow. Kitty jumps up on the sofa, nestling close to her. She pets him while looking at me intently.

"The only way I'll forgive you is if you tell me sordid details of you doing the nasty with Hot Daddy. So, *spill*," she says, her eyes locked on me while she shoves popcorn in her face.

I flush from head to toe.

"There's really not that much to tell," I say. She lowers her chin and stares at me wide-eyed.

I try to avoid it, but a slow, beaming smile slides onto my face.

"Okay, well, maybe there's a little bit to tell."

"I knew it!" She bounces on the sofa. "Oh, my God, did you bump uglies? I want, nay, *need* to know!"

She's vibrating with excitement.

"No, we did not 'bump uglies,' as you so eloquently put it." I shake my head in amusement. "But we did a lot of other things that were a lot of fun."

"*Biiiiitch,* like what?" She picks up speed shoveling popcorn into her mouth, chewing sloppily.

"Girl, slow down before you choke. And let's just say that

Hot Daddy lives up to his name. And many orgasms were had."

She squeals.

"And that's all you're getting out of me," I say.

I head to the kitchen, noting the stacks of mail on the island.

Ugh, I should open those.

I shuffle through the piles I've ignored over the past few days while soaking in my time with Hunter, absently thumbing through them. I set aside the ones that look important, chucking aside the ads and credit card offers. I pause when I come across an envelope that's starkly different from the other mailers. My name stands out across the front of the card, the blocky handwriting strange against the elegant feel of the paper. I flip it over, noting there isn't a return address.

"So now that you've pretty much popped your cherry," Veronica says, and I look at her over my shoulder. "Let's talk about getting you out there. You need to play the field."

I look up from what I'm doing to consider her words. Do I want to play the field?

The idea of being with anyone else immediately fills me with a sick feeling.

In my heart, I know that Hunter is the one for me. I know that I love him.

But does he love you?

A thread of tension weaves through me, but I shake it off. I know Hunter cares about me. I know he cares deeply about me. It feels like he loves me.

But can I trust that feeling?

"I don't think I want to play the field," I say to Veronica softly, not meeting her eyes. She tilts her head to the side as if I said something perplexing.

"What do you mean? You can't go back to being a nun."

"No, I don't plan on doing that. I just…" I start wiping

invisible crumbs off the countertop. "I think he and I are the real thing. We're in love."

Veronica's gaze turns soft, clearly radiating pity.

After a long moment of discomfort, she says, "Have you said, 'I love you' to each other?" She folds her hands over her belly. It's crazy to think she has more of her pregnancy behind her than in front of her.

I struggle to answer her. "Well, no…" I stop talking at her look. I know by the crease of her eyebrows that she's concerned.

"Winter," she says quietly. "You can't possibly be in love with him. It's too soon. You barely know the man. Hell, *I* don't know the man—not even his name." She gets up more quietly than ever and pads over to where I stand in the kitchen.

I consider her words, staring off to the corner of my apartment. I set up the saddest Christmas tree. It's only about four feet tall, and I drag the same fake tree out year after year, even though I generally spend Christmas elsewhere. It comes with pre-strung Christmas lights, and besides assembling it, I do nothing to it to add to the festive atmosphere.

"I…" My face starts to tingle, and my chest feels tight. I shake my head quickly to dislodge my thoughts.

Maybe I have this all wrong. Maybe…

You're smarter than this.

Kitty pads over to me, putting his front paws on my leg. The simple touch shakes me out of the spiral.

What am I doing? What am I really doing here?

"You know, you're probably right. I mean, I'm damn near a doctoral-level psychologist. I know what infatuation is." I busy myself straightening up the already clean kitchen. "This is just lust at this point."

Veronica nods. "Lust is good. But don't get caught up in this whirlwind. Hot Daddy is, well, hot, I'm sure. But you should do more than screw around with *just* him. You should go date other people. See what kind of guys you like. Or girls. Are you attracted to women? You've never mentioned an interest in swimming on the other side of the pond. It could be fun if you're into it."

I laugh, but it's forced.

"I don't want you to get hurt, Winter. Because if he hurts you, he won't be Hot Daddy anymore. He'll be Dickless Daddy." The side eye she gives me makes me laugh for real this time.

"I won't get hurt, Rons. I promise. My eyes are wide open," I say. Now, if I can believe my own words.

A knock sounds at the front door, and Veronica and I look at each other. When Kitty pads over and puts his paws on the door, sniffing, I decide that I should be the one to answer it, even though I'm not expecting any more guests.

I look through the peephole and whirl around to press my back to the door.

"It's him," I say.

"Who?" Veronica rasps urgently. She grabs her purse and moves closer to me. Presumably, to whack any intruders in the head.

"Hot Daddy," I say. My eyes are wide, and I'm caught off guard. A few things are happening right now. One, I didn't expect him to show up to my apartment unannounced, and the flannel pjs and camisole with the mystery stain near the hip is the last thing I want him to see me in. Two, Veronica looks way too eager to open the door and meet him, and that's another step I'm not prepared for.

Especially if this is just a phase. I don't want her to see him—see us—and know from the jump that it's not real.

"Open it!" she hisses, pulling me away from the door. When I don't make a move to open it, she rolls her eyes and mutters, "I have to do every damn thing around here."

Swinging the door open, she says, "Helloooooooo!" and Hunter takes a step back from the doorway.

"Um," he says. "Is Winter home?"

"I'm here," I say meekly, waving at him from behind Veronica's shoulder.

"So, you're..."

Please God, Veronica. Please do not call this man Hot Daddy to his face.

"I'm sorry, what's your name?"

I release my breath.

"Hunter Brigham," he says, sticking his hand out to shake Veronica's.

"Hunter Brigham," she emphasizes, shaking his hand. I can see she's putting all the strength in her 5'3" body into squeezing the life out of Hunter's hand. "It's lovely to put a name to the face. Veronica Palmer. Best friend to Winter Vaughan and professional ass-kicker," she says.

"Veronica!" I hiss.

She looks over her shoulder at me. "What?" she says. She even bats her eyelashes for extra effect.

"It's nice to meet you, Veronica. Do you mind if I come in?" He addresses his request to both of us—Veronica, because she's quite literally barricading the door. Me, because it's my damn apartment.

"Come in," Veronica and I say at the same time.

Hunter steps inside and closes the door.

"So, Hunter Brigham," Veronica says, and I groan, dropping my face into my hands.

"Veronica, quit it," I say in a low voice.

She looks at me, and I look at her—we're having a whole conversation with our eyes.

Me: Quit your shit.

Veronica: Make me. I don't know this man!

Me: Leave him alone! Stop badgering him!

Veronica: I guess.

She gives me a rueful smile, and looking at the both of us, she shrugs her shoulders and pulls her purse up higher.

"All right, you two, I'mma head out."

I mouth, "thank you" to her; she mouths back, "yeah, yeah."

Walking her to the door, she gives me a tight hug. Well, as tight as it can be with her belly between us. Speaking close to my ear, she says, "Stay safe and keep your head about you. I see why you're so tied up over him. He's fawkin' hot."

I playfully pat her on the butt, and she turns to do the same.

When she's out the door, I don't turn around right away. It's for sure the conversation Veronica and I just had and the way she lovingly eviscerated my beliefs about my relationship with Hunter that makes me pause. I'm shook. Uncertain.

"I missed you today, Sunbeam," he says softly. I lower my head to the cool door.

I've missed him too. Today was the first day that we've spent completely apart from each other since we've started dating. We both work from Amelia Manor: him with BwP on the other side of the estate and I with August, usually in his game room. Still, I've felt off-kilter all day. And that further unsettles me.

I turn to face him.

Exhaustion etches lines on his face, and he looks more tired than I've ever seen him. Sadness colors his words, and the longer I look into his fathomless eyes, the more clearly I see the storm clouds gathering in his expression.

"I missed you too, H."

We stand there looking at each other, the tension thick between us. I take the first step, and he's there in front of me in a second. I'm in his arms.

He holds me tight with something that feels so much like desperation—it's thick in his every inhalation and exhalation.

And I don't know why, but I hold him just as tightly.

"Bad night?" I run my fingers up and down his back and smile into his chest at the fine tremor that runs through him.

"Something like that," he says, his voice strained.

"Do you want to talk about it?" Up and down. Up and down.

He inhales deeply, holds his breath, and then exhales. His body relaxes, and he rests his head on top of mine. "No, I don't, Winter." His hand runs up the back of my neck, resting in the tangle of my hair. "I need you. I need you so badly."

I tilt my head to look into his eyes.

"I'm here," I say. And he lowers his lips to mine.

There's too much left unsaid in the urgency of this kiss. I feel it in the press of his lips and the way his hands tremble as they clutch at my flesh.

It's clear that something is wrong. Terribly wrong. I just hope it doesn't mean the end of us.

"Come on, H," I whisper, taking his hand and leading him through my tiny apartment. I flick off the lights before I sit him on my bed.

"Wait here for a second," I say, my tone muted.

Moving in the dim glow coming off the Christmas tree, I get Kitty settled for the night. When I stop by the nightstand, I light the wood wick of a soy candle. Lavender, jasmine, and lemon verbena diffuse in the air. It's a candle he purchased for me on our first all-day date.

I haven't lit it in the weeks since he purchased it for me, feeling that I wanted to do so when the moment was significant.

This moment feels significant.

I move in front of him. He leans forward, resting his elbows on his thighs and he cradles his head in his right hand. His eyes fix on me.

You can't tell me that look in his eyes isn't love.

I move closer, placing my hands on his shoulders. He wraps his arms around my waist, burying his face in my stomach.

"What do you need, Hunter?"

He doesn't answer. Instead, he slowly moves my tank top up until it's off my body. My breasts bounce when they're free from the built-in bra.

"Winter," he says on a breath, taking my nipple in his mouth.

I arch my back, plunging my fingers into his hair. "H, please talk to me," I whisper. Tears well in my eyes, and I don't know why.

Don't you?

He buries his face into my stomach again. "I don't know where to start. Everything is fucked-up." He shivers.

"Hunter, please. We're friends, remember?" I pull his head back by tugging his hair. When I get a clear look at his face, he's closed his eyes. Shutting me out.

So I kiss him. I put all my love and desire and promise and fears into the kiss. Then I step back and take off my remaining clothes.

His eyes are open now, trained on my body.

"I'm ready, H," I whisper.

He swallows, and it's clear on his face that he's contemplating which step to take. What is right? What is wrong?

He takes my hand, pulling me down on him. We're back on each other as the icy silence between us turns into a conflagration.

"Winter," he says, his voice so low it's almost a growl.

The sound makes my toes curl and floods my pussy. I straddle him, rushing to remove his shirt.

He lifts his hips, removing his pants.

Now, we're both naked, chest to chest, and I shiver when he runs a hand down my stomach and between my legs.

His touch is feather-light on my clit, and when he finds the wetness of my arousal between my lips, he groans again, tilting forward to suck on the skin above my breast.

"Winter," he says urgently. I move, running my hand up and down the entire length of the hard flesh of his cock.

"Hunter." I moan his name, transforming the broken syllables into a prayer. I remove my hand from his manhood, putting both hands on his cheeks and forcing him to look at me.

His blue eyes crash into mine.

"I'm ready," I say on a faint breath.

We stare at each other for several heartbeats.

One.

Two.

Three.

Then he says, "Put me inside you, Winter."

I bite my lip and reach down for his cock again. Rubbing the tip along my seam, I moan when I rub his length across my hard nub. I rock my hips over and over.

There's no urge to pause, to hesitate, within my spirit. This moment has always been inevitable. This was always meant to happen between Hunter and me.

I put him at my entrance, and torturously, I lower myself on top of him.

My eyes cross. The stretch is unimaginable—burning, pulsing. My womanhood accepting both Hunter's presence and the significance of this reclamation of my sex.

I choose Hunter. I choose this.

Power surges through me, electric in the inherent current of our connection. I feel completely full. And when I look down to see him stretching me, breaching me, filling me, I want to weep at the pure eroticism of the moment.

His body shakes as he puts his hands on my hips. I can tell he is struggling to stay completely still and let me control the pace. He's letting me control everything about this moment.

"Winter," he says, "I want this to last forever."

I lower myself more and test moving up and down and back and forth on his cock. He leans back to rest on his elbows, and I resettle myself on top of him, putting the pressure on my knees.

At this angle, he bottoms out, and I quickly learn I love the feeling of him so deep inside me.

This feels right. This feels so right.

"Who says it can't, H?" I pant as I pick up the pace, rocking back and forth and hitting my clit on every pass over his pubic bone. I'm taking all of him now, and I can feel my wetness dripping down, slicking over both of us.

He doesn't say anything. Instead, he rubs his thumb over my clit.

"Come for me, Sunbeam," he says, and I pick up the pace quickly learning the movements that feel the best. He leans back all the way, pulling my arm to have me tilt over him, and I'm ricocheted to another level of pleasure.

"Oh, fuck, Hunter," I moan, and he grabs my breast with his free hand and picks up the pace with the other hand that's adding to the pleasure radiating from my core.

"Make it feel good, Winter. You feel like heaven to me," he whispers.

I'm wild on top of him now, racing after the orgasm that's right within my reach.

"You're not wearing a condom, H," I say between pants. My eyes screw shut.

"Do you want me to stop, Sunbeam?" He's breathing hard now. We're both sweaty, and the sounds of our lovemaking are obscene in the small apartment.

"Oh, God, no." The thought trips me to the precipice, heating me so thoroughly. I've never ever ever wanted a man to come inside me. The idea was so vile to me that I never considered it. I'm on birth control, but with H…

"On the pill," I choke out.

He groans from deep inside his chest, and I feel the vibration where my thighs press against his sides.

"I won't. I won't ever stop, Winter."

That's all I need to explode over him. I squeeze down on him, strangling his cock and fighting to push him out with the intensity of my orgasm.

"Oh, fuck!" he roars, and gripping my hip with one hand, he pulls me down with the other into a brutal kiss. His cock throbs inside me, and I feel the warmth of his cum coating my walls.

My pussy squeezes him again, completely out of my control.

I rock against him softly, coming down, and a primal part of me preens as his hands run up and down my back while he's still inside me.

I turn my head and kiss his chest. His breathing slows.

"Hunter, you can talk to me. Tell me what's wrong." I'm still whispering, even though my throat is dry from yelling out my release.

He just kisses my head and doesn't say a word.

THREE A.M. never brings good news. So when my phone rings, waking me from my sleep in Hunter's arms, I know something is terribly wrong.

"Rons, what's happening? Is it the baby?" I'm immediately wide awake.

"Are you alone?" Veronica says with a strange, solemn tone.

I look back at Hunter. He's still asleep, and I pad over to the bathroom.

I sit on the closed toilet seat.

"Now I am. What's going on?" I say, keeping my voice low.

"Hunter is there?" she replies.

I'm quiet for a moment, then I say, "Yes, he spent the night."

Veronica audibly blows out a breath.

"But I'm in the bathroom right now. What's...what's happening, Veronica?"

"Let's switch to FaceTime," she says, and I move my phone from my face when it beeps.

"You're scaring me, Veronica. Please tell me what's going on." I'm embarrassed when my voice cracks, and I look away when tears well in my eyes.

I can feel it.

I have been feeling it. The *tick-tock* of the countdown on my happiness. It's not pessimism—it's the reality that I know something horrible will shatter my fragile hold on my bliss.

"Winter, I don't want to tell you this. But..." she breathes out again. "It's about Hunter."

I shake my head, still not looking at her through the phone screen.

"You looked him up, didn't you?" I knew she'd look him up as soon as she left. And I knew she'd do so without the rose-colored glasses I have firmly affixed to my face. The same glasses that have prevented me from digging deeper into the Brigham family beyond my initial pre-interview research.

She's silent except for a small whimper. I slide my gaze to look at her. She nods her head in the affirmative. Tears pool in her eyes.

"Rons, don't." I screw my eyes shut again, squeezing my lids together so firmly that my ocular muscles resist the action.

Don't...what? Don't cry? Don't tell me the truth? Don't

take away this bubble of happiness that I haven't felt since my parents were alive?

She pauses for a minute. "Will you look at me, Winter?" she says softly.

I release the tension in my face, and when I allow my eyes to open a slit, I'm mortified at the tears spilling down my face. "What did you find?" I ask.

She takes a deep breath. "Winter, he's engaged," she says. She's crying alongside me, and I shut my eyes at the news.

Engaged. Engaged. Engaged.

"How do you know?" My phone pings with an incoming text message. It's an article from *The Herald*.

Billionaire MedTech CEO Hunter Brigham to wed socialite and philanthropist Blair Winthrope

My hands shake, and it takes all my strength to keep the phone propped up. Veronica says something I don't register while I tap to expand the webpage.

I need to know everything. So I scroll through the article.

Hunter and his…fiancée Blair make a pretty couple. He looks completely different in the pictures. Regal and aloof in his navy-colored three-piece suit. It looks similar to the one he wore on our date.

His fiancée stands next to him, smiling gently with her hand pressed against his chest. Her leg peeks from the high slit in her emerald silk dress. The massive pear-shaped diamond on her hand looks stunning in the photo.

"This could be old," I say, grasping at anything to make this not real.

"There are other articles, Winter. And…just check the date. You'll see," she says on a rushed whisper.

My blood turns to ice when I read the publication date. I force myself to read the date over and over and over.

It was published last night.

After I told him about the darkest moment in my life.

After he promised I would always have him.

After he saw me so intimately.

After I gave myself to him.

Anger nudges my despair to the side, blooming hot in my chest and rushing to flush my face.

"Veronica, get some rest. I'll call you in the morning."

"What are you going to do, Winter?" Redness rings her tired eyes.

"I'm going to handle this situation," I say.

She looks at me steadily. "You've been through hell and back, and this won't wreck you." She sniffs. "I love you. Please call me later in the morning."

When the screen goes black, I sit on the toilet for a few more minutes, staring at nothing.

One thought repeats in my head: it was published last night.

Even knowing he promised himself to another woman, he still fucked me.

And I let him. I let him have everything.

"I want this to last forever," he said to me just hours ago.

Lies. All a bunch of pretty lies.

My movements are mechanical, done by muscle memory, as I wash my hands and face. I put hand cream on to give myself something to do. It's the same brand my mother used, and I take comfort in inhaling the familiar scent.

I leave the safe haven of my bathroom.

Hunter sits on the edge of the bed, facing the bathroom door and fully dressed. His head hangs low, and the light from the bathroom illuminates his face when he raises it to look at me. His eyes are bloodshot.

Wordlessly, I walk toward him and hand him my phone.

"Is this true?" I ask, already knowing the answer but hoping he'll tell me it's not.

Praying he'll tell me that it's just a horrible misunderstanding.

Pleading with the heavens that everything I thought was real is real.

Instead, he doesn't look at the screen. He meets my gaze and nods. "Yes. It's true."

I stand there for a moment, proud that my legs still hold me upright as tears crest my eyelids. My chest tightens with the inability to breathe.

I spin the phone around in my hand, clutching it to have something to anchor myself in reality.

"Well, thank you for the fuck. But you can get out now." I turn around to go back into the bathroom, desperate to go anywhere but in the same airspace as him, and before I can close the door, he's there.

"Let me just explain," he says.

I cross my arms. "Please do. I've been waiting all night for you to explain *anything*—to use your words. So, speak," I say. And I wait.

When he gapes at me for several tense moments, I say, "Right. You can't." I push past him and out of the bathroom.

"For your safety, there are things you can't know."

"Oh, why don't you try me, Hunter? I'm pretty smart, according to some people."

"Winter, I—"

"Listen, it's a simple question, yes or no. Are you currently engaged to be married?"

He doesn't answer right away. Finally, he says, "Yes."

"Then we're done here. There's nothing further to discuss."

"I know you deserve answers, something to help you understand that if you just wait—"

"Wait? Wait for what?" I spit out. I feel myself losing it. Losing my composure. Losing ground. Losing myself.

"Fuck this," he says, and I feel my heart drop to my

stomach because he's finally figured out that I'm not worth all this drama.

He got what he wanted.

Instead of leaving, he's in front of me, crowding me against the door. My lips tremble, and I want to kiss every part of his stupid face. I hate myself for wanting that, even after all this.

"Winter." He lets out a slow breath, his arms caging me in as I press firmly against the door. "I'm so sorry." He reaches a hand to touch the side of my face, and I hate myself more that I let him.

"I'm so sorry I hurt you. I should have explained everything to you earlier. Things are messy right now, but I will make it right. Just wait for me."

I raise my eyes to his, not caring that he sees the devastation that must be in them. Because I feel wrecked right now.

I knew it would come to this and still.

His lips are on mine. Pressing, coaxing, sliding his tongue to caress mine. My hands go to his chest, grasping his shirt.

I want to push him away. I want him to leave.

Lies. Everything is a lie.

"Winter, please don't," he whispers against my lips. "Please don't break us apart."

The words pull me out of the trance. In a flash, I push him back with my arm straight and my palm hard against his chest.

"You can't do this to me, Hunter."

He closes his eyes, pushing back against my hand that's keeping us separated.

"I'm sorry, Winter. I'll do whatever I need to do to have you forgive me. To make this right."

"Make it right?" I snort. There's no making this right.

"Eh, it's okay," I say nonchalantly. "It was just a bit of fun, right? I wanted to be wild, and that's what I did. I got wild. It doesn't have to mean anything."

My chest tightens, and my throat feels like it's closing up. I'm sure I'm having a heart attack. Or maybe I'm simply dying. I spin around, breaking the connection between our gazes.

"I'll be there for August. Let him know I'll see him on Monday."

He pulls my body back against his, and the hard chest I felt beneath my fingers is now pressed fully against my spine. He bands his arms around my waist, and all I can do is freeze.

"I'm trying to keep you safe, Winter." His words are hard and low, whispered urgently. "There are people who would revel in dancing in your blood just to see me hurt. Just to make me do what they want me to do. I'm trying to protect you. Protect August. Protect our love. Please, just be patient with me. I'm going to fix this, and we can continue our lives. Because I want you forever. You're it for me, Winter." He's breathing double time, and I feel like he's making up for my lack of inhalation and exhalation.

Because he just said he loves me.

He loves me. He wants to protect me.

This is toxic. This is possession. This is…

"There you go sounding like you're in the fucking mob again. Should I expect to find a horse head in my bed?" My words are firm and clear, but the resolve in them is lost when my voice trembles at the last few words.

"There is so much I want to tell you, but I can't right now. I will tell you *soon,* but I can't right now. But this situation with Blair—"

I jerk when he says her name.

Blair, Blair, Blair. A perfect name for someone like Hunter Brigham to be married to.

"This engagement is completely fake. It's a means to an end. I can't share all the details. But just know that everything I do is for you. For you and August. I need you to wait for me." He runs a hand up and places it over my breast. Over my heart. I know he can feel it racing.

"I love you, Winter Leigh Vaughan."

I close my eyes at the declaration. It's everything I could have hoped for. And I feel so, so, so empty.

"You love me?" I whisper.

"Yes, I love you. I have loved you since I saw you on the floor of my home, protecting my son."

The quaking I feel radiating from my heart travels to my arms.

"If you love me…" I breathe in deeply. "Answer me this, Hunter. How can you fuck me, say you love me, and be promised to someone else?"

"Winter, it's not even like that." His voice is rough, strained.

"Even with everything you've said to me, will you still go through with this marriage if whatever you're waiting for doesn't pan out before next spring? Your wedding is right around the corner from what the tabloids say. Will you bring her into your home? Into your bed? And you want me to wait for you? Wait for you until *when*? Wait for *what?* How long will I have to watch you with another woman?"

I'm choking. Sobbing. Trying to grapple back my composure, my upper hand. But I'm failing. I'm falling.

He pulls me in closer, nearly crushing me with his strength. His desperation.

"No, it's—goddamn it, Winter, it's complicated, but it's not at all what you think. I'm fucking this up, not explaining things right. Let's just sit down. Cool off and talk."

I put my hand over his as he continues to hold my heart.

For a moment, with our bodies silent in the moonlight and only a shaft of illumination coming from the bathroom, I let myself revel in the feeling and knowledge and truth of loving Hunter Brigham.

I soak it into my skin, let it encode into my DNA.

And then I pull away.

"I love you too, Hunter. I love you so much. But this is messy. Hurtful. I can't subscribe to this life. I need more. I need better than this."

I unlock the door, opening it. The security guard outside my door looks up from his cell phone at the movement.

"Winter, I won't accept this being the end of us." His voice is hoarse, but the look on his face would be terrifying if I didn't know him.

Do I know him?

I look away from his beautiful, stupid, lying face.

And even though tears blur my vision, I say, "Well, unfortunately for you, I will accept it.

I look away from him, still stubbornly holding the door open.

"I'll see August on Monday, but I think we should keep our interactions to a minimum."

I pull the door wider, and he moves through it, taking my heart with him.

I immediately shut the door when he clears the threshold, slamming the locks home.

I touch the lock one more time. Then again. Then again. Then again and again and again until I collapse on the floor, sobbing.

Kitty trots over to me.

I bury my face in his fur and wail.

TWENTY-EIGHT
WINTER

A week later, August and I are firmly settled into a new routine. I'm grateful he's been able to manage the transition well.

Christmas sucked. I spent the entire day alone. Veronica wanted to stay behind with me, but I begged her to go to the Poconos with James as planned. She needed that alone time with her husband, and I've derailed too many of their plans over the years.

I can handle this myself.

So I spent the day on my sofa watching *Last Holiday* and *The Preacher's Wife* and sobbing into Kitty's fur until my eyes seared from my tears.

I cried again when I opened my door to take out the trash and learned that Hunter still had security sitting outside my apartment. Further adding to my devastation, Hunter had a gift delivered to me via the security. When the beefy man handed it to me, I chucked it into my apartment and demanded they leave. The man simply shrugged and went back to scrolling through his phone. His refusal to listen to me brought a new wave of frustrated rage-tears to my eyes.

I told Alexa to play "You Oughta Know" by Alanis Morissette on repeat until my neighbor started banging on my door to turn it down.

I made it to 1 a.m. before caving and opening Hunter's gift. Of course he got me jewelry, but of course he didn't get me a diamond bracelet like any normal person. He selected a handcrafted white gold ring. Dark musgravite stones surround a large color-changing alexandrite. A ridiculously expensive and thoughtful gift, knowing the meanings of the two stones: musgravite for boundless joy and alexandrite for balance between the spiritual and physical worlds.

Now I sit at the gates of Amelia Manor in the car Veronica's coordinated for me using James' account. The driver, a serious-faced man from Romania, hasn't spoken to me for the entire ride. I appreciate his silence.

I'm outside. Ready?

I tap my fingers on my glossy black phone case until August replies two minutes later.

Yes.

Ten minutes later, he rolls down the drive in the grounds cart with Rex by his side.

We drive to a small private airfield and head inside August's hangar. Hunter apparently purchased it last summer, but August has just recently decided to use it for storing and working on all his RC stuff.

The small hangar is a teenage boy's dream. August decked the place out with shelves and tables to work on the dozens of remote-controlled aircraft he owns. He has a sofa and chairs, and posters on the walls of characters I vaguely remember from the games he's introduced me to. A fridge, microwave, and string lights complete the scene.

"I need to charge these batteries," August says, already

fiddling with his tools. "Please pull the chairs and the heater to the edge of the hangar."

It seems like August isn't bothered by the bitter temperatures at all, but I feel like my fingers are a few minutes away from frostbite.

I do what he asks, and once done, I beeline for a chair and thank the heavens for the powerful space heater next to my seat, protecting me from the freezing temperatures. Kitty seeks my body heat beneath the several layers of clothing, and I hold his trembling body close.

More hangars spot the far side of the airstrip, and three bays down I see a couple working on a small two-seater airplane.

Besides the couple, our driver, and Rex, August and I are the only people here. The solitude feels nice.

It's cold, but bright today. Someone cleared the airfield of all the snow that's accumulated over the last forty-eight hours, and August stands at the opening of the hangar, preparing his electric RC helicopter for flight.

Before the holiday, August told me about discovering RC helicopters when he was a young kid before he could use AAC to communicate.

"I used to watch YouTube videos about all kinds of stuff. I didn't understand how you could hold a helicopter in your hand and make it fly," he told me.

Today, he performs tricks in the air, flipping the helicopter in smooth circles and racing at top speed. After fifteen minutes, he sits next to me, assessing his batteries.

His nose is red, and the beanie he wears sits haphazardly on top of his head. He doesn't wear gloves because he hates the feeling, he says. I bet his fingers are nearly frozen.

I'm under two blankets, a space heater, and three layers of clothing including my wool coat, hat, and scarf, and I'm still shivering.

Or maybe that chill is coming from my bleeding soul.

"How have you been feeling this last week, August?" I perch my sunglasses on my face under the guise of protecting them from snow blindness.

He shrugs. "It has been weird not having you in the house. But I like going places with you. I spend a lot of time in my room, but I like doing things."

"A social butterfly, are you?" I tease. He looks in my direction with an expression I've come to understand is confusion.

"I have many friends," he says.

Seeing an opening to dive deeper, I say, "Tell me more about them."

He taps his cheek a few times. "I have my RC group. There are four of us, and we met at an Autism meetup for kids that mom's church held."

"Your mom went to church?" I ask.

"Yes, she did. She would go to church a lot, actually. Especially in the last year before she died."

"Did you go with her to church?"

"No. I do not believe in God. It is a logical impracticality."

"Very interesting. Care to share more about that?"

"No."

I throw my hands up. "Fair enough. So you have your RC friends. You have others?"

I wait for him to formulate his response. "Yes, there are my gamer friends and my schoolmates." He shakes his hand, flicking his fingers back and forth. "I have not spoken with them in a very long time now that I do not go to school anymore."

I think about his schooling. And mine too, for that matter.

"Have you asked your dad about going back to school?"

His eyes shift toward me, then back out toward the airstrip. He rocks gently from side to side. "Hunter and I do not communicate."

"Why? You both were making so much progress."

His body stills, and he looks in my direction for a long

minute. "I do not like what he did to you. I know about him being engaged. I am not dumb."

My cheeks heat.

"August..." I don't know what else to say. I'd promised myself that I'd keep my world with August and my world with Hunter separate. It's better for everyone involved.

"You appear sad."

I take my glasses off and lean forward to talk with him.

"I won't insult your intelligence by lying or hiding things from you. Your father and I are no longer together. But please believe me when I say I'm okay. I wish him and his fiancée well."

He doesn't say anything. He puts his tablet in his lap, and we sit for several long minutes. "Their engagement party is tomorrow," he says.

I try to fight the tears welling up in my throat, and I put my glasses back on in case I embarrass myself and start crying.

"Oh?" I say. "New Year's Eve. Nice. How do you feel about that?"

He rolls his eyes. I'm unsure if he's rolling them at me or at them.

"I hate it. I do not want to be around a crowd of people, and I do not want to go because I know how they will treat me."

I tilt my head to the side. "They? Who is 'they,' August?"

"The guests. They will either treat me like a baby or talk at me slowly as if I cannot comprehend their speech. Also, people are loud or smell offensive. It is likely the lights will be too bright. It is stressful. When I get stressed, I cannot control my body sometimes, even if I really want my body to be calm."

He looks at me earnestly now.

He taps his cheek again. "Will you come with me, Winter?"

My initial instinct is to scream no. It's to wail and stomp my foot at the unfairness of it all.

"I can't do that, August. That would be really inappropriate for me to do."

He snorts, and I know he's directing that one at me.

"Was dating Hunter not inappropriate?"

I rear back and put my hand on my chest. "I'm insulted," I say. I smile to let him know I'm being sarcastic. I'm not sure he picks up on it, so I add, "I'm joking."

He shrugs.

"Really though, August, that wouldn't be a good idea."

He gets up from his chair and paces a few steps away from our seats. A few minutes later, after tapping his cheek and flicking his wrist several times, he returns to his chair and grabs his forgotten tablet.

"I do not feel safe going alone. I really need you, Winter. Aunt Ella will be there, but she will also be busy. My grandfather will be there." He holds his tablet to his chest, his head downcast.

I breathe in deeply, analyzing the situation. I know that it will be gut-wrenching if I go to the party. I know I'm not invited. I know I'm not wanted.

And I also know that—even with Ella running interference—for August, attending a party like this one is torture. He's expected to go, but who will he lean on while he's there?

I think about all the tools for managing sensory assault that we've established over the past few weeks. Taking those brand-new skills for a test drive in a high-stress situation isn't the best move.

As a practitioner, I know that's only asking for overwhelming distress.

"Okay, August. I'll go. I know you don't want to be there, so let's limit this to thirty minutes tops. If you get an urge to stay longer than that, I can't commit to staying, though. Deal?"

He smiles and starts pacing again, vocalizing happily.

"Deal," he says.

I smile too, but on the inside, I feel like I'm walking to my death.

WALKING into the country club's ballroom is like teleporting into an alternate dimension. My past, the one where I used to attend events at country clubs all around D.C. with my mom and dad, collides with the strange luxury of the Appleton Country Club.

I didn't think twice about not bringing Kitty, even though his presence would make this hellscape at least seventy percent more tolerable.

But I didn't want more eyes on me than necessary. Plus, I think I saw it as a challenge: will I be able to make it through this without leaning on my supports?

Genevieve's wise voice echoes in my brain, telling me, lovingly, that that's a dumb thing to aspire to.

Everything is pure white, gold, and crystals. There must be two hundred guests milling around the ballroom, and at the center of them is Hunter Brigham and his fiancée, Blair Winthrope.

I beg my eyes to move from looking at him. They fail to listen.

"I think thirty minutes is long enough." The accent August uses, an overly proper lady who sounds a little like Maggie Smith, feels hilariously perfectly imperfect.

"I agree, friend." A waiter passes out champagne, and I snag one, resisting the urge to grab a second. When August reaches for one, I say, "Not on your life, home skillet."

He rolls his eyes. We arrived as late as we dared. It's

eleven thirty, and we planned to stay through the countdown to the new year, and then we'll bounce.

I feel an arm link with mine and jump at the unexpected touch. Looking to my right, Ella's bowed head leans on my shoulder.

"Doesn't this blow?" she asks. "They're all so disgusting."

She looks beautiful tonight. Her long black hair wraps into an elegant chignon and a diamond necklace gleams from her neck. The floor-length strapless silk maroon dress looks molded to her body. The corseted top makes her bust pop. She straightens, facing me.

"At least you look beautiful, Ella." I try to smile, but I know my face is doing weird things.

Thirty minutes, tops.

"How are you here?" she asks in a low voice. Not why, but how.

"I'm here purely on the strength of my love for August," I say.

"I get it. Sometimes, I only run on rage and Warheads." She nods sagely.

I suppress the first laugh I've felt enough to utter in the last week. Looking around the room, I see a few faces I recognize. Security staff from Amelia Manor. August's guard, Rex. The goddamn Vice President.

And Hunter.

Suddenly, the lights are too bright, the sounds too percussive. I look back at Ella but still see Hunter in the periphery. He's looking straight at me. His eyes reflect shock. Then longing. My throat feels like it's closing, and I struggle to keep a calm appearance. I don't want to stress August out more. I also don't want Hunter to see me lose it.

You will not have a panic attack here. You will not give him the privilege of seeing you break down.

"Excuse me. I need to go to the ladies' room. August, you're good here with your aunt, right?"

August's eyes narrow slightly, but he nods.

I smile as brightly as I can. "I'll be back in a minute."

I turn around and try to temper my pace toward the restrooms. I saw them when we entered the club, and I pray my muscle memory will bring me to the right place.

I rush into the bathroom, rejoicing when I see it empty. Locking myself in, I thank the club's over-the-top design when I see a small sitting area next to the stall.

Breathe in. *I am calm.*

Breathe out. *I am safe.*

Breathe in. *I am protected.*

Breathe out. *I am love.*

Love.

Love, love, love.

I put my hand on my heart, wondering if I can feel the breaks in it.

One day, when you are old and gray and looking back on your life, you will laugh at how impossible getting over this feels.

Right now, every breath hurts.

I've got to get out of here. I pull my phone out of my clutch and pray Ella has her phone on her.

Ella?

Five minutes pass, and I'm about to give up and search for August and Ella when a reply comes.

Are you okay?

I let out a breath.

Yes, I am, but…this is really tough for me. I need to go home. Can you get August home? I feel terrible for bailing on him, but I just can't.

Dots appear on her side immediately.

Of course, Winter. I've got it covered.

Please tell August I will see him Monday.

I muster up my courage, leave the stall, and re-enter the empty bathroom. I wash my hands and look at my reflection. Besides my nose being slightly rosier than it usually is, I don't look like I've been crying.

Score one, Winter.

In the background, I hear someone announce that there's twenty minutes until the new year. I pull my phone out to schedule an Uber and rejoice when I see one forty-five minutes down the road. Reserving the car, I tuck my phone back in my clutch and exit the bathroom.

And walk right into the chest of the one human I'd desperately wanted to avoid.

TWENTY-NINE
HUNTER

When I see her in the ballroom, I'm convinced my mind is playing tricks on me. Maybe the multi-day alcohol binge I went on after leaving Winter's apartment has caused brain damage and I'm entering psychosis.

But she isn't a figment of my imagination. She's here. In the middle of this fucked-up engagement party.

"Look happy," Blair says through gritted teeth, parodying a smile.

"What's there to be happy about, Blair?" I say back just as tensely.

"There's plenty to smile about, actually. You're rich. You're about to marry me, and you still have your life."

I clear my throat and stay silent.

"Son."

Just fucking great.

Blair beams at my father, turning to him fully, and he takes her hand and kisses the back of it. The look that passes between the two of them lets me know that they're undoubtedly fucking.

Not that I actually give a shit. They could have a three-way with Satan for all I care. If they'd just leave me the fuck alone.

"Father," I say, forcing myself to shake his hand.

"I thought you'd be a little more discerning with your invites," he says. If you'd look at the three of us from the outside, you'd see us all smiling, relaxed. But we're anything but.

"Do you have a problem with my guests, *Dad*?" I look him dead in the eye. He smiles at the unmistakable sign of aggression.

"Surely not," he replies after a beat. "Well, I see people I need to talk to. Duty calls," he says. He waves to the Vice President, who stands surrounded by a mass of Secret Service agents.

He nods to the both of us and walks off.

"That does beg the question. What do you plan on doing with the child?"

I arch my eyebrow at Blair's question. "Meaning?"

"Well, he won't be living with us. Will you give him to Ella or send him away?"

White hot fury shoots through my body like a lightning bolt from God.

"Excuse me?" I smile brightly to counter the action I want to take, which is to snap her neck in front of every single one of these people. I catch Leo's eye. He's lurking in the shadows, as are at least twenty of our security detail. Tonight isn't the night. But if something were to happen, they'd be here to take it down.

This is all temporary. It's a means to an end.

"Surely you heard me, Hunter." She waves gently at a guest who walks near us.

I move closer to her, pulling her arm so that anyone who sees us will think we're in a lover's embrace. When I lean close to her ear, I say, "If you so much as mention my son ever again in your life, I will put a bullet in your brain myself."

Then to drive the point home, I kiss her cheek and turn to walk away without another word.

I step down from the platform where Blair and I stand and look through the crowd for August—and Winter. I see August with Ella and move toward them. August seems annoyed, and when he turns his head to the side, I see he has earbuds to dampen the noise.

Smart move.

"Enjoying yourself, brother?" Ella lifts her champagne glass to her mouth and takes a healthy sip.

"Can I go now?" August says. I nod at August since I know he won't be able to hear me.

"Where's Winter?" I ask Ella.

She kicks up one side of her mouth. She looks at me for a moment, then says, "I thought about telling you to fuck off, but I like you tonight. She's in the restroom near the front entrance."

"Get August out of here, will you?" I ask.

She rolls her eyes. "Sure," she grumbles.

I walk through the crowd and toward the front women's restroom. Most guests don't use this one, as the closer bathroom is on the other side of the ballroom.

Once outside the bathroom, I pause against the wall, cherishing the silence.

And when you see her, what will you say to her? Will you beg her to take you back again?

I just want a minute alone with her.

After several heavy moments, I turn to enter the room, questioning if she's even in there. Right when my hand touches the door, she opens it.

We both stare at each other; the moment is tense. But I can't begrudge it for anything. Because the second I look at her beautiful face, I realize I can breathe again.

"Winter," I say.

"Hunter," she replies. Her lips tremble. And then, she's crying.

I cannot stand the sight. I push her back into the bathroom and lock the door as soon as we're both through the threshold. I pull her into my arms.

"Is there anyone in here?" I whisper in her ear.

She shakes her head no.

"Hunter, this hurts." Her voice breaks with every word, and she's clinging to me just as I'm clinging to her.

"I know it does, baby." I'm rubbing circles on her back, and the rose smell of her hair causes something significant to crack in my chest.

"Why are you doing this to me? To us?" She looks up at me. Her mascara runs down her cheek, and her lipstick is smudged in one corner.

"Sunbeam," I sigh.

"Just give me something here, Hunter. Some explanation as to why you'd string me along like this."

I look at her face. She's shaking in my arms. And then I realize that I can't keep her out of this. I never could.

"Okay, Sunbeam. Let me tell you a story," I begin. "It starts with a young boy. He's pretty spoiled because he was born into unimaginable wealth. His mother was a beautiful person. Happy. Always smiling. Always saying I love you. But his father was evil. Pure evil."

I look past her face and to the far side of the restroom. The picture framed on the wall should be a cheap replica, but it's a real Seurat. In a bathroom. The waste, greed, and disregard of the people I've spent my whole life around churns my stomach.

"His father was the type of evil that was remorseless. He enjoyed and thrived off hurting people. And the fucked-up part is because he was so wealthy, he could do whatever he wanted at scale. Think of funding wars and genocides and selling people into slavery. But that stuff…a lot of people have a hand in those things. But he was even more depraved. He'd rape and sell children he knew. People he knew. He would hunt people for sport like wild animals. He was a proud, unrepentant slave master."

Winter gasps, and her fingers flex against my chest.

"Let's say this boy's father wants his son to follow in his footsteps. Because that's what's expected of him. So his father shows him what being part of this family means. He tells him the family secrets. He teaches him how to kill, and eventually has the boy kill people, one after the other, dozens. All because the father wanted it done. Because it entertained him. He gives the boy women to fuck at twelve years old. His father's friends introduce him to drugs."

She slams her face into my chest, and her shoulders shake with sobs.

"He is entrenched in what his father does, how he acts, and what he knows. But his mother…his beautiful mother wants out. She was tired of being beaten and abused by her powerful husband. She couldn't look away once she knew of the horrors he inflicted on others. So she tries to stop his father and put him away. But his father is so powerful. Too powerful." I suck in a breath, knowing that this moment could truly tear her from me forever. But I'm resigned that there will be no more secrets. Not anymore.

"His father learns of his mother's betrayal, and he tortures the boy until he tells him his mother's plans. The boy's father burns him, whips him, starves him…."

I pause. Swallow.

"So the boy cracks. He just wants the pain to end. And the next day, his mother is dead."

Another shudder passes through her, and she stills. Stills for several seconds. Her fingers flex against my chest.

There's so much more that happened.

No more secrets, Hunter.

I clear my throat, trying to ease the tightness. Trying to say the words.

But the idea of telling her all of it?

I stare at the top of her head, catching a glimpse of her long eyelashes.

I can't tell her *that*.

"Imagine that boy is changed forever. He hates himself every single day. He does drugs. He gets drunk. He fucks. He gets a girl pregnant. He's a shithead to her and to everyone. He craves the power of providing pain—of hurting people—because in his fucked up life, that's the only thing that makes sense. But when his baby is born, the boy is so, so, so scared. Because he has someone to care about. To cherish. To protect. And he doesn't think he can protect his child at all. His father will destroy his son just for the right to make the boy hurt. So the boy runs away. Runs away to the farthest-flung parts of the world. Runs away even though he knows he's running on borrowed time. And while he's running, the only thing he really wants is to have someone care about him. To have a family. But he knows he can't have that."

I kiss the top of her head, breathing in her scent.

"And then, that boy's carefully orchestrated escape plan blows to pieces…but, in the midst of that chaos he meets a woman. A woman who embodies the sun."

I put my cheek to the top of her head. Everything feels right for the first time since I left her apartment. Finally.

"That boy falls in love with the sunshine. Deeply, madly in love. So now, the boy has so much to lose. And he'll do everything he can to keep the people he loves safe. Even if that means finishing what his mother started all those years ago."

I push my hands into her hair, satisfied as pins fall from her curls. I rub a lock of her hair between my fingers.

She slowly pulls her face from my chest. Her swollen eyes and red nose only add to her beauty because they highlight the rawness of her emotions.

"My father is a terrible, terrible human, Winter. And he's threatened not just me but Leo, Ella, my company, and August. Everyone is at risk, and I didn't want to add you to the list of targets, plus if shit went sideways...I wanted you to have plausible deniability. I've been trying to protect you. I didn't want you to get caught up in all my shit. But I see that shutting you out is not how to do that."

"Thank you for telling me, H."

I don't reply. I just keep looking at her face and rubbing the back of her neck. In the main hall, someone calls out a one-minute warning to the new year.

"Does it..." She bites her lip.

"Does it what, Sunbeam?" She closes her eyes when I call her Sunbeam.

"Does it make me crazy," she opens her eyes, "that I still want to be with you knowing all that?"

My heart thuds in my chest.

"No. Because I'm crazy for you."

"Will you kiss me, H? Will you make it better? I don't care anymore. I just want to be with you."

I rub her cheek, taking in every part of her radiance.

"No," I say.

"No?" She takes one step back, then another.

"No, Sunbeam. Because I want you to be sure. I want you to know that you're a hundred percent mine the next time I kiss you. And that nothing and no one will stop you from being mine."

Her breath hitches.

"Ten!" the crowd chants from outside our sanctuary. We stare at each other; the space between our bodies is electric, pulsing.

"I want to know that we're in this together, facing down the bullshit together. And that when I'm inside you in the next five seconds, you're completely committed to me. Just like I'm completely committed to you. So think, baby."

She bites her lip, and the five-second countdown begins in the hall.

"Five," I count.

"I have missed you so much, H."

"Four," I say. I step closer to her.

"It's been like part of my body is missing every day we've been apart."

"Me too. Three."

"I won't let you marry that bitch. You're not hers to have."

"Of course not. Because I belong to you. Two," I say. I take another step closer to her.

"I love you so much, Hunter Brigham. It's crazy, but I do."

I take the final step, which places her back in my arms. "One."

"Times up, H." She smiles. And I crash my mouth against hers as the crowd cheers.

We battle each other, fighting to breathe in each other's air and merge into one with our mouths. She doesn't bother with my shirt, reaching down to unbuckle my pants and then sliding her warm hand in to caress my already hard cock.

She groans in my mouth, and I push her back against the wall, pulling the skirt of her dress up past her waist. I waste no time pulling her thong aside and plunging a finger into her wet warmth.

"H, please, God," she whispers into my mouth. She bites my lip.

I can't help but release a growl. "I'm going to fuck you, Winter," I say in reply.

"Please," she begs.

Pulling my fingers from her drenched slit, I push them into her mouth. "See how good you taste," I grind out, and she sucks eagerly on my fingers.

Her hand spasms on my cock, squeezing it.

I turn her around to face the wall. She splays her fingers

flat on the wallpaper and arches her back, sticking her ass out toward me.

If there's anything I want to see right before I die, it's this image.

I palm her ass, squeezing it in my hands. "One day, I'm going to fuck this too."

She pants. "I want you to fuck me everywhere, H," she says. "But if you don't get inside me in the next five seconds, I'm gonna take matters into my own hands." She wiggles her ass for emphasis. I lean over her back and nip her ear.

"Patience, love." I turn her face into mine and kiss her hungrily.

I pull my dick out of my pants, stroking it twice before taking one hand to lift her left leg up and using my right to place my cock at the mouth of her pussy.

"Let's do this together," I whisper. Reaching down the front of her body, she curls a hand around my dick and slowly pushes back until I'm fully seated inside her.

"Hold on to the wall, Sunbeam," I growl. She trembles and places both hands flat on the wall again, lowering her chest to rest flush against it.

"Fuck me like I'm yours, my love," she says, and I snap my hips forward to do just that.

When she moans, the sound causes all my thoughts, emotions, and anxieties from the days we've been apart to surface. I press my fingers into her hips, pulling her back on my dick with a punishing slap.

Leaning over her, my lips graze the shell of her ear when I say, "You think you can end us, Winter?"

I stroke my cock in and out of her, slapping my balls against her clit with every thrust. "Ending us is impossible, Sunbeam." She releases a choked sob, and I tilt her back more to hit her spot.

"Even when we're both dead and in the ground, my soul

will find yours." I rub her clit in circles, pressing hard to give her the firm pressure I know she craves.

"Our children and children's children will know about our love."

Her cries escalate.

"Shhh, love, you don't want them to hear you. Or do you?"

Her head tilts back, rocking from side to side on my shoulder.

"Come for me, baby." I pick up the pace, not letting up on her clit, and she reaches to grip the back of my head.

"Hunter, come in me." She's panting after every word, and I feel my balls draw up tight at the command.

"Ah, Hunter!" She spasms around me, squeezing my dick so hard that I feel the strangle in my throat. She's coming. Hard. "H, it's too much!"

I'm rubbing her pussy and slamming into her so hard that I'm bottoming out inside her.

"Again," I say, and I deliver a slap to her clit. She jerks and screams as she slides up to that peak again. Her entire body trembles, her voice caught in her throat until moments later she's keening into the fist she's pressed to her mouth. I want to rejoice at the sensation of wetness drenching my cock and slacks.

I don't give a fuck about a stain.

"Winter," I groan. The base of my spine tingles, and before I erupt, I say, "Are you sure you want my cum, baby?"

"Yes! Yes, yes, yes, please," she pleads, and that's all it takes for me to shoot deep inside her.

She's milking me, squeezing the cum out of my dick as I empty my balls.

I move my hand to rest over her lower stomach. Dreaming.

I lean an arm against the wall in front of us and lower her

leg to the ground. Slowly, I pull out of her and hold her close to me.

"What do we do now, Hunter?" she whispers.

"Now, we move forward together."

THIRTY
WINTER

When Hunter spins me around and moves my panties back into their appropriate place, patting the fabric reverently, I want to laugh.

But I have a feeling any laughter I utter will turn into hysteria, and we don't have the time for that.

I'm trying to reconcile the fact that:

1. Hunter just told me some incredibly sordid shit.
2. I've lost my mind because I want to be with him anyway.
3. I just let him fuck me raw in a bathroom.

"Hunter, I'm..." I move to the sink and lather the expensive-smelling liquid soap over my palms. "Don't you want to wash your hands?" I ask, looking at his hands as I rinse.

The hands that were just inside me.

"I might never wash my hands again," he says. He smiles at me. He's got himself back together, but I can see the stain I left on his pants when I...

I groan, burying my face in my wet hands.

"What's wrong, Sunbeam?" He walks over to me, lowering my hands from my face.

Unable to look at him directly, I whisper, "I squirted on you."

His smile grows even wider. "Yeah, you did."

"Hunter!" I slap a hand across his chest. "I am *mortified,*" I say.

He kisses my hands. "I'm not," he replies.

I lean into him again, taking strength from the in and out of his breath. He does eventually wash his hands, even though he grumbles while he does so.

Grabbing one of the linen towels, I choke when he says, "Move in with me."

"What?" I ask.

"Right now. Move in with me." I blink at him.

"So that sounds great, but don't you have a few loose ends to tie up? Like, the whole fiancée thing?"

"I do," he says. "That ends right now."

I arch an eyebrow. "Right now?"

"Yes, baby. I can't tolerate any scenario that causes you pain. I've tried to be patient, but—" He rubs his hand over his mouth with a determined look, and his jaw hardens before he kisses my forehead. "There's more I want to tell you. But I need to know you'll be safe in the meantime. And you're safest right by my side."

I look away from him, logic settling into my brain. "Let me get Kitty," I say.

"Can I send someone to get him for you?" Hunter's mouth is pressed to my forehead again.

"I need to get my stuff too. Look at my apartment for a minute. Think about this massive change you're asking of me."

"But you're not second-guessing us?"

I reach my hand up to his cheek. "No, I'm not second-guessing us. I want us. I just want to be the one to do this. I need a second for closure, okay?"

He nods. "I don't like it, but okay."

He pulls his phone out of his pocket and taps the screen. "I'll have one of the guys bring you to your apartment. He'll stay with you while you pack. Unless..." He looks up at me, done texting. "I can meet you there? We can spend the night at your place. Maybe I could eat you out on your kitchen island again. You know, for closure." He gives me his best innocent look.

I laugh a little. "Absolutely not, H." I kiss his cheek.

He sighs.

"We can't be seen leaving this bathroom together," he murmurs when he pulls me in for another hug.

"I can only imagine the scandal. You and your other woman having a bathroom tryst at your engagement party." I move to re-pin my hair.

"You're not my other woman. You're my only woman. This whole situation is just an...inconvenience," he says.

I bite my lip. What if things don't work out how he plans? What if things are more complicated or dangerous than he knows? What if he gets hurt? August? Ella?

"Hey," he says, pulling my lip from between my teeth. "It's all going to be okay."

He kisses me gently, and I relax into it.

"I'll leave first," he says. He peppers kisses along my jaw and my eyelids. His phone beeps, and he looks at the screen. "Great, we've got Jose to bring you. Have you met him?"

I shake my head no. "Go out the front doors, and he'll be waiting for you with the Tahoe."

He pulls away from me.

"Wait," I say, and he turns back around. "I love you, Hunter James Brigham."

He smiles. "I love you more, Winter Leigh Vaughan."

And then he's out the door.

I wait three minutes just to make sure he is far from the bathroom before I walk out the door. Turning to the front entrance, I praise the gods for the deserted lobby. Even the reception desk is empty. Through the glass doors, I see a tall man with dark skin standing on the passenger side of the Tahoe with the door open. I haven't seen him before, but he's dressed in black cargo pants, a black jacket, and a black baseball cap. His back faces the automatic doors as he fiddles with the windshield wipers.

"Jose?" I ask as I walk through the doors. My phone chirps with an Uber notification just as my foot hits the rug embossed with the Appleton Country Club insignia. I look down at my phone while walking toward the vehicle, focusing on quickly pulling up the app to cancel my ride. He nods in my periphery. "Thanks for the ride," I say, closing the app with a few taps as I slide into the back seat.

He's silent as he drives us away from the country club, and I'm honestly grateful for the time to think.

Everything Hunter shared with me…all of it is horrifying. What he's been through and what his father forced him to do is…there are no words. He didn't call it abuse by name, but all those details…is there any other way to look at his history?

My heart aches. My mind churns. Only one thought is clear.

I love him, and he is mine.

I pull out my phone to text Veronica.

No reception.

I wave the phone around, hoping to catch a signal if I change positions. I'm in a complete dead zone. I look around at my surroundings, but everything is dark.

"Jose, do you have reception out here?"

He doesn't respond.

Anxiety settles in my chest.

"Jose?" I ask, scooting closer to the front seat. Anxiety morphs into terror as he slams on the accelerator.

"What the fuck!" I yell, and I scream when he takes a sharp left, my head cracking soundly into the side window. I scramble to open the door, but it won't budge. Same for the other one.

I start to fling my body over the seat and nearly vomit when I see the lifeless body of a stranger in the trunk area. His head rests at an unnatural angle as the slit in his throat nearly separates his head from the rest of his body.

I can't help the scream that exits my throat.

Gasping for air, I collect myself to assess the situation.

"Who are you?" I demand through quivering lips.

Finally, he speaks. "Aw. You couldn't have forgotten about me. Right, princess?"

Want to know what happens next?

Keep reading for a sneak peek from *Oathbreaker*, Book Two in The Devils in D.C. Saga.

OATHBREAKER

CHAPTER TWO: HUNTER

"Happy New Year!" An unfamiliar woman slings her arm around my neck once I push through the ballroom's double doors. The party is in full swing—the celebration slated to go well into the early morning hours. The woman hanging off me smells like a nauseating mix of champagne, gin, and olive brine.

"Yeah, you too," I mutter, pushing her away. She gives me a drunken smile and saunters away when her partner pulls her arm.

Just give it fifteen more minutes, and then you'll be out of here.

A glance at my watch shows I've been gone for more than half an hour, and as I face the wall of people milling around the room and spilling out into the foyer, I want to turn right around and run away with Winter.

My chest grows tight at the thought of the intimacy we just shared. It's not even about the sex, although that was... everything.

It's deeper than that.

She is everything.

I never expected her love. I never expected to feel this way about anyone. But I do. Besides Leo, she's the only person I've been able to share the entirety of my darkness with. And instead of writing me off—writing *us* off—she opened her arms and her heart to me.

"You missed the ball drop," Leo murmurs, coming up behind me. He's dressed in a nondescript black tuxedo, intending to blend into the crowd. But at 6'3" and with his dark hair slicked back, he looks like a goddamn Latin movie star. He sticks out in the white-washed ballroom. Giving a side eye as he moves next to me, the corner of his mouth kicks up in a slight smile. He knows what I've been up to.

When I don't respond, he says, "Misha Hroshko wants to meet tomorrow."

"Oh?" I ask, still not looking at him. I scan the room for threats. Specifically, the biggest danger of all—Benjamin Brigham. My father.

"We're going to him," Leo says, talking about Misha. I nod as my palms tingle. This is what we need—to get a formidable adversary on our side. We can nullify my father's power if we can convince Misha Hroshko to join us.

"Excuse me," a young male voice cuts in. We both look to our left and see a pimple-faced teenager standing near us in an ill-fitting uniform.

"Mr. Brigham has requested your presence, sir," he says.

I turn to look at Leo. The subtle tick of his jaw is my only indication of what he's thinking. He doesn't like this. With his mouth pressed into a thin line, Leo nods with a slight tilt of his head.

"Lead the way," I say to the boy.

"Mr. Brigham requested you come alone," the boy says, stammering. His hands shake. When I give him a withering glare, he looks like he's two seconds away from pissing his pants.

"He comes," I say with a flat tone.

"R-Right. Right this way." The kid sprints down the hall, and Leo and I look at each other before following.

When we reach the private room, our usher stops and opens the double doors with a flourish.

We're on the other side of the country club, opposite the main entrance and the restroom where Winter and I stole moments together. There are more than a dozen suites for the most prominent members to use between golf rounds, sipping brandy, and smoking cigars.

The room before me is one of the largest if I remember the layout correctly—second only to the President's private wing. On one end is a desk with an oversized leather chair and two low-back seats for visitors. Across the room is a fireplace and a seating area.

That's where I find Father.

"Hunter," my father says. He's seated with his ankle resting on his knee, slouched. He and Blair sit across from each other, a decanter and two full tumblers on the table between them. Near the lit fireplace, Morris Winthrope stands with his back to the room. He gives me the barest acknowledgment with a glance over his shoulder.

"Father," I say back, just as formally.

"You missed the countdown. I believe Blair was waiting for a kiss." He reaches for his drink, bringing it to his lips. "It would have been a great photo for the press," he adds, looking at me over the rim of the Waterford crystal. In one gulp, he downs almost half the glass.

He stares at me with bloodshot eyes, and his hair doesn't look quite as perfect as usual.

In the face of my silence, he says, "Is there a reason why you need backup?" He tilts his head in Leo's direction.

I don't respond.

He sighs.

"Have it your way," he says.

"I'm glad you called for me, actually," I say. "I wanted to tell you that this—" I wave my hand between Blair and me "is over."

Blair sits straight in her seat, stiff.

Morris finally turns around, his face impassive—as if he already expected this to happen.

My father smiles. He's amused. He's annoyed. But his grin also holds an edge of something else unreadable.

"I am unsure if you've considered the ramifications of that decision," Father says, bringing the glass back to his lips.

The tremble in his hand as he lowers it again makes everything clear: My father *needs* me to follow through.

He's not in control. My eyes slide to Morris Winthrope.

He is.

"Hunter, really. This is what you want to choose? Think about it before you throw everything away—"

"No," I grind out, the single syllable landing hard in the room. "I've considered all of it. And here's what I see: a man losing his grip on power. I see a man who thinks he can manipulate any situation to feed his objective. But the thing that gives you power? Your ability to instill fear." I take slow, measured steps toward him. From where he sits, I tower over him.

I don't know what reaction to expect. In the past, he would backhand me for my insubordination. Beat me to the floor and singe my skin with the end of a lit cigar.

Maybe he'll attack. Maybe he'll ignore me—wave off my aggression.

But he does the one thing I don't expect.

He looks at me, our gazes clashing. And says not a single word.

That's when it clicks. My father only has power over me because I've let him have it. Yes, he can manipulate events and circumstances, but me? He can only run *me* if I let him. I'm not a kid anymore.

Control. I am in control.

"I'm not afraid of you." The words are low, measured. My voice is just for his ears. It doesn't need to be a bombastic declaration. It simply needs to be said.

He blinks. And remains silent for a long moment.

For the millionth time, I feel loathing poison every cell in my body as my eyes shift from my father to Blair's impassive face.

I despise him.

I detest her.

They set the price for my freedom as part of the fucked-up game they want me to play. The cost is the sale of my soul. But they can't have it—Father can't have it.

Not anymore.

So if I want to get on the other side of this and get to a place where everyone is safe, my father can't hurt any more people, and I can go forward and live my life with Winter and August in peace…I have to get past *this* part.

I have to sack up and stand up to my father.

Because every last one of them can fuck all the way off.

Even if it means going to war.

Father blinks again. As if coming out of a fog, he stands and tilts his head to the side, considering me. "Afraid? Why would you be afraid of your own father, Hunter? I've always wanted the best for you." His eyes, so much like mine, are frosty, and the skin around his mouth is tense, blanched.

A throat clears across the room. "That's well and good, Hunter, but unfortunately, I cannot accept your decision. The ball has gone too far down the court," Morris says, gesturing to the massive space around us. He leaves his perch next to the fireplace, coming closer and crowding me in a display of dominance.

My father moves to stand shoulder to shoulder with Morris Winthrope.

Benjamin Brigham, for once, seems small. Unimpressive.

A smirk crawls across my face, and it must do something to my father. He straightens his back, his shoulders broadening.

Now he looks more like the imposing man the world knows.

Fake. It's all fake.

"You're distracted," my father says, and I smell his cologne as he moves even closer. The sweet scent of whiskey fans across my face.

I hold my ground.

With a quirked eyebrow, Morris moves to Blair and places a hand on her shoulder. Ice glazes over her green eyes, but she doesn't look at all upset that I just dissolved all wedding plans at our engagement party.

"Now, that's not to say that I haven't had my dalliances in the past. A little strange here and there keeps you young." My father taps my arm with the back of his hand to punctuate his words.

"But you can't let pussy take you under, Hunter. So I'm going to help you clear the distractions. Help you understand the bigger picture."

He claps a hand on my shoulder.

And smiles.

Vibrations of foreboding center in my chest. I am going to murder him right here, right now. Forget the rest of the plan.

I feel the shift of air as Leo takes a step closer to me.

Father sighs.

"Enough with the theatrics," Morris says. "If that will be all, I'll leave you to make your rounds. The Senator from Virginia would love to speak with you, Benjamin." Morris turns back to Blair, ignoring my father and cutting me out.

Winter. August. Ella.

Clearing out distractions.

What has he done?

What have *I* done?

Resisting the urge to run, I leave the room with Leo following behind me. As soon as we clear the doors, I say, "We need locations on everyone now. Where are Ella, August, and Winter?" I book it to the club door, aiming for the G-wagon, not stopping to grab my coat.

"I need to get Winter *now*."

"Agreed," he says.

Fuck her clothes. I'll have someone get her dog and buy her new clothes.

I need her with me, in my home. Safe.

Leo and I break into the bitter chill of the dead night. It's stopped sleeting, at least.

I pull my phone out to call Winter. When she doesn't answer, I look at the time. She should be home by now. I send her a text and try to ignore the apprehension manifesting behind my breastbone.

On my way to get you. I know you want space, but you'll be safest at Amelia Manor.

A few seconds later, I send another text.

I love you.

We reach the G-wagon. Seconds later, Leo stomps on the gas and we launch out of the portico and down the winding drive. Leo frowns with his phone up to his ear as he navigates the vehicle through the slick turns. He pulls the phone away before tapping the screen and putting the call on hands-free mode through the car's system.

"Rio, what's the location on Jose?" Leo says as soon as the man answers.

We pull out onto the main road. Leo taps the brakes but doesn't stop for the right turn.

Rio has always been more than Winter's driver and protection detail—he's the head of our security team. While we assembled a crew to attend the party tonight, we left Rio behind to monitor everything at Amelia Manor.

"Checking now, boss," Rio says over the line. He sounds alert, serious. And he should be—any fuck-ups security-wise are on his head.

My palms itch as my anger rises.

Leo pulls out of the spot, and we head toward the interstate entrance.

I check my messages to Winter.

The last two say "delivered," not read.

"Leo." Dread sits like a stone in my stomach.

He grips the steering wheel with tight fists—his knuckles blanch.

"Boss, his beacon is stationary. Jose's stopped on some back road. Southbound."

I pull up the GPS location app for Winter's phone and push back the tinge of guilt cropping up. I haven't told her I installed the tech, but I don't consider it a violation. It's my way of keeping her safe. I haven't used it beyond checking the set-up weeks ago.

This is why she wants space. You're running all over her.

I refresh the screen on my phone, pure terror filling all the empty spaces within my body.

Location: Not Found

I should have put a tracker in her. I should have—I'd know where she is right now.

There's commotion over the line as other voices join and doors slam.

"Send me the location you have now," Leo commands.

"Sent," Rio says half a second after Leo's edict leaves his lips. The map pulls up on the screen in the center console. "I have confirmation that Ella and August are back at Amelia Manor with Rex and Jared," Rio adds.

I tap to call Winter, and when she doesn't answer, I call her again.

And again.

And again, and again, and again—

"Winter's not answering her phone, Rio. I can't find her location. Do you have her location?" The side buttons leave deep indents in my flesh as I grasp the device in a tight fist.

Anxiety is a noose around my neck.

Tighter.

Tighter.

"Working on it," Rio says. His voice is sharp, brittle. Crackling comes over the line, and then his voice is clearer. He put on a headset.

"Max," Rio yells, and Max's voice sounds far away from the microphone.

Rio gives tense orders to Max, who makes an affirmative noise in response.

"Rio! Do you see Winter's location?" I repeat, pressing every word through tingling lips.

"No," he snaps, "I'm trying to figure out what *the fuck* happened." There's silence over the line for a beat.

"Well, fucking find her!" I roar.

My hand stings. I look down, and it's flat on the dashboard. I must have hit it.

Control.

"Hunter, breathe," Leo says. When I look at him, his eyes fix on the road. But he takes shallow breaths.

He's trying to stay calm so *he* can remain in control.

I want to collect myself.

But every part of my being screams with the chaos.

"Fuck!" I bellow, hitting the dashboard again. "Get me to Winter now!" I yell at Leo. At Rio and Max.

At the Universe.

Something is wrong, wrong, wrong. They have her. She's gone. They've killed her.

I try to regain my senses—to reach a feeling of calm necessary to fix this situation.

Flashes of my mother's face as unknown men dragged her away from my bloodied body rotate through my mind. My mouth dries with the memory of Isla Cara's sea breeze.

I try to blink the thoughts away; nothing works.

You promised to protect her.

You promised, and you failed.

You failed.

You. Fucking. Failed.

My gut clenches, horror bubbling up like vomit.

Leo makes a sharp U-turn at the next intersection, gunning it in the direction of the country club. "Check Winter's location again and give me the coordinates for—"

An SUV rams into the back of the G-wagon. In a second, the world rocks, and our vehicle lists onto the passenger-side tires for a millisecond before slamming back onto the pavement. We fishtail, shifting so hard from side to side that my head cracks against the window.

"Shit!" Leo shouts, and I grip the seat belt where it cuts into my chest. Punching the accelerator, Leo revs the engine to get distance between us and our attackers.

"Rio, you still with me? We're being rammed," Leo yells into the speaker.

"I have three cars approaching your location right now. Do you have a description of the vehicle?" As the tension rises, Rio becomes calmer. There's a deadly focus in his tone. Maybe it's the black ops training.

Maybe it's something else. How did *he* lose Winter?

"Black SUV. Looks like a Suburban or a Tahoe," Leo says.

I look behind us and see two more SUVs swerving around the car gunning for us.

"Those our guys, Rio?" I yell over my shoulder.

This is my father or Blair or Morris or all of them trying to send me a message. Or maybe they're over me and my resistance and decided it's time I become a non-factor.

"Those aren't my guys," Rio says.

We get hit hard on the driver's side; the back end of the SUV skids off the pavement.

"Shit!" Leo curses and tries to regain control of the vehicle.

Fuck this. I pull the gun from beneath the seat as a bullet shatters the back window.

Leo shifts and swerves again, evading the cars following us.

Using the back of my seat as a shield, I pop three rounds into the front of the SUV following us.

A crack forms in their windshield, and the car closest to us veers into its partner.

Crash.

Two cars remain.

"Our guys have your position," Rio says over the speaker.

"Mother*fucker*," Leo shouts. His face is all sharp angles; his eyes rage filled.

This is the Leo who hunts—the Leo who maims and kills. I haven't seen this side of him since we left Isla Cara years ago.

He's gonna kill somebody tonight.

And so am I.

Leo cuts another right down a farm-to-market road, and I reach for the dashboard to steady myself against the sharp movement.

The car closest to us tries to make the turn but fails on the slick curve, popping on its driver-side tires before skidding down the opposite lane for several feet on its side. It stops when it careens into a thicket of trees.

The final car makes the turn and accelerates toward us.

We bounce over the ill-maintained road, headlights on bright as we navigate the two-lane path. Out here, we're too exposed. Nothing but barren trees, farmland, and snowbanks surround us.

"We gotta lose 'em," I yell. Everything is so fucking loud —the wind whips into the damaged SUV, slicing at my skin. Or maybe that's broken glass.

"I know," Leo says, voice hard.

The speedometer goes past ninety just as a concrete barrier materializes a half mile ahead. We draw closer to it in one second.

Two.

Three.

"Hold on!" Leo slams on the brakes. The car behind us stops short, cutting its wheel to the right and toppling over, rolling to a stop as it slides into an icy ditch.

The turn signal on the car flashes as the headlights hang from their housings.

For several moments, the only sound is our breathing. Leo clutches the steering wheel, and I sit there, gun still in my hand.

The sharp, sucking sound of Leo's inhalation tears through the cabin before he jerks open the driver's door. He pulls both guns out: one from the side compartment of the driver's seat, the other from his waistband.

He starts over to the crash.

"Rio. Winter?" I feel wild when my voice cracks, and he breathes in and out over the line.

"Nothing, sir." He sounds…incredulous. Angry.

Lost.

Air seizes in my chest as I grip the gun in one hand.

Winter. Gone. Winter is gone.

I rush out the door toward the scene of the wreck.

Leo has pulled the driver out of the car. Blood runs from the guy's head, but he's conscious.

I peer into the crushed vehicle.

The passenger hangs upside down against the seat belt, with his neck at a sharp angle.

"Who sent you?" Leo barks out. His voice is rough but steady.

"Fuck you," the man spits. Leo kicks him in the side, and the driver groans, rolling over. He coughs up blood.

"I'm gonna put a bullet in your brain either way. Might as well tell the truth. A point in your favor when you meet God," Leo says, his voice deceptively calm.

"You already know who sent me," the man says with labored breathing.

I do know. I do fucking know.

A sheen of pain and resolute defiance glazes over the driver's eyes. I've seen that look before in a man who's about to die—in a man who knew his time was up but didn't give a fuck anyway.

"Winter Vaughan. Where is she?" I must look deranged as I speak. With absent awareness, I notice a trickle of moisture rolling down the side of my face. A copper scent fills the air.

"Her?" The man smiles, baring his blood-coated teeth. "You'll never find her again," he says.

I shoot him right between the eyes.

In the shot's reverberation. I am quiet.

Up. Down.

Goes my chest.

And every single part of my mind breaks.

Morris. Blair. Father.

Winter, Winter, Winter.

Gone.

In the darkness, my vision shrinks to a pinpoint—stops. Feeling ceases to register in my brain as my hands numb.

In the distance, Leo yells at me. He's so far. So far away.

"Drop the gun, Hunter."

Winter. Winter. I need to get to Winter.

What do I do? What do I do first?

"Drop the gun, Hunter," Leo says. He's closer now. Close. Grabbing my wrist. I look down. Bullets riddle the driver's face and chest, transforming his body into a pockmarked monstrosity.

Did I do that?

With Leo's hand on my wrist, I squeeze the trigger again.

Crack. One more shot.

Click. Silence.

My entire clip is empty with the slide of the gun pulled back—the rounds released into the dead driver's body.

"H," Leo says, squeezing my wrist. The gun falls from my hand and onto the rocky asphalt.

"Hunter," Leo tries again. He moves into my field of vision. He's giving me a look I recognize.

It's the look of him saving me from myself.

"We're going to find her," he says. His voice is clear.

But in his eyes is the thing I don't want to see.

Doubt.

"We're going to find Winter. You've got to get it together so we can save her." His voice hardens.

"Yes," I rasp. My voice doesn't sound like my own.

Winter. Winter. Winter.

Gone.

My phone buzzes in my pocket, and I rush to remove it. Winter. It could be Winter.

But my muscles rebel as I read the message from an unknown sender.

You were warned.

I lose control; the phone joins the gun on the ground.

Outside of myself, I hear Leo calling for me. I feel him reaching for me, attempting to pull me back into our dented vehicle.

But I resist, every part of me locked tight.
I scream into the blackness of the night sky.

Preorder *Oathbreaker*, book two in The Devils in D.C. Saga now!

AFTERWORD

I'm so honored you've chosen to read *Shadowplay*. I hope you loved it! If you did, please leave a review wherever you purchased your book from. Want to really make this indie author's heart soar? A Goodreads or BookBub review from you would make my entire life.

Book Two in The Devils in D.C. Saga, *Oathbreaker*, comes out very soon, so be sure to pre-order to get it when it drops! In the meantime, join my newsletter to receive the latest news about Hunter, Winter, and The Devils in D.C. Saga!

www.angelmshaw.com/eob-signup

ACKNOWLEDGMENTS

From the bottom of my heart, thank you for reading *Shadowplay*. After decades of stops and starts, it's only fitting that Winter and Hunter's story would be the first one birthed into this world.

First and foremost, all my love and thanks to my husband, Mr. S. You are the best hype man a woman could ever have, and your unwavering belief in me, my talent, and my abilities keep me going on my lowest days. I love you more. (Also, thank you for answering and researching all my questions about firearms, aircraft, and RC stuff.)

Daddy, you give me the straight talk and the "Deepak stuff" when I need it (even when I don't want it). You always believe in me and help me shoot for the stars. I'm so blessed to have a dad like you. (I always listen to you, by the way.)

A major, major thank you to my co-writing buddies, Ashley, Stephanie, and Meg. Body doubling is LIFE, and without your virtual presence on my laptop screen, this book would not exist. I'm grateful for you.

A special thank you to my sorority sister and fellow romance book lover, Lauren. You always tell me the raw truth, and knowing you loved Winter and Hunter's story gave me such a boost of confidence. Xily, sis!

A HUGE thank you to the Author Ever After community and my mentor, author Danika Bloom. The universe always gives me what I need, and it saw fit to give me you and the AEA community.

Thank you, thank you, thank you to my beta readers who

gave excellent notes and hyped me all the way up to Mars. Your feedback and support gave me the courage to push publish.

To Chinelo and Sarah, thank you for providing your unique insight into August's character. Getting his character right and doing service to the Autistic community is critical to me. I am grateful for your meticulous evaluation of this book.

Rosa, thank you for checking and re-checking my Spanish so I don't go out in the world with my proverbial ass showing. Love you, sis!

Wendee, my amazing, amazing editor—I am so grateful that we connected more than a decade ago and get to do this editing thing again…this time with me as your client! To the moon!

Finally, to my sisters Danielle and Nikita. Y'all know what y'all do for me. I love you. Saying thank you isn't enough.

ABOUT THE AUTHOR

Angel M. Shaw (she/they) writes spicy suspense with lots of heat and heart. A New Orleanian by birth, she lives in Texas with her three children and spouse, where she spends as much time outside as she can, eats lots of crawfish, and people watches to find inspiration for her next novel. You can follow Angel on Instagram, TikTok, or YouTube or visit her website at www.angelmshaw.com to connect.

Find Angel's social media links and email address here:
http://social.angelmshaw.com

instagram.com/angelmshaw_writes
tiktok.com/@angelmshaw_writes
youtube.com/@AngelMShawWrites

ALSO BY ANGEL M. SHAW

The Devils in D.C. Series

Shadowplay

Coming soon:

Oathbreaker (August 27, 2024)

Reverie (September 24, 2024)

Made in the USA
Columbia, SC
21 June 2024